THE SPIRAL

THE SPIRAL

BITTERSWEET EMPATHY: THE TRAGEDY OF AMY DURENE

NIKKI DEKEUSTER

PHOENIX ROSE PUBLISHING

CONTENT WARNING

Mature content and themes. Graphic language. Graphic sex. Graphic violence. Graphic design. Graphic ellipses use…

For Brian, my granite: with the constitution of a mountain, you are the lighthouse to my turbulent sea.

For Aisling, my sweet bear: Mama's finally done, here's that sibling you always wanted.

In memory of Kevin DeKeuster, the engine beneath so much of the car-speak within these pages, and one of the finest human beings I've ever had the privilege to know.

"Go then if you must, but remember, no matter how foolish your deeds, those who **love** you will **love** you still."

— ANTIGONE

CHAPTER ONE

*B*oots make a distinct sound when you step on shattered glass. There's a heaviness to it you just don't get with sneakers or bare feet.

I would come to know this intimately in time.

It's the little things that make up life.

And it was the little things that shone and crunched beneath my boots as I jumped from the rotted window pane they'd once called home. Dust kicked up in tiny cyclones around me, coating my long blonde hair in a fine powder before settling back down into the prevailing winter stillness.

My best friend, Kayla, who'd come in before me, wiped away the cobwebs on a wall calendar, tapping at it with her forefinger. The faded name of Ms. November 1975 called out to us through the ages. Either someone had a hint of nostalgia or no one had been here for a very long time.

Kayla put all one hundred pounds of her weight into opening the double doors leading out of the cramped office we were in and into the barn proper. The doors buckled under decades of warp and rot, clutching the concrete with each shove of her elbow.

"You aren't even going to knock?" I mumbled through my filtered face mask, the kind bikers used in big cities and that made us look like ninjas of the highest order. Putting down the ancient MAD magazine I was rifling through, I went to lend a shoulder to her struggle. I had two inches and twenty-five pounds on her—but being a farm girl since birth, what Kayla lacked in stature she made up for in muscle and grit. By the time I reached her I was little more than moral support.

"It's only the spook's place after dark." She peeked her head through the door, which was now propped open enough for us to squeeze through. "Assuming anybody dwells here at all." A massive barn owl hooted and drifted through the rafters, no doubt getting a better view of the two masked intruders. "That's a good sign," she said, disappearing through the door.

Kayla, bless her ginger soul, had a love for exploring old, abandoned buildings in our little corner of Albion, Maine. I went along out of curiosity and the obligations that come with being best friends with someone since the age of five. Although the thrill of the hunt excited her, we had yet to find any tangible evidence of the paranormal, her constant prey. She believed in spirits and the mystical and, while open to it all, I had yet to be convinced one way or the other.

If I'm honest, I got a thrill out of breaking into places and rediscovering what time had forgotten. I wanted to take videos and put them up for everyone to see, but Kayla thought the better of it. She said cops trolled for that sort of thing and it was inviting trouble. She was probably right; it wasn't like we ever got permission to lurk in these lost hovels.

Light streamed through gaps and holes in the outer walls of the barn in ribbons, letting in more than enough of the afternoon sun for us to see by. The space was huge and didn't seem to know what it wanted to be. Along the far side ran

2

several concrete slabs that were once stalls, and the half mezzanine above overlooked a cluttered workbench with heaps of rusted farm equipment strewn about. A faded old muscle car parked in the corner had been mercilessly cannibalized for parts. The deflated wheels had dug down into the bare earth over time. Clumps of matted fur, gnawed spine, and shining viscera, which might have once been a rat, writhed near the trunk and I was at once grateful for my mask. We wore them as a precaution against mold and the rotting animal stench that frequented most of the places we explored.

"Why do you think this place is haunted, again?" I asked, taking it all in.

"Look at it, Amy. It's creepy as all shit." Kayla gestured around, as if presenting one of the great art galleries of the millennia.

"So's your abuela's house, but we aren't sifting through her dusty relics and unmentionables." A smile hung in my voice.

Kayla's eyebrows rose up and down. "That'll be our next stop then." She laughed and I followed suit. Her abuela, or grandmother, was about two hundred and fifty-eight thousand years old and had the largest collection of misshapen Jesus and the Blessed Virgin statues in the nine realms. They were the work of many a well-meaning child, grandchild, and great grandchild, but the effect was no less disturbing for this revelation. Add to it an ever-accusing glare, not unlike that of a featherless crow appraising a carcass, that the old woman displayed whenever her red-haired, half-Irish granddaughter was present, and the atmosphere at Abuela's home got quite frosty on its own; no paranormal influence needed. Three DNA tests and a headless chicken had to make their way through the US postal system before she'd begrudgingly accepted Kayla into the family.

My best friend was an only child, same as me. Her dad

passed away when she was three, but she held clear memories of continuing to play with him until she was five. This was the fuel behind her paranormal interest, and why we frequented the forgotten haunts of Maine.

Still chuckling, she added, "No, but look at this place, tucked away in an overgrown forest, hasn't been touched since the Mesozoic. I just know there's a dead body buried under the floorboards." Kicking the dirt that made up the floor throughout most of the barn, she amended, "Figurative floorboards."

"Could be something in the concrete..." I motioned toward the crumbled livestock stalls with a nod of my head.

"That's the spirit! I knew there was a reason I married you," she teased. We often joked back and forth about being each other's wives. It was a measure of our closeness rather than our physical attraction to one another. She was practically my sister, and I was most certainly into men, even as I only ever seemed to find boys. Kayla tried her heart in both fields and at present had chosen a drama-free existence via the single life. My single status wasn't by choice so much as a lack thereof.

We were on an exploratory mission, charting the place out before coming back for a series of nighttime vigils, when ghosts were supposed to be at their strongest. Mostly we just spooked the be-jesused tar out of each other all night before crossing another "haunted place" off our list as...well...dead. It was the better part of a week into March, a little past my sixteenth birthday, and we were happy to have the weather warm to the point that we could come check the creepy barn out. Kayla had spotted it while out snowmobiling with her cousin and had been waiting for the snow to melt so our tracks wouldn't betray our presence. An internet search of the property revealed the owner to be someone from Wisconsin who paid his taxes but was otherwise a ghost himself.

While Kayla tested the sturdiness of the stairs to the loft, I studied an oversized sign on the wall above the workbench that commanded me to "Drink Coca Cola." Climbing onto the creaking bench, I took a gloved finger to the metal sign and wrote "Pepsi" over the accumulated grunge of centuries.

"Now you're just askin' for some poltergeist activity," Kayla quipped with a disapproving shake of her head. The shelves surrounding the work area were filled with over-turned and exploded spray paint cans, giving the area the ambiance of a sloppily tagged train yard.

"Looks like we already missed it." I kicked a can across the barn and the owl screeched its disapproval. "Have ghosts ever communicated through graffiti or would this place be a first?"

Kayla took out her camera and snapped pictures of the chaotic artwork. Nothing was immediately visible, but she would run it through her computer programs later to be sure. For my part, I jumped down and walked over to the muscle car as the space behind me lit up with her intermit-tent flashes. What was left of the vehicle was partially covered by a moth-eaten drop cloth, as though someone had once given a damn about the car's condition.

I wrote "Love Me" in big letters through the grit on the car's blackish-gray hood and was leaning over to start on a giant heart when I froze in my tracks, a sinuous, icy current gripping my spine. Adrenaline steamrolled through my system with the finesse of a fire hose, and I could taste my heart beating in my mouth. I would either throw it up or choke on it—either way I was dead.

I was dead, and there was no getting away.

My terror spun on a feedback loop, entrenching further with each passing rotation.

"K-Kayla…?" I stumbled back from the car, every sense on high alert, until her warm hand settled on my shoulder. "There's something here." My voice trembled.

5

"No shit—are you serious?" She met my wild eyes and squealed. "You are!"

"Over there, by the car!" I squealed alongside her, bouncing on my feet and pointing. Who said anything about getting away? I had to see what it was!

Kayla steeled herself and made her way to the drop cloth, pulling it to the floor in one freakishly strong motion. Eyes glinted in the shadows of the backseat for only a breath before something lunged at us, snarling, vicious, and desperate. Not the nightmarish abominations of a Wes Craven film, but the skittering, clamoring claws of a family of raccoons. Cute, fluffy, foaming at the mouth raccoons.

A deafening gunshot lit up the barn, silencing everything but my instinct to flee. The critter who had been coming right for me veered onto the workbench, knocking over the remnants of a buzz saw as it scurried to safety under a rusted-out tiller.

Scrambling backwards, I found refuge behind the workbench, pleading with my heart to stay in my chest. Ripping off my gloves, I focused on my tingling fingers and frantic breathing. But why should I be the one to back down? To cower from those diseased, flea ridden—

Strange...I wasn't generally quick to anger. I left that sort of thing to my trigger-happy other half.

Kayla unleashed a volley of curse words over the ringing in my ears. "What a bunch of stupid assholes! We made enough fucking noise! Why didn't you leave?!"

I peered over the table, shivering with shock, fear, and anger, a dog-pile of emotions. Kayla sat on the floor, her legs splayed out in front of her and her mother's forty-five smoking at her side. My friend had "borrowed" it for the last four years in case we ever ran into trouble. This was the first time she'd needed to use it outside of her makeshift Coke can firing range back home.

"No way the spirits will show themselves now." She wiped

her forehead on the crook of her elbow. "And hell among us, we better get our high and proud asses out of here. Remote or not, that sound is gonna carry." Rising to her feet, she asked, "Amy? You okay?"

I was about to scream at her. No, I wasn't okay! What was she thinking firing that gun at such close range?! Did she want me to be deaf for the rest of my life? But my emotional dog-pile splintered into jittery nerves and breathless worry. Lava and ice melted over my brain and dripped down my spine in sparks, sputtering like an emotional short circuit. What was the correct line of feelings to follow?

What...what kind of question is that?

My mouth opened and a small, unintelligible sound came out, followed by the remains of my lunch. Thankfully—and I sincerely mean this—I pulled my mask off my face before-hand. My naturally ghost-white skin had washed out, giving my hands the anemic, ashen appearance of a cadaver. And just last week I'd been saying I couldn't possibly get any whiter this winter. My fault for jinxing myself.

As Kayla helped me up and put my mask back on, one feeling topped the din—worry. Had I been bitten? Was there something in the dust here that was making me sick? What in blue blazes happened? With a secure arm around me, my friend led us back the way we had come, through the double doors and into the small office. She unlatched the outer door, and we were rewarded with a gust of fresh air and a shower of sunlight.

After she looked me over and was satisfied I hadn't been hurt, Kayla let out a contagious sigh of relief. Her ease, coupled with the change of scenery, quieted my heart, and we beat a hasty retreat to her truck. The likelihood someone would hear the gunshot and call the sheriff was low, but not nonexistent; no need to tempt fate.

Kayla drove out, stopping to latch the entrance gate behind us. It wasn't until we were well on the main highway that we smirked at one another and broke into hysterical laughter. "First time we get a hit in all these years and it ends up being raccoons that knock us both on our asses!" Kayla howled, "High holy hell that's hilarious!"

"And you shot, you shot at them!" I interjected, barely able to form the sentence as my face turned red. "Did you hit one?"

"I hope so! Little fuckers!" Kayla wiped a few tears away, trying to get control of herself and concentrate on the road. How many accidents happened because of merriment?

Taking a deep breath and calming along with her, I gave voice to what ended our expedition. "It was so weird, like I sensed them or something, before you ripped the sheet off."

"You the raccoon whisperer now?" Kayla raised an eyebrow at me.

"Yeah, they can be my minions, going into the night to tip over the garbage cans of my enemies." I waved a dismissive hand.

"Infinitely useful and often overlooked," she pondered, suppressing another chuckle.

"Well we'll wait a few weeks before goin' back for the night. Maybe what you felt wasn't the raccoons. Maybe they were meant to drive us away."

"They sure earned their keep then. I about pissed myself."

"You threw up!" Kayla gave me the eye and I nodded. "Ah well, could've been so much worse, so let's count our blessings, eh?"

"Yeah, I'm not foaming at the mouth…" I pulled down the visor and looked in the mirror. "Am I?"

"No rabies for you I'm afraid," Kayla said with mock sympathy.

"I'm still feelin' out of sorts though. I wouldn't say no to a nap." I rested my head on Kayla's shoulder as she drove, and she kissed the top of it. Before I knew it, we were in her driveway and she was fighting with the ancient green Ford to get it to stay in park. It required a very specific ritual involving an old Irish prayer and the sign of the cross. Any old Irish prayer would do—the Green Goblin, as we called her truck, wasn't picky.

I zombied up the stairs of her farmhouse and into the tiny bathroom, stripping off my dirty clothes and oozing into the shower. The grime of the day spiraled down the drain and my emotional vertigo faded into the woodwork, but by the time Kayla joined me in her bedroom, it returned.

She'd showered in the downstairs bathroom and was rummaging through her drawer for some clean socks while I changed into the spare clothes I always kept with her, getting as far as a Breaking Benjamin t-shirt before I had to sit on her bed and clutch my temples.

The light from her table lamp, the solar candles behind her curtains, and even the bathroom nightlight flared with menacing brightness. I shut my eyes hard against it.

"Still not feelin' good?" Kayla asked.

Shaking my head "no" was all I could manage.

She pulled back the plush covers on her full-size bed. "Here, get in."

I didn't argue and was asleep before my head hit the pillow.

CHAPTER TWO

*K*ayla won a giant stuffed raccoon at the Fryeburg Fair two years back. I woke snuggled two inches deep into its fur. I smiled at the humor of it before setting the beast on the floor and sneaking into the bathroom, careful not to wake the prankster-in-chief sleeping beside me.

A note, stuck to the bathroom mirror, showcased a realistic drawing of a chicken, a bowl of hot soup, and a refrigerator. Kayla's mom, or *Ma* as we called her, was a good artist and an even better mother. Not wanting her drawing to be in vain, I plucked it free and snuck downstairs to heat up some breakfast. I felt a thousand times better—but you were never too healthy for a bowl of Mrs. Rodriguez's soup. It had actually won prizes at the State Fair, prizes which decorated her kitchen with extreme care. I set a pot on the stove—Ma didn't allow microwaves in her house—something about them giving off radiation or some such. We all have our quirks.

The chickens, clucking out of their henhouse and into their wire enclosure one by one, entertained me as I ate. Ma butchered her own birds, so the one warming my belly had once tumbled down into that same enclosure on mornings similar to this one. I never tired of observing them—it was almost therapeutic. When the roosters were on their thirtieth crow, Kayla bounded down the stairs, full of energy as always. She grabbed a bowl of soup and joined me at the table.

"Amy, when you weren't beside me I thought maybe you'd become a walker, dead as you were to the world last night."

"I feel great." My smile showed that I meant it. "A little nookie from 'Ralph the Love Raccoon' was just what the doctor ordered." I picked up my spoon and toasted to the air. "And Ma came through like a champion."

"She made it special for you last night when she got home. I don't think she was countin' on it being breakfast though." Kayla smirked, raising her spoon in return.

"It's cold out again." I looked out the window at the breath steaming from the chickens. "I'll need it to get through the day...especially since I didn't do my history homework." History annoyed me. I preferred to live in the now, while daydreaming about the future. Oh, sometimes what happened in the past was interesting enough, until the fun was ripped out of it by making us memorize names, titles, and dates for some test, instead of making sure we grasped the bigger picture.

"You can copy mine on the way in." Kayla shrugged. "Just change the answers up a bit."

"I love you," I hummed.

"More than a lobotomy." She smiled, sweetly. "You know, you could stay home—you were pretty sick last night."

"Nah, my mother will insist on bringing me to ol' Doc Carrington. I'm not taking the next week to scrub the smell of piss and whiskey out of my skin from being near the guy for thirty seconds. Besides, if I have to spend the day with her, I'll relapse." I shook my head and Kayla chuckled. "Nope, school is the lesser evil today."

"So not fair." There was genuine sympathy in her tone as she joined me in staring out the window. We ate the rest of our soup in silence, enjoying the peaceful dawn, before clearing the table and loading the dishwasher. Ma held a full-time job as a nurse while also running the farm, which meant Kayla took care of the early morning and evening chores. When I was there, which was often enough to have my own set of muck boots and a working jacket, I didn't balk at pitching in.

"Fawk it's wicked cold!" The air stung my nose and cheeks raw as I let the chickens out to free range, and refilled their food. The water for all the animals was on a heated hose system, so even on the most frigid of nights it remained liquid. It had been Kayla's design, though she insisted it was nothing special. On mornings like this however, I was glad for her genius, modest or not.

Samson and Delilah, two gigantic balls of great white Pyreneesian fluff, rocketed toward us in anticipation of breakfast. They slept wherever the cattle slept and were unfazed by the temperatures. Kayla ran them through a series of tricks before giving them their chow. The two dogs were as smart as they were cuddly, protecting two dozen head of cattle from predators all day every day, with no weekends or holidays.

Two years back we'd watched in amusement as they'd escorted a large bull moose to the edge of the property line with relentless teamwork. They took their jobs very seriously, and would only allow for five-minute play breaks scattered conservatively throughout the day. Both were remarkably wonderful dogs.

While I fed the milking goats, Kayla let the cattle out of the barn and filled their troughs. As soon as we finished, we ran squealing back into the house to get warm again. "Your mother should just let you come live here," Kayla said as we washed up. "Chores would be done in half the time and we'd get up to twice the mischief."

"That's why she'd never allow it. The work part she'd be more than happy with, but the fun...well we can't be having that now can we? I'm surprised she let me stay over on a school night as is."

"Why do you suppose I had Ma call? If it was me she'd think you were drunk on moonshine for sure."

"Pff," I huffed. "If she had any sense she'd know your moonshine is terrible. I haven't touched it in years." We laughed, remembering a time when we were twelve and had attempted to make the substance out of potatoes and licorice sticks in one of the old tool sheds out back. The result was something tar-like and distressingly offensive to mankind.

"Just you wait, we've got cherry trees comin' into bloom this year and I'll have another go at it. You'll be my guinea pig whether you like it or not."

"Such threats," I mused.

A few minutes later we were back outside and heading to my house to grab my school things. I lived just down the road from The Willows, Kayla's farm, in a poorly planned and hastily thrown together subdivision. It had once been farmland and resembled the layout you might get by allowing a small child to scatter Monopoly houses onto a map. The house itself was cavernous. You could spend your whole life in it and barely find another human being. Thankfully my mother and father had already left for work, so I avoided even the sparse chance of unnecessary drama and the Fifth Inquisition.

We had a bit of time, so I sat at the ornate mahogany dining table we seldom dined on and vigorously copied Kayla's history homework. Meanwhile, she looted our kitchen cupboards and pocketed an array of junk food she wasn't allowed to eat at home; our relationship was symbiotic that way.

"What's a plausible wrong answer for 'What did Sir Leonard Woolley find?'" My voice was raised so she would be able to hear in the next room, and it echoed off the walls ever so slightly.

"Jesus?" Kayla laughed. "I almost put 'Jesus' but my OCD wouldn't let me. *You* do it Amy! Live free where I have failed!"

I typed in Jesus. "Mr. Feeney is a Baptist, so maybe I'll get partial credit for that one." Jesus was always the answer to those folks, wasn't he? I read the next question with puzzlement, tapping the tabletop with my forefinger. "What did Adad-Nirari like to do? You put that he liked to torture and murder but I bet there was so much more to him. I bet he liked to sunbathe and eat...what did they eat back then? Figs? Yeah, he liked to sunbathe, eat figs, and...drink the blood of his enemies."

"That last one is close enough to torture...maybe you'll get partial credit there too. Careful Amy, or you might eke out a B!" Kayla snickered, finishing her glass of chocolate milk and grabbing her keys. "You'll have to do the rest on the way in."

We were the odd couple in many ways—she was studious and motivated, I was a chaotic daydreamer—but we both let fun and silliness be our compass, and neither of us tried to change the other. I guess that's what love is: acceptance without judgment. She only ever let me copy from her when I had a good reason, and in return I didn't push her to let me without one. The funny part is I always learned the most, truly retained and understood it, when I copied from her. They say everyone learns differently—I just happened to be at my best thirty minutes before school began as I feverishly plagiarized my best friend's work. Didn't the end justify the means?

Whenever I did "borrow her thoughts" I had to make sure not to get too many right. I was an average student at best

14

while Kayla was a super brain. I suppose I could tell you that my average grades and general lack of ambition were passive aggressive middle fingers to my mother's insistence that I excel at everything in order to make her look good, and there would be some truth there, but I'm also just not that smart. My talents lie outside of academia, such as my uncanny ability to build a tall and sturdy house of cards out of any kind of deck.

Yes, even the round kind.

Time warped like it always did when I needed more of it, and we pulled into the parking lot at Waterville High (Go Cougars!) with three questions left undone. But that would only help ensure I got a C, even with my potential partial credit. Fate was fate.

"See you in third!" Kayla cheerily jogged off to her first period art class, likely a result of so much morning sugar. My stomach was already regretting not downing a glass of chocolate milk along with her.

Soldier on.

I had biology first period, which was rather cruel as these things went—asking people to "science" first thing in the morning. Luckily, Mrs. Randall was of the same mind and barely sentient herself, so I could wander through my thoughts and sometimes get an occasional nap in without her noticing. It wasn't a large class by American standards, maybe twenty of us total, but the layout allowed savvy students—such as myself—strategic cover in several spots. Behind Mr. Skullhead, the anatomy skeleton, was my particular haunt.

Then it was on to second period geometry, where I had to at least look like I was paying attention or Mr. Clazmer would have a small aneurysm, so by the time I met up with Kayla for our third period history class I was dragging. Two grueling hours until lunch still, and gym loomed next on the horizon, asking me to expend more energy I didn't have.

Should I have stayed home after all?

"Who the fuck said that? Who's the slimy little communist shit twinkle-toed cocksucker down here who just signed his own death warrant?" The siren call of the drill sergeant from *Full Metal Jacket* shook me abruptly from my daydream...or had I actually nodded off? The room and everyone in it grew hazy and disconnected, as if on the cusp of a dream.

The class laughed and turned their focus to the boy in front of me. It was his phone that had made the offending remark, the result of an unfortunately timed text message. Mr. Feeney, my history teacher, walked over and held out his hand for the device. "We won't be covering the Vietnam War in this class, Brian." Despite trying to sound authoritative, the curled corners of his lips betrayed him. There were no points for making him laugh, though—the school had a strict no cell phone policy.

The excitement was short lived and soon Mr. Feeney was back droning on about some dead Mesopotamian king. Brian sneered at the teacher, his cheeks flushed red, and I sneered at Brian. He'd woken me from a perfectly good daydream, even if I couldn't remember it...it had to be better than this. At the same time, an iron ball sank in the pit of my stomach. They'd all seen me daydreaming; that's what they were laughing at. I'd never live this down.

Since when did I give a fuck if they caught me daydreaming or not?

Heat flooded my cheeks, sweat pooled at the edges of my brows, and my skin was too tight...too damn confining...

Pain stabbed through my chest, sucking the breath from me and staking me in place. A guttural howl strangled in my throat before it could begin, coming out as a short hum. No one would hear, no one ever heard! Silent tears warmed the back of my hand. I touched my cheek and rubbed the droplets between my fingertips. Was I crying?

The pain lifted and I took in a slow, steady breath. Everything was fine. It would all work out.

Had I actually cried?

I stared at my wet fingers.

I must have.

Flaring my nostrils, I leaned back in my chair. What the fuck was going on, and when was this death sentence of a class going to end? My eyes flicked around the room, unable to focus on anything for long. When did it get so hot in here? I should take my shirt off and...sit in Brian's lap, let us both overheat as we...

Doesn't he have a girlfriend?

No, that's boring too.

What?

What's the correct line of feelings to follow?

The ball in the pit of my stomach grew, shifted into butterflies, and fell like iron rain seconds later. This wasn't my rain, wasn't my butterfly!

It was though, wasn't it?

I have to get out of here, now, before I...

"Mr. Feeney." My hand trembled as it rose. *Curious...* Was I the one moving it? The teacher stopped mid-sentence, turning to raise his bushy gray eyebrows at me. "I'm sick," I continued. "I n-need to go to the nurse."

With a saccharin smile he remarked, "You can wait five minutes, Amy."

Five minutes? I'd be dead in five minutes! Oh...what was wrong with me? A lump formed in my throat and I choked on worry that wouldn't go down the right pipe...

And how dare he tell me I can't leave!

He can't keep me here!

My mouth opened, possibly to say just that, when Kayla snapped up from her desk. "No, she can't. Or do you want her passing out here and really puttin' a wrench in it?"

17

Patting me on the shoulder, she beckoned me to stand. "Come on, I'll go down with you."

I jerked my arm from her, she couldn't touch me! I'd burn, I'd melt away, I'd—

"Amy? Is it you?" she whispered, a thousand times at once.

But I didn't respond. I couldn't respond. If I stopped clutching my chest, if my nails weren't digging into my temple, I would scatter. I'd slip into the spaces between spaces. Students crowded around me, bringing more heat, more pressure. My body shook, each heartbeat magnified and echoing, over a dry tongue, wet panties, and cold, iron butterflies.

This must be what death is.

How my mind tries to make sense of it.

I am dying.

And I am not me.

CHAPTER THREE

I never did make it to my funeral. Instead, I came to lying on a stiff, elevated bed, with the steady blip of a heart monitor in my ear and eyes too swollen to open without protest. Rubbing at them gently with my fingertips, I felt something tug at my arm. An IV line?

So it was.

Interesting.

I should care about this, but—

"For heaven's sake Amy, what did you take?" My mother sat in the chair opposite my hospital bed. Her sandy blonde hair was swept back into a ponytail, and the sleeves of her crisp white dress shirt were rolled up as always, giving her the carefully crafted appearance of a business woman who wasn't afraid to get dirty. She worked for Freedom Timber, bilking people out of their land rights and having them thank her for the privilege. She also spent a fair amount of time in the field, either scouting prospects or cleaning up disputes firsthand. As a result she had a healthy tan, a modestly fit physique, and looked to be seven years younger than her actual age of thirty-five.

On a small end table to her right lay her laptop, open no

doubt to the files of some important land acquisition. Her demeanor conveyed more annoyance at the situation than concern as she unglued her eyes from the glowing screen. Ordinarily this would have upset me. Now though, I felt nothing, only managing a passionless observation. "You assume the worst. What if I have a tumor?"

"Then I'll be relieved my daughter isn't on drugs. Tumors can be cut out," she said curtly.

"Then you'll be relieved and I'll be terrified...unless they keep me on this *government approved* drug." I pulled on the IV line, straining to see the writing on the bag hanging above me. "Peroxide?"

"Paraxopram," Mother corrected me.

"Then I'll be likely to walk into traffic out of apathy." I should have been scared, I should have been crying, or angry, or something, after what I'd been through. But I was just...empty.

"Cut the bullshit Amy. Your blood work is already being tested so it's just a matter of time before they tell me what you took. The sooner you fess up, the sooner they can counter the effects." She was so sure of herself.

"I'm not on anything but peroxide, Mother," robot me replied.

The condescension in her voice amped up along with her volume. "You were screaming, 'I'm not me!' in your classroom for ten minutes before they finally had the sense to call an ambulance and bring you here for treatment. Don't think I won't be talking to Martin about their negligence as soon as you're released." My mother was on a first name basis with her lawyer, giving him more business in a year than is healthy for someone who isn't a career criminal.

"The last thing I remember is a queasy stomach and"—I squinted—"wanting to get away from...Kayla?" Was that right?

"Mmm, so this drug you're on isn't all bad," Mother interrupted, partially speaking to herself.

"Where is she?" I asked.

"I wouldn't let her in here," she snorted. "And I advised her mother to test her too, since she's the likely source." Did I mention that my mother didn't like Kayla and was always looking for a reason to separate us? I'd be an Olympic athlete by now if it weren't for Kayla's bad influence. As if my friendship with her was all that was holding me back from fulfilling some potential only seen through Mother's rose-colored glasses. Never mind her own giant boot cutting off my circulation.

"And when you're wrong I look forward to your apology." Logically I should be yelling at her for the things she was saying, but it was like my inner fire had been snuffed out. I twiddled my IV line. "What does this do? I feel like the walking dead."

"It's a sedative; you were crying and incoherent when they brought you in. They were afraid you might hurt yourself." Mother's tone was as emotionless as my own. "Don't take it out until they tell you."

I hit the nurse call button and Ma's warm and friendly face greeted me within moments. She looked like Kayla, save for a longer nose, dark auburn hair, and some crow's feet around her eyes. "Amy! What a blessing you're up. How're you feeling?"

"I'm not," I said, shoving my cheeks up with my fingertips to induce a smile.

Mother tilted her head and smirked. "She wants to take the tube out of her arm, Faye, though I think it's a much more pleasant atmosphere in here with it in."

Ma gave her an irreverent smile and shook her head with a small laugh. "If only raising children were that easy, Angela." My mother doubtless took her words as agreement. I was a difficult daughter, but Ma wasn't laughing with her, she was laughing at her and her desire to control me. Faye Rodriguez danced a fine line with my parents, holding back her true thoughts and maintaining a friendly relationship with them for the sake of me and Kayla. With some of the things Mother had said to her over the years about her daughter, she'd have been well within her rights to deck her.

"It's a powerful sedative," she said, checking one of the machines that went ping. "Now that she's rested and calmed down it's best to remove it." She unplugged the IV from my arm but left the connector attached. "We're going to keep that on you for a while, until we've got everything sorted out. Okay?" I didn't really have a choice but the illusion of one was nice and I nodded.

Ma called up my chart on the computer. "We got your initial blood work back from the lab and found no traces of any drugs in your system." She turned from me to my mother, leaving a silence just long enough to make things awkward before continuing. "There are increased cytokines in the blood which indicates her body is fighting something off, but none of the usual suspects came back positive. Doctor Nimans would like to run some more tests that will help us get to the bottom of things."

As a birthday gift to myself, I'd dropped a twelve-pound bowling ball on my foot last week. Ma had worked her magic on the spot, with ice from the soda fountain and warm oil from the Splitz deep fryer. I smelled like onion rings for three days afterwards, but finished my free game and even went to a party that night. If Ma could work miracles under bowling alley conditions, I'd be out of Waterville Memorial, with all their beeping machines, within the hour.

I might have been relieved, if I could feel such a thing.

Typed in bold letters at the end of my chart was the word "Exhaustion." Exhaustion? Wasn't that something house-wives in the 1940s used to suffer from? What did I have to be exhausted about? I was a middle-class girl from rural Maine.

Ma logged out, unfolded a nearby wheelchair, and gestured for me to get in it.

"Free rides." She smiled and helped me sit on the frigid faux leather seat. When we reached the door she called back, "Angela, are you coming?"

Mother pressed her phone to her ear. "I'm calling Matthew to update him. Let me know when the results are in or if I need to make a decision." She sat back in her chair, eyes trailing out the window. "Hey, your daughter isn't on drugs…"

My apology for that assumption would never come. I had smoked pot now and again, but luckily not recently, or the "devil-weed" would have been a scapegoat.

Doctor Nimans met us in the frigid MRI room—couldn't this place afford heat? She was a pudgy middle-aged woman, with brown hair pulled up in a hasty bun, and wrinkles that suggested she had worried herself into old age before her time. The bottom part of her glasses was hidden by the creases of her cheeks.

"How are you feeling?" she asked, closing the door behind her. A poster of a monkey juggling fruit cheerfully instructed us to "Go bananas for fruits and veggies." All the produce was smiling, and for a moment I pondered the sinister nature of eating fruit with a face.

"I'm hungry," I replied. "And cold."

"Well that's a good sign." Taking out her flashlight, she looked into both my eyes. "Follow my finger without moving your head." She wagged her pointer at me and I did as requested.

"Here, drink this." Ma handed me a cup of blue liquid.

"What is it?" I asked.

"Radioactive Kool-Aid." She pursed her lips together.

Not exactly the meal I had in mind, but I downed it with a slight gag and cough. "Store brand, radioactive flavored, powdered beverage like substance," I corrected her as she handed me a blessedly heated blanket for my journey.

Laying on the platform, I slid inside the metal tube and into a world of following Pac-man with my eyes while he gobbled up little round souls and blinking ghosts for the better part of an hour. By the end, a ball of nerves had formed in the pit of my stomach.

But it was *my* ball.

My anxiety.

I am me.

The Paraxopram had worn off.

"Everything looks normal." Under the weight of her furrowed brow, the top half of Doctor Nimans's glasses disappeared. She stood in the doorway, some distance away, as the machine slid me back out.

"So it's not a tumor?" I asked, slipping off the platform before it stopped. It was still bouncing when my head and heart seized. I steadied myself against the bed as Ma, Doctor Nimans, and a group of technicians filed into the room. The weight in my stomach evaporated and I took a deep, easy breath, my fingers curling, vice-like, around the platform.

Whatever this is, I can handle it. I'm just hungr—

A bowling ball dropped on my insides, rolling off my heart and spinning through my guts.

No! No, I can't! My mouth went dry, even as drool oozed from the edges.

"I see no evidence here." Nimans flipped through my chart. "Although some results will need to be sent out for interpretation, it will be a few days before we have the complete picture. I'm going to discharge you unti—"

I fell forward under the weight of worry, clinging to Ma as she held me up. "It'll be okay." Tears broiled in my eyes, and I choked out a smile before springing to my feet. "Yes! Yes, it will!" I patted the face of one of the technicians and tweaked his nose, with a grin.

Claws shredded into my heart and mind, ripping trenches that bubbled and filled in with—my teeth chattered—*excitement? Worry?*

Not mine.

None of it mine.

Color bled from the eyes of the people above me and from the red squared patterns of the carpet in the hallway. Darkness flooded in, eager to take its place.

CHAPTER FOUR

*D*arkness still encircled me when I awoke, save for the glow of the machines around me and the night light over the nurses' station. My view was partially obstructed out of both eyes by something running down the middle of my face—a ribbon of some kind. I made to move it aside, but my arms jerked against leather straps. An IV line once again ran the length of my arm, pumping numbness into me. I wanted to crawl out of my skin and into someone else's.

A small shape lay curled in the big gray chair opposite me. "Kayla," I whispered. A giant wooden cross around my neck swayed to the side and clanged against the metal bars of the bed. One of Abuela's monstrosities.

After my fourth call, Kayla sat up, rubbing her eyes and taking a hard look around. "Amy? Is it you?"

"Mostly...I think," I blew out, and the ribbon briefly rode the updraft. "What is this?"

"How long were you grounded when your mother found out we went cliff diving off Frye's Leap?"

"I wasn't grounded because she never found out," I replied flatly. She yanked the ribbon off in one motion and I grit my teeth. She'd stuck it on with a hospital grade bandage. "Besides, you chickened out so there was no we."

Kayla turned on the overhead light and undid my wrist straps. "With any luck you'll always be you from here on out." She gestured to the ribbon. "That's a talisman to kick out hitchhiking spirits. I had to borrow some of your blood and mix it with mine to make it. Must have lanced you twenty times and you didn't wake up."

With my left hand free, I picked up the ribbon and examined the intricate pictograms painted down its length.

Still focused on my straps, she chided, "And I didn't chicken out, but I did scream like a yeti all the way down."

"I know, I had to make sure you were you, too." The shadow of a smile attempted to surface. "It's pretty." I rubbed the satin talisman through my fingertips, which somehow weren't sore after Kayla's butchering. What happened before I blacked out this time? Had I finished the MRI scans? "I certainly feel empty. There's barely one of me in here, let alone two, but that could be from the liquid sunshine flowing in my veins. I feel like an unfrosted Pop-Tart. Like one of those girls who hang out in the bathroom by the auditorium —emotionally dead."

My eyes moved from the talisman to the balloon hovering above me. It boasted a silvery reflective clown honking a horn that told me to get well. "See, you know something is wrong because I should be terrified of that thing but it isn't bothering me. Seriously, I can see why people kill themselves on these meds, you're already halfway there."

"Maybe I made the talisman wrong?" Kayla took the ribbon and squinted at it in the dim light.

"I was like this earlier too. It is definitely the Paramore, or whatever it's called." With my right hand I worked at unhooking the IV line, but they had made it a two-handed process precisely to thwart me.

Kayla pinched the line between a paperclip, stopping the drip while leaving the needle as it was.

"I can't even appreciate you," I said, with a dry sigh. But I couldn't be afraid either, not like how I should be. Was that a good thing?

From her bag she pulled an extra-large take-out cup with a picture of a scheming cartoon leprechaun on it. He'd get all your gold. You'd give it voluntarily on account of how good his shake was. We never missed out on the seasonal delicacy from Clifford's ice cream shop. Crawling into my bed beside me, she shoved the straw in and tilted the cup toward my lips.

"How 'bout now?" She laughed.

The shake was a warm melted puddle of utter mint perfection. We swapped it back and forth, along with our versions of the day's events. My adventures at school hadn't ended where I thought they had.

"So you don't remember flipping Mr. Feeney the bird and telling him to shove his potatoes up his ass?" She stifled a laugh as I shook my head. "We barely made it to the hallway when the bell rang anyway, he should have just let us go."

I had no memory of it, but Mr. Feeney sure wouldn't forget.

"Anyway, you backed away from me like I was on fire until you slammed into the lockers. Then you clutched your head and went fetal, repeating, 'I'm not me,' over and over again. Whispered at first, but by the time the paramedics got there you were screamin' it and thrashing around."

"They had to sedate me," I finished, stating a fact.

"Yeah, you wouldn't even let me near you."

I chewed on the straw. "Maybe, I was protecting you?"

Or me?

"Pfft. You couldn't kick my ass, even if there were two of you in there." She nudged me with her shoulder. "But it seems like the kinda thing you'd think of while fighting a possession." My unwitting chivalry earned me a kiss on the cheek.

Possession? Was that what this was?

Excitement and worry that weren't mine.

I'm not me.

"Is that what happened in the MRI room too? Why'd they strap me down? Did I hurt Ma?"

"Ma's good, but yeah, it was similar." She opened the cup, ran her finger along the inside, and licked it clean.

"I get the talisman and the cross, but what's with the clown?" I asked. "How does it factor into your hoodoo?"

"I'm tryin' to ward off evil spirits, not encourage them." Kayla frowned. "Your dad brought it."

"He left his man-cave to go somewhere other than work? That's a minor miracle right there."

Both my parents acted as though they were reading a tattered copy of *How to Raise Your Child in 15 Easy Steps*, where some of the steps had been ripped out and used for kindling. Visiting your child in the hospital to scare the crap out of her with a hovering clown must have been on one of the surviving pages.

Still, it was the thought that counted. I was immune to fear for now, but he didn't know that.

The nurses, all friends of Ma's, looked the other way and let my best girl stay the night so long as she was gone by visiting hours the next morning. She stayed home from school the following day, throwing herself into paranormal research in case the talisman and rosary weren't enough. Meanwhile, in addition to calling in her daughter, Ma called in favors to have my labs bumped up, making sure they were analyzed by the guy with the most experience and the least Baileys in his coffee.

We had the results by the end of the day. Aside from the increased cytokines in my blood, which had fallen substantially in subsequent tests, I was the picture of health. I would have been overjoyed to hear the news, but they had forced the sedative back on me sometime in the night.

The trouble with a conclusion of godlike vitality was that the doctors fell to their all-purpose junk diagnosis of it being "all in my head"—and faster than you can say Paraxopram, I was given the home version, Paraxil, judged to have "social anxiety disorder," and sentenced to a lifetime of pharmaceuticals.

CHAPTER FIVE

*I*n the days that followed, the blank, cod-like expression I wore kept gossip at school to a minimum, and Kayla's raised fist took care of any stragglers. No more episodes happened, but the only way to know if the reprieve was due to Kayla's talisman, or the soul-destroying meds, was to go off them. However, if I had another episode and Mother found out, I'd be gawking at a padded cell in County Psyche.

"I can't stay on these pills," I said to Kayla as we left school Thursday afternoon. "I'd rather drown in emotion, or figure out a timeshare agreement with the hitchhiker, than never feel again. Only thing I've felt in the past three days is *wrong*. Like I'm outta phase or not even here at all. Like I'm a ghost in my own skin."

"Stay at my house this weekend. You can stop the meds and we'll see if the talisman worked. Worse comes to worse, you can go back on the Paraxil again." Her truck creaked as she got in.

"No. If I have another breakdown we need to find a better way to handle it." I crawled onto the passenger's side. "I won't go back on that shit, it's suicide."

She nodded and reached under her seat, coming up with a screwdriver. "There's more than one way to unskin a ghost. If my talisman didn't work we've got options, don't you worry."

"No risk there. But you don't want to ask it any questions before booting it?"

"Time for questions passed when it put my best friend in the hospital." She jammed the screwdriver into the ignition, twisted it, and Goblin's engine turned over, stopped, clicked, turned over again, sputtered, clanked, and begrudgingly rattled awake.

I sympathized with it.

"Now, you sound possessed," I droned. "After all this, I might like to at least get a name."

"We'll see how things go." She smirked and gave me the eye. "I might like to know where my keys wandered off to."

I tapered off the pills Friday night, during a "Slumber Party Massacre" marathon at Kayla's. I didn't scream, I didn't laugh; I just sat there, watching as if through several panes of ash smudged glass. The whole of me was buried, brain deep, in dry earth, my bones rusting from within, and if I sat on that squeaky couch one more minute I would become it.

At least it squeaked in an interesting way, which was more than I could say for myself.

"I'm going to bed," I said in my monotone voice, walking with my monotone shuffle up a monotonous set of stairs. One more step to the top, but if I missed it and tumbled back and broke my neck it would be all the same.

Kayla nudged me from behind, and I cleared the step. Two minutes later I fell asleep instead of down the stairs.

The next morning, I drifted awake to the pleasant feeling of my feelings—and only my feelings. No weird pressure, no claws, no oblivionic void sucking the color out of life—one pill, one IV drip at a time.

Grinning ear to ear, I sat up and made a duck face in Kayla's bedside mirror. "Hello beautiful." I transferred a kiss from my fingers to the mirror and it spun in place several times from the force of it. Outside, the cattle chuffed and stomped at the gate. Kayla would be feeding them soon, so I hurried down the stairs in my Scooby Doo pajamas to help and give her the good news.

Halfway across the kitchen, my skin prickled and a new butterfly hatched in my stomach. Reflexively, I took a few steps backward and the butterfly evaporated. Cocking my head to the side, I walked forward again and the sensation returned.

I was crossing a barrier of some kind.

Sliding back again, I called to Kayla, her mud boots and coat hung by the door, so she had to still be in the house. "Hey! Kayla! You've gotta come check this out!" Moments after the words left me, adrenaline flooded through my ankles, then on up through my knees. More excitement merging with my own...but not mine.

Kayla appeared in the kitchen door, a burst dam of adrenaline gushing from her. Bringing my hands up against the pressure, and heat, I stumbled back and fell on the stairs, crab crawling up them as Kayla rushed toward me.

"Stay back!" I shouted and my friend froze where she stood. By the time I reached the first landing, the excess excitement had gone out with the tide.

"Amy, talk to me!" Kayla's quivering voice came from below.

"I'm alright...just stay where you are." One by one I descended the stairs on my butt until the adrenaline lapped at my feet and a lead butterfly unfurled in my stomach. After a deep breath, I said, "Take one step forward." As she did, the butterflies multiplied and my calves submerged in hot adrenaline. Vice grips tightened against my mind and chest. "Now back," I huffed through gritted teeth. She complied and the feelings receded incrementally.

The house was laid out in such a way that we could only see one another's feet as we talked. Sunlight danced through the white curtains of the stairwell window, making lacey patterns on my legs. *My* legs. "So, um, this is interesting. I'm getting some kind of emotional feedback, but it's tied to you. The closer you get, the more my brain wants to pop."

"And you're fine up there on the steps?" Kayla asked tentatively.

"Perfectly. Well, no, not really. I kinda wanna throw up but it's because of my butterflies, not yours...I think. Fuck, I don't know!" My heart thrummed an unpleasant rhythm against my ribs.

"Alright, let me grab my Proton Pack and we can continue our Hokey Pokey." Her feet disappeared from view only to reappear a second later. "Urm, if you're up for it?"

"God yes! But let's go out to the barn. Less chance we'll be interrupted when Ma gets home." I bolted up the stairs, two by two, and threw on jeans and a t-shirt while Kayla loaded her backpack with cameras that saw in multiple wavelengths and several small boxes adorned with colorful lights that sometimes beeped. There were good beeps and bad beeps, but I could never tell which was which. Kayla had spent a small fortune on the stuff over the years and spoke their language fluently.

My desire to find out what was really going on, and more importantly how to stop, or at least control it, was slightly stronger than my desire to run screaming up the hillside and bury my head in mud. The suffocating violation of drowning in another person's emotions, even those of my sister, wasn't something I was keen to experience again, but what choice was there?

This twisted empathy seemed to have intensified since getting off the drugs. Maybe whatever was inside me knew it could be shut away and so was trying harder to break free while it still could? Maybe it was trying to jump to Kayla? We'd really be screwed then. She'd forgotten more about the paranormal world than I'd ever learned.

Right then, I just wouldn't let this thing out of my clutches; simple as that.

Was it even an it? If it was, then it only responded to other people, because as I sat alone in the front hall, half into one boot, I felt nothing out of the ordinary. No, I didn't like the idea of it being an it—there had to be something else going on. Kayla's tests were strictly a formality. Get it out of her system.

By the time I opened the side door I almost believed it.

The chickens were clustered at the door as I exited; they heard me getting ready and congregated expectantly. "There's a whole world of bugs out there to eat." I shook my head, smiled, and gestured to the front yard. "The world is your banquet." Halting at the end of the stairs, I looked down at my chest and frowned. "Not you...you need to behave yourself."

It felt good to assert myself out loud like that. Never mind, I wasn't sure who I was talking to. Hadn't I just decided what was happening to me was a "what" and not an "it" less than a minute before?

One of the heifers, Selene, rubbed her nose on the fence beside the barn door, and as I approached, a gentle pressure made my ears pop. I procrastinated by assisting in the scratching, and my heart beat slowed to a relaxed pace. A faint yet pleasant calmness drifted around the animal. Rather than forcing itself upon me, like had happened with Kayla, it was more of a slow tide, coming and going with ease.

After a few moments, she snorted and walked away, leaving me free and excuse-less. I took a steadying breath and went into the barn. Kayla futzed with one of her cameras some forty feet away, and I shouted to explain what happened with Selene. My voice echoed and distorted throughout the place.

"So it appears to be more human focused," she yelled.

"If it is an 'it.'" I surveyed what she had set up so far. Lots of flashing black boxes, a digital clock with giant numbers, multicolored strips of tape at regular intervals on the floor, and stacks of hay bales at the far end.

"Would you prefer he, or she, or Casper?" She cackled.

"No. I mean what if '*it*' is '*me*'? Like I'm some kinda mutant or something, instead of being possessed."

"Then you get to have a low-cut uniform and fight crime, with me as your beautiful sidekick. As a matter of fact, that sounds like fun no matter how things turn out. We should make it happen." One of the machines beeped when she set it on the ground. Was it a good beep? It must have been; Kayla didn't pay it any mind.

"I hate Spandex," I said.

"Leather then." Her face was deadpan perfection.

"I haven't ruled out that I'm just a figment of your imagination, either." Chuckling, I peeled a bit of paint off the wood beside me. "Because that totally sounds like something you'd do."

"If that was true you'd already be in Spandex." She smirked.

"Now you just became the villain." How could she make me laugh when so much of me was mid-scream?

"Good. They have the best lines. Speakin' of, go stand over by that red one." I did, and she came gradually closer to me. "Let me know when you start to feel something, anything at all."

"There!" I shouted. "Pressure on me and…" I narrowed my eyes. "…excitement, a little bit of nerves…but maybe that's me?"

She made a mark on the floor and measured from the nearest piece of tape. "Twenty-two and a quarter feet."

"One quarter?"

"Yeah, you're apparently an empathic overachiever." She smiled and backed up to the starting line to repeat the process several more times, with the same results. Even her excitement stayed exactly the same.

Then she vaulted over the hay bales and disappeared behind them. "Okay! Now, I'm gonna try to change my emotions! The white line marks the edge of your range from me. Step over it and tell me when you feel the pressure, and what I'm feeling. I've got a checklist!" She held up her green spiral bound notebook and flapped it around. Her pen fell out and stuck in the hay.

"Eager, giddy, about to bust a nut. That's low hanging fruit." I laughed. "How are you going to be anything else right now?"

Revulsion punched me in the gut, and skittered up my spine, my lip curling in an involuntary response seconds later. "Oh God." I bent over and spat. "What are you doing over there? I feel like I'm gonna be sick, while punching something."

"Reading through my spam, and you are spot on. I'm definitely NOT going to be downloading THAT." Her tone was even, though her emotions up-ticked steadily into mischievous, happy territory.

"That's better. Now you've got a Loki vibe going on. Goddess of Mischief." My hands rested on my knees.

"I'm trolling a fascist with a spelling impediment. Damn, that lead in the baby rattles, paint, and gasoline really reached across the decades with some of these assholes."

An emotion, too radiant for me to make sense of, flared out from her. I stumbled back, over the white line, and crashed onto my butt while the world needled into black. Three minutes later, I sucked in a short deep breath, while whispering, "I'm not me." Kayla was still behind the hay bales; she hadn't come to my side. "I-I don't know about that last one, it was too…bright."

"I was tryin' to be peaceful," she said. "You alright?"

"Ah, peaceful, that explains it, I have no frame of reference!" I giggled uneasily, stood, and brushed myself off as I stepped back over the white line. "It's nice to feel your relief though, like a summer's breeze. A summer's breeze in the heat of the Mojave desert, but still a breeze."

"I didn't come check on you, didn't want to make it worse."

"Probably the right call." I sighed, rubbing sweat from my cool skin. "Give me some breathing room."

She took her phone down from one of her rigs and flipped through some images. "Amy! I recorded us on my thermal app and you can see your temperature change to match mine!" She sent me the video files, which translated into a bunch of rainbow blobs to me. Still, I couldn't help but share her excitement. If she said the blobs were in harmony, then the blobs were in harmony. "This is HUGE! We've got outside verification!"

In my/her excitement, I ran toward her, intent on hugging her, but hugged the floor instead, losing consciousness for five minutes this time.

Imagine a stadium floodlight hanging ten feet above your head. It wouldn't immediately fry you to a crisp, but you wouldn't want to sit and play jacks under it, either. The same was true for me and my ability to be near my best friend for too long; the intensity of her emotions was blinding.

Ma popped in, not long after I came to, with some well-timed fruit and almonds for us while we played our "ghost busting game." There was a marked difference between the bleed over from her and the bleed over from Kayla. Kayla was far brighter, so to speak, than her mother, or indeed anyone else I would ever come to encounter. Maybe because we were so close, so it stood to reason our connection would be that much more intense?

It was only a guess.

Something also might have happened to her, along with me, and it hadn't shown itself yet.

To that end, none of her machines beeped in any of the ways that indicated an entity other than the two of us was involved. Not letting me sit with that relief for long, Kayla insisted she needed to upgrade her equipment before we could rule it out.

She anointed me with funny smelling oils, read to me in Latin, and smudged me with sage smoke until the smoke detector in the barn went ballistic.

That beep I understood.

"Here, put this on." Kayla set a silver butterfly ring on one of the fence posts and backed away.

"A mood ring?" I slipped it on and the blue wings shifted and mottled to pink.

"Yeah, I found it in my bottom dresser drawer, along with my freakin' keys! Divine guidance. I want you to concentrate on it when you start feeling overwhelmed. Hold onto the color on display and tell yourself it's yours and no one else's." She shrugged. "I don't know if it'll work but, it's worth a try and it'll class up your wardrobe."

Kayla started out twenty-three feet away, coming ever closer as I focused on the ring. The nearer she got, the more intense her emotions became and the harder it was to distinguish them from my own. Like drops of food coloring in a bowl of water. After a few hours and many, many more black outs, she could be two feet from me without me losing consciousness, as long as I kept my focus on that ring. I couldn't concentrate on anything else to save my life, but I stayed upright.

Maybe it was divine guidance that led Kayla to that mood ring; maybe she'd just kicked off her jeans with her keys in

39

the pocket and they'd fallen into her drawer. Either way, it was a welcome pressure relief valve. I would continue working on control and refinement, while Kayla threw herself into research with the new data we'd collected. But for now, we had met our immediate goal. I could get through school on Monday.

I had no idea what I was getting myself into.

CHAPTER SIX

$\mathcal{B}$y the time we made it to school Monday, I was already exhausted from repeating "I am orange," like a deranged Buddhist, for the thirty minute drive with Kayla. Orange was the color of anxiety, so I at least knew the thing was functioning properly, but in those moments it was such an understated color.

Walking down the nearly empty hall at school, I was bombarded with emotions seeping into the corridor from the different classrooms; boredom, anxiety, infatuation, and lust. I eyed my mood ring, kept my head down, and shuffled inside biology class just as the bell sounded. Outwardly, there wasn't much difference between how I behaved on Paraxil and how I was now without it. In both cases I appeared to match wits with a vacant zombie. At least I'd keep up expected appearances.

Small miracles.

It was impossible for me to distinguish who owned any particular emotion in the room, but there was a nearly constant undercurrent of lust, except when anything having to do with sex was mentioned, then that same stream would shift towards embarrassment. Every now and again there would be a noticeably intense emotion and I could tell the general area it was coming from, but in those times I was too preoccupied with keeping myself upright to work on pinpointing the source.

I am orange.

I made it through the entire class as a citrus fruit. Not that I learned a damn thing about biology, other than teenagers are horny and confused, which I already knew, but I held it together like a champ. When the bell rang, I ran to my second period math class in order to secure a place by the door. I had it all figured out; such a spot in every class would allow me to have the least amount of people in my bubble—but it wasn't my usual pick, so I would have to usurp whoever's butt had grown comfortable there over the semester. Their angst and frustration would just end up blending right in with everyone else's.

The bell rang again, sealing us all into Mr. Clazmer's geometry class. The overweight, middle-aged, deceptively jovial looking man surveyed us with sadistic glee before saying in a cheery voice, "Put everything under your desks except your pencils and your brilliant minds. Let's see what pops out!" He hadn't even finished speaking when I was hit with wave after wave of panic, anxiety, frustration, and fear.

Pop quiz indeed. *Let's see how you fare with such intensity Amy…why not…it's only your second class on your first day back—you should be an old pro at this by now.*

I breathed deeply and focused on my ring, but it wasn't enough to keep the feelings out. They rang through me like slow motion bullets: punching holes through my heart and mind, filling the empty spaces with their respective emotions. This had the jarring effect of me not knowing which vein of emotions belonged to me…because they all did.

In the distance, Mr. Clazmer called time, and the barrage of anxiety began to curl away. Time? Only a minute had passed. Why was he asking us to bring our papers to the front? My eyes fluttered open and I stared down at my quiz. It wasn't blank. The word "**Black**," written in disheveled, blocky letters, was scattered haphazardly around the page. The same color as my mood ring. The color of fear and overwhelming stress.

I am black.

A shockwave of my own terror and confusion pulsed through me. Needles tingled across my limbs. My limbs? I had a body?

Of course.

When had I lost the connection?

I crumpled the quiz into my purse and bolted from the room, not stopping until I reached the auditorium bathroom at the far end of school.

A thunderous creak echoed through the girls' bathroom as I shouldered the door open and stumbled inside. My eyes burned with tears so thick the world became a canvas of vague shapes and muted colors. The pressure in my head threatened to drop me where I stood. They would find me with my head cracked open on this dirty floor, torrents of "black" streaming out in place of blood. What in the fuck had I been thinking trying to pull this off? Maybe a nice padded cell somewhere wouldn't be so bad—at least there'd be fewer people around...right?

Right?

Legs wobbling, I clutched the sink and squinted at the blurred mirror. Was that face even mine? Why was it even in question? Gasping, I crawled to the toilet seat in the farthest stall, shut the door, and leaned my head against the cold tile wall. I hadn't allowed myself to cry much since this shit storm began—I was too focused on keeping in control and figuring out what was going on. Now I howled like a lost puppy, releasing pent up stress from the past week, alongside abrasive foreign emotions that had become almost indistinguishable from my own. They trickled out like tar, and hollow, unyielding despair filled in the fissures. I was either out of my depth, or out of my mind, or both. Either way, I wasn't leaving that stall under my own power.

Was that the door creaking open?

Is someone here?

What does it matter? I either can't or won't quiet myself for their benefit.

Their emotions were...distant and hazy, as though they were a walking dose of Paraxil. I would have to go back on the drug, at least until the summer, when I could work on being around people on my own terms. A fresh cry escaped me. Summer was over two months away.

The person walked straight to the stall next to mine, latched the door shut, and straddled the seat. Black leggings, a black floor length, shredded skirt, and black military boots —scuffed and scraped, yet polished to perfection—settled in place and stilled. Rainbow shoelaces offered a playful swatch of color in the otherwise drab attire.

Sulfur burned.

A match?

Cigarette smoke wafted over the door. A long breath in and slow exhale came from the figure beside me. Two slender fingers jutted under the divider, a lit cigarette held between them. "It helps me take the edge off the bullshit." Her voice was soft, but detached, stating a fact rather than offering pity or sympathy.

With a shaky hand I reached down and plucked it from her, sure I would burn myself, but I didn't. I stared at the smoking stick in abject fascination for a moment before putting it to my lips and inhaling. What the fuck did I have to lose at this point? Maybe the emo girl was onto something?

A sense of calm euphoria washed through me, loosening each of the sticky, pent up, parasitical emotions I'd been carrying. They slipped out of me like water through a sieve. I let out a moan as I took another drag. This was exactly what I needed.

"Most people hack a lung up the first time, you're one tough bitch," my mysterious benefactor remarked. She didn't have the usual Maine accent.

I puffed out a short laugh. My lungs burned slightly with each inhalation, but that was all. Now the first time I had smoked pot two years back, that was another story. I coughed so loud and so long I spooked a squirrel out of its tree. It climbed halfway down the trunk and chattered at me in such a way that I was sure it was calling my virtue into question. This, of course, set my friends and I to a good half hour of hysterics, during which the offended critter bounded across the tree tops and disappeared.

"I'm Leilani," my new found drug dealer said, breaking me from my memories.

"Amy. And thanks," the words trembled out, followed by a quick breath in.

"It's nothin'. You'll get me back." Her tone was sure and steady; maybe she was from Colorado or somewhere out West? Was Heaven out West? At some point she lit up another cigarette and we smoked in silence for a while, my face tightening up as the tears evaporated and I returned to myself again.

Only myself.

"There's no need to fear the wolves, Amy..." She rapped on the divider with her knuckles as she spoke, and I thought I heard her head lay against it as she paused. "...You're a lioness." An underlying wistfulness caressed each sober word.

Nothing like it touched her emotions. They remained distant.

A pack of smokes hit the floor and she kicked them under the stall to me before standing and opening her door. "Happy Birthday."

With a smile, I picked up the pack of Green menthols. Two lions faced each other on the logo. Bizarre, as pep talks went, but I appreciated it, and the fact that she hadn't asked me what was wrong. These auditorium bathroom girls were all right.

I squinted at her reflection in the mirror through the crack in my door as she scrubbed her hands with enough vigor to draw blood. Her jet black hair was swept neatly behind her to her waist and sported a streak of rainbow down one side. Her features were delicately chiseled, a doll on the top shelf poised to fall and break at the slightest wobble. Full lips mouthed silent trembling words without fully closing, and her angular eyes were white. Only white.

Where are her pupils?!

Blinking in rapid succession, I narrowed my eyes and peered again. Her pupils were there, vibrant, black irises that gripped me through her reflection.

"The janitor is on her rounds, you might want to recede to the shadows." She headed for the exit, pausing at the door with a smile in her voice. "Work on your roar, alright?" The door creaked open and she disappeared into the hall.

I didn't get to thank her for lending me the lifeline, though my gratitude was self-evident. I *would* get her back—I had some money saved from my birthday—but cigarettes were expensive, and it wouldn't last long. I'd have to get a job for sure now, something my mother had been on me about since I'd turned sixteen. All supposing these little miracles held up their end of the bargain and continued helping me function.

A book of matches tucked into the cellophane of the cigarette pack read, "Crime Scene Clean-Up Kit. Just add gasoline, strike, drop, and run." I chuckled, flushed my cigarette butt, and opened the stall door. At the very sink Leilani had been a minute before, I looked at my reflection in the warped mirror and splashed cool water on my face. She'd always had pupils; these mirrors just sucked.

"Shit's spooky enough without you adding to it," I said to myself. As I left the girls' bathroom, the janitor had just entered the boys. The hall was clear for miles in either direction.

Cigarettes. How do I love thee? Let me count my doomed bank balance. It turned out the little cancer sticks took just enough edge off my empathy for me to be able to breathe a little. As long as I smoked regularly, it was sort of like putting on headphones to drown out a fire alarm. You can still hear it blaring like a banshee, but it sucks a little less. This effect lasted anywhere from half an hour to an hour per cigarette, depending on what was going on around me, but I reveled in every minute of it.

We tried the nicotine patch, some gum, vaping, and even some straight nicotine pills, but they didn't have the same effect. Even chewing tobacco, which I thought would be nice since I could do it on the sly in class, did nothing but make me want to puke. Smoking weed made everyone's emotions about as bright as Kayla's on a good day and super sticky; they stuck to me long after I'd retreated. It wasn't pleasant.

As near as we could figure, there must have been something unique to the tobacco smoking process. If I chain smoked, I could stay close to Kayla for an hour each night; however, watching her cough and turn green was just as daunting as not smoking at all in many ways. Still, things were steadily improving, and Kayla was sure it would be a matter of time before I held the reins on this empathy thing and could toss the smokes aside for good.

CHAPTER SEVEN

*W*hen a few days passed, and I had yet to run into Leilani again to pay her back, hug her, and worship at her feet, I put Kayla to work digging up her address from the school records. When classes let out, we met in the parking lot to discuss what she'd found.

She was a mixture of frustration and excitement as she hit the hood of her truck with both palms. "We're chasing a ghost!"

"Aren't we always?" I quipped.

"I put in every possible spelling of Leilani, looked through all of the names starting with *L*, and went back five fawkin' years and nothin' even came close! I even talked to the head of maintenance and crusty old Linda in the office to see about temporary staff who may have had that name. She damn near caught me going through the Vice's computer too, I didn't think the search would take so long." Kayla drew in a long breath, leaned against the Goblin's driver's side door and leveled her gaze at me. "Are you *positive* it was Leilani and not something else?"

I took in my own deep breath filled with tar, nicotine, and fiberglass. "Yeah, because it sounded like lei lines, and we were just talking about those last month." I was growing increasingly agitated along with her, despite the anchor of my cigarette. My eyes closed while I attempted to center myself, and the day I met Leilani played back through my mind.

Had I heard her name right? Yes, I had. *We're chasing a ghost.* Kayla used the term in the sense of someone who has vanished but—my eyes shot open.

"Kayla...there's somethin' I forgot to tell you, but now I wonder if it might not be important. Urm, if it even happened at all but, I should really know better, considering how freaky all this is..." My best friend waited patiently for me to gather my words. No small feat in her current agitated state. "...I think maybe her eyes went all white, just for a second, or it may have been a flash of the mirror or some-thing, I don't know..."

Kayla nodded, took another measured breath, and exhaled, coughing as the chilly wind shifted and blew my smoke in her direction. "You said her emotions were different too, like she was on Paraxil or something like it."

"You think she was a spirit?" I asked, seeking validation that I might be on to something.

"Explains that weird thing she said to you about you being a lioness. Ghosts are always saying cryptic shit." Her irritation shifted to elation and her smile curled up at the edges.

The hunt was on.

"Are spirits always smoking Marlboro Greens?" I pondered my cigarette.

"I don't know—depends on how strong they are." She laughed. "But I wanna look into it some more, see if I can't pull the surveillance footage. She had to come in some-where." Her eyebrows raised. "Unless she didn't..."

My smile grew as I flicked my cigarette into the road,

49

showering sparks like mini fireworks. "You're lovin' this, aren't you?"

"You already know the answer to that—even without your freaky ability." She kissed me on the forehead. "There's no way this isn't connected to what's going on with you. Could be the break we're lookin' for. Let's go charm our way into Chuck's office and take a look at Monday's footage." My girl grinned from ear to ear.

With the school nearly empty, it was easy for me to find and follow officer Chuck as he made his rounds and made sure all the doors were locked for the night, checking them each neatly off his clipboard list as he went. He was not a small man, and the whole event seemed to wind him, so he was relieved to be able to head back to his waiting chair and log on for his nightly report. As soon as boredom slogged from him, I figured he was well into the system and went into action.

"Chuck! Thank goodness you're still here!" Panting, I ran into his office, amazed and a little disgusted/flattered at how quickly his emotions went from bored to horny. I could use that. Keep his eyes on me. "I *stupidly* left my keys in the auditorium and now it's locked and I can't get in!" My hips shifted toward him. "I know it was dumb of me but, can you help me out?" Wasn't this how several porn movies started? Judging by his flustered, yet hopeful reaction, I thought that must be the case.

"You're in luck." He puffed out his massive chest and cleared his throat. "Another five minutes and I'd have been gone."

"Thank you!" I managed a demure smile and held his eyes, all but willing him to leave his computer on and come with me. He was right: I was in luck. He grabbed his cabal of keys and beckoned me out the door without another glance at the device. Once we were outside he turned and closed the door behind him, at least having the presence of mind to not leave his office completely vulnerable. He wasn't an officer for nothing.

"The auditorium you say?" He sighed—it was all the way on the other end of the building. My smile showed fake sympathy as we rounded the corner.

Kayla set about picking the lock on his door in our absence. I made small talk and got to know Chuck as we strolled. He was married with three young kids, whom he genuinely adored, and a wife who elicited bitterness from him as he spoke of her. I didn't press the issue. I also didn't find my damn keys—I looked under *every* seat in the place *twice*, but they *just* weren't there. Chuck didn't seem to mind one bit; the pervert was getting a rise out of me crawling around on all fours.

Finally, my phone played "Freak Like Me," Kayla's little ditty, and I was beyond overjoyed that she had found my keys! I thanked Chuck profusely and apologized for wasting his time, but he was more sad to see me go than angry. Kayla, for her part, had managed to download footage for the last three weeks in the bountiful time I'd bought her.

"And I added a nice little backdoor for me, in case I need to look at something else in the future." With closed eyes, my girl held up three fingers next to her impish smirk, adding, "I solemnly swear to use this power only for the greater good."

"Don't you dare," I crooned, and we laughed the rest of the way back to her truck.

CHAPTER EIGHT

It was going to take Kayla some time to sift through the files, so I set about doing her evening chores. Sampson and Delilah were holding a vigil on the east end of the property and declined to come in for dinner. It wasn't unheard of, and they were probably just keeping a pack of coyotes at bay, but my imagination ran wildly through the X-files for other possibilities. I chuckled to the goats as I closed up their pen. "I am the X-file this time, aren't I?"

They bleated.

The last rays of sunshine melted past the horizon and I lit up a cigarette, taking in the peace and tranquility of the Willows. Maybe I should try to find the real-life Mulder and Scully? Or would that just end in me being put on a slab and dissected? In all likelihood, yes. But I couldn't be the only one, could I? What Leilani had said about smoking helping her deal with the bullshit suggested she was at least a kindred spirit, if not an actual one.

The screen door clattered open and slammed behind Kayla as she waved me to the patio. The mottled glass table reflected the glow from her laptop. She sat in one of the rusting metal chairs and pressed play on a set of time synced videos showing two different angles. Leilani entered the school on the auditorium side and veered casually into the girls' bathroom, emerging seven minutes and fifty-six seconds later and exiting the way she had come.

"If she's a ghost she doesn't know how to act like it." Kayla's head shook, a sense of flustered confusion hanging palpably around her. "She walks with a sense of gravity, casts a shadow, opens doors like a pro, and otherwise appears to be very much alive."

I watched as the video looped and played back again, pausing and having Kayla enlarge it when her face was at its most visible. "And yet...she's still a ghost to us..." Her pixelated and grainy face gave me goosebumps in the silent, cool air of the Willows. "We know more now than we did before at least. We aren't looking for a dead girl, just one that knows more than she's letting on."

An ill thought occurred to me and my stomach soured. "I hope she's not dead. I mean maybe that's why she hasn't been around?"

Kayla looked up at me, concern and fear topping her emotions. Before she could answer, my phone belted out "Whooooooo are you? Who? Who? Who? Who?" We both raised an eyebrow and stared at it with wide eyes while I brought it out of my pocket. That particular song was reserved for unknown callers.

Moving away from Kayla, whose spike in fear was seriously clouding my head, I answered with a wince. "H...hello?"

"Is this Amy Durene?" It was a woman's voice, raspy and with a definite Maine country inflection.

The overwhelming urge to throw the phone like it was on fire skittered through my frayed nerves. Where might this conversation go? "Y-yes." I worked to swallow down Kayla's fear.

"This is Kamrie, owner of the Gilded Gelding. I'd like ya ta come in so's I can take a look atcha, tomorrow, 'round four?" She was sharp and to the point.

I slumped to the cold ground, letting out a tiny murmur of a laugh that the call was about something so mundane. It had only been one day since I'd submitted my application, and I never imagined they'd be calling so soon.

"If four don't work I can make it six-thirty but I'll be a might more cranky by then so I'd advise against it." There might have been humor buried in that tone, but I couldn't be sure just then.

"Um...yeah...four will be good...I can do four." Catching Kayla's curious eyes, I gave her a pensive thumb up to go with my absent-minded smirk.

"Dress ta get dirty, no need fer fancy clothes on this un."

"Okay. I will. Thank you very much!"

"Tomorrah then." She hung up.

Staring down at my phone like it had just teleported me to Mars, I chuckled. "I've got an interview at the Gilded Gelding tomorrow at four."

Kayla made the sign of the cross over herself. "Well, Heavenly Father, do they ever have the worst timin'! I thought for sure it was heavy breathing and death threats on the other end."

"Right? Or that it'd be Leilani herself all like, 'Bitch, I told you it was nothing, why you stalkin' me?'" Another relieved laugh swam through me, loosening my locked muscles. This was the problem with carrying tension for two...something that shouldn't have been so damn scary had conspired to give me a coronary. Sitting on that frigid earth I resented the intrusion, even if it hadn't been intentional on Kayla's part.

My best friend stayed back, giving me necessary space and time to recover. What kind of friend was I to put this on her? She had less control over this craziness than I did. Reaching in the pocket of my flannel shirt, I plucked a cigarette from its resting spot and smoked until I felt like myself again.

Seeming to sense the shift, Kayla broke the silence in a low, contemplative voice: "Wish Ma could afford to hire you on here. But with feed prices skyrocketing, we'll be lucky to bring our ends together this year as is."

Things had been hard since her father's death. Ma taking work as a nurse had helped, but then the bottom dropped out of the US economy. As near as I could tell, it had been propped up with duct tape and bailing wire ever since.

"She's the reason I got an interview I bet." Having asked her for a reference, she had insisted I put her down as a previous employer who let me go due to cutbacks. So what if she paid me in hugs and chicken soup?

Both were more valuable than money anyway.

"Shit, I can't give you a ride tomorrow Amy, it's Abuela's bi-monthly doctor's appointment and it's my turn to take her."

"Didn't she throw a king fit when she found out you didn't have a license?" Have I mentioned Kayla was only fifteen and operating on her temps? She'd been driving since she was eleven, but the law didn't take that kind of thing into account.

Kayla shrugged. "She's forgotten all about that by now." With Alzheimer's fast setting in for the ancient woman, it was a fair assumption.

"My mother'll give me a ride...she'll be overjoyed I have an interview somewhere." I took in a drag and gazed at the swaying willow trees lining the driveway. "It's probably for the best anyway, today was pretty brutal on me. The smokes make it easier but you're just too damn hot for me to handle and still be good for an interview." Looking back at her, I attempted a playful smile that fell apart at the edges. "Besides, you're not my chauffeur."

"I don't mind giving you rides at all." She returned such a sweet smile, my eyes warmed with tears.

"I know you don't…" *But I do.* This last part was left unspoken but perfectly understood between us.

We had both been deluding ourselves into thinking we could just slip back into things as they were, with the slight advantage smoking granted us. Now, for the first time, the sense of adventure, novelty, and adrenaline that we'd been coasting on since this weirdness began faced an uphill slope and gravity's relentless strain.

Kayla moved as if to hug me, before tensing and jerking to a stop.

"Fear's the worst…" I continued, "…it comes in like a sledgehammer."

"I'm sorry." She hugged herself, more for comfort than because of the cold, though it was turning chillier by the minute.

"Hey, this isn't a sprint, that's all. It's a marathon." If my words could reassure her, maybe they'd have the same effect on me. "Give me a sec to pull myself together and then I'll hit you up for a ride home. I'd walk but the dogs seem to think there's somethin' out there tonight, and fawk I'm spooked enough."

Kayla relaxed at this. "I think Sam and Dee have been catching rabbits lately, they haven't been too keen on their kibble." She grabbed her laptop and made to head back inside, giving me a wide berth.

"Kayla…what are you afraid of?" The question stopped her mid-reach for the screen door. "It bled into me somethin' fierce right before my phone rang."

She turned partially toward me without meeting my eyes. "Losing you." Opening the door, she stepped one foot inside and called over her shoulder, "And that we're in over our heads." With that the door clanged shut, leaving me alone in the gravel driveway.

CHAPTER NINE

*D*ad's apathy slid over the front walkway like coagulating lime jello as I made my way up to the house. He was probably drinking in front of some recorded sporting event or another. Not that he was an alcoholic, but he did pound a few back after getting home from his considerably long days at the accounting firm of Patrick and Hume.

The sad truth was that I hardly knew him. I had to glance at our family portrait from time to time just to remember what he looked like: tall, with short, full, salt and pepper hair, a lean face, large cloudy blue eyes, and an ever-present sweater vest. I got my eyes from him...so we shared that much at least.

We took family vacations twice a year during which he tried to act like we were closer than we were. If I was in good enough spirits, I even obliged him. Maybe, if we could just look like a cohesive family for the camera, it would leak into our reality. But it never did, and year after year I didn't learn my lesson, so I would make the same wish again this summer when we went off to—shit I didn't even know where, but there would be a beach involved because there was always a beach.

I know, right? First world problems.

Mother was in her office typing away at some super important and urgent document, or maybe she was looking at porn. I liked to think she must do that from time to time; it humanized her. I'll leave it to you to speculate what type she got enthusiastic about—my twisted mind will only go so far on the subject. I knocked on the door good and loud and waited to be sure to give her time to close anything that needed closing.

"You're home earlier than I thought you would be," her disinterested voice called out. She didn't so much as look at me as I came in, transfixed as she was with the figures on some spreadsheet. Her large oak desk dominated the room and was bursting with files and papers, not one of which was out of place.

"Is that a problem? I didn't catch you watching something racy did I?" My eyebrows rose up and down and I suppressed a ridiculous giggle at the joke only I would get.

"I don't watch the races," she replied, and judging from the confusion rippling from her I don't think she understood what I had actually said. That or she just didn't want to deal with it, which was entirely possible.

"Well, maybe you should start." I tapped the door frame. "It might relax you." A blank stare greeted me and she opened her mouth to respond when I interrupted her. "Speaking of races, I have an interview tomorrow at four o'clock at the Gilded Gelding Horse Ranch in Brooks. I'm respectfully and humbly asking for a ride." I offered a slight curtsy.

"Hey, that's great!" She swiveled her overstuffed brown leather chair toward me. "Yeah, of course I'll give you a ride." Opening her calendar, she paged to the following day's itinerary. Without looking up she asked, "Why can't Kayla take you?" There was an arrogance to her emotions that was masked by her words.

"She's busy." My response was matter of fact, not giving her any length of rope to use if I could help it.

"You need me to pick you up from school?" Her finger traced an appointment.

"Yeah." You know things were bleak if I was preferring spending any amount of time with my mother over getting a ride home with Kayla. I couldn't afford to be emotionally spent by the time I got to the interview. And since my mother was happy I had an interview, she would likely be in a good mood, at least for the ride out there.

"I can do it, but I'll have to take you straight there and drop you off at three-thirty, so make sure you bring everything you need to school tomorrow or put it in my car tonight." Her tone was business like, just another transaction in a day filled with them. But then she turned to me, her tongue in her cheek: "They're gonna make you shovel shit, you know?"

"No different than writing a paper for English class." *Or what I do around here every day*, I wanted to say, but held back my snark. She was doing me a solid favor after all.

She laughed as she penciled me into her schedule. My very own entry; that counted as a show of love and affection, didn't it? Funny as it would have been to point out, I stayed my tongue.

"Make sure you wear something nice and presentable, maybe that outfit I got you for Easter."

I said nothing, only smiled at her. "It's not going to be the same as working with Kayla you know. You can't slack off when you're on someone's payroll." It was her turn to raise an eyebrow to me.

Smiling. Still smiling. Always smiling.

"I really hope you get this job!" She closed her schedule and set it aside. "Those cigarettes aren't going to pay for themselves." Her chair crinkled and squeaked as she turned back to me, taking in my reaction. "Honestly, with how

59

expensive those damn things are I'm surprised anyone picks up the habit anymore."

"It helps with the bullshit," I stammered. How had she found out?

She pressed her lips together and nodded. "That it does. You should try to quit before you turn eighteen though, it isn't as much fun when it's legal." With that she returned to the cultish glow of her laptop. "Anything else?"

I stood there scratching my shoulder and blinking. Why was she not reaming me out? She smoked when she was younger, and I'd been prepared to bring that up as a defense if she ever figured out I started; but apparently she didn't feel like being an ash-black kettle today. Not that I was complaining.

"No. I'll meet you out front of school tomorrow, and... thanks," I said.

"Goodnight," she said, her mouse already mid-click. It was only eight, and neither of us would be in bed until midnight at least.

Did she even know that?

I made myself dinner, cleaned up, and did the bare minimum of homework in the cavernous dining room, but didn't see either of my parents until Mother picked me up at school the following afternoon.

CHAPTER TEN

"*You* reek like cigarette smoke!" Mother spritzed me with an essential oil mixture. I popped out of the car and into the parking lot of the Gilded Gelding, fresh as a peppermint breeze.

As soon as she was out of sight I lit up a cigarette, taking the place in. It was a mixture of wooded areas and vast fields with electrical fencing running the length of them. Hills rolled in giant waves throughout, with the main house and stables sitting warm and inviting at the highest visible point. The shadows cast by the light of the waning sun made it look like an old painting.

The closer I got to the stables the more emotions I sensed, only they were subdued and pastel, not unlike the ones I'd experienced from the cows at the Willows. But whereas the cattle had been calming, these were…refreshing, like the distilled essence of freedom. I stuck my head into the stable to confirm with my eyes what my sixth sense already knew. Half a dozen horses lazily chewed on their hay or played with bits and bobbles hanging around their stalls. The stable, built of dark wood and trimmed with golden, embossed vines at each entrance, could easily hold three times that number.

Every horse looked at me when I entered, save for one transfixed by his own image in a mirror clipped to his stall. Could they tell there was something "off" about me? They always could in the movies. In fear of spooking them, I kept my distance, moving further into the grounds.

There were three more stables, with twenty stalls apiece. The others had maybe fifteen horses in each and they gave me a similar reception. Taking a deep breath, I stepped inside the last one. Better to find out how they would react now than risk a possible incident with Kamrie later. Before my second step could land, a colorful curse thundered from the far end of the stable.

A stout woman clutched the handles of a wheelbarrow that lay on its side. Its contents, which matched said curse perfectly, were still settling all over the road. Without thinking, I ran through the center of the stable to see what I could do to help. A few of the horses snorted and stepped back, but just as many stepped forward, watching me pass with interest. A mixture of apprehension and curiosity flowed from them, but was so watered down I didn't have to concentrate to keep it separate from me.

"Are you alright?" I asked the woman, whose crimped brown hair was speckled with gray.

Wide, bright eyes looked up at me, then to the pile on the ground, and then back to me again, her mouth flush with an exaggerated, upturned O. It would have been infectious even without my ability to sense the irreverent cheerfulness behind it. Licking her lips, the woman let out a huff. "Well...shit!" She gave me a wink and turned back to her broken barrow, examining the busted axle at the center of the...ahem...shitstorm.

"Chinese parts I betcha," she chided, and I knew without a doubt this was Kamrie. Was this a good first impression to make or not? "I'm careful ta buy American, but they slip those parts in from all over by God."

I nodded. "Do you have another barrow?"

"I do." Straightening up, she walked toward the house. It was a hodgepodge of add-ons, but the exterior was well maintained. Part of the building was constructed of time-weathered stone, likely from when the area was first settled. Not knowing what else to do, I followed her.

We rounded the stone section of the house and kept going until we reached a gigantic three-chambered compost bin. Wheelbarrows and an assortment of rakes and shovels leaned against it. She tossed me a shovel which I caught one handed.

Though her face was stern and focused, her emotions told me she was impressed and just as impish as ever. "Ya just get right intah the shit, doncha girl? Not so much as an intro-duction."

"I'm Amy." I smiled, putting the shovel in the barrow before lifting it and licking my grinning lips. "Your new stable hand."

Kamrie burst out laughing, put a second shovel in the barrow, and gestured for me to lead the way. Cautious opti-mism hummed like an electric fence around her, but genuine affection was already creeping along the outer rim. She'd likely been burned before, and I'd do well to keep that in mind.

"So does the ownah of this place know she hired ya?" Kamrie kept pace beside me.

"Not yet, but I'm hopeful she'll come around by the end of my interview." My eyes sparkled back at her.

"Ya know the funny thing is I was gonna have ya shovel some o' this sweet stuff as part of ya interview. I've had it too many times that a young gal applies ta work here thinkin' she'll get ta ride and pet horsies all day, so now I add a dose of reality first off and save us time." We stopped at the mess and each grabbed a shovel.

"I practically grew up on the Willows cattle farm in Albion, so I know what goes into—and comes out of—taking care of barnyard critters."

"I get their beef now and again, solidly good stuff that, if on the pricey side." She flipped the broken barrow completely over and emptied it onto the ground before moving it out of the way. "So if I give 'em a call, what will they have ta say about you?" Her lightheartedness fell to the wayside, replaced now with a serious curiosity.

"That I'm a hard worker and she wishes they could afford to hire me on this year." Ma might also tell her the name of my favorite stuffed animal, but sensing that Kamrie saw a time and a place for humor at work, and that we'd passed that line, I kept it to myself. Instead, I discussed the chores I helped with around the farm, shoveling shit among them.

The interview proceeded with the normal volley of questions as we worked side by side. The further I got from my last cigarette the harder it became to divide my attention between answering her, working, and making sure my emotions were my own. I'm sure I seemed a little slow on the uptake, but it didn't appear to bother Kamrie. Maybe she was tired too?

Once all the manure was picked up and safely with its brethren, we went to visit a black and gray mare in need of some grooming. Her name was Jigsaw, and she and Kamrie taught me the basics of horse handling. Jigsaw initially kept her distance from me, but after a few hardy sniffs of my undershirt she relaxed, nudged me with her head, and let out a raucous snort. I dropped the brush in the water bucket, soaking my pant leg, but after that I found my footing.

Jigsaw's coat was radiant by the end.

As the sun set, Kamrie and I walked the grounds together and I got lost in the beauty and presence of the landscape. I missed a vital direction from Kamrie on how to open one of the gates and had to be shown again. "Sorry, it's just this place..." Soaking in the hilltop view, I continued, "...I can imagine working here so bad it hurts." Inspired optimism sprang up around her caution and I rode the wave with her. It seemed she could imagine it too.

"If I spent half the time starin' at these hills as I'd like, this place'd fall to ruin 'round my ankles fastah than a mule can spit." She chuckled. "That you see the same thing as me and have the same work ethic besides tells me I'd be a fool to letcha go wand'rin' ta anothah pasture. No need to hurt none on my account, I'd have ya join us just as well."

I stared at her with an uncertain grin, still very much high on her optimism. Was I hearing her correctly? Had I been offered the job?

When understanding of my confusion dawned on Kamrie, she let out a sigh that said she was used to her manner of speech confusing people. "Job's yers, Darlin'."

Before I knew it, my arms were around her in a ridiculously unprofessional hug. She patted me on the back with one hand, deeply heartened by the gesture. "Thank you," I said.

"You ken thank me by keepin' up the hard work, Sugah Cube." Pointing to my face, she walked toward the house. "And keepin' that smile, right there." On the way, we discussed pay, hours, and who would be training me. She had three full-time and two part-time stable hands she kept on year round, with two seasonal helpers for the busier summer and fall seasons. Seasonal workers had a way of becoming year rounders, too, so there was room for advancement.

I was on the front porch, finishing the paperwork, when my mother pulled up. Kamrie insisted on greeting her.

"How'd it go?" Mother asked after pleasantries were exchanged.

Leaning down next to my mother's partially opened

window, her elbow resting on the lip of it, my new boss raised her eyebrows in my direction as I rounded the front of the car. Then she gave my mother a sly, energetic smirk while shaking her head in mock disbelief. "I ain't nevah seen a girl jump that enthusiastically into a barrow full of horse shit in all my—not inconsiderable—years on this planet."

Mother followed my movement with comically wide eyes, her voice squeaking over clenched teeth and shallow laughter. "Not literally, I hope."

An unruly grin pounced on Kamrie. "Well now…I'll let ya nose be the judge a that." Slapping the top of the car, she caught my eye right before I ducked inside. "I'll see ya Saturday, Amy!" She winked at me and nodded to my mother. "Ma'am."

Mother filled with dread, wincing when I sat down on the tan leather seats of her precious Audi sedan. I was in too good a mood to let her bring me down. I'd have to bring her up instead.

"I got the job!!!" I squealed, closing the door and doing a little dance in place.

I was ecstatic on my own, but Kamrie's infectious boisterousness was an over-the-top upper, and it wasted no time spreading to my mother. She took my hands, without regard for how dirty they might have been, and danced along with me, pausing to change the station from talk radio to something with a beat.

"Let's celebrate with some frozen custard! I've heard great things about Frozen Jim's down the road a ways," she said, slamming the car into gear and pulling a quick U-turn in the lot.

Suspicion, you ask? Where was I supposed to find room for that?

rozen Jim's wasn't open for the season yet, so we made do with Choco Tacos from the On the Run gas station instead. We ate them as we drove, something she *never* allowed under normal circumstances. She didn't even care when a big chunk of hers inevitably fell to the carpet at her feet. I braced for her to go ballistic, but she remained in high spirits, playfully scolding the rest of her taco to stay in line.

I had just breathed a sigh of relief when she let out a sinister laugh, looking half at the road and half at the melting treat underneath her. "Oh, you aren't getting away from me *that* easy, taco man!" Taking her eyes from the road, she attempted to scoop up the wayward piece. The car kicked up gravel as it veered toward the ditch to our right.

Without thinking, my hand shot out and grabbed the wheel, easing us back onto the pavement. "Ummm...I can get that if you want!" My heartbeat thrummed in my fingertips. She popped up, holding her prize victoriously in one hand and taking back control of the car with the other.

"I got it!" she sang, but after one long look at the sticky mass in her hand in the light of a passing semi, her mood curdled and a deep frown replaced her once gleeful grin. Opening her window, she threw out the chunk that kissed the floor, followed shortly by the rest of the chocolate treat, wrapper and all.

Her dread gaze seized upon the Choco Taco in my hand. With a sigh, I rolled down my window and chucked the ice cream out.

"Ugh!" she cried, "I don't know what I was thinking bringing those things in here!" She shook her head, enunciating her next words. "There is a reason I don't allow food in my Audi!" Gesturing to the glove box, her impatience spiked. "Hand me some tissues."

I did as she asked.

"I guess you got caught up in my moment." The jarring change in her emotions was a bulldozer to my system, but I smiled anyway, desperate to lighten the atmosphere. It was slowly sinking in just how out of character she'd been acting since I got in the car. I had been too swept up in my own euphoria to scrutinize things until the adrenaline of having to take the wheel snapped me out of it. A few excruciating moments passed where she shifted from confusion, to uneasiness, and finally to embarrassment and alarm, in rapid succession.

My stomach churned and I opened my cigarettes, bringing one to my mouth.

"What do you think you're doing?" Mother shrieked. "You're not smoking that in here!"

"Fine," I huffed, banging my now throbbing head against the window and fighting the urge to expel the remainder of my Choco Taco down the inner door. "Pull over."

"We're not stopping so you can smoke." Incredulity piled on to the emotional heap.

"How 'bout so I can puke then?" I swallowed hard.

She laughed and shook her head. "Nice try, but you'll just have to wait until we get home."

"MOTHER!" I snarled, whipping open the glove box. "If you don't pull this car over right now I'm going to use your glove box as a sick bag!"

She narrowed her eyes at me, as though attempting to gauge my level of sincerity. In seconds the car was slowing down and riding the shoulder. As soon as my door would open, I was out, running across the gravel and into the tall grass that lined the country road. When I reached a safe distance, some twenty feet away from her, I collapsed to the ground and lit up the cigarette that was still hanging from my mouth.

Taking in a long drag, I stared up at the sky and exhaled slow and steady. "Faaaawk me!" I shook my head and suppressed another spasm in my stomach. "I thought I was doing better with this shit!"

And I was, so long as I could chain smoke like a convict in front of a firing squad.

No...that wasn't true...something was different tonight... it was almost like I had emotional whiplash, and that was new. A super ball bounced into my thoughts when I tried to remember what happened after I got in the car. Try as I might, I couldn't catch the damn thing. The lights from a passing car seared into my retinas. Was this because I let Kamrie's emotions take over and rode the wave? An emotional hangover? Had I simply gotten too high on life?

If that was the case, then so had my mother. She'd been acting in a similar way, as though those same emotions had bled into her. Did she have the same condition as me? It was an angle I hadn't considered...that whatever was going on with me was something that ran in my family. Hadn't she vehemently agreed that cigarettes help with the bullshit? But then, why hadn't she been more understanding and told me the truth when I was in the hospital?

After precisely how long it would take for someone to scrub a bit of chocolate and crumbs out of a carpet with club soda (one of the few beverages allowed in the Audi), Mother's voice interrupted my inner ramblings. I didn't have to be within range to tell she was pissed. "Amy Rachael Durene! Are you smoking out there?! Did you seriously just cry wolf so you could have your cigarette?"

"No," I called back, the cigarette dangling from my lips. "It's just a pleasant side effect!"

"Well, if you aren't back in this car in the next minute I'm leaving without you." She meant it too, but considering her current emotional state and the fault lines in my head, I had a better chance of becoming a Choco Taco than getting back in that car.

I should be careful with that thought. This was Maine after all, and such an idea could easily become the premise of a Stephen King novel if dwelled on too long. Legend had it that he scoured our brains in the night, and whatever he wrote about came true. Frankly, I didn't think I'd fare well as a snack treat in this locality. Or worse, in Derry.

Smirking at the odd notion, I responded, "It's okay, I'll walk home." We were only maybe four miles from my house, and I could use the time to think and be blessedly alone.

"I'm not coming back to get you if you get cold or tired!"

Looking down at my outfit I sneered. I hadn't dressed for a lengthy nocturnal walk through King country and would be both tired and freezing before too long.

Damn.

I called Mother on her phone rather than continuing to shout, and she answered without a word.

"You do know that the side effects of the meds *you* authorized include nausea and vomiting right?" Reproach oozed from each syllable. Mothers were supposed to know that sort of thing, and I was betting I had just flustered the anger out of her. It was best to follow up with a softer, more reasonable tone now. "I just need a few minutes, okay? Let me finish this smoke and get some air and it'll pass."

She let out a frustrated sigh. "You aren't getting much air if you're smoking."

"I can always see if Kayla can come get me." Fat chance she was back from Abuela's house, but Mother didn't know that.

There was a pause before she responded curtly, "Don't be too long." She hung up, and the little valley I sat in echoed with the slamming of her car door. Might she leave me anyway? I strained for the sound of the engine starting, but all was silent.

Mercifully silent.

Focusing on keeping myself calm, I finished my cigarette. All thought of what happened tonight floated out of my fractured mind and into the starry night. As I walked back to the car, Mother's sadness crackled in like an out of tune radio. Her inner station flipped to stoicism upon seeing me, though the background sadness was still seeping through. She often admonished me for crying, saying my energy was better spent elsewhere. I'd only seen her cry once, at my uncle Jerry's funeral, but her eyes blared puffy and red when I climbed into my seat.

I looked out the window and pretended not to notice.

CHAPTER TWELVE

The strangeness of the day swirled down the shower drain, but I held on to the happy fact that I had a job. Things with Mother would work themselves out, but for now I had cleared one of the hurdles in my path. I didn't have to worry about how I was going to afford my new life saving habit.

The Corner Store in Albion provided my cigarettes with the express understanding that I didn't get them from them. They also added on a hefty two-dollar-a-pack surcharge. I hoped to eventually get my mother to pick me up a carton at the local smoke shop for far less, but was waiting for the right time to broach the subject. At the rate we were going, I would be eighteen long before that happened.

Kayla and I attempted to set up a video chat, but she had the bare minimum for internet speed, only marginally better than the fabled dial-up of yore, and we kept getting disconnected. After the sixth time, we called each other. She was ecstatic I got the job, and just as perplexed as me about what happened with my mother.

"You wouldn't think she could be so cruel, but I wouldn't

rule it out," she said, after I floated the idea that what was happening with me was genetic.

"Somethin's definitely going on with her, she was crying before I got in the car." I laid back on my bed and stared at the poster of Cormack Skerrett from the *Dusk* series that hung on my ceiling. *Dusk* was a dark tale about a girl named Rowan who finds out she's one of the Fae. Cormack is her infatuated and sexy lover, played by Reese Myers. His skin shifted from white to green to brown depending on the angle you looked at it from, and I tossed my head from side to side to create the effect.

"I didn't know robots could cry." Kayla snickered.

Normally, I would have made some snarky comment about oil being harder to get out of the carpet than chocolate so that's why my mother rarely cried, but her sadness was still too raw, so I chuckled instead.

Kayla had me repeat everything that happened around the time my mother came to pick me up.

"I wonder if it's comin' from you…" she said thoughtfully when I'd finished, "…like you willed her emotions to change into something more palatable."

"And the whiplash I felt was from her emotions correcting themselves…" My eyes widened. "Fawk, that would be a game changer!"

"I'll be your guinea pig. Give me five minutes and I'll be over." Was that giddiness in her voice?

"Maybe I could find your dimmer switch!" But, could I really handle her tonight? Tired as I was? "Not now though."

"Mmm, long day eh?" She let out a low sigh. "Okay, tomorrow then, before school."

"I love you more than Cormack Skerrett."

"Don't go sayin' stuff you'll be regrettin' later," she mused. "Now it's my turn for good news!"

"You have good news comin' out of an afternoon with Abuela?"

73

"Ayeah. So there I am, stuck at the world's longest red light, when I look over to find those beady little black crow eyes boring into me. 'What's troubling you Kayla?' she asks, 'And don't bother lying cuz I'm far too deaf for it.' She's so tiny I swear she should be in a booster seat for safety, but she's got some powerful juju about her because I found my mouth moving in spite of myself! Now, I didn't tell her nothin' about you, that much I managed to keep, but I did tell her some about Leilani and how I'm looking for her. Turns out I have a second cousin, Javier, who's a cop over in Belfast, and she's going to have him call me about our mystery girl. He has access to all kinds of databases I don't!"

"Whoa, Abuela with the unexpected hook up."

"She's growin' softer the older she gets. Doc says at ninety-eight she's as spry as some of his patients half her age though, and he won't think of puttin' her in a home." This was said with no small amount of pride in her voice.

"She'd just bust out and he'd be missing his vitals by sundown." I laughed. "It's self preservation on his part."

"So then, on the way back to her apartment, I get third degree burns from her eyes again, so I ask her to tell me everything she knows about exorcisms. 'Exorcisms aren't for white girls to do,' she tells me, and I spit back that I'll have my Mexican half perform one should it ever become necessary. This sets her into, I shit you not, seven straight minutes of cacklin' laughter that set my bones on edge. I don't know how I didn't drive us both into oncoming traffic. But when she finally stops, she tells me that you have to have ironclad faith for an exorcism to work and that she loves me, but I have a skeptic's heart, and that's why all of my mad searchings find nothing."

Kayla's voice tightened—this kind of thing got to her more than she let on. "Then she said if I ever needed an exorcism, to call her or her priest and not attempt to do it myself. 'Even if you manage to pull it out' she says, 'the demon would only jump right into you and that's no way for my grand-daughter to be behaving. And don't you forget! It's your roots that ground you girl, 'cept yours are all knotted up.' To which I replied, 'Celtic knotted up, Grandma.'"

"Oh, I bet she loved that." I could see Abuela's eyebrows tripling their anger wrinkles.

"You know...I think she really did. The older I get, the more I feel like she dishes it out in hopes someone'll dish it back to her. Maybe the fire in her blood is what keeps her going?" Kayla yawned.

"Why'd you ask her about exorcisms?" That was a road we already went down and I'd been given a clean bill of health. Hadn't I?

"I don't know, she threw me off guard and I grasped for somethin' to talk about. Plus...part of me worries I got some-thin' wrong, or maybe I really am too white, and it's good to keep all our options on the table."

She yawned a second time. "Anyway, I did manage to get out of there without confessing all my sins to her, and now we have another route to look for Leilani, so I consider it a win."

"Yes! I'd say today was a good day." I smiled.

"It'll be even better tomorrow."

But tomorrow seldom lives up to its potential, any more than it never dies. It didn't help any that I was as tense as a bra clasp on a Bond girl when morning rolled around. "I don't know about this Kayla...what if I blow your brain up or something?"

"You think we should put down some garbage bags?" Kayla looked around my room in mock wide-eyed assess-ment before rolling her eyes at me with a smirk. "Besides, you'll probably blow your brain up before mine."

I shot her a hard look and she returned an innocent smile, adding, "I trust you."

That made one of us.

We sat cross legged in the middle of my bed, a cigarette smoldering on the edge of my nightstand. Rays of Kayla's excitement baked into me. A blanket of nervous fear provided some shade as I envisioned her as a nice, lukewarm, inviting calm—not the Sahara sun, blazing down to burn me to ash, not the fires of Mount Doom leaving no trace of me behind—calm. CALM!

Calm!

Sweat beaded on my throbbing temples and my heart did a somersault in my chest.

I should stop.

No, just a little bit more…this could be it!

Could be—

Kayla slid from fevered hope, to scorching disappointment, to boiling worry, and my world disintegrated to frigid black.

At least I was already on the bed, so there wasn't far to fall this time.

My brain was a pallet of burned rubber when I came to, some fifteen minutes later.

"How're you feeling?" Kayla's voice popped through my phone on the nightstand. She must have set it up to keep an eye on me while giving me space to recover. My cigarette had also been removed.

"Like Old Turnpike Road in July." I scratched my head and winced. "I don't think I'm gonna be able to handle the drive in with you, let alone all day at school."

"I'm sorry, I should have seen the warning signs." She bit her lip.

"Hey, I wanted it to work too." Every word sent a rail spike through my head. "I won't be goin' to school though."

No way could I handle the drive in with her. I winced. "No more morning experiments, okay?"

"You want me to stay? Or will I just make things worse?"

"Yes, to both." I gritted my teeth and laughed through the pain. "I need alone time."

"I understand. Hate it, but understand." Kayla's lips blurred out her screen as she made smacking kissing sounds against it. "I'll call you at lunch. Make sure you answer, slacker, or I'll be on my way whether it bursts your brain or not." The chat winked out and the Goblin's stuttering whine filtered in through my window a minute later.

Slowly, and with the help of some aspirin, my head stopped revolting. I dedicated the remainder of the day to shooting fungus zombies on my X-Station and not thinking about anything too hard.

It was the first time I hadn't been around anyone for such a long stretch, and that was precisely what the doctor ordered.

Of course, that doctor neglected to call me in to school... so I got the following text from Mother.

10:06 AM: 😡 😡 😡 🤬 🤬 🤬 ??????

To which, I replied,

10:12 AM: HTTP://WWW.PARAXIL.COM/SIDEEFFECTS 😴

And went back to my fungus zombies.

CHAPTER THIRTEEN

On Saturday, Mother drove me to my first day at the Gelding. As we listened to some old guy getting overly excited about his azalea bushes on Garden Talk, I concentrated on lowering her nervous tension while being a blue butterfly. It was a risk to try it in the car, but my first day should be chipper and happy, not filled with the blundering mistakes her mood would bring out in me if I let it.

As with Kayla, nothing budged.

So, I was back to wondering if dear Mother had the same ability as me or not. Was she in denial about it? It would certainly make her stand out from the Joneses. Couldn't have that, could we? I'd bring it up to her directly, after work.

Kamrie waved at me from the office as Mother pulled away without a word. "Eager for your first day?" my new boss asked.

I soaked in her boisterousness and beamed at her. "I am now!"

She rubbed her hands together, cackled, and beckoned me to follow her.

For eight hours, I ping-ponged from job to job and

person to person, doing a slice of everything. I cleaned the stalls, aisles, and tack; groomed, fed, watered, turned the horses out; and picked their feet. I composted, marked inventory, filled in mud holes, and even got to drive the tractor.

"We're heavin' shit at the wall to see what sticks," Kamrie eloquently pointed out.

I stuck the longest to disinfecting the stalls with Mr. Bubble's caustic cousin Larry Lye.

"It don't burn your lungs?" Kamrie narrowed her eyes while I refilled the mixture from concentrate. "Stuff works powerful good, but the smell sets my hair so stiff I can play 'Johnny B. Goode' on it."

"No, it doesn't bother me at all." I laughed. Why didn't it bother me? Had smoking fried my sense of smell? That happened to my great aunt, though she had smoked for half a century before then. So, maybe it ran in the family, like my empathy might?

Whatever, I was just happy to get a pair of mad scientist gloves and goggles and be left to my own devices. Most of my time was spent mucking out the stables from then on. I would clear out the manure and urine soaked bedding, put fresh stuff down, refresh the water buckets, rinse and repeat. It was a never-ending process that had to be done two or three times per day, per stall.

With music cranked up in my earbuds, lye keeping people away, and the horses for company, I could almost fool myself into thinking things were normal and I wasn't drowning in the deep end of the crazy pool.

The Gelding became my oasis, from which I barely looked up for the following three weeks. I took extra shifts, stayed late, and came home too exhausted to do more than crawl into bed. This was fine by me; I couldn't stress if I was asleep.

I could stay in my dreamland, where I snuggled with

Kayla, where emotions were internal things, and where Javier had found Leilani.

But I'd inevitably wake alone, too focused on being a blue butterfly to enjoy what little time I had with my best friend, who tried to understand my need for isolation but couldn't hide her hurt—not from me. And Javier…

Two days ago, Javier hit us with the news that his extensive searches of the national criminal and missing persons databases yielded nothing. This went over like a bucket of frozen fish. Fish we'd pinned what fragile hope we had on, and which now lay sprawled and rotting on increasingly unstable flooring: my cracked linoleum psyche, turning up at the corners and fading in the bright light of day…of Kayla.

It had been nearly an hour since my shift ended at eight, and I was most of the way through my history homework when the screen door of my mind creaked open, letting in the stray thought that I had promised to call Kayla. A thought that had wavered in the doorway for the better part of an hour, flicking its tail. I mean…history homework? You know I had some serious procrastination issues going on if that was my choice of escape.

Setting my text book down on the soft peat moss bedding of the empty stall I sat in, I ran my fingers through my hair and brought my elbows to rest on my knees. The only light in the place came from the aluminum lamp clipped to the side of the stall and pointed in my direction. The horses didn't care for the brightness of the overhead fluorescents this late at night.

I empathized.

After a minute, I pulled out my phone, staring down at my best friend's picture next to her contact information. In it, she had stuffed her mouth full of discounted Valentine's Day chocolates and was laughing with puffed out cheeks as drool dribbled down her chin. That was taken less than two months ago when things had been so much simpler, before being in the same room as her became a struggle.

I miss you.

The girl with the chocolate face and the Kayla of right now both loved me, so what was I procrastinating for? What was I afraid of? That she would ream me out for not helping with the research, following up with Mother, or working harder to get a handle on my ability? That she would be right to do so?

Or was I afraid she would see I was cracking? Terrified I'd take her down with me? If I was descending into madness she'd never let me go alone. Blinking back tears, I let my head rest against the stall, staring into the blackness of the rafters.

I pressed and held the icon to dial her number for several heartbeats before releasing it. Come what may, I wouldn't live in fear of talking to my best friend.

Silence greeted me, followed by a ping and a robotic message stating, "You have no signal."

A clock on my phone counted down how long it would be until I went on a rampage owing to withdrawals. It had me pegged at forty-five minutes. Cell coverage was hit or miss on the ranch on the best of days, but tonight there was a dry thunderstorm rolling through the hills. I had heard it in the distance and felt the horses' unease, but now it had reached us.

"Well...that was anticlimactic," I said to Kayla's picture as I swiped the apocalyptic clock away.

"Oh, I don't know, it seems to me like it's only just beginning." From somewhere in the darkness came a smooth, resonant male voice and I gave a tremendous start, dropping my phone and scrambling to turn toward the source of the sound. Nearby, horses stirred in their pens as my heart, unaccustomed to being caught off guard, cleared three laps and jumped the fence.

Standing in the doorway to my little sanctuary was a boy, not much older than myself, dressed in dark blue jeans and a white, long sleeved thermal top with something printed on it. He had a warm, sly smile, a shaved head, fair skin, and the kind of hazel eyes that could haunt a girl's dreams.

"But you aren't going to see anything sitting in there." He held out his hand with the intention of helping me to my feet.

I didn't move.

I didn't even breathe.

I just peered up at him, blindly groping for any hint of an emotion…and finding none.

CHAPTER FOURTEEN

*S*weet Jesus, I hadn't realized how much I'd come to rely on my sixth sense until that very moment. It was, in many ways, like seeing a ghost suddenly appear before you, or turning toward the sound of someone's voice and discovering you're alone; in other words—creepy as fuck. But you don't spend the night in as many "haunted" locations as I have without building up some brass, and so after the initial adrenaline spike settled itself into a dull background hum, I took his offered hand.

I braced myself to pass right through, but it was rough, calloused, and solid, the hand of someone who works for a living. Spirits, as I understood it, were quite unable to do so. Locking my hand around his, I surprised us both by pulling him toward me. He momentarily flailed from the suddenness of it, but was soon down on one knee in front of me, his left hand firmly splayed on the horse bedding for balance. His wide eyes settled on mine, which combed over him in the intensity of the 100 watt light above us, searching for anything out of place.

His chest rose and fell. He smelled of artificial earth, a deodorant of some kind, intermingled with motor oil or grease. There was an underlying, arousing scent wrapped within his natural sweat…pheromones maybe? When at last I was satisfied he was at least substantial and without tail or horns, my eyes worked their way back to his, and I let him go. His initial look of shock had been replaced with one of playful amusement.

It must have been invasive and unnerving, me staring him down like that, but he didn't miss a beat. "So, do I pass inspection?" He brought his recently liberated hand up to his neck and face, rubbing the small amount of stubble that was gaining ground. Stopping mid-stroke, he raised an eyebrow at me in sudden, mock worry. "Or do you have to take me out back and shoot me?"

A light laugh broke from my otherwise stone facade, in spite of myself. Did aliens know how to make jokes? Oh, and I had the urge to take him alright, just not out back…necessarily. My cheeks warmed. "That remains to be seen…" I said, lips turning up in a feline smirk. "But I'll need a name to put on the Certificate of Dea…Health."

"Daniel Varrick." He looked at himself, still down on one knee, and then back up at me while flashing a set of gleaming white teeth. "Apparently at your service."

"That could be dangerous." I was fixed on his canines now. They were larger than most but still well within normal human parameters…at least I was pretty sure.

"So now I know you're beautiful and wise. How 'bout a name?"

"Amy."

He paused. "Is it *your* name?"

"One of 'em," I mused. "I also answer to 'beautiful and wise'…"

Daniel chuckled, rose to his feet, and gestured to the northern entrance of the stable with a nod. "There's one helluva storm happenin' just out there I think you should throw an eye at, Amy." Turning to point toward the southern entrance with his thumb, he continued, "Much better than the view from here."

"I don't know...the view from here seems pretty nice..." I grinned, not bothering to take my eyes from him. That smile of his lit up the night as bright as lightning once he realized I wasn't talking about the storm. I extended my hand toward him. "Help me up?" There was no hesitation on his part; he wrapped his hand around mine and pulled me to my feet in one swift motion. I lifted clean off the ground from the force of it, letting out a joyful little squeak as I landed back down.

"That's how it was supposed to go." He smiled down at me, releasing me from his grip and stepping backwards into the darkness. Masculine edges highlighted his face, but whenever he smiled, his boyish charm broke through. I would have found him infinitely intriguing even without the emotional silence, but with it, he was quite simply intoxicating.

His silhouette dominated each stall he passed as he made his way toward the northern entrance, leaving me to ponder whether or not to follow.

There was a part of me that thought this was all too good to be true, and there must be something wrong with him. This part of me knew if I followed him outside just then he would slam me against the side of the stable, drain my blood, and roll my body down the infinite hillside into the muddy ravine below. The crazy thing was...I didn't much care if that was exactly where my story ended. Being in the presence of someone—without having to divide my attention between the conversation and sifting through whose emotions I was feeling—was precisely the life preserver I needed and worth the risk.

And so, much like Alice after her white rabbit, I ran to catch up.

The storm, rolling from west to east, had dipped into the valley below us, giving the odd impression we were watching it from the side. Lightning cascaded through the clouds in never-ending streams that turned night into day.

My jaw hung open as I caught up with Daniel. "Holy hell. You weren't kiddin'!" I continued past him in a daze until I reached the little wooden half fence that kept people from tumbling down that aforementioned hillside. Without ceremony, I climbed it and sat snuggly on the top rung, keeping my eyes on the storm.

My white rabbit walked up and I braced myself to be thrown down the hill, but he only joined me while hooting and whistling at a particularly bright series of flashes. Sitting a foot and a half away from me, he was clearly excited and not one lick of it was coming through to my sixth sense. Meanwhile, the horses were cycling through various shades of apprehension, so my ability was definitely working.

He was an alien…that had to be it. And this was his mothership. Any moment now I was going to be zapped up there by one of those lightning bolts and dissected on a table made of some unknown magnetic element that conformed to my body and held me in place.

Aliens could look human…they had whole labs set up to make hybrids and fit in. Coast to Coast AM did a show about it not long ago. They knew I could blow their cover and so they had come to collect me. Or maybe I was one of them and they were here to take me home? I glanced over at Daniel. If he was going to be there I might just go willingly.

Might.

But probably not.

Why can't I feel you? The question danced at the edges of my lips, but I swallowed it down. Best to keep that hand of crazy eights close to my chest, for now.

Noticing me looking at him, my alien leaned in toward me. "You know you scared me? I thought I was alone until I heard you." There was an air of light-hearted embarrassment in his voice, which was slightly raised so as to be heard over the thunder.

"That makes two of us." I smiled, shaking off the notion that he was a little gray man in a tall white body, with a chuckle.

"Well then, I owe you an apology." His eyes held a quiet sincerity.

"No you don't. I'd have missed all this. It'd be a crime against humanity." Assuming I was human...

I looked out over the valley in admiration before returning to him. "I owe you my thanks."

"Nah, I'm at your service, remember?" He inclined his head in a chivalrous manner.

"I won't be forgetting a thing like that. I'll probably abuse it though, so fair warning." My shoulder bumped into his and he rewarded me with another playful smile. "What nefarious thing were you up to that I spooked you?" I asked.

"Horse thievin'. How 'bout you?" His manner was deadpan and matter of fact.

I looked at him for a long moment before responding in kind, "History homework."

Smirking, he took on a professorial tone. "'We learn from history, that we learn nothing from history.' One of my favorite quotes right next to, 'the shorter the tether the sooner the goat starves.'" The printing on his shirt was actually a series of numbers and letters that appeared to be stamped across the front. Maybe he'd escaped from some sort of experimental lab...which also didn't preclude him being of alien origin. "So, what have you been learning?" he continued.

"Hmm?" I had lost myself both in thought and in the contours of his chest through the fabric of his shirt. His physique was well cared for without being overbearing, a consequence of work, rather than working out.

"From history? What have you learned from it?" He repeated with a sense of genuine curiosity.

I tried to remember what I was supposed to be writing about, but drew a blank. "Apparently not a damn thing."

Daniel must have liked my answer because his smile deepened. "Wise woman."

"That's what it says on my birth certificate." I grinned and could have gone on talking but was interrupted just then by strong feelings of agitation, anxiety, and zeal. Yes...zeal. My defenses were completely down, and it was like taking a hard slap to the head. I pitched forward, reflexively cursing, "The fuck?"

Daniel's hand pressed against my stomach. He was the only thing between me and a tumble down the hill.

"Daaaaanoooo!" a young man's voice yodeled from somewhere behind us. I whipped around as another boy my age rounded the corner of the stable. Short, lanky, and drowning in a green hoodie, he had light brown hair that resembled a shredded feather duster. "Daaaannnooo!" he called again, spotting us both a moment later.

The horses bantered in protest; it was late and they were already freaked out enough on account of the storm without adding this moron to the mix. Relief was now working its way through the boy's agitation, but not into me: I had sealed myself off after the first wave.

I am red.

"Where you been, man? I tried your cell forever ago!" he said.

Daniel, who had yet to take his eyes from me, just pointed toward the storm in an overly pronounced gesture. His friend gaped, as if he were only now noticing it. I, meanwhile, was resisting the urge to throttle the little bastard for damaging my calm.

I reached into my back pocket and pulled out a smoke, lighting it up and dismissing Daniel's hand with a nod as I brought my hand to my temple. I met his eyes with a small smile. The excess emotions drained away much faster than usual. Was there more at play here than just my cigarette?

"Thanks," I whispered, so only my savior could hear.

"That is fuck-king cool." The boy's agitation melted away, replaced by a momentary sense of wonder and then harrowingly fierce pride. "You know what else is cool?" Neither of us had a chance to respond before he blurted out, "You're looking at the owner of a Geee-en-uuine Thurrew-bread Hurse. And this here..." He stared out at the storm, putting an arm around each of us. "...Is a sign I'm doing the right thing."

He looked first to Daniel and then to me. "You're in the presence of the future winner of the Ken-tuck-y Derby." Yup, that's how he talked, placing a comically redneck twang every few words. Well...that he found it to be comical was in evidence, anyway. He had an ever-present, underlying river of arrogance to match his charm. It flowed, sludge-like, beneath whatever emotions bubbled to the top.

"Soon as he learns how to ride that is." Daniel smirked, placing a hand on the intruder's chest and pushing him slowly backwards until his arms were no longer around us. "Amy, this is Trevor. He's what passes as my friend in these parts."

Grateful for the distance Daniel put between us, I faced Trevor. Electric blue eyes and long, fine features, while still masculine, made him more beautiful than handsome. I perked up in recognition of his name. "Oh! You bought Nyla!"

Nyla was a gorgeous brown and white thoroughbred with white face markings that gave her the illusion of having a skull for a head. She was highly spirited and had been for sale at the Gelding for the past four months after being transferred all over the Northeast. Everyone who worked at the ranch knew a newbie had bought her, and there was a pool going around regarding how long he would last as her owner. After meeting Trevor in person, my money was on a month and a week.

Perhaps too generous.

"Congratulations!" I said, but my beaming smile faded at the sight of Mother's car pulling up. Her headlights came to rest directly on the three of us, with her horn sounding shortly thereafter.

"Who's this now?" Daniel asked me as he turned towards the storm again so as not to be blinded. The backlighting made him look otherworldly and angelic. An angel? In all my assumptions of ill intent, that was something I hadn't considered. Maybe he'd been sent to help make things more bearable for me, to give me someone to talk to without the maddening pressure in my head.

It had already been easier to deal with Trevor's deluge in the short time I had known Daniel...and hadn't he saved me from a nasty fall minutes before? That was exactly the kind of thing angels did. It might also explain why I was having such a hard time taking my eyes off him.

"My mother." Taking a drag from my cigarette, I did little to hide my disappointment.

"Tell her I'll give you a ride home later," he said, nonchalantly, and the angel theory gained further prominence.

My eyes bulged. "Oh yeah, that'll go over like a sack of wet cats."

"Walk you to her car then?" In one easy movement, he swiveled around and jumped off the fence, holding out his hand to help me down. I didn't need the help but took it anyway, following his lead in one crisp motion.

"It's the Green Mile..." I sighed, giving a glance toward the Audi.

"Can't be more than one hundred feet," Daniel said, gauging it with his thumb.

"Yeah but with these shackles on...feels like a mile."
Showing off my ankles, I modeled nonexistent restraints.

"They're pink with green polka dots. Wouldn't have expected that." Eyebrow raised in mock surprise, he started forward and I followed.

"Yes well...just because you're going to your death doesn't mean you can't be fashionable," I replied. Turning momentarily back toward Trevor, I waved. "Nice meetin' you!" Okay, not precisely true, but he was a patron of the Gilded Gelding so it was best to keep things cordial. He managed a grunt in response and went back to watching the storm, annoyance and a twinge of slimy envy at the forefront of his emotions.

As we left Trevor's range there was a blissful swath of time where it was only Daniel and me again. I had to keep looking at him to remind myself he was really there, and all too soon my mother's feelings of anxious intrigue came hammering in. "Daniel?" I stopped and backed up a few steps until I could no longer feel her. "I don't wanna get too close, if it's all the same."

He smiled sympathetically, retracing his steps until he was beside me. With a slight bow, he took my free hand and brought it to his lips, placing a slow, deliberate kiss on the knuckles. "I appreciate you sharing the night with me." His eyes met mine as he released me and stood tall once more.

"I appreciate you saving my life..." I did my best to act coy, batting my lashes and twisting my boot in the dirt, but quickly devolved into a giant cheese-eating grin.

"I'd like to do it again sometime—save your life I mean." His tone was soft and irreverent.

"Thought you said your name was Daniel, not Clark."

He brought his finger to his lips in a quieting gesture. "Secret identity."

Putting my smoke out on the bottom of my shoe, I pocketed the filter and took out my phone. "Well, Clark...are you on Baseline?" Baseline was a social media site that synced up all the social platforms so you didn't have to check more than one place per day.

"Ah uh." His eyes locked with mine again, and a mischievous smile spread across his face while he shook his head "no." Walking backwards in the direction of his friend he said firmly, "I'll find you."

My eyes, along with a few other choice organs, went wild. The sheer devilishness of his behavior made me giddy, but was he actually leaving without exchanging anything other than our names? He didn't even have mine in full!

Seeing my look of amused confusion, he pointed to his chest with both hands and added, "Superman, remember?"

Flush with exhilaration, and confident it wouldn't be too long before I saw him again, I turned on my heel and skipped the rest of the way to the waiting Audi.

CHAPTER FIFTEEN

*M*other's anxious intrigue was at operatic levels when I got in the car. "Who's the boy? He's cute," she said, the millisecond my door shut.

"I'm not even sure myself." This was said half in truth and half in jest. The Audi sported tinted windows and I stared at Daniel shamelessly from every direction until he was no longer visible. "Damn trees." I sneered, flipping back around in my seat and clicking on my seatbelt.

"Ooooh, you've got it bad for this one..." Mother teased. "Does he work at the ranch?"

"No, he was out there with a friend who owns one of the stabled horses, I think." I was beginning to wonder if I had done something to remove her anxiety, when it spiked again. As usual, she could only ever seem to be happy for me for the length of time it took to suck the flavor from a stick of Juicy Fruit. The other night notwithstanding.

"Well that may be for the best. I don't think getting involved with a boy is such a good idea given your...state. Boys are trouble as is."

Now, you should know that my mother had me put on the birth control shot for my thirteenth birthday out of fear I would get pregnant. 'Happy birthday, Amy! Here's a shot in the arm and a look of derision!' Understand, this was less to keep me from ruining my life and more to keep her carefully maintained, illusionary bubble intact. There was no way she was going to be a grandmother at the tender age of thirty-two.

And I have to say that despite my own grandmother's scornful looks and insistence that being on birth control would make me promiscuous, I hadn't ever gone beyond oral sex. I had, in fact, gotten quite good at it over time, if my sources were to be believed. After the first traumatic incident involving my teeth and an overly eager Liam Garner, I had run to Ramburglarz, a prominent gay men's forum, to learn how to give a good blowjob; so such accounts were probably accurate. Increasing my skills in this way helped keep the pressure for sex, from subsequent boyfriends, to a minimum. Let's face it: they were just happy I was touching their bishop at all.

There were only three guys I had ever "played chess" with to any extent, and by the time we broke up I was exceedingly thankful I hadn't allowed any of them to take my queen. Mind you, I wasn't exactly saving myself for some hallowed place or time, but I didn't want to have any regrets either. Kayla had lost her queen in a raging comedy of errors that was the catalyst for her exploring girls as an option. She can still be heard grumbling under her breath, on nights when the moon is full, about how girls at least know basic female anatomy.

"You were just drooling over him a minute ago and now you're telling me to back off?" I looked at her like she was nuts.

"I'm saying you don't need any more complications." Her tone patted me on the head like I was an eight-year-old.

"Yeah, well…I don't even know if I'm into this guy…I

can't get a read on him." Another half-truth—I was ridiculously into him.

"He wants sex," she said bluntly. "There, I saved you the trouble."

"You don't know that. What if he's gay?" I snorted.

"No gay man kisses a woman's hand that way…"

There was a musical certainty in her voice, and her anxious annoyance took such a sharp turn into untouchable conceit that I had to steady myself against the armrest.

"Oh, and you're an expert on the subject then?" I chided, though she was right: the way he'd looked at me, no way was he batting for the other team.

She gave me a knowing smile but didn't go any further on the subject. "I don't want you blowing all the hard work we've done these past few weeks because of some boy, no matter how weak in the knees he makes you. If Dr. Siva gives you the okay to date, then we can talk about it."

Dr. Siva was my psychiatrist, and I didn't see her for another two weeks. But arguing the point with my mother would only make it harder for me to sneak around and do whatever I was going to do anyway, so I nodded and rested my head against the passenger's side window. My lack of resistance at first made her suspicious, but before too long, she settled into a comfortably smug satisfaction.

I could work with satisfaction.

Now would be an opportune time to flip the conversation sideways and see what spilled out. "You remember the night I got the job at the Gelding?" I asked.

"Yes. I was, and still am, very happy for you. They've been really great for your recovery." Pride and a sense of superiority outshone her happiness, but to be fair, it was present.

"They have been," I agreed. "You were happier than I ever remember seein' you, almost like…well…do you ever have issues with taking on other people's emotions?" There, the question was blurted out. I gripped the seat, bracing for impact.

"I care about people, Amy, you know that." Confusion swirled into her pride, without a hint of panic, shame, or guilt to indicate she was keeping something from me. Of course it was possible she had some sort of mastery over her emotions, but after what happened the other night I didn't think so. More to the point, she didn't seem to understand what I was asking. Maybe if I tried a different angle?

"Is there anything about our family that's...unusual..." I asked.

"Ha!" she laughed, before replying in a bone dry tone, "Plenty." There was something there...an uptick in her suspicion and anxiety, though on the outside she seemed to be having fun with it. "You'll have to be more specific."

"Did anyone ever claim to have any ESP, or psychic abilities, or anything like that?"

Relief flooded through her—whatever she had been afraid of me finding out, it wasn't within this line of questioning. "Nothing. Well, besides talking to God of course, but that's hardly unusual." The disbelief that flared up then was deliciously telling for the self-proclaimed "good Catholic woman." She went to church each Sunday not out of any sense of piety, but because it bolstered her image within the community—and that meant more sales for Freedom Timber.

I chuckled to myself at the confirmation of what I had known all my life.

Hey, I was a human lie detector, too! There were some potentially huge benefits to my ability, if I could get it under control.

"Yeah, I suppose even if you did have some kind of empathy or somethin' there's no way you could have brought it up to Grandma..." I said. No surprise or bitterness came from her.

Nothing indicating I'd hit on anything secretive, just more confusion, and the irritation that was always present when my grandmother was mentioned. I brought her into the conversation in hopes of throwing my mother off balance and kicking up any of the emotions that would come with being repressed.

"First she'd have had to look up what empathy means, and then she'd have probably sent me to a nunnery." She snickered.

"What about…emotional issues? Do they run in the family?" I wanted to be thorough; after all, one woman's empathy was another woman's mental breakdown.

"No." She paused before adding in an off-hand manner, "Just you." Embarrassment mixed into her emotions then, but nothing else, and the appearance of that particular feeling wasn't surprising. She had hidden the entire hospital incident from the rest of my family and instructed me to do the same.

Her words stung, but the salt on the wound was that they got to me at all. Without thinking, I bit back. "You know you nearly drove us off the road the other night in your euphoria over a Choco Taco. How sure are you that it doesn't run in the family and straight through you?" Not exactly diplomatic, but this was good; I needed to confront her on the specifics of that night, and if anger was my medium, then so be it.

"I did nothing of the kind!" She was disturbed and befuddled underneath her budding fury and incredulity. "And you are on dangerous ground, young lady."

"You seriously don't remember that? I had to dive for the wheel!" I exclaimed. Her turbulent and disorienting emotions answered my question for me. No. She didn't. Had she been possessed or something? What had she made of her emotions snapping back into place?

Risking her further ire, I pressed on. "After we stopped,

97

your emotions were bouncing all over the place, you were crying. Do you remember why?"

"Because it's always a fight with you lately!" She shook her head and a cup of misery and indignation tipped onto her confusion, melting it away. "I know you're feeling alone, Amy, but lots of people go through what you're going through and go on to live perfectly normal lives." And because that was a decent thing to say, she added, with a huff and a roll of her eyes, "You don't have to try to make me seem crazy, too."

I stared at her for a while, holding onto a quip about her doing a fine enough job of that on her own, before gazing out the window again. I had what I wanted and was now painfully convinced that my mother knew less than nothing about what happened that night. She seemed to be subconsciously dismissing anything out of the ordinary, and not just to save face...but to preserve her sanity.

The emotional whiplash I got from her must have been much worse on her end. Her brain was probably scrambled...at least when it came to that particular memory. I didn't rule out that what was going on with me was genetic, but I wouldn't be getting any answers from my mother.

Still, as the miles rolled past us in silence, I was grateful to have made it through the dreaded conversation relatively unscathed. It was silly to have put it off as long as I had. She hadn't threatened to put me in an institution or up my dosage of Paraxil or anything of the sort.

Not yet, anyway.

CHAPTER SIXTEEN

*a*fter we got home, I threw together a turkey and swiss sandwich and ran upstairs to call Kayla.

"I met another ghost tonight." Immediately after blurting it out I took a gigantic bite of my sandwich and waited, now with a literal cheese-eating grin on my face.

"Are you destroyin' a sandwich while breaking this spine melting news to me?" Kayla's voice conveyed both awe and annoyed amusement.

In between muffled smacks I said, "Mmmfyesshh."

"Is it at least a good sandwich?"

"Nyyoh." Swallowing down what I had just laboriously chewed, I made a disgusted face at the remains of the meal. "I think this turkey may have died twice." Undaunted by the prospect of food poisoning, I took another bite.

"Well it's about to have you for company if you don't tell me what in the four rooms you're talkin' about!" she shouted.

"I told you! I met a ghost tonight...one who was also an alien and a vampire and an angel all wrapped up in the body of a god." After a third, smaller bite, I spilled everything about my close encounter of the Daniel kind.

"I can't believe you let him go!" Kayla cried when I'd finished.

"What was I supposed to do? My mother would have noticed if I stuffed him in the trunk."

She sighed. "Yeah, well, we need some answers!" It was easy for me to forget that this whole situation had been affecting her too.

"I know...but if he knows somethin', why didn't he just say? Why keep it from me?"

"Why'd Leilani? That's the sweet pot o' honey right there." I could practically hear the gears spinning in her head. "Maybe you're bein' put through some kinda gauntlet, or test. It's just too freaky a coincidence, him and Leilani." Pencil scratched against paper on her end. "Their names are even similar...hers starts with L E I and his ends in I E L... and they both have an A and an N...it's like they wanna be palindromes..."

"Their names sharin' some letters doesn't mean they're friends, Kayla..."

"Not pals Amy, *palindromes*. Words spelled the same way backwards as forwards."

"Oh. How can you remember English class at a time like this? You're sick, you know that?"

"Mmmmmhmmm. But you're right, it could be irrelevant. Let's shelve it for now and go onto what else we know. What did you say his last name was again?" A loud squeaking noise dominated the call—she'd just sat forward on her rickety couch, ready to really get down to business.

"Varrick."

"As in Varrick Construction?"

"I don't know who they are." *Did I?*

"Yeah, you do—they have the signs with that giant eagle head that looks like it disapproves of your life choices."

"Oh yeah!" I said, laughing. "The way his muscles

stretched over him, it would make sense for him to be in construction."

Kayla clacked away on her laptop. "Let's see what I can find out about him. Well he isn't a forty-three-year-old black guy who's into photography, is he?"

"I'm pretty sure he isn't, though I wouldn't rule anything out." I snickered, stuffing the remainder of my sandwich into my mouth.

"There's a book about a post-apocalyptic survivor named Daniel Varrick...could that be your guy?"

My bedroom window stuck and squealed under my attempts to open it. "I'll ask him the next time he sneaks up and scares the life out of me." Triumphant, I lit up a cigarette and blew the smoke through the screen. Mother was not okay with me smoking in my room. This was me meeting her halfway.

"There's a Baseline profile for just 'Varrick,' and he seems to be obsessed with the Avatar anime...seriously that is all this profile is...on and on and on..."

"It's a good show." An opossum crawled along the roof of the back porch, directly beneath my window. The thing was remarkable in its ability to be repulsively cute. It stared at me, a flare of something like curiosity curling from it, but it was hard to pin down. The further removed animals were from people, the harder it was to speak their emotional language—so to speak. Fear and anger were universal, but anything beyond that got muddied.

"Here we go! Varrick Custom Builders Inc. out of Monroe. It's a family owned business. Daniel has his very own write-up on their website, but no picture."

"That's a crime," I lamented, flicking my ashes into a mug that proclaimed I was the "World's Greatest Dad."

Kayla read the website word for word. "Daniel is the only boy in our merry brood and has been a crucial cog in the family business since he could hold a hammer. He is a quick draw with both the nail and staple guns and assists in maintaining our fleet and keeping it strong. When not working tirelessly alongside his father, Daniel enjoys hanging out with his friends, snowboarding, and hunting." She made the tsk noise. "He's jus' a regulah ol' good ol' boy, ain't he? All he needs is a beat up ol' pickup truck."

"You mean like yours?"

"No! Green Goblin's one of a kind," Kayla said with finality. "Well okay, at least now we know he's real, but we're just supposed to wait around for him to stalk you? That doesn't sit right with me. I mean, who does that?"

"Superman." My grin translated through the phone and Kayla groaned. "He's just havin' some fun, and it's totally somethin' you would do and you know it!" I reminded her.

"Maybe…but that's me…" She laughed.

"Kayla, it was so nice to be able to be close to someone without…" My eyes filled with unexpected tears and my throat caught. So often we're strong about a situation until we say it aloud. Then it becomes real.

"I know." The sympathy in her voice reached through the line and wrapped itself around me. "I just want you to be careful, which you weren't tonight by the way, floatin' after him all starry-eyed."

"Hey…you haven't seen him…I apologize for nothing!" Wiping away a few tears, I cleared my throat. "And why do we have to immediately assume the worst? Why can't he just be an angel?"

"Because the world is shit." Bluntness was her scalpel, and it cut through me deep and direct. I had been careless, willfully so at some points. "You still have that pen knife?" Her tone softened.

My pen knife was exactly what it sounds like, a small knife hidden inside a working pen: a gift from my uncle Jerry the Christmas before he passed four years ago. He taught me how to use it safely and said I was to keep it from my parents at all costs. Which, of course, made it ten times cooler. I carried it with me everywhere until Mother borrowed it, thinking it was an ordinary pen. She buggered off to work, and I spent the whole day dreading an inevitable outcome that never came. The pen hadn't given up its secrets but, not wanting to tempt fate, I kept it safely tucked away in the false bottom of my jewelry box ever since.

Walking over to said box, I took the penknife out and checked the sharpness against my pointer finger, drawing a small amount of blood. "Yeah, still sharp too. I'll start carryin' it again." My thumb traced the wound, waiting for more of the red stuff to trickle out, but I apparently hadn't cut that deep and nothing more came.

As I cleaned my knife, I gave Kayla the Cliff Notes version of the conversation with my mother. She agreed with my assessment that Mother didn't know anything and confessed she was relieved I had finally asked. Now we could rule out her active involvement and move forward.

My best girl had spent the day plastering Leilani's picture all over the internet and researching some shiny new equipment to take out to the Whitaker barn where this whole mess began.

It would be a few weeks before we had enough money to buy the thermal camera, aura reader, and full spectrum lighting Kayla was eyeing. That suited me fine. I was in no rush to go back there, not because it gave me the creeps—which it did—but because I couldn't shake the feeling that I had somehow gotten off light; the feeling that things hadn't gone as planned inside that barn for more than just Kayla and me.

CHAPTER SEVENTEEN

ollowing the beauty of that dry thunderstorm, we were treated to three days of torrential rain that transformed the entire Northeast region into one giant mud pit. Everyone at the ranch was in a bad mood, with the notable exception of the horses. They loved it. At times it seemed as though they were reveling in the knowledge that the mud made our jobs tougher. They still had to run; it was cruel to keep them locked up for days at a time, and we had to hose them down after every outing on the off chance that their owners came for a visit. With over fifty horses at the stable, things got extremely time consuming.

While dealing with my empathy had been easier immediately after meeting Daniel, the days that followed were that much harder for me. After the reminder of what life could/should be like, reality was a tyrannical S.O.B. Coping with the negative emotions from my usually chipper coworkers was especially challenging since they popped in and out of my empathy field sporadically throughout the day.

Keeping my "mental shield" up with no one pressing on it was something I hadn't mastered, so I was caught unaware, and cussing like a sailor, more times than I can count. I'd be alone for twenty minutes just to have someone run through all flustered and angry, and then I'd be flustered and angry and have to deal with refocusing—which also made me flustered and angry. Needless to say, I was relieved when most of the employees went home that afternoon.

That is, until I saw Nyla.

Nyla had rolled herself completely in one of the mud pits in the east pasture. The horses weren't supposed to have access to that section, but somehow the mare managed to find her way out there. If that wasn't bad enough, the rain gods picked that moment to graciously ease their assault, so no help there.

Dejected as I was, I couldn't help but laugh. "You look like a chocolate covered horse, Nyla." She snorted, indisputably proud of herself.

Two mud-caked hours later, she was as beautiful as she'd ever been; I was another story. Kamrie had come out to help and give me some pointers but was called away to other tasks before long. She was always busy, but never hesitated to put aside time for a "teachable moment." As I finished toweling down Nyla, I daydreamed that Kamrie was my mom and we lived happily ever after in this fairytale life of hers.

"If you buff that bum anymore I'll be able ta see myself in it!" My employer's voice and infectious cheeriness floated through the haze of my mind. I snapped to and found her beckoning for someone to join us. Trevor walked over, adjusting the straps on a helmet. A silver and black jockey outfit clung to his every feature, and he felt as awkward as he looked. Of course, he hid it well behind an outer facade of self confidence, standing tall with his chin out.

Impish thoughts were evident in Kamrie's eyes, and it was all she could do to keep from laughing hysterically. "Come on ovah Trevah! Nyla's ya horse and she's expectin' ya ta take her reins and show her you know it!"

My heart sank. After all my hard work, Nyla would get dirty again in minutes. No, Kamrie wouldn't let that happen. "Trevah got all trussed up for his first ridin' lesson with me. If I didn't know bettah, I'd think you were tryin' ta impress," she added to him.

"I might be." Trevor swayed over to Nyla and patted her down. The horse looked at him with indignant disdain and nickered.

"Nyla's a stickler for fashion." I stepped aside, smirking at Kamrie, and let her take over instructing Trevor on how best to approach and saddle up his horse.

Remember that pool I mentioned? The one about how long Trevor would last as Nyla's owner? Kamrie had gotten wind of it and thrown herself all-in as a matter of pride. She'd see him in racing shape by summer's end, have bragging rights, and the $100 pot to boot. Had I known she was going to be giving him lessons personally, I would have lengthened the time I threw in for. As it was, we were all sure we would be out our twenty bucks.

He hadn't brought Daniel...

The butterflies in my stomach began to sour just as my white rabbit rounded the corner into the stable at a jog. Above his head, he held an expensive looking camera, announcing triumphantly, "Got it!"

Eager excitement fluttered through me, but not only through me. Trevor had the same butterflies. He was standing right next to Kamrie and radiating them. For the first time, I was separating two or more people within my 22 ¼ foot bubble.

I gawked at the two of them, switching back and forth between each set of distinct emotions. It was sort of like scrolling through pictures on a phone, but using my mind and heart instead of my fingers. There was a pressure in my head and a corresponding small jolt in my heart with each "swipe."

A bright flash pulled me from my reverie and dissolved the distinction. Daniel snapped photos of Trevor from different angles. "Doesn't matter what I do." He shook his head as he adjusted something on the device and lined up another shot. "You still look like a tool." There was some humor in his tone, but his expression was stoic.

I concentrated, but couldn't get Trevor and Kamrie's emotions to separate again.

Damn.

The wanna-be jockey retorted in an over-the-top Irish accent, "You'll beh saingin a deffarhent tune when I'm rawlin' en thah dough!" Leading Nyla out of the stable with Kamrie at his side, Trevor shouted back at his friend, "Are ya shar you'll beh alright here by yarself?"

Daniel grinned, his eye catching mine. "I'll manage to occupy myself, somehow."

The butterflies were a swarm, and I was suddenly painfully aware of how I looked. Mud, grit, and plant matter slid down the front of my apron, and my hair, tight in a ponytail, dripped with it as well. Nothing to be done; the only option was to play it cool.

"I was just indulging in a relaxing and refreshing mud bath, if you care to join me." I extended my mud-caked hand and he took it, closing the gap between us.

"I do," he answered.

He actually took my hand? My nasty muddy, sudsy hand?

Oh, and those eyes...those eyes will be the death of me...

"Ah...but first." Grinning like the Cheshire cat, I peered at him. "What's my name?" I decided a long time ago that if a guy can't be bothered to remember a girl's name, he isn't worth the skin he's sitting in. It was a litmus test for me. After our first encounter, I didn't think he'd forget, but I was a creature of habit, and so the question hung in the damp air.

His brow furrowed as though he were in deep thought and struggling to remember. We had only met briefly days ago…maybe he forgot…oh, why did he have to forget? I let go of his hand, my voice dripping with faux sympathy: "Aw, and I had such high hopes for you, Daniel Varrick." Bending down, I started picking up the shampoo bottles Nyla had lovingly kicked everywhere.

He watched me casually for a few moments while swinging one of the horse stall doors back and forth on its hinges. "How 'bout a deal? I get three guesses and for each wrong one I help you clean up for another hour. If I guess right, you have to drop what you're doing and come keep me company."

What was up his sleeve? Did it matter? Either way I won. "Okay Daniel, shoot me with it."

"Shake?" He reached for my hand again and I complied. "A pleasure doing business with you…Amy Rachael Durene, the beautiful, and wise." Somewhere under his smile were the feathers of a canary.

Like candles at the end of their wicks, Trevor and Kamrie's emotions chose that moment to fade, at first into whispers and then into blissful silence. I was truly alone with Daniel. Of course, the horses were there, but they were so much background noise by then. I laughed and cried in the same breath, from the same sense of relief.

My eyes were taken in by his for several heart beats. "Are you real?" I whispered, my lips betraying a slight quiver as I wiped at my tears with my free hand. "I should call you Daniel the resourceful."

If he thought I was the mad woman I felt like, he gave no sign. "What's my prize for getting all three right?" There was something in that smug smile he threw at me that broke my inner trickster out of its paper thin cell.

Opening his palm, I pulled a clump of mud from my hair and slapped it into his hand. "You get the play-at-home version of a Gilded Gelding mud bath." With that I backed away, taking off my apron and swallowing a small yellow bird of my own. "I'm off in fifteen—just let me clean up, and I'll meet you back out here." I placed the supply bucket back in its closet and headed up to the main house with a spring in my step and without looking back. Mercifully, Kamrie had an employee shower, complete with attached mudroom for use in just such an emergency.

When I was sufficiently human again, I bounded out to meet Daniel, nervous as a vampire in a tanning booth. Was this a date? I wasn't exactly dressed to the nines in my black jeans, gray shirt, and blue flannel, but it'd have to do. You take what you get when you show up unannounced.

My canary-eating white rabbit was nowhere to be seen when I reached the stable. Had he gone out front? Maybe to our fence? *"Our fence?" Moving a bit fast there, aren't we, Amy?*

Wait a second. What's got the horses' undies in a bunch? I followed their gazes to the rafters. Daniel sat on one of the beams, greeting me with his boyish smile.

"I did a bit of dusting while I waited." He adjusted himself so his legs dangled over the side. "You don't mind, do you?"

"Nnn...o, but you won the bet. You shouldn't be cleaning." I searched around. How had he gotten up there?

"Well...in my defense, I didn't do a very good job," he responded dryly.

Daniel watched in amusement as I figured out which pillars and cross beams he used and started up them myself. "I'll be the judge of that." Thankfully, after three weeks of hard labor at the ranch, I had the muscles to pull it off and was soon straddling the same beam he was sitting on, only safely on the opposite end. I rubbed some dust from the top of the beam between my fingers and concluded, "You're right, you didn't."

The ease with which I could talk to him was both liberating and unsettling. I stared at him for a time. There were disadvantages to being completely blind to his true intentions. I'd have to proceed the old fashioned way...by getting to know him. "Okay, Spiderman…so how'd you discover my secret identity?"

With a slow smirk he answered, "I used my spider minions to bring me a copy of the schedule hanging up in the main office."

"Please tell me the spiders Xeroxed their little butts in your copy."

He nodded. "All sixteen of them."

"How'd you know I didn't have plans?"

"I didn't." He chuckled. "You could've left me holdin' mud."

"Yeah, but then I wouldn't be up here entertainin' the horses." I looked at my charges, who were still eyeing us from time to time, some with wonder, some with suspicion, and raised an eyebrow at Daniel. "Why are you up here, anyway?"

Shrugging, he rose to his feet. "Just passin' the time." Without a single glance down he navigated the length of the two-foot-wide beam and sat next to me. We weren't touching, but I could feel his warmth, and my temperature went up a few degrees. "What is it about horses for you?" he asked.

"They make me feel free…just bein' around 'em." *Not unlike you…*

"You have a horse here?"

"Not yet…someday maybe, but for now I just take care of 'em. You?"

Shaking his head he surveyed our equine audience. "All my horses live inside engines. But I wouldn't say no to a Mustang. I'd name her Shelby and ride her every day."

"You know your way around more than just construction equipment then?" There might have been something like mischief in my tone.

"Someone's been stalking…" Daniel gave me the side eye.

"Did you know there's a post-apocalyptic series written about you?"

"Oh, that?" He smiled. "It's a true story. Wait 'til they get to the part where I travel backwards through time to right now. I get up to some mean shenanigans." Laughing as he again got to his feet, my date grabbed one of the supports and made his way back down as fluidly as ol' Spidey himself. "Show me around the place," he said as he hit the ground.

My descent was nowhere near as poetic, but I managed not to fall on my ass—which was good—or to wind up in his arms—which was a terrible injustice. It left me with the bizarre thought that klutzy girls got all the breaks.

It had stopped raining but a thick mist hung in the air as we walked the grounds, continuing to get to know one another. Daniel worked a lot, but the weather had put a halt to their latest project, and he'd been on maintenance duty in the garage. He had turned eighteen in January and graduated high school a semester early so he could be free by the time adulthood came around. He said it had less to do with him being smart and more to do with not taking study hall. I wondered when he'd found time to sleep but kept the comment to myself.

After a while I started to get cold, so we hopped in his truck. I gave Kayla a mental point since he did indeed have one, a white Dodge Ram in great condition. We listened to music off my phone and discovered we had the same taste; he was even into some of the local indie bands, like Dead Operation and Mushroom Beard. We were hard pressed to find a television show or movie we didn't agree on, with the notable exception of my beloved Dusk movies. Daniel thought the mud clump I handed him earlier was both a more engaging story than my favorite series, and a better actor than Reese Myers. He wouldn't be getting lost in Cormack Skerrett's eyes in the poster above my bed. Oddly, the little battle made me feel more at ease with my alien angel…I was beginning to worry that he might be a little too perfect.

I kept a sharp eye out the entire time for anything suspicious or out of the ordinary, but aside from the stunt with the rafters, which only indicated he was in good shape, there was nothing alarming. There were times I swore we were picking up right where we left off in some past life, ironically, just like Rowan and Cormack. Even the silences between us were natural; there was no struggle to find something to say next. But the cherry on top? I'd gone two hours without a cigarette while carrying on with someone less than three feet from me the entire time. And I gotta tell ya, a girl could get used to that.

When my stomach began to growl, Daniel opened up the glove box and produced a package of Rustic Ray's beef jerky. As we both chewed, I commented thoughtfully, "I think this is the most redneck date I've ever been on." With nothing but a half-crazed smile to serve as a warning, my date started the truck and peeled out, spraying gravel every which way. I was too busy cracking up and enjoying the ride to bother asking where we were going.

Whipping into a muddy field three-and-a-half miles down the road, Daniel grinned. "After the day you've had, this here's a bit of cosmic justice for you." The truck's tires slipped and scoured through the mud, weaving all manner of patterns. My cheeks, already sore from so much laughing throughout the day, actually went numb from it now.

After a while, Daniel put the truck into park and asked with a twinkle in his eye, "You want a go at it? I just modified the U-joints on the drive train so she's handlin' like a dream." I slid over his lap and took the wheel with gusto, vowing to make an absolute disaster of a mess. After stalling the truck no less than five times, I finally got the hang of driving stick shift and made mincemeat of the remaining field.

Daniel took the wheel back and slid onto the main road, turning to me with a satisfied smirk. "Now you can be *sure* this is the most redneck date you've ever been on."

"Until next time..." My devious eyes washed over him,

holding onto his reciprocating gaze long enough for the truck to kick up gravel on the shoulder. He refocused on the road, and, to the chagrin of my poor, weary sides, we lost ourselves in laughter again.

Trevor, whose mud-soaked body rivaled the trucks, was waiting for us when we pulled into the parking lot. His anger and frustration were palpable, and served as an ugly reminder of my reality after two-and-a-half hours of relative normalcy.

Nyla hadn't taken kindly to Trevor on their ride, and she rubbed into a tree until he fell off into the mud. Kamrie calmed her immediately, but not before poor Trevor's right ankle was sprained. He had been waiting for Daniel for the better part of an hour and laid into him.

He leaves Daniel to go horse riding and then has the nerve to get mad at him for taking a short joyride in his own truck?! Where does this guy get off?! Let me add a sore jaw to go with that sprained ankle!

No, these aren't my feelings zipping through my brain, they're Trevor's. In lieu of going homicidal, I hopped out of the truck and lit up a cigarette. This was between two friends; I wasn't getting in the middle.

A substantial maple tree dominated the center of the parking area and I made my way slowly over to it, listening as I went. Over the course of their "conversation," it was revealed that the truck actually belonged to Trevor, not Daniel. To be fair, he hadn't claimed otherwise, I'd just assumed. When Trevor finally registered all the mud on his truck, he added jealousy to his cornucopia of emotions. By the time I reached the tree and ducked behind its trunk, only the occasional word reached me and I had to make do with emotional eavesdropping.

Judging from the distance, my range had increased as of late.

For his part, Daniel remained remarkably calm in tone

through his friend's tirade, and over the next few minutes, he somehow managed to appease him, even bringing about a twinge of guilt in the arrogant S.O.B. When Trevor's emotions began to fade, I chanced a look around the tree; Daniel was helping him into the truck. Once his injured friend was secured, Daniel closed the door and walked in my direction.

Trevor promptly opened the window and shouted, "Yeah well...you're still a wanker!" Without looking back Daniel flipped him the bird, keeping his pace towards me. I acted overly startled when his eyes fell on me, ducking back behind the tree trunk in a playful attempt to hide.

It was dusk and the stable lights were flickering on around us. The fog, still heavy in the air, added to the illusion that we were entirely alone. The only intruder was a gentle, if chilly, breeze.

"You know, smoking is bad for you." Daniel was on the opposite side from where I'd expected him, and his sudden appearance made me jump. He cocked his head to one side, considering me as I took another hit. "But it does make you look bad-girl sexy...so I'll forgive it."

"Hmm...well stealin' a truck makes you bad-boy sexy, so we should be just about even," I replied, reveling in the light of his savory smile.

"I was hoping to hang out with you a bit more, but I need to take T-bone to get his ankle checked out. At the very least, I owe him for bringin' me to see you." Normally, I would have gagged at such a line, but that night my swooning was unrepentant. What's more...I knew he meant every syllable.

I was working on stitching together a cohesive thought when Daniel cupped the side of my face in his hand—gently, but firmly—and leaned in. Without a moment's hesitation I met him halfway, parting his lips as he parted mine. My breath caught in my throat with each new taste of him and he pressed in further in response. I brought my hand up to caress his jawline before running my fingertips along the nape of his neck. Our kisses grew in intensity, and the rough bark of the tree scraped against my back as his tongue slid into my mouth. A growl wrapped in a moan rumbled through him, sending ripples of fire my way and being echoed in kind.

Never in my life had I been kissed with such conviction; all sense of the world melted away as I melded into him. I'm not sure how much time passed, but it wasn't enough...

An icy rush of air replaced Daniel's warmth as he pulled away, abject satisfaction in his every feature. My trembling lower lip drew the attention of one last kiss, and the next thing I knew, his fingers were slipping from my outstretched hand.

Somehow, I let him go, hanging onto the ghost of his touch long after the roar of the truck's engine faded into the night.

CHAPTER EIGHTEEN

$\mathcal{T}$he shrill sound of my Tigger alarm clock rang through my room at a most unpleasant hour the next morning. I was sore from all that scrubbing the day before and loath to get out of bed. Who the hell set my alarm clock on my Sunday off, anyway? I was having a good dream, though I couldn't recall the specifics. It was one of those dreams that was so much better than reality that your brain resists waking, out of some primal sense of self preservation. I punched Tigger's tail to shut him up as he gave off one final and defiant "Woohoohoohoo!"

Sleep's loving arms had just begun to embrace me again when Mother ripped off my covers. "I don't care how much you hurt today, you are going to make good on your promise." My promise? What promise? My brain grasped futilely for the answer before dread set in. In a moment of weakness a few months back, I had agreed to help out at the Church of the Divine Heart's spring carnival. Mother had pressured me to do it as a good "networking" opportunity when I was looking for work.

"The carnival doesn't start for another four hours!" I moaned.

"Well, we have to go to Mass before it starts, and we have to get set up before Mass, so, out of bed with you!"

Mass? That wasn't part of the deal! Catholic Masses were the worst. A whole hour of some crusty old man telling us all about how we are going to burn in hell. I'd pass, thanks. "I didn't agree to Mass!" I pulled the covers back over myself. "I'll take Dad's car and meet you out there."

"Your father has his golf game today!" she snapped. My dad's lack of "faith" was a bit of a sore spot for her. "Besides, you don't have your license, and if you aren't downstairs and ready to go in twenty minutes, you won't until you're eighteen."

Checkmate.

I rolled my carcass out of bed, kicking aside the preppy outfit my mother had set out for me and grabbing my Slayer shirt. How could last night have been so great and this morning so horrific? It defied some law of physics.

The church was nearly an hour away. I tried to sleep in the car but my mother was way too uptight to allow for that. She spent the first half hour of our ride bitching about my dad and what a bad influence he was on me. How could I be expected to love and respect God with such a role model? The funny thing was, she could have just as easily been talking about herself.

I popped a message off to Kayla letting her know I was dead for the day and scrolled through my previous message to her.

8:22 PM: DANIEL'S NOT A VAMPIRE...

8:22 PM: ...NO FANGS...

8:22 PM: ...I CHECKED...

8:23 PM: ...WITH MY TONGUE. 😈

There was no typed response: she had called me less than a minute after I sent it, and we talked well into the night, with her insisting I go through every insignificant detail. Somewhere in all that she seemed happy for me, but she also

117

thought I had been reckless to let him take me away from the ranch like I had. I understood, but I'd be damned if I was going to let paranoia dictate how I lived my life.

I'd rather die first.

Five minutes into Mass, death was looking like a mighty tempting option. It was excruciatingly boring, and easily half of the people around me shared my suicidal inclination. My phone vibrated and I checked it discreetly. Bumblebees waltzed through my stomach and my chest tightened...it was Daniel. My mother didn't give me a second look when I slid out of the pew; she was too busy pretending to sing.

"Morning, Daniel," I answered quietly, my smile shining through the phone. An older couple gave me the evil eye, and I shot it right back at them as I escaped into the main foyer.

"What are you up to today?" he asked.

"Stuck at church, if you'd believe it." I rolled my eyes. Could he hear my heartbeat over the phone?

"I didn't think you believed in Jeebus."

"I don't. I agreed to help with their stupid carnival a few months ago, and I can't back out now, much as it pains me. I'm afraid I'm a lady of my word."

"How long will you be there?"

"Well, the carnival ends at three, but knowing my mother and how she likes to socialize, I can expect to be here *much* longer." It was only ten past nine.

"Unacceptable." Daniel's voice grew narrow. "What church is it?"

"Divine Heart, in Waterville," I replied.

Keys jangled in the background. "Have no fear, Amy, I'm gonna save you. I'll be there soon."

My heart skipped a beat. He lived in Monroe, an hour and a half from the church, and he was willing to drive all that way just to see me. I'd never known such dedication from a boyfriend before. Was he even my boyfriend? We hadn't

118

talked about it; he hadn't asked me to go steady or out to the ice cream social, but he had taken me muddin'...which was pretty well the same thing in our parts. I squelched the question on my lips. Why not see where the day took us?

We continued talking as he drove, but with the priest intoning the final blessing, I had to let him go and get back to my mother. She wouldn't care how long I was gone as long as I could be seen shaking hands by her side at the end.

It had been decided, not by me, that I would be in charge of one of the kids' games. When Mass let out, I made my way over to that section of the carnival; the toss game was lame and off in a corner, so before anyone could tell me different, I took that one. With all the anxious, excited, haughty energy flying around, I needed a quieter location to center myself. At least it was a relatively nice day, so everything was set up outside instead of being crammed into the gym. I could sneak a smoke in as needed.

My game was *Daniel and the Lion's Den.* I laughed to myself as I walked up to the large wooden lion with holes in its mouth, tail, and paws. Different points were awarded depending on which hole you tossed the multicolored bean bags into. It didn't end up being an issue for most of the kids, who couldn't land a shot if they were about to be eaten by a real lion. I'm telling you, these kids were either anomalies of nature or there was no hope for the future of mankind.

"Is this the line for the kissing booth?" I looked up from messing with my ticket pouch to find Daniel standing in front of me.

"You have any tickets?" My cheeks flushed with my smile.

"Yeah, there's a whole mess of them right here." He grabbed me by the pouch and brought me in close.

Everything in me wanted to continue where we left off the previous night, but given our immediate surroundings, I composed myself. "As much as I would love to, and believe me *I would love to*, I can't. Not here. We'd probably give that old lady a heart attack."

Daniel took my right hand in his and brought it resolutely to his lips, his eyes never leaving mine. I blushed a little at his chivalry but was interrupted shortly thereafter by some kids. "Is this the bean toss game?" They were *way* too excited at the prospect. I looked at Daniel, sighed, and proceeded to take their tickets in a cheerful manner. Ten minutes later they had exhausted all hope of winning and ran off to the bouncy room. It could have been worse, I could have been stuck with *that* job for the day. The operator spent as much time inside the rubber room, with a mop and bucket, as he did outside, taking tickets.

Picking a bean bag off of the fence a few yards away, I turned back to Daniel; he was examining the steadily growing crowd, probably wondering what he had gotten himself into. "Great, Daniel, we can be bored together at least." I offered a smile. "It was very sweet of you to come all the way out here just to save me."

"Oh, I have no intention of being bored." He smirked, gave another quick look around, and with his back turned to the wooden lion, kicked it as hard as he could. It splintered in several places and I jumped back from the suddenness of it. "Life's too short for boredom." He picked up the game and beckoned me to follow. Still in a bit of shock, I obliged, and we headed towards the church.

On the way, Father Merkel, the generally upbeat, white haired old priest, stopped us to ask what had happened to the poor lion. "I broke it," Daniel confessed. "I'm going to go see if I can fix it now." Father Merkel thanked him for his help and commented about what a fine young man he was. I had to bite my tongue to keep from laughing.

Upon entering the church, we ducked into a side room and Daniel threw the broken lion behind some old furniture.

"Oops, I guess it can't be fixed. It seems you no longer have a game to run, Amy, I've freed you from your obligations."

I probably should have been bothered by what he'd done, but all I could feel was relief at my liberation. Besides, someone would fix the game...eventually. "You defeated a lion for me. You really are my hero."

"Does the hero get a kiss? Or do I still need tickets?" he asked, roguishly.

Reaching into my pouch, I scooped out a handful of tickets, scattering a number on the floor in the process. I strolled over, opened his shirt, and dropped the lot of them down it, looking up at him expectantly. His lips were on me in seconds, hand wrapped tightly around the back of my neck... as if I were going anywhere...

We hadn't left the maple tree at all...the time in between had only been an illusion.

He closed the door and we moved to the couch where I straddled him, continuing to give him his "tickets worth." A quarter of an hour passed in this way until a ball of agitation neared the door. "Daniel..." I said between kisses, "someone's coming..." *More kisses...like breathing...*

"We should..." *Really though...there's no way to know for sure they'll come in here...*

He flipped me onto my back, nuzzling my neck, before stopping abruptly to listen. In an instant, he pulled me to my feet, and we slipped through the door to the adjoining classroom just as the main door to where we had been opened.

Daniel pressed me against the wall next to our exit and held me there as we both strove to control our breathing. We hadn't had time to close the connecting door. The person, a woman by the sound of her heels, was befuddled and rifling through the cabinets while muttering to herself. Daniel smirked at me, coming in for a single succulent kiss before leading us silently out the main door of the classroom.

121

"You're observant." He gave me the eye when we were safely in the hallway.

"I've got a sixth sense." I wasn't sure I wanted to get into my ability with him just yet, it might scare him off...but there it was.

"I like this church." He didn't seem to register the full weight of what I'd just told him. Why would he? It was a common enough turn of phrase. My secret identity would remain safe. "The architecture has an old, surreal feel to it." He panned from floor to ceiling, walking slowly, and reaching back for my hand. "I bet there are hidden passages —wanna go explorin', see what we can find?"

My eyes gave him the answer: of course I did.

We spent the next hour checking every nook and cranny we came across. My adrenaline was up; it was deliciously wrong to be poking around all these previously off-limits areas. Kayla and I had stuck to investigating abandoned places, but some of the quiet spots Daniel and I found had a definite spook factor to them. Maybe we should rethink that policy?

Hidden in the ornate woodwork against one wall of the audiovisual room was a secret set of stairs that spiraled upward. It was a tight squeeze, ending in a locked door. Kayla and I would definitely have to come back here; the ancient lock wouldn't stand a chance against—

A small but audible clank filled the space, and Daniel swung the door open. He'd straight up broken the lock...not that I let a thing like breaking and entering stop me from following him inside. An open balcony, some twenty feet in circumference, welcomed us, offering a view of the pulpit and pews that went unnoticed by the people below. Indeed, I had grown up attending Divine Heart every week and never noticed it.

Creepy, stalker balcony.

We watched the people underneath us for a time,

marveling at what folks did when they thought no one was looking. No less than three kids spit in the holy water in the span of ten minutes.

"I think we've found the best seats in the house," I told Daniel.

"Yes, but something is missing...we need more blasphemy." There was that mischievous grin again.

Moments later we were headed for the kitchen, plunging me into an ocean of feelings from the densely packed lunch crowd. As usual, it was a shock to my system, but with Daniel leading me through by the hand, the emotional waters were noticeably warmer. Brain power that would have gone into navigating the throng was now dedicated solely to shielding myself from it. A girl could get used to this, indeed.

As we grew closer to the kitchen, an agitated sledgehammer slammed against my mental armor, sending spider webbed cracks through it. I felt increasingly on edge, nervous, angry, and self assured, all from a single source. There was no mistaking it, my mother was in there!

I stopped dead, jerking Daniel back to me. "I can't go in there," I said, "My mother's in there. If she sees me away from the games she'll ask questions, and I don't wanna deal with one of her freak-outs." With each panicked breath, I lost my ability to sense her; her moody shark swam back into the murk, blending in with the ambient melodrama.

But for how long? Was she on her way out now?!

Daniel surveyed the crowd. "Did you take the Audi here today?" He remembered the car my mother drove, though he had only seen it at a distance, in the dark.

"Yeah." What did that have to do with anything?

He approached the next lady to come out of the kitchen and explained that there was a black Audi sedan in the parking lot, and it looked like someone might have broken into it. The woman re-entered the kitchen and less than thirty seconds later my mother came rushing out, making a beeline for the parking lot while Daniel and I slipped in the secondary entrance.

"Stay focused on me." He led me straight down the stairs and into the wine cellar. No one questioned us. Daniel would later say that it was because we carried ourselves like we were supposed to be there, and I would be surprised by how often the direct approach worked best. People wanted to believe you had the best of intentions, especially in a church setting.

We each grabbed a bottle of sacramental wine, running up the stairs and back through the kitchen. Daniel snatched a pizza that was sitting on the counter, and we headed back to our perch with the spoils.

Taking out his Swiss army knife, he uncorked the first bottle while snickering. "I love Catholics." The gentleman that he was, he offered me the first swig.

Laying with our backs against the outer edge of the balcony, we indulged in our ill-gotten goods under the watchful gaze of a giant crucified Christ. There wasn't much alcohol in the wine, but that was far from the only thing I was drunk on. I snuggled into Daniel, feeling his chest rise and fall, the tension I'd been carrying evaporating with each successive breath. "You're exactly what I needed," I hummed without thinking, but without regret.

He kissed the top of my head, playing with a strand of my hair. "I could say the same about you…"

My hand wriggled under his shirt, outlining defined, but not quite chiseled, abs. In one graceful motion, he pulled the shirt over his head and tossed it to the side.

"You tryin' to impress me?" I asked.

"I'm leading by example…" He eyed me.

"I suppose it *is* only fair…" My shirt was cast aside, revealing a plain white bra underneath. If I would have known what the day had in store, I would have worn my little red satin number.

Daniel studied me. "*And?*" Clear expectation swayed in his voice.

"And what?" I mused, "That's where your example ends...I can't help it if you aren't into cross dressing..."

Smirking, he bit his lower lip. "Can I borrow yours?"

"You'll have to come get it..." I laughed and sprang to my feet for a game of keep away around the balcony. The hardest part was holding in my shrieks and squeals as he attempted to catch me; it was no good drawing an audience if we could help it. Each time he got near enough, he deftly unhooked one clasp until my bra sprung open. I halted, my lungs burning, and instinctively criss-crossed my arms over my chest to keep my girls covered by the bra.

In the muted light of the stained-glass window, Daniel came up behind me, sliding his fingertips softly up my back. I didn't run away this time, allowing the sensation of his touch to resonate through me. The loose straps on either side gave way to him, falling to the crooks of my elbows. He kissed each of the places they had been, and I turned around to face him, letting the casualty of war slip to the floor.

"Now we're even...though, you're far nicer to look at." He studied me appreciatively.

Appraising him in equal measure, I raised my eyebrows. "I disagree." There were several noticeable scars scattered around his physique, each one a story waiting to be told, and I traced one with my thumb.

His fingers slid over my chest. "Mmmm...but I've got the evidence right here in front of me..." One hand cupped and gently toyed with my breast, the other held me firmly by the waist. "You're gorgeous..." The warmth of his lips nestled into my shoulder. "And witty..." With a short laugh, his teeth brushed against my neck. "Fearless..." My breath caught as his tongue swept up to the base of my ear. "Tasty..." His heat spread over me and he bit my earlobe, tugging playfully before kissing down my jaw line, his confidence demanding the attention of every cell in my body.

Hanging onto a feline smirk, I closed my eyes and swallowed. "You don't have any more tickets left...do you...?" I'd never wanted someone so much...

"No." It ached not to breathe him in...until his mouth returned to mine.

It was drafty up on that balcony, but we managed to work up a considerable sweat. My fingernails raked the small of his back, enticing him closer and increasing the fervor of his kisses. Without reservation I brought my arms up and around his neck, pressing myself into him and feeling his heartbeat on top of mine. He lifted me into the air and devoured each breast in turn while placing me on the ledge that jutted out from the stained-glass window.

Oh my God...I'm getting in way over my head...

My penknife seemed to agree. It dug into Daniel's side as he pressed me against the glass. He removed it from my pocket, tossing it to the floor as an afterthought. So much for that defense mechanism...

His hands worked their way down, fiddling with the button on my jeans. I forced a bit of blood back into my head...if I wasn't careful I'd end up losing my virginity right here and now...

My lower half pleaded that this wouldn't be such a bad thing...and it'd make for one hell of a story even if it all went wrong. But no...I'd only known Daniel for five days...five days...or a lifetime...whichever was shorter.

"Here...let me..." I managed between kisses, pushing him up and hopping from the ledge onto unsteady legs. My pen knife was gone, but I did have one more ace up my sleeve... or rather...down his pants. Holding onto his trembling gaze, I unzipped his pants and rubbed his cock through his dark purple boxers. He was already rock hard, moaning as I touched him and fell to my knees. I freed his little soldier, hungrily licking him from base to tip before taking him deep into my mouth.

Between bouts of delirium Daniel's hands caressed my face, assisting with whatever rhythm he desired. "Amy...I feel like a god..." He half laughed, half moaned, stretching his arms out and mocking the statue in front of us. Like some sacrilegious communion, my savior anointed me a few moments later, and with pious devotion, I swallowed every last drop.

When he finally came to his senses, his face could scarcely contain its gratified smile. "If church was always like this, I'd be a *very* devout man..." He helped me up off my knees before pulling his pants back up.

"I don't know what got into me..." I said, my eyes darting to the statue. "Must've been the power of Jesus."

Daniel lifted my chin, adoration in his eyes. "Well, thank you." He hugged me close to him. "That was fucking amazing." Seconds later he shouted, "Hallelujah!" from the bottom of his toes. It echoed through the cathedral and was met by several "Amens" and a "that's right brother!" from the crowd.

We ducked down and didn't stop laughing for I don't know how long. My diversion had worked. Daniel may have been infinitely more intriguing than any other guy I had been with, but it was refreshing to know that be he ghost, vampire, alien, or angel, he was still male. I had soothed the beast for now. Oh sure, I could have just said no, slapped his hand away, and kept making out with him, but then I wouldn't have gotten to see his eyes roll up into the back of his head...and I rather enjoyed that part.

With Daniel by my side, the time passed quickly and I almost didn't notice it was quarter to three. The carnival would be over soon and I would be off the hook. Not that our time at the church hadn't been wonderful, but it did smell like old people and death. "In about fifteen minutes, I'm all yours, Daniel," I chimed.

"You're already mine," he said, giving me a quick kiss before standing. "You wrap up what you need to around here, I'll get the car and wait for you by that angel statue out back. Look for a metallic blue Dodge Avenger, with me driving it." He gave a salute to the Jesus statue before bounding down the stairs.

I made my way out to the carnival and found Father Merkel. "Hi Father, I'm sorry but we weren't able to repair the lion."

"Oh, that is unfortunate," the kindly old man said. "I'll have Stephen take a look at it and see what can be done. Where did you put it?"

"In room one-ten, behind some old furniture—we didn't want one of the kids to hurt themselves on it." *Lying to a priest, go directly to hell, do not pass go.*

"Thank you for your help today, Amy." He put his hand on my shoulder and bowed slightly before moving on. Luckily for me, I didn't believe in hell—although a conversation with my mother was the next best thing.

I opened the kitchen door to find her cleaning up with two other women. Well, mostly they were just talking and making the same hypnotic swirling pattern with their wash rags over and over again. My stomach soured. Mother was going on about what a good time she had that day doing the Lord's work. When she finally stopped to take a breath, I interrupted. "I'm all done, Mother. Kayla's waiting for me out back, so I'll see you when I get home later on tonight, okay!?" I turned to leave, but Mother had other plans.

"Oh Amy! Amy, come in here! Poor girl's been kept so busy, I haven't been able to find her *all* day." She smiled broadly in the direction of the two ladies and I was left with the unpleasant aftertaste of seething anger beneath her happy facade.

"This is my daughter Amy, she's a sophomore in high school and works with horses part-time!" Introductions were made and a few minor pleasantries exchanged before I figured out the real reason my mother had called me over. The door swung open and in walked a mousy boy carrying a stack of dishes. "Amy, this is Reid, Beth's son. You two are the same age!"

We looked at each other; he was mortified, and so was I. My mother was trying to set me up! And after that bullshit rant about me being too unstable for a boyfriend not one week ago! No disrespect to Reid, but I turned green. Still, I didn't want to be rude. "Hi, Reid."

"Hi," he squeaked out, growing more terrified by the minute. Meanwhile my mother was going on about how much we supposedly had in common, half of which hadn't been true since I was six. I just wanted to get out of there. Why was God punishing me? ...Oh...right...

"Why don't I help you collect some more dishes?" I asked Reid.

"But that was the la—"

"Great! Come on," I interrupted him and dragged him out the door.

"Um...you didn't let me finish. That was the last of the dishes," he said sluggishly.

"Oh. Well, it was nice meeting you Reid! I believe Father Merkel was looking for you earlier, though I could be mistaken. You might want to check with him and see. I've gotta run! Bye!"

Would I make it out? Or would my mother's claw extend preternaturally from the kitchen to drag me back in for another round of torture? I pushed through the heavy wooden doors. There was Daniel, fiddling with the radio.

Twenty-five feet to freedom.

Fifteen.

Five.

The car door clicked shut just as Mother came running out, a five alarm fire of anger pouring from her.

I ducked down in my seat and Daniel threw the Avenger into drive. Three blocks later, I sat up and we both laughed. I'd hear an earful when I got home, but that was in some distant galaxy, and we had a whole night of stars ahead of us.

Time for the real fun to begin.

CHAPTER NINETEEN

"*A* my..."

"Aaaaaamy..."

"Get up, get up, get down with the sickness!" Disturbed ripped into my ears, a cacophony of mad guitar riffs and screaming vocals.

"Ahhhhhh!" I jolted up, knocking something heavy onto the floor.

Where am I?

What the—

The aforementioned song still blared away on the carpet, with all the bass Kayla's phone could muster—which was surprisingly a lot—at least, first thing in the morning.

So was Kayla's luminosity. She sat sprawled on my floor, beams of anxiety shooting from her in every direction. My mind raced with a dozen doomsday scenarios faster than I could process any of them. What was she doing in here? What had gone wrong? Was she okay? Was Ma? Had I slept all day?

How did she live with this level of anxiety? I'd seen it most of my life, but to actually feel it, to walk in her skin, no wonder she had such a sensitive stomach. I wanted to throw up after fifteen seconds of what she'd lived a lifetime with.

"Well, you're alive at least." Kayla stared up at me, her worry shifting into annoyance and then blissful relief. She was genuinely worried something had happened to me.

"Shit!" I didn't have time to bask in the sweetness of it, with the problem of the moment cycling into place. I was late! How late? My Tigger alarm clock lay in pieces among the clothes and clutter of my bedroom closet, the bent prongs of the cord barely attached to the electrical outlet. It displayed the time as 13:72. I didn't remember throwing him, but he had decidedly not bounced.

"I tried callin' you." The song ended with a flick of her thumb and I focused on the orange half of Tigger's tail until the apocalyptic frustration I felt was solely mine. Son of a bitch, I'd had that alarm clock since I was seven!

Sneering at myself, I rubbed my eyes. "Phone's grounded. I'm on the Fugitive 'til I'm back in her Majesty's good graces." The Fugitive was what I called my secret throw away phone that I kept for just such emergencies. I acted like taking my phone from me was the worst punishment imaginable when it happened, but it was a mild inconvenience at best. "I forgot to message you before I fell asleep. I'm sorry, last night was—"

"Apologize in the Goblin, slacker," Kayla interrupted. "I'll grab you some grub while you unnakify yo-self."

At the foot of my bed was the preppy outfit Mother had laid out for me the previous morning. It was close and clean so on it went. I snatched up my brush, make-up kit, and school bag—which was precisely where I'd left it on Friday—and headed down the stairs still half asleep. Kayla pointed an entire box of Lil Susie donuts at me when I climbed into her truck, and I rifled through until I found a strawberry one. With any luck, the sugar would jar me awake.

"Is it picture day or somethin'?" She gave me the eye. "What's with the outfit?"

"Just give me a sec to wake up...or somethin' in the area..." Why'd she have to be so wretchedly bright! I held up a hand, flashing my mood ring.

A "sec" stretched into the rest of the drive with me half asleep, and half yellow. Yellow was tired. Daniel and I had stayed out until one in the morning, and between my fanciful imagination and Mother's residual rage, I was up far later than that. At a guess, I'd gotten two hours of sleep, so dealing with the emotional onslaught of my angsty, lusty peers that morning turned out to be a special kind of hell. The kind reserved for puppy murderers and guys who wear Hitler mustaches.

However, daydreams of Daniel proved to be an asset as well as a liability, and were surprisingly effective at holding me together. With the focus on me and my desires, it stood to reason it would be harder to get lost in the choppy emotional sea around me. He wasn't even there, and he was still making things easier for me.

That, ladies and gentlemen, took talent.

Even with my new trick, I wound up pulling out the "period emergency" card in every class just so I could go have a smoke. And you know, it wasn't lost on me how much smoother the whole transaction went thanks to my preppy attire. Teachers who normally second guessed everything out of my mouth waved me out the door without question. Still, I was beyond grateful when lunch time finally rolled around and I could go someplace quiet.

Grease splattered onto my pastel pink skirt as I took a bite of my bacon burger, reminding me why I didn't dress up more often. Kayla and I were sitting in her truck in a secluded part of the parking lot of the Fiery Bull. It boasted the juiciest burgers in all of Waterville, and didn't disappoint.

Throughout my narrative of the previous day's events,

Kayla alternated between laughing and smacking me, and in all cases was thoroughly convinced I was going to Satan's hot tub. She and Ma weren't big on the Catholic institution, but they were a rare breed of believers who actually lived the values it supposedly espoused. Be kind, do unto others as you would have done unto you, love thy neighbor, that sort of outlandish thing.

To Kayla, loving thy neighbor did not extend to giving him fellatio in a church…at least not on the second date. Was it a naughty thing to do? Yeah. But by now you should be realizing I'm no saint, and neither is Kayla. More than the locale, it was the speed at which Daniel and I were moving that was raising alarm bells in her head. Perhaps not without reason, but she hadn't been there—the whole thing had been as natural as breathing. I worked as vigorously as my sleep-deprived brain would allow to get this point across to her.

"He's not like anyone I've ever been with…I mean, he's still a guy and was finished in two minutes, but everything he does just oozes intensity and purpose. Every kiss, every touch, every look, he's…he's right there…" I brought my fingertips together and interlocked them, adding a little shake for emphasis. "…fully present. There's no second guessing, no timidness…and he brings the same out of me." I dipped a fry in some mayo, watching it drip off. "It's like I'm all shot up on adrenaline when I'm with him…and I fuckin' love it." Popping the fry in my mouth, I continued, "And then you add in that the bullshit's easier to deal with when he's around and—"

"Or he is the bullshit," Kayla interrupted. "It doesn't seem convenient to you?" She shook her head in the shadow of the vacant stare I gave her. "This guy shows up a month after you get these freaky empath super powers, he's everything you've been wanting, and has you so swoony your brain's melting out through your ears." She squeezed my mayo cup, making a gelatinous mess all over the foil on which it sat.

"Hey! I managed not to lose my virginity in front of voyeur Jesus…give me some credit." Dunking another fry in the entrails of my melted "brain," I tried to keep my tone light, but I was tired and it came off as defensive.

"Okay…credit given." She put her hands up in a gesture of temporary acquiescence. "But why haven't you asked him what he is and why you can't feel him? That would've been the first thing I asked."

I gave her a cursory wave, replying in a flippant, mocking tone, "Hey Daniel, I can't feel your emotions, what are you, some kind of cyborg?" Hmmm, I hadn't considered that angle…

I scrunched my face up. "Did I swallow nanites?"

"That's probably the least of your STD worries…" Kayla threw me a look that just about curdled the mayonnaise. "I can't believe you don't see how reckless you're being. It's like he's got you under an insta-love spell."

Wizard? I hadn't considered wizard either…

I had felt like I was in over my head and I might drown without him. Was she onto something? Or was it all hormones?

"Insta-lust, maybe." I snorted, playing it off. "I don't love the guy…we just really click. Why can't you be happy for me?" The question was genuine, but I'd be lying if I said there wasn't a hint of passive aggression swirling around in it.

"If it was any other situation, if this had been two months ago, I would be, but it isn't, and there's too much strange shit going on to be accepting anything at face value." Her response was resolute, bearing all the stubborn finality of one of her bulls.

"Well, I already told him I have a sixth sense and he just blew it off—have you considered he really might not have any idea why I can't feel him? That it might disturb him to know? I mean, we don't know why you're lighting up the outfield compared to everyone else…"

"I figured it's because you love me so much," she said, fluttering her eyes and trying to ease the tension between us.

It worked, and I managed a small smile. "Could be...or there might be somethin' goin' on with you too. You were out in that barn, same as me."

Cold fear squirmed in, the edges of each of her emotions fraying up one by one at its frigid touch. "I feel fine..." she lied, "...and I'm not the one on trial here. Daniel is."

"Nobody should be on trial. That's my point. I'm not all super suspicious of you and your motives, am I?"

"You've known me since we were five and him for five minutes!" Her rising temper was already beginning to burn away the fear. Primal emotions were the hardest for me to keep out, and here two of them stood side by side.

"And you don't know him at all. I'm tellin' you he just doesn't seem sinister. If anything, he's been like an angel." Having lost my appetite, I dropped the rest of my second burger back into the bag and took a deep breath. I didn't want to fight with her.

She raised her voice, cheeks reddening. "Do angels get blowjobs in churches, Amy? *Really* think about that. Do angels steal things, break and enter, lie about car burglaries?"

Closing my eyes, I pictured all the vandalism and deceit in the short time I'd known him. Was I just seeing what I wanted to see? "I was right there with him..." I said softly, coming to his defense. It all sounded so much more ominous when she summed it up like that. At the time it had been innocent fun.

It was innocent fun.

I won't get angry...

Fear leads to anger...

...anger to hate...

...hate to...what does hate lead to? Herpes?

Sympathy flowed around Kayla's anger when she noticed me struggling. She half laughed, attempting to put a lighter spin back into the conversation. "Yeah, and as we discussed you're going to hell."

It helped, but I kept my eyes closed and my breathing steady as I continued. "Honestly, I didn't think about any of it too much...I just wanted to relax and break a few harmless rules. When the time is right, I promise I'll bring it up with him...but I wanna get to know him better...I don't want him to immediately bolt and think I'm some head case." It all seemed perfectly reasonable to me, but Kayla's anger flared again.

"Amy, you know if he can't handle your crazy, it's best to know right now and be done with him." Her blunt assessment of the situation, as if it were all so simple, was something Mother would say.

"No." My eyes shot open and I glared at her, speaking through gritted teeth. "I like him, he's cute, he makes me laugh, he's silent...I'm *not* giving that up." The air grew still for a few moments, the gravity of my words sinking in. "And what if I *am* wrong and I tell him and he really *can't* be trusted and I end up on a slab getting my brain dissected? Then what? I might even have gotten lucky that he blew me off before. What ever happened to sleuthing around anyway? Investigating? Having patience?"

"Exactly." Kayla gave me a hard stare and we returned to silence while I tried not to let her irritation mix with mine to create "Mecha-hostility," destroyer of worlds. It was a battle I was about to lose. I opened the truck door and bolted until I was a safe distance away.

Safe and alone.

Plucking out a cigarette, I lit it up, kicked a chunk of asphalt, and sat down with a "hrumpf" on a broken cement parking bumper, two decades past its prime. I concentrated on my ring, on all the love and support it represented. Kayla always had my back...I loved her...I just had to help her understand. And how could I do that when I hadn't been entirely honest with her?

A sullen glance over at my best friend's truck found her watching me in the side mirror. When our eyes met I took out my phone to call her, but she beat me to it.

"Overload?" she asked.

"Yeah." My bottom lip quivered at the admission.

"Want me to sit on your French fries to keep 'em warm for you?" There was a sluggish playfulness to her tone.

My laugh was stifled by a catch in my throat. Damn it…I was going to cry. "No."

"Well, too late…" Her smile soon soured when she registered the quaver in my voice.

"Kayla…I need you to understand…I just wanted to have a normal day where I didn't have to stress about this…" I made a gun symbol with my forefinger and thumb and "shot" my temple.

"I know…" Her eyes held sympathy.

"No…I don't think you do. Not really…and that's my fault. I've been tryin' to be strong, take it one day at a time like we talked about, but it's getting harder. When we talk, I can't really just be there with you…or anybody…it's like…" I looked at the gray, cloudy sky, blinking back tears. "…Talkin' to you through a wall…only I have to keep pressed against it the whole time or it'll fall in and crush me." The trembling in my lips worsened and I took in a deep breath.

Kayla pressed her fingertips against the driver's side window before lowering it. It was an odd thing to hear her so close in my ear and again at a distance. "Amy…"

"There's cracks formin' in here and I can't tell if I'm keepin' things out…or in…" The taste of warm salt touched my mouth and dripped off my nose, as I told her things I hadn't yet fully admitted to myself. "I was thinkin' about giving up, lettin' my mind just…crumble to dust…but then Daniel came…and…"

"...And that's why you see him as a guardian angel." She finished my sentence for me, her own face glistening with tears, and I nodded. "You stubborn bitch...I didn't know things were so bad, why didn't you say something?"

"Because, I don't want it to be like this...and sayin' it out loud turns it into a thing." I wiped at my cheeks with my sleeves, smearing a bit of ketchup and mustard onto the white blouse. "And I don't see the point in cryin' over it; we're already doing everything we can..."

"Crying releases stress hormones...so it's never pointless."

"What I need you to understand in all this drama is that Daniel is more than just a hot piece of meat to me...he's helping my grill stay lit. Hell, I was down to a single wet match when he showed up. However he's doin' it, whether he knows or not, he was an outstretched hand as I fell off a cliff. We can't just discard that...I won't."

"I'm here...you don't have to shoulder this alone...you know that," Kayla said in a low voice. I'd hurt her somewhere along the way, though it wasn't my intent.

"Of course I know that...no way in all of Hades would I have lasted this long without you. And that doesn't even touch on any of this...weirdness. You've been savin' me from cliffs my whole life. You're my angel too, Kayla...I bet that's why you're so bright."

"If I've got some heavenly powers comin', they better hurry up already, cuz I feel mighty helpless. I wish I could do somethin'. Can't even give you a hug right now, not without making things worse."

"You can let me sleep in the Goblin 'til classes get out... and take me into work later..." I grinned, wide enough to showcase the piece of pickle stuck between my lower right molars.

This seemed to brighten her mood considerably. "What-ever you need."

"Thanks." I stood up, and stuck out my tongue at a couple

of boys from my school who'd been watching me break down from across the lot. The whole school knew I was crazy anyway, so I was just playing to my audience at that point. I'd never gotten flak from anyone for my maniacal behavior; if anything, they were eager to not be in the same room with me if they could help it. Since the feeling was mutual, I hadn't begrudged them. A blank mannequin who might pass, or freak out, at any moment makes for a lousy science partner.

"So, you're startin' to be able to distinguish between people?" Kayla asked as I got back in the truck. She was trying to keep herself calm, but it felt artificial, like a bunch of other emotions pasted together to resemble calm.

"Yeah, but I don't have the hang of it, and it seems to be only when Daniel is around." I wasn't sure I should bring him up, but she didn't waver. "It's like separating mud with a pair of tongs."

"I want to meet him."

"I'll see what I can do, maybe this Wednesday? I don't work, and can see if he'll come out to your place. If you didn't keep old lady hours, we could come by tonight. I'm actually anxious to see if he helps make you less...radiant."

She took on a haughty air and winked at me. "Not likely. You can't dull this shine." I snickered and she continued, "Of course, this all supposes your mother doesn't ground you for missing class today... You should just go, be a zombie and get through the day, you can nap on the way home, and out to work."

I pointed in the direction of the school, my finger shaking. "I can't take any more today. If I go in there, I'm gonna end up in a padded cell. I'll deal with my mother."

I know, I know, infamous last words...

CHAPTER TWENTY

*W*ednesday afternoon I popped home for a quick shower and was greeted by a friendly smiley face note stuck to my bedroom door. Mother's perfect penmanship glistened up at me in blue ink: "Plant your feet. You're grounded."

I promptly crumpled it up and threw it in my trash can, where it rolled back down the mountain of junk that had gathered there and came to rest at my feet. "I don't have time to be grounded," I said to it in an almost apologetic manner. It was just doing its job after all, and with cheer, no less. But today was the day Daniel was coming to meet Kayla, so there was zero chance I'd be missing that. As long as I was back by the time Mother got home at seven I'd be good. She could yell at me—probably for skipping my afternoon classes all week—and then I could slip out my window and be back with Daniel and Kayla by seven thirty, eight at the latest.

I wasn't without my reasons for giving the one-fingered salute to my classes. Lack of sleep had made it impossible for me to get through an entire day of *Teen Turmoil: The Musical* without an intermission. Why wasn't I sleeping? Well…that may have had something to do with staying out every night until one or two in the morning with a certain hot construction worker. Every morning, I'd promise myself I wasn't going to stay out late again, and every evening, by the whites of Daniel's gleaming eyes, I'd shred that promise into a fine mist.

The Willows was less than a mile away if you knew which yards to cut through, so I popped in my earbuds and took a jog, making a game out of avoiding feeling anyone as I went. Most folks were still at work so it wasn't as hard as you might think, but I had fun pretending I was in a training montage anyway.

Kayla and Daniel had each been built up to be larger than life to one another in the past week...because they were, to me. But would they see that in each other? Daniel always seemed interested when I rambled on about the misadventures of Amy and Kayla, laughing at appropriate parts and asking questions as I went along. Lesser guys checked out part way through and were singularly focused on getting back to snogging. My white rabbit had even agreed to ditch work early to make sure he could meet us before sundown without question.

And well, you know how Kayla felt about him already. I carried a nervous excitement tinged with optimism as I walked up the Willows' driveway, catching my breath.

My ginger rabbit held out a pair of '80s cop sunglasses at my approach. "Here, put these on and don't take 'em off 'til I do."

I put them on, half my face now in hiding. "Why are we too cool today?"

"In case he has to make eye contact to work his spell." She put on a matching pair. "It's how vampires dominate their victims."

"I've already seen him in the daylight, Kayla. The only thing that sparkles are his eyes, and if he burst into flames, he was discreet about it."

"The drool on your chin is sparkling," she teased. There was no downside to humoring her—one day soon we'd look back on the whole thing and laugh—so I kept them on as I helped with the chores. Ma had been picking up extra hours at the hospital, placing even more responsibility on Kayla's petite shoulders. I was glad to be able to help when I could.

I had a bucket full of chicken eggs when Daniel pulled up in a white pickup truck with the Varrick Custom Builders eagle logo emblazoned on the side. With a smirk, I sauntered up to the driver's side window, a single egg held between the tips of my fingers. "You eat yet?"

"Nah, I'm savin' room for later…" From the look he gave me, I was clearly on the menu. My pulse quickened and the redness in my cheeks came from more than the nip in the air.

A sweetly sensual kiss awaited him as he got out of the truck, which was meticulously clean for a construction vehicle. Once the door closed, I swiveled around and glared at the eagle. "Why is that eagle so judgmental? I feel like it knows my darkest secrets."

Daniel laughed. "My dad made it, and he's a judgmental asshole. Stands to reason it would ooze into his artwork." He flipped it off, holding his middle finger against the door for a five count before urging me towards Kayla. He hadn't talked about his family much, and I hadn't pushed it, but now I understood a little better why that might be. My best friend had just come out of the house and was propping herself up on the patio table. Beside her sat a small black case, the one that housed Ma's handgun and cleaning kit.

As we came within range, she flashed as emotionally bright as she'd ever been. Her calm demeanor was riddled with mirth, suspicion, fear, and even a dab of jealous insecurity right below the surface. Kayla leveled her gaze at Daniel, chambering open the stocky 45 with a loud clack. "What are your intentions with my daughter, Mr. Varrick?"

"Mr. Varrick" stopped about six feet away, his eyes

making an appraising sweep over her. "Well, Mrs. Durene, I intend to make Amy smile as frequently, and in as many ways as possible, whenever, and wherever, I can. And might I add, you're looking remarkably young for a woman of thirty-six."

Whew. He was taking all this with gentle good humor. I laughed: Mother was actually somewhere around that age. Kayla had a reflexive flare up of annoyance at him calling her by my mother's name, but it quickly passed—she was playing the role after all.

Ignoring the "compliment" on her age, she set about disassembling the gun. "Is there some reason you can't seem to get her home 'til well after the witching hour?"

"Are marshmallows a reason?" He looked to me for the answer.

"I'd allow it." I shrugged with a mischievous glance at "Mrs. Durene."

"I'm gonna go with s'mores then." Daniel turned back to Kayla, who frowned, her mouth agape. "That's a nice forty-five," he continued in a steady tone. "You shoot that for sport or are you just unhappy to see me?"

She cocked her head. "Does it have to be an either or?"

"That a Taurus?" He motioned to the gun.

"What else would a cattle rancher have...?" Kayla's hard edges softened slightly. Was I imagining things, or was she less bright than she had been only a minute before?

"A wicked sense of humor." He offered out his hand, causing a sizable spike in her anxiety. "I'm Daniel." Though she could have easily set everything down, she brandished the gun parts like a shield, indicating her hands were too full to oblige him. My boyfriend nodded at the gesture, not making a big deal of it one way or the other. "You got any targets besides me to shoot at?"

"Nope." Kayla's mammoth shades added to her air of authority.

"Well, we'll have to change that. There's a field over in Freedom that has a range. It's officially abandoned but still has some workable targets, and folks add new ones all the time. There was a Stormtrooper wearing a Santa hat stuck up in a tree this past January." Ordinarily, he would have had Kayla at the word abandoned, but her resolve only doubled at the mention of it.

"Taking out the Empire sounds loaded with Christmas cheer," I chimed in.

Kayla set a few drops of oil onto her gun and worked them in with a small white rag that quickly transformed to black. "What is it you like about my Amy?" she asked.

"That she has a best friend who cares enough to put me on the firing line." He smiled at me. "I do the same thing with my sisters' gentleman callers, 'cept I use my shotgun and shovel. I've only had to dig three graves, so far."

"Keep talkin', you're workin' on a fourth…" But her harsh exterior was betrayed by the undercurrent of amusement struggling to surface. She did find him charming, and it was bothering the stuffing out of her. As if summoned by their master's distress, Sampson and Delilah came trotting up, each giving a woof and sniffing my boyfriend, who turned and walked back to his truck without acknowledging them. He pulled a frayed length of rope from his truck bed and worked two giant knots into either end.

"Who are these magnificent creatures?" Daniel made his way toward us, giving eye contact to the canines and offering each one end of the rope.

"Those are my other weapons…Sampson and Delilah," Kayla beamed.

The Great Pyrenees dogs chomped down on the makeshift toy and began a fierce game of tug-of-war with Daniel, right there on the spot. They weren't small dogs by any means, but he managed to hold his own and even swung them up off the ground for brief periods of time.

"Sam and Dee approve of him." Leaning against the patio table next to Kayla, I relaxed a smidge and enjoyed the acrobatics, with a raised eyebrow in my friend's direction.

"Traitors." She smirked. "He cheated…they can't resist the siren song of the rope."

"Aw, come on Kayla, when are you gonna let up on him?" I scooped up an inner spring she'd just set down and bounced it in between my fingers. "I think he's taken this whole imminent death thing pretty well."

"I don't see it…" Squinting one eye shut, she looked down the barrel of the disassembled gun straight at my dog whisperer. "I was expecting some Adonis with the way you went on about him, and I just don't see it…" She tilted her head in my direction. "Then again, I didn't shake his hand or make eye contact with him, now did I…?"

We'd never shared the same taste in boys—it was probably a contributing factor in us staying friends for so long. I let out an exasperated sigh. "Is there anything he can do to get you to lower your hackles?" I bit my lip. "You want your own rope toy?" The three amigos were now rough housing in the gravel, Sam and Dee barking like puppies as they all tackled one another.

Kayla backhanded my arm, though it didn't hurt. "Can I use it to gag you?"

"Kinky." I snickered.

"He can answer my questions straight, not keep you out so late you end up missin' school…maybe…let me take a look at him with my equipment."

Cupping my hands to the sides of my mouth, I shouted, "Hey Daniel! You wanna see Kayla's ghosty equipment in action?!"

"Hmm?" He was coated in white dog fur, such that he could have passed for one of them at a distance. Once he stopped playing, the two actual dogs shook themselves off, briefly nudged up against Kayla, and took off back into the field.

Daniel did his own interpretation of a shedding dog while he walked our way, becoming somewhat human again by the time he reached us.

"None of it gives you cancer does it?" he asked.

"I don't think so…" I answered, but it hadn't really come up. Should I have been worried all this time?

"No." The question hadn't done much to help Kayla's overall irritation level. She'd tried to be jovial about her dog's "betrayal," but the annoyance stuck to her ribs like peanut butter in a Kong.

"Well, you do have it out for me. I have to be sure." Daniel flashed his canines in his signature boyish grin.

Kayla grinned back in an over exaggerated manner. "If I really had it out for you, you'd already be dog chow." Her irritation flared, and I moved to help Daniel groom himself.

"I'd love to see what equipment you have. Ever pick anything up?" He acknowledged my help by licking the side of my face and making me shriek with laughter.

My best friend's eagerness bore into me. She wanted to shout "YES" from the rooftops, to show him all the data we'd collected on me, if only to "best" him. But she swallowed it down out of respect for me.

"Not yet," she choked.

"How do you know it works then?" Daniel asked.

"Other people have had success." Kayla took the spring from me and slammed it back into the gun.

"These other people wouldn't happen to sell this equipment would they?"

"Not all of them," I interjected before Kayla could come uncoiled. "There's this whole world of spirit hunters out there who share what works and what doesn't, purely in the name of discovery."

Daniel looked from me to her and back again; his curiosity piqued. "Well then, lead the way."

Kayla's tension let up as she showed him her equipment out in the barn. The two of them spoke in lingo that flew right over my head and out into the night. She wasn't at five alarm levels around him anymore, but she was far from relaxed. Watching her dodge every pat on the back, or chance touch, was a thing of comedic genius when you knew what you were looking for. Did Daniel see it? I certainly laughed out loud on more than one occasion. After a while, I noticed she was less bright than she had been when we started. No doubt about it, Daniel dulled her shine.

How would she feel about my hypothesis coming true? Would she like him more or less because of it? Either way, I used the opportunity to get as close to her as we always used to be, and this made us both genuinely happy. So happy, in fact, that I plum forgot about the time. The ghosty camera displayed 8:30 p.m.—an hour and a half past my grounding.

"Aw shit!" I said, under my breath. But I didn't want to stop the good thing we had going, and at that point, late as it was, I might as well stay out all night. Fuck it. I'd enjoy my time with Kayla and Daniel while I could. No matter when I went home, it would be the last time I'd see either of them for a while.

Hopefully, my exclamation went unnoticed and—

"Amy, what'd you step in?" Kayla grew bright again and each second I didn't answer brought stronger waves of aggravation, so I told them about the adventures of Mr. Smiley, the Post-it note.

"This could've all been avoided if you weren't staying out so late, you know." She glared first at me and then at Daniel. "Tell her to stop skipping school and bring her home at a decent hour, would you?" It wasn't so much a question as a directive. There went my tranquil scene.

Daniel shook his head, tweaking something on the

machine that gave you epileptic seizures. "I'm not about to tell Amy what to do. Besides, school's overrated—you can always get your equivalency when you turn eighteen."

Kayla's nostrils flared. "Yeah well, those blowjobs are gonna be pretty hard to come by when she's shackled to her bedroom floor!"

Daniel took my hand, holding my eyes with his, and chuckled. "You've got a window..." He kissed my hand. "...I'll bring the shackles..." When he put it that way, grounding might not be so bad...

"Ha! Her mother will weld that shit shut," Kayla interceded. "You have *no* idea."

"There's a blowtorch in the back of my truck..." He raised his eyebrows with a suggestive smirk.

"Come on, Amy, I'll give you a ride home. You can tell your mother you helped me wrangle up some cattle that got loose, she might buy it." Kayla patted my shoulder, and I winced from the intensity of her frustration.

She was right, it was my best shot.

I looked to Daniel—he'd come a long way—was he expecting us to hang out again tonight?

As if sensing my indecision, he made up my mind for me. Raising his palms in a placating gesture, he said, "I'm not gonna argue with the lady with a gun." Kayla's anger amped down a notch. "Amy, walk me to my truck." He turned to my friend. "Thanks for the enlightening tour, been a pleasure gettin' to know you better."

"I appreciate you stoppin' by." She nodded to him. "I gotta go grab my keys, and I'll be back out to take you home." Her eyes warned me not to leave with him, which made me temporarily inclined to do just that. I'd just had a fucking circle pissed around me.

Daniel and I walked to his truck, me dragging my feet a little every few steps. "I'm sorry you came all this way and I have to duck out early...I don't want to, but Mother's going to grow another head if I don't lop 'em all off now."

"Let me know if you need help hidin' the body, I know a few foundations getting poured tomorrow." We laughed and he tweaked my chin, bringing it up until I was staring into his endless eyes. "You take care of what you need to here and I'll see you soon. No matter what happens she won't keep us apart." We shared a series of deep kisses while a guilty part of me wondered if he was talking about my mother or Kayla. The whole meeting could have gone worse, but I had my work cut out for me if the three of us were ever going to play Horseshoes together.

"I don't like him." The screen door banged shut behind Kayla, echoing out into the courtyard and adding a sense of finality to her blunt words.

I lit up a smoke, watching Daniel's tail lights fade out of sight before facing her. "I know. You took out a billboard." It was my turn to be annoyed. "You never like any of the guys I date—"

"Yeah, and you aren't still with any of 'em are you? You should listen to me," she said dryly.

"You should give him an actual chance and let your guard down with someone other than me for five seconds." I swiped the sunglasses off of her face and threw them in the cab of the truck. "If all he needed was skin or eye contact to make you like him, he could've just ripped the sunglasses off your head or taken you by the arm at any point. But he didn't even try, and you saw how strong he is, liftin' Sam and Dee like that..." I stifled a laugh. "Not that it wasn't hilarious watchin' you stumble over yourself to avoid touchin' him. Clever use of a cow by the way."

"Thank you, I'm sure they'll be wary of me for the next week or so, but it was worth it."

"Did you notice how long I was able to stay close to you

with him around?" My tone was conversational; I was terrible at staying mad at Kayla.

"Yeah, makes me wanna dissect him on a slab all the more, but see how I refrained from knockin' him out. That was for you." She made a kissy face at me.

"Let's not lose sight that this is a good thing. We could hang out more...maybe get to a point where I don't need these." I held up my cigarette. "That's one thing you both agree on by the way, he doesn't want me smokin' either and I told him the same thing I told you...tough shit. So if he really had some kind of spell on me why wouldn't he make me chuck these?" I flicked my cigarette into the tall grass and got into the truck.

"Even a penguin can fly in a hurricane." Kayla slid in beside me and started up ol' faithful on the second try. "I can't believe I'm in agreement with your mother that you should be grounded...you see what he's reduced me to?" She shuddered. "I also can't believe my equipment didn't pick up anything strange about him. Maybe some of the new stuff will...so okay...keep him around for a little bit longer. But you definitely need to put some ice on it."

A queasy feeling burbled up into my stomach the closer we got to my impending doom, and I didn't respond. Was I ready for this confrontation? Would I ever be? Why was I always so damn short sighted?

I jumped out of the idling truck, but before closing the door I said, "I thought he handled himself really well. If he had anything supernatural to hide, I don't think he'd have let you scan him."

"Just tells us he's not a ghost." She looked at me gravely. "Good luck in there...I'll see you tomorrow." We blew each other kisses and I slammed the door shut, leaving bits of rust flakes at my feet.

I stared at the house as she drove off; the light above the garage had gone out. Shadows leached into every crevice, giving it all the loving glow of a mausoleum. Under my breath I rehearsed what I'd say to Mother, stooping to coat myself in a good layer of dirt; cattle wrangling was dirty business after all. Before I could finish, I heard the front door open and the unmistakable sound of Mother's slippers scuffing against the brick walkway.

I rose with a sigh, turning on my heel to go meet her, only to find myself face to face with Daniel.

CHAPTER TWENTY-ONE

*D*aniel brought a finger to his lips and grabbed my wrist, pulling me into the darkness of the hedges that lined our property just as my mother rounded the corner. He held me still against the bush, seemingly willing my breath to slow with the intensity of his gaze. Mother's long shadow fell into the neighboring yard. She was wearing her robe and swaying from side to side as if searching for something...or someone.

"Amy!" she shouted, "You out here?"

When I didn't respond, Daniel smiled wryly and came in for a sweet, soft kiss. I put my hand around his neck and gave into the embrace. Mother started down the stairs towards the driveway, angry, smug, and apprehensive. My eyes went wide and I broke off from my boyfriend; a few more steps and she might be able to see us.

Taking his wrist now, I led him towards the back of the property, my heart thrumming with each footfall on the slick mulch beneath us. At the end of the hedge row stood a small garden where I promptly knocked over a ceramic gnome wielding a set of mushroom bagpipes. The small clink sound it made as it hit a nearby rock made me cringe—I was pretty sure that was good for seven years of bad luck.

Judging from the velociraptor-like sounds coming from my mother, it was effective immediately. "Amy! Stop messing around and get your butt in this house!"

And yet there was still some doubt frothing in her sea of anger, she didn't know for certain I was out here. So long as I could sense Mother, I could stay two steps ahead of her and we might have a chance of escaping. So, of course that's why my neighbor chose that moment to come into my empathy field with a mixture of humiliated glee and arousal. Thank God the curtains were drawn. Those feelings spread out and melded into Mother's puddle of emotions, muddying up the waters.

Alright gnome...challenge accepted.

The whites of Daniel's eyes and teeth shone in the rapidly diminishing light; he was enjoying this right alongside me. I was *alive*—all my senses on high alert and in prime working order...except for one. Number six would just have to fall in line. I closed my eyes and concentrated on the different emotions, what was unique in each of them, and yet the same. Anger and apprehension surfaced: they were Mother's but how to trace them back to her? How to untangle the kite strings?

That underlying subfrequency...the one that makes me ill at ease...if I can just...follow that back to its source...yes...there!!!

The two sets of emotions snapped back to their respective owners, turning the ground to gelatin beneath my feet for the briefest of seconds. Pressure on my brain and heart told me how close Mother was, with something like emotional echolocation. Daniel tensed, taking my sweaty hand in his. Our fingers had barely clasped together when I pulled him to the other side of the bushes, missing Mother by a gnome's breath as she crossed over to where we had been moments before.

I did it!

Fuck yeah!

It took an act of will not to squeal with delight right there on the spot. How cool was it to be able to "see" in the dark? No, it was better than seeing: I didn't have to be facing her to sense her.

Sight beyond sight!

Leilani had said I was a lioness...

Wait, was that what was going on here, was I a Thunder-cat? That would be both incredibly awesome and danger-ously cheesy.

Before I could get too lost in giddiness over my kick ass new "night vision," Daniel tugged me behind one of the medium sized pine trees that dotted my backyard. The motion sensitive front porch light went out, leaving all of us in relative darkness. Mother stopped, a hefty dose of primal fear bubbling up and wrapping itself around her anger, threatening to snuff it out. She apparently didn't relish being out here in the pitch black.

Who could blame her? There might be monsters—I might be one of them.

With my mental defenses up, I wasn't precisely feeling what she was, it was more like looking at fish through aquarium glass. You can tell which ones would be rough or smooth to the touch without needing to reach in. She swatted her fear aside and continued forward, a T-rex on the scent. What would she do if she found me here with Daniel? I couldn't expose him to those levels of crazy.

How were we going to get out of this? Fences boxed us in on two sides, with Mother and the house completing the square. She'd see us if we went for the house, or tried to pass her, and one of the fences was chain link. It would rattle awake the dead if we jumped it. But the other fence was wooden, sturdy, and only eight feet tall. We'd climbed the beams at the stable without a problem. We could clear it.

Holding in a deep breath, I yanked Daniel toward it at a run, letting go of his hand and vaulting myself up. My shoes scuffed the planks for purchase, but I was over in one stride. The fence shook alongside me. My partner in crime had gotten the message. I'd be willing to bet there was a beauty, and synchronicity to the flailing plunge into the neighbor's above ground swimming pool that followed.

I was too frozen and in shock that brisk spring evening to fully appreciate it.

While underwater, I let out an involuntary scream, stifling a second one as I surfaced. My teeth chattered over an otherwise rigid body and I squeaked into the cold night, "Sh...iiii...tttt." Was it possible to drown with your head above water? I couldn't seem to suck in enough air.

Daniel popped up in front of me, took me by the shoulders, and whispered in my ear, through his clicking teeth, "You're in sh...hhock. Ffff...ocus on my brrr...eathhh...ing and just feellll the fuck off...ff ccc...c...old." Small plumes of condensation coming from each breath made it easy to do as he instructed, and after a panicked minute, I began to calm down. It was all we could do to keep from laughing as our eyes met and we listened for signs we'd been detected.

I took heart that Mother would have been cackling with laughter by now if she would have heard what happened, and no lights flicked on from the neighbor's house. Judging from the open earth around the pool, they had recently moved the whole thing and were building a larger deck. We swam to the ladder and climbed out into the unforgiving night air. Had we jumped over that fence anywhere else we would have landed on mounds of nice soft earth.

The gnomes would need to be appeased as soon as possible.

I'd heard it on good authority that they liked pizza. A whole pepperoni pizza would be left at the bearded figure's feet tomorrow. Assuming I didn't die of hypothermia, or asphyxiation by Mother before then.

Maybe if I went back now, looking like a drowned rat popsicle, she'd be too busy laughing to punish me too severely? We slipped through the torn up yard and let ourselves out the front gate. Daniel kicked dirt over our muddy shoe prints in our wake.

"Truck'sssss hhhup this www...aaay." He headed down the road, having cleverly parked one block behind my house, in the shadowy space between street lamps.

"But we need to get ddd...rry...my mother's a bear but shhhh...eeee isn't cruel enoughhhh to let either of us fff... reeeezzzze to death." If I was honest, that was really more of a working theory.

"You gonna let hh...hh...er win after such a daring escape? I've got emergggg...ency blankets and a working heater. You won't fff...reeeezzzze to death on my wwww...aaatch."

He had a point...wasn't it the principal of the thing? When we reached the truck the eagle logo bore down on me as if to say, "You damn fool girl. Now you're about to be naked, with a dire need to conserve body heat, in a tightly confined space with him. Good luck keeping that queen of yours." I glared at the bird and removed my soaking wet clothes while Daniel handed me two blankets, one thermal and one wool, from underneath the back seat.

"I swear I didn't plan this." He smirked, stripping down to his birthday suit and gesturing to his little man huddled tightly against his body: "It isn't exactly flattering." He showed no reservations about being buck naked in the street, but jumped inside the truck and started it with haste none-theless. I joined him, wrapping both blankets firmly around me and leaving *everything* to the imagination...

Fuck that eagle.

"Woooo!" Daniel let out a raucous cry as soon as my door

closed. "That'll wake you right the fuck up! Makes me glad I did the radiator flush on you and the crew this week." He tapped the steering wheel before reaching over and turning the heat on low. It blew out cool air and he opened his blanket up for me to share in his body heat. I did the same with my wool blanket but kept the thermal between us. "I've got a thermostat installed in this truck, we'll be crisp in no time." I waited to shoot down some sexual innuendo about body heat generation, but it never came.

Instead, he laid his wet clothes on the dash to dry and I followed his lead, staring at my cell phone with a frown. The Fugitive had taken a dive with me, but at least my real phone was safely locked in Mother's desk drawer. I'd never been so happy to have been grounded from it.

Daniel plucked the waterlogged corpse from my hand and tipped it this way and that. "Open the glove box and hand me the little red case." Pushing past a first aid kit, a heavy-duty flashlight, a box of Legos, and a copy of Hustler, I found the red tool case and gave it to him.

"Your lunch breaks must be interesting..." I noted, placing my dripping cigarettes near one of the vents. He smiled and lifted his eyebrows suggestively before popping the cover off my phone, and placing the innards on a dry napkin by another heating vent. Warm air trickled out now, and he cranked the heating dial to maximum.

"There. Should be good as new in a bit."

"Thank you...what about yours?"

"I kept it in the truck." His eyes fell on the catch-all next to the stick shift. "Didn't want it goin' off while I was sneakin' up on you."

"Lucky." I shivered into him. "Do you think pepperoni is okay for gnomes or should I stick with vegetarian? I don't want to offend them any more than I already have."

"Offend them?" he asked.

"Yes," I answered, and laid out my ideas on gnomish curses.

He listened to my ramblings thoughtfully, nodding and pursing his lips together. "Well, I know what I'm strappin' my M80s to this fourth of July. All gnomes, all the time, startin' with that lil fucker."

"Do you know how many pizzas I'm gonna have to order if you start doin' that?" I tried to do the math but gave up at triple digits. "Unless we put an M80 on top of a pizza...then we can reach more gnomes with it!" The thought of my neighbor's lawn furniture dripping in six different toppings made me laugh.

"As long as I get to blow something up, I'll be happy."

Happy? What did that feel like coming from him? Each person had their own distinct rhythm. A large part of my initial attraction to Daniel had been because I couldn't sense his emotions; I lamented that absence now.

"So, why'd you come back for me? I thought you agreed with Kayla's plan..."

"I said I wasn't gonna *argue* with her, not that I agreed with her." He traced my jaw line with his knuckles. "There'll be plenty of yellin' no matter what time you get home. Besides, surprisin' you was much more fun than fightin' with your friend."

"Kayla wasn't very nice to you...I'm sorry she's..."

"Lookin' out for you. For all she knows I'm a serial killer."

"Are you?" I shot him the side eye.

"Only on weekends and I haven't had time for it lately... someone's been keepin' me out past the witching hour."

"Does that make me a good or a bad influence on you?"

"I don't care...long as you're on me..." He pulled me in tighter, not flinching as I rested my cold hair on his chest.

"Anyone givin' you flak about the hours we been keepin'?" I asked.

"No one worth mentionin'." He laughed. "So, did I pass the second round of inspections?"

I nodded, looking up at him. "And the bonus round…"

"Your friend wasn't just showin' me her equipment, she was testing me. She think I'm a ghoul or somethin'?"

An uneasy chuckle rolled over me. "Kayla thought maybe…you had me under some kinda voodoo spell. She's worried I'm movin' too fast…"

"Are you worried?"

My head shook. "Not really."

He gazed out the window, his jaw set. "I am. Sometimes, it's like you've got this gravitational pull on me and I can't get enough of you."

In all our worrying about *what* Daniel was, Kayla and I hadn't once stopped to consider the weird effects I might be having on him. I was the confirmed supernatural one after all; was I making him be attracted to me? There was this feeling, a tugging, swirling sort of vertigo around my heart. I'd been so lonely when I'd met him…had I caught him up in it? Was I the reason I couldn't sense him?

You're going to make yourself crazy, Amy.

Going to? That train has sailed.

It's probably just a smooth line designed to make you swoon…

He looked down at me, shaking his head. "I mean, I don't understand how it is that you can make shrivelin' my manhood into a coma fun, but here we are."

I reached between his legs, anxious to lighten my thoughts. "That's pretty simple actually…" And down I went until the lil man's mood had warmed significantly. Daniel growled and pulled at my blanket when I came up for air and switched over to using my hand. I had to slap his away several times before he stopped trying to remove the barrier between us.

"Why don't you…let me…return the favor?" It was an effort for him to string the words together.

"If I let you down here all hell's gonna break loose..." Fact...plain and simple.

"And that'd be...terrible because?"

I snickered, peering down my nose at him with a half smile. "'Cause I ain't ready..."

Ladies, don't ever forget that you hold all the cards, every last one, including the rules for drawing stud poker. Hmm... perhaps especially that one. I might not have had book smarts, but a bit of wisdom threaded through my mind from time to time.

Daniel closed his eyes, laying his head back and letting out a moan tinged with laughter while I continued stroking him. "That just makes me want you *all* the more."

My tongue ran up his neck and along his jaw, stopping at his ear long enough for me to whisper, "Good...I want you fantasizing about what you can't have..." In one fluid motion my naked thigh added to the friction, my lips hovering just over his. For that fraction of a second I held fast to the illusion that my muscles held him firmly against the seat of that truck. He wasn't going anywhere without my permission. Then his lips claimed mine and my back was arching into the steering wheel. The blankets still somehow covered most of my body—but now so did he. A sharp, familiar intake of breath seized him, and I bit his bottom lip to keep his eyes fixed on mine as he came. No rolling away—not this time.

And that was the first time I really saw it.

Right there, within those fathomless eyes, sitting on its haunches and straining against bent, nearly broken chains, sat a beast. I didn't need my empathy to work on him to see he was suppressing the desire to disregard what I wanted, and in my prone position, there would be nothing I could do to stop him. I'd been playing a pickup game of hockey with weapons-grade plutonium. Each light-hearted, innocent tease on my part drained a little more coolant from his reactor. And while he had his playful side, this wasn't a game to him…or at least not one that would be allowed to go into extra rounds.

This revelation gave me pause, yes…but I also couldn't help but wonder what shoe size the beast wore, and whether or not it liked pepperoni pizza. I held an overwhelming, and borderline suicidal, urge to reach in and break those last few chains just to see what would happen. And then, there was the sensible part of me that advised breaking off eye contact, backing away slowly, and high-tailing it home.

I split the difference, closing my eyes while continuing to taste his lips as though they were coated with zesty tomato sauce. He gripped either side of my blankets to bring himself in closer, moving from my lips to the nape of my neck, heating me with each unsteady breath.

"You're evil, Amy Durene…pure evil…" An unsettling statement coming from a plutonium dragon, but given my recent insight into his point of view, not without merit. With a hefty sigh he rested his forehead against mine. "But one of these nights I'm gonna get those defenses down and then…" I swear I heard the clattering of chains, though it may have been the low snarl that escaped his lips.

"All hell will break loose…and I suspect I'll enjoy myself." I refused to look away from his eyes this time, kissing him daintily on his nose, which was slightly out of alignment. Had he broken it in the past? Cool air rushed over my breasts and down my navel, followed immediately by the comforting warmth of my blankets being secured around me. He lifted me and returned me to my place next to him, where I promptly opened my outermost blanket to continue sharing our body heat and snuggling into him.

"And Daniel Varrick," I said softly, "you'll have earned it…"

We ended up driving to an all-night laundromat in Waterville to finish drying our clothes. Wearing our blankets didn't garner as many odd looks as you might think, but we did get a resounding thumbs up and accompanying toothless grin from a woman old enough to be Abuela. A few shenanigans involving the laundry buggies and some late-night tacos later, and time caught up with us.

I debated the advantages of life in a laundromat in lieu of going back to my house to face Mother. I'd always smell fresh, never run out of food from the fully stocked vending machines, and the privy was kept relatively clean.

"We'll be fine." Daniel handed me my now working cell phone as we pulled into my driveway. "She locks you in your tower and I'll climb your golden hair. Or pull it…at your request, of course." He flashed a smile.

I plucked a hair from my head and handed it to him. "This'll have to tide you over 'til then…"

We shared a kiss that left me humming some long forgotten tune as I wafted up my front steps. His confidence put me at ease, and I was now much more relaxed going into the house than I had been several hours earlier.

Yes, it would all work out.

Hurricane Mother held a different view.

CHAPTER TWENTY-TWO

I hesitated at the door, the knob twisted ninety degrees in my hand, ready to be pushed open into a dark and certain foyer. It would make a small whooshing noise that couldn't be helped, but stealth was only a pretense anyway. Even through the stone walls, Mother's anger, indignation, and contempt lit up my sixth sense like a gnome strapped to an M80. She was sequestered in the shadows of the living room, no doubt waiting for the most dramatic moment to turn on the overhead light and scare the holy Christmas out of me. Holding back until I'd made it halfway up the stairs would have been a nice touch.

Out of habit, or maybe as a stall tactic, I took my time entering, going through the motions with all the speed of a sloth. This was a bad idea…if I left now I could be asleep on Kayla's squeaky couch in another fifteen minutes. I could deal with Mother better in the morning.

Except…she already knows you're here Amy…so that's an even worse idea. Plus, you're already inside…

The dead bolt echoed through the house like a gavel sounding out some final verdict, and Mother's icy words hung on its heels. "I hope that kiss was worth it." Even as I

164

knew it was coming, that damned light disoriented me—had she put a brighter bulb in just for the occasion? It was the kind of thing she'd do, little torture techniques squirreled away over the years.

It had been worth it, of course, but I didn't answer—or more correctly, I couldn't answer. It was all I could do to keep her emotions on their side of the dividing line.

I need to go. Unlock this door and just go. Now.

"He's that boy I told you not to see, isn't he?" she hissed, and by then it was too late. Her raw vitriol streamed into me with the inevitability of a lava flow. My stalwart and hard-fought wall melted and twisted under the pressure. Shutting my eyes, I focused on my craving to see Daniel again, just as I had in school. That was *my* desire, not hers. *My* high ground.

"Answer me!" she spat, engulfing me in concentrated anger and setting what little defenses remained to kindling. Who did this bitch think she was? Breaking down my fucking wall!

I flipped around, glaring at my mother with her own contempt. "Because I'm too crazy for a boyfriend right?"

"With the way you've been acting, you damn well must be!" Her eyes narrowed to match mine.

"Not too crazy for Reid, though, what family does he belong to? Must be one with influence or you wouldn't give a shit!" Her initial shock at the gall of my words cooled things enough to allow some of my own regret and horror to surface within me. That was a nasty, if painfully true, thing to say, and I really didn't want to poke the bear any further. The bear needed a picnic basket and a nap.

I put my hands out in a placating gesture as I made my way towards the stairs. "Look...I'm tired...you're tired...why don't we both get some sleep and talk about this in the morning?" I was halfway there, only ten more feet to go.

"You don't get to dictate to a pile of dust in this house!" Through clenched teeth and atop a writhing coil of defiance, she pointed to the sofa. "Sit your ass down while I tell you what your life is going to be like from now on!" She clicked on the small table lamp, granting the room the warm, loving glow of an interrogation scene. In keeping with the crappy mood I was now in, I chose to sit where I stood.

As I've mentioned, Mother kept up a good physique as part of her business image with Freedom Timber. She had to be able to chop wood and play with the big boys, at least for a little while, and so I was pulled off my butt with some amount of force and thrown into the place she had highlighted for me with minimal effort on her part. She wasn't often physical with me, but I'd seldom been so openly obstinate with her, either. This was new territory for us both.

I rubbed my arm where she'd grabbed me and reached for a cigarette, which was promptly knocked out of my hand and across the shiny hardwood floor. "This. This is done," she spouted, "You're not mature enough to smoke."

An unenforceable threat, and she knew it. What a waste of time and tobacco.

"I had to rearrange my schedule significantly..." She paced back and forth with the air of someone expecting their every word to be written down as sacrosanct. "...But I will be taking you to and from school every day and instructing them that you are not to leave the campus at lunch time. When you aren't catching up on your school work, you will be doing bookkeeping for me, to help make up for my lost time and productivity. You will reduce your hours at the stable to Saturday and Sunday only and we'll be having a talk with Cassie about how you've been spending your time lately."

"Kamrie," I corrected. She ignored me and kept right on reciting her line items.

"There will be no more Kayla, and certainly no more of this boy...what's his name?"

"You wouldn't remember it anyway," I scoffed.

166

"It hardly matters, he's a worse influence on you than Kayla." She was so damned sure she had it all figured out.

"Ever think maybe I'm the one keeping him out late?" Let that burst her pretentious bubble.

"Well, then his parents can have this lovely one a.m. conversation with him."

"He's eighteen."

"Have you had sex with him yet?" she asked, and when it became apparent by my flat gaze that I wasn't going to dignify her with a response, she doubled down. "Have you been remembering to take your birth control or is it just your Paraxopram you've been forgetting?"

How'd she know I wasn't taking it?! I'd been throwing out my Paraxopram every day…except for yesterday…and Tuesday…oh yeah and Monday too. I'd been too tired to bother… but what the hell was she doing going through my things?! A low growl rumbled from me. "Who and what I put into my body are none of your business!"

"Oh, it's my business alright, an exhausting side-hustle with crummy pay and lousy hours!" she hissed. "But someone's got to give a shit about your future, because you're obviously incapable!"

"It's not my future you're giving a shit about! Don't confuse the two."

I could have said anything to her, and her internal file would have played on. "Tomorrow after school I'm taking you to get the shot version of Paraxopram. It has to be done once a week, but I think it will be worth the drive to improve your shit attitude." She sneered down at me. "We'll throw in an STD panel while we're at it…"

"Like hell I'm gonna let you inject that poison into me!" I leapt to my feet, intent on leaving.

"You don't have to LET me do anything! You are my MINOR sixteen-year-old daughter! You don't have a say!" She shoved me back onto the sofa, trapping me between her outstretched arms, and getting in my face so close my mascara might have rubbed off on her chin. "If you *ever* leave this house without me again, I will call the police and report you as a runaway. They'll take you to jail and you can rest your head on concrete for the night. Maybe it'll help you appreciate the home you have!"

I stared blankly past her at the unplugged faux fireplace embedded into the wall. "What's the difference, it'll be just as cold and lifeless!"

"Probably not actually, you'd have a TV in the rec room down at Juvi. I've already sold yours, along with your X-Station and all your games." Smugness coated her anger, as fine as ash.

Raising my chin, I blew the ash right back at her. "You won't call the cops on me, you won't talk to my boss, and you won't keep me from seeing Kayla, or anyone else. If you did, word might get out about what kind of family we *really* have!"

"Oh? *Try* me." Mother's tone could have curdled milk, but there was a telling jump in her anxiety. Brushing her arm aside I got up; I was done being threatened. Two steps were as far as I made it before she dug into the sore spot on my arm and whipped me around on my heels to face her. "I'm not finished with you yet, child!"

As we scowled at each other in righteous indignation, the fragile silence was broken by a bubblegum pop jingle, courtesy of my freshly rebooted Fugitive phone. The first sixty seconds of "I Love You" by Avril Lavigne played out; I had a message from Kayla.

Mother's eyes went wide with disbelief, and in her temporary confusion, I wrested free of her. I managed three steps backwards before she slammed me into the decorative bookshelf to the right of the picture window. A fake copy of *Lord of the Flies* fell onto the floor with a resounding clack, opening on one of the vacant pages in the middle. She held me against the shelf with one arm while patting my pockets. I squirmed and twisted while screaming through gritted teeth.

Somehow, she came out of the scuffle with my phone in her hand. Another ill-timed "La la, la la la la," started anew. There were multiple messages.

Mother shook her head, her lip curled. "Who's messaging you this late? Hmm? Is it him? Unlock it!"

"Never going to happen." My arms folded across my chest.

"I'll take it to Jeremy tomorrow, along with your other one. Whatever's been going on with you I'll bet your texts will be enlightening."

"You can't!" I seethed.

"I can!" Another notification piped in.

"Give. It. To. Me." The look I gave her could have melted sand.

Her blood boiled at my insubordination, pouring directly into my already stoked inferno. "Never. Going. To. Happen. And you know what?! If this is how you spend your money, buying extra phones, and cigarettes, you don't need a job." Waving my phone in front of my face, she bared her teeth. "Just for this little straw, tomorrow you'll call Carlie on it and let her know you are no longer working there and why. Effective immedi—"

"It's Kamrie!" I snatched up her wrist, sinking my nails into it and forcing her grip to loosen. "K. A. M. R. I. E!" For each enunciated letter, I peeled one of her fingers from my property until it was returned to me. I'd break the thing into pieces before I'd let her touch it again. It was MINE! "Jesus-fucking-Christ! So I skipped a couple classes, you need to calm the fuck—" My head whipped to one side from the force of Mother's slap. Half my face went numb, and my vision blurred. She was saying something, but the ringing in my ears and adrenaline in my blood were louder. By the

169

time things came back into focus, red was the only color left.

I was slightly outside of myself then, as if I were watching a video of what was happening rather than being in the director's chair.

Mother is knocked backwards over the couch. I stand over her, the phone raised above my head with every intention of smashing it against her temple until either it breaks, or she does. She won't get what she's after! I'll win! A distant part of me screams at myself to stop, and Mother uses my weak hesitation to tangle me in her legs, sending me careening into the glass coffee table. It doesn't shatter like you see in the movies, but several long cracks form an outline around me.

Mother's briefcase tips off the side, sending her laptop and file folders sprawling across the floor. The shine of her keys catches my eye, and I roll off the table, ripping them free of the leather lanyard they're attached to. Something unintelligible is screamed at me. If I can make it to her office, I can lock myself inside...I can get MY other phone back...at least I think that's the plan. So then...why am I holding the keys between my knuckles like a weapon?

I hit the ground hard on my shoulder, pinned under Mother's weight as I strike out blindly with the keys. She bludgeons my hand against the floor again and again, trying to make me drop them.

The pain brings me somewhat to my senses.

"Ahhhh! God!" I howled, straining against her until my muscles might snap, and not moving her more than half an inch. "Why can't you just go back to ignoring me like you do every other fucking day!" At the center of Mother's looming vortex of outrage and anger, a miniscule twinge of indifference emerged...as if in response to my plea. I'd no sooner recognized what it was, than it came flying to the forefront, snuffing out first her anger, and then mine, under an avalanche of perfect apathy.

If you've ever had the wind knocked out of you, or come to a sudden stop on a roller coaster, you have some idea of what it felt like. The tension in my body dropped and the emotion drained from my mother's eyes; her once tight jaw slackened as she rolled off me.

"You know what Amy? You're right...live your life how you want. I'm done staying up 'til all hours of the night worrying about you." She got up, leaving her keys, her laptop, and me on the polished hardwood floor.

Up the stairs she shuffled, quick as a zombie, while I lay there slowly absorbing the surreal nature of my situation. Her and my dad talked in low, muffled tones at the top of the stairs. We'd actually managed to wake the dead with our racket. I couldn't make out what they were saying, but he didn't come down.

After a time, I sat up, rubbing at the back of my right hand and expecting to find bruises and scratches, but wiping away only dirt. The feeling of her smashing it into the floor was still raw, but she hadn't done any lasting damage. Flipping my hand around, I studied the hard-won set of keys, unable to truly enjoy the victory. It just didn't seem important anymore...and I knew that wasn't right.

Ah well...fuck it...where'd that cigarette get off to? Ah there it is, under the end table.

Propping my back up against the foot of the arm chair, I lit up the smoke, taking in a pleasant drag and letting my mind play over the events of the last few minutes while surveying the damage. As the pile of ashes grew at my feet I became something of myself again, increasingly horrified by what I'd done...and what I'd nearly done.

I had attacked my mother—with her own anger, true— and there was some poetic justice to that, but still...if she hadn't tripped me...

My blood turned to slush at the thought. I didn't get along with Mother, but I'd never wanted her dead, well...not really. Besides, the whole thing was more like attempted suicide than murder when you reasoned it all out. So, there you go, there was nothing to feel guilty about. If anything, I'd saved her from herself at the end there when I made her apathetic.

And I *had* made her apathetic, there was no mistaking it this time. I'd manipulated her emotions, just like I suspected I had out at the Gelding. It was stupidly easy too, like shooting a barrel full of monkeys. I laughed, stopping just short of putting my cigarette out on the floor. I wasn't quite *that* apathetic anymore. "All this time, I've been working to keep the door shut when all I had to do was reach through it," I said.

In order to control her emotions, I had to open myself up to what she was feeling in the moment, so of course it hadn't worked since that first time. I'd been strengthening my mental barrier right alongside trying to control Mother's and Kayla's emotions. I might as well have been trying to take an x-ray through a lead vault.

"So fuckin' simple..." I whispered. "But, the key will be not to lose myself in the process..." My eyes fell on the cracked coffee table. "I don't want to do that again." My fingertips started to burn from the spent cigarette, and I got to my feet to find a place to pitch it. Mother's keys jangled under my boot, sliding two feet across the floor. I smiled down at the spoils of war. "Speaking of keys...let's not waste this opportunity, shall we?" Picking them up, I headed into the kitchen.

The garbage disposal grumbled as it devoured my lone cigarette butt, as if to say, "You woke me up for this puny sacrifice?" The water spiraled down the drain, conjuring memories of Mother's emotional cyclone, and how satisfying it had been to reach in and mold her internal landscape to my liking, to wipe that smug look off her face with a thought. My stomach rumbled and I broke from my flashback to find my hand hovering at the mouth of the disposal, my fingertips an inch from the whirling blades, as though trying to grasp them. I pulled my hand back and stared at it, switching the disposal off.

Curious…

Was I just tired or was there something more going on here? Maybe I really was possessed…

It wasn't the first time my hand had done its own thing. I'd raised it without being sure it was me, written things I didn't remember writing, and damn near smashed the Fugitive to bits on Mother's head.

"You really need to stop going off on your own. That time you almost got yourself killed!" I scolded my wayward appendage, trying to mask my fear through anger. If I was truly possessed, such an effort was pointless…it would know, but it made me feel better and more in control of the situation.

"And you!" It was the sink's turn now. "You don't get to have my hand." Opening the cupboard, I took down a box of peanut butter crackers and emptied some of them into the disposal until it was less grumbly. "There! Happy?" It thankfully didn't reply, but my stomach, having registered there were crackers, did…and loudly. Hadn't I just eaten two hours ago?

"Great crickets of mercy, what's going on with me?" My voice was shallow, my head swimming. I stuffed a few crackers in my mouth while leaning against the kitchen counter and waiting to see if my hand tried anything else. And yes, next to the knife block in a darkened kitchen was *not* the smartest location for this exercise.

"How 'bout you just cut the shit and tell me, hmm?"

Only silence followed.

CHAPTER TWENTY-THREE

*W*ith my meal fit for a queen and the keys to the kingdom in my more cooperative left hand, I made my way to Mother's office. How long would she remain apathetic? It certainly wasn't her normal state when challenged, so it was best to get my phone out of prison while the getting was good.

Into the lion's den I strode.

Mother always made a show of locking things up in her file cabinet, mostly noise-toys of mine that had driven her to the brink over the years—which my phone still technically counted as. Seeing as how she also locked her office door, it was grandiose overkill. My phone was waiting right there on top, dead as a man with thirteen life insurance policies. I plugged it in to recharge and plumbed the depths of the drawer for more treasures, invading the privacy of the woman who had been so ready to do the same to me.

Among stacks of Freedom Timber legal documents lay a flask wrapped in black leather with an embossed angel on it, a favored symbol for my mother. Sloshing it around and opening it up revealed it to be one quarter filled with something that smelled like shoe polish. I took a swig, gagged, and slid it back into its dark crevice.

It tasted like shoe polish too.

There was a small photo album from Mother's younger days, in which she was smoking, drinking, and posing in a lewd manner with various men and women. I took pictures of some of the more incriminating ones, just in case, and put the album to the side.

A handsomely carved wooden box caught my eye. It was the kind of thing you'd expect to find a magic lamp or pair of ambitious eyes in, but all that awaited me were piles of receipts and old airline and cruise stubs going back fifteen years. Mother was always going off on business trips and conferences that took her to exotic locales; who knew she was so sentimental about them? Underneath the box, a Maine Black Bears football jersey, number thirty-five, gave off the slightest hint of cologne. Who might she still be pining over to keep such a treasure?

I dropped the shirt in a heap on the ground at the sight of the sweetest plum of all. Sweeter even than my dear phone. It was red and plastic, and after six years of separation it was again pressed to my lips. My kazoo. Settling into Mother's all too comfortable chair, I lit up a cigarette and blew smoke through my once estranged kazoo in utter triumph.

It still worked.

"Freak Like Me" played as my phone reached a sufficient charge. There was a message from Kayla on Monday morning, wanting to know if I'd been struck by lightning at church, and threatening that if I was sleeping she was going to come up there with a magic marker and turn me into Frida Kahlo...whatever that was. It was three a.m.; if I didn't want to be a Frida in the morning I needed to go to sleep right then. It wasn't a hard sell, I was exhausted...and probably had shoe polish poisoning. My eyes closed...a girl could sleep forty years in this comfy chair...

Kayla will Kahlo you!

My eyes shot back open, and I picked up the Fugitive to set the alarm. Kayla's previous messages lay waiting to be read. I'd nearly killed Mother over those texts, and while it might make my best friend happy to know she was almost an accomplice, that wasn't the reason she sent them.

11:46 PM: YOU UP?

The first text had come three hours after she'd dropped me off. Why was she still up?

11:48 PM: HAVE YOU SEEN THIS GIRL?

Attached was a picture of a teenage girl with shiny, long black hair. She was young, and beautiful, with delicate features, and a light sprinkling of make-up that she didn't need. Her genuine smile brightened the photo, though her eyes were distant, and somehow older than the face which held them.

"Leilani..." I whispered, sitting up straight in the chair and clutching my phone.

So much for getting any sleep. It was probably best that Mother didn't catch me passed out in her office, next to her open drawer of keepsakes and plunder, anyway. There was no telling what mood she'd be in—though I could always change it—couldn't I? Maybe, providing it didn't backfire on me. I'd gotten a fourth wind, but it was more a light breeze than anything.

Come to think of it, I probably shouldn't be in this house come morning. I didn't know how long the apathy would last and she was sure to rip me out of bed if it wore off. Putting everything back where I'd found it, aside from my phone and kazoo, I crept up the stairs to grab a few things. At the top of the landing I could feel both my parents were asleep.

Emotions while sleeping are naturally subdued, as you might expect, but they jump around and change up in unpredictable ways. It's sort of like stirring up a stew pot.

I took a gamble that Mother's emotions were the ones

176

with a slight edge to them and dove in, consciously calling for her indifference to surface. It was slippery, like trying to pick a carrot out of that stew pot with a butter knife. I'd bring it up only to have it sink back down again. My own emotions started to swirl and bubble along with hers until I had to back away—or risk losing my balance and falling down the stairs.

Worse yet would be losing control. Would I come to, having stabbed my parents to death with my trusty penknife as they slept? No, I had to stop tempting fate. I gathered a change of clothes, some make-up, and my backpack, and left a note about needing to cool off at Kayla's wedged in my door.

I'd need to clean up the carnage downstairs before I left. The fancy table cloth reserved for high end guests made a good cover for the cracked coffee table when folded three times over. It would at least help Mother to not be immediately enraged in the morning…in theory.

I walked to Kayla's in the pre-dawn stillness of a sleeping world. A journey I'd taken thousands of times before, only now I didn't feel entirely alone, even as I knew there was nobody there. It isn't like I could sense anyone. Whether to calm my jittery nerves or to keep things friendly between me and…"It"…I struck up a song.

"I'm Henry the Eighth I am…Henry the Eighth I am, I am. I got married to the widow next door, she's been married seven times before…" And on I went.

No one else joined in.

Thankfully.

Exhaustion settled in my bones around the fiftieth verse, when it would have taken the same amount of effort to turn back as to keep going. My flashlight gleamed off the eyes of something in the distance and I tensed, shining the light in its direction. Being eaten by a pack of coyotes would be just the way to end this bizarre night. I was reaching for my lighter when the great white yeti that was Sampson came into view. He trotted over, and sniffed me with a familiarity usually reserved for my gynecologist. I fell to my knees and hugged him tightly, as much in self-defense as because I was relieved to see him.

"You smell anyone else inside me, Sam?" I asked. He sneezed several times in quick succession, coating the sleeve of my jacket in mucus. "How am I supposed to take this? Hmm?" He wagged his tail at me, sending great tufts of fur flying. "Is that your seal of approval, or a signal that I'm contaminated?" He cocked his head to one side. "You'd attack me if something was wrong? Wouldn't you, boy?" His head cocked back the other way.

I steadied myself against the big brute to stand. What had I been thinking? I was too tired to be walking so far in the dead of night. My fifth wind had died down to a stagnant, wheezing breath. But at least Sampson's hackles were down; that offered peace of mind. In the movies, the animals always growled at the infected person—they didn't cover them in kisses. Sam stayed by my side until I was safely inside Kayla's house, then he disappeared back into the shadows. There'd be a steak in his future, I'd see to it.

The kitchen was black, save for the green light coming from the oven clock. I made my way to the living room by memory; the old couch called to me with false promises of sleeping on a cloud. Kayla's laptop kicked on as I carefully moved it from the cushions to the metal coffee table, bathing the room in a soft, blue-white glow. Leilani's haunting brown eyes stared back at me from the pages of a forum: "Paranormal Coffee Cake."

I squinted to read the accompanying words as the couch let out a protest squeal under my weight. "Looks kinda like this Leilani, but that is a pretty crappy video. You should send it to T-Rex for clean up. Anyway, if it is her let me know because that would make your already creepy story give me a coronary!"

The first link pulled up a tab that was already open. Once again Leilani stared back at me, only this time she was smaller, on a background of roses, and accompanied by a wall of text.

Leilani Polumya, local youth leader, was given unto God's loving arms on Saturday. She is survived by her mother, Cassandra Polumya, father Bane Polumya, brother Kai Polumya, sister in law, Emma, and niece, Makani. She had a love and zest for life and touched the lives of so many St. George residents. An active member of the Youth City Council and Captain of the Youth Rugby Team, she was committed to making the world around her a better place and she succeeded in doing so with the short time she was given to us. Leilani had recently received a scholarship to attend Wayne State University, in Michigan, where she was to pursue a degree in Biomedical Physics.

Funeral Services will be held March 24th at the Temple of Latter Day Saints. In lieu of flowers the family asks that you make a donation to the Leilani Polumya rugby scholarship fund.

March 24th?

A few days after I'd met her?

"Oh my God..." Bringing my fingers to my mouth, I slowly exhaled through them, my heart quickening. Why hadn't Kayla said anything about this in her message? I might have been prepared. As it was, my stomach clenched in my throat.

The header of a third open tab read, "Brutal murder..." Licking my sandpaper lips, I clicked on it.

Brutal murder rocks St. George Community. Police say it bears the marks of an honor killing.

In the early morning hours, a man out for a run with his dog discovered the remains of a young woman who had been badly muti-lated and left lying in the road. The body was later identified through

dental records as that of Leilani Polumya, an 18-year-old youth
activist from St. George. Given the severe acid burns on the victim's
face, throat, and upper body, police suspect that this may be an honor
killing. Her father has been taken in for questioning, though the
family lawyer, Anansi Hussad, insists that the family is Mormon and
loved their daughter. "They are distraught and in need of community
support, not accusations," he told an AP reporter this morning.

The creak of a floorboard in the kitchen tore me out of the article. Kayla's fear rammed into me a millisecond later and I clawed into the edge of the couch. "It's me! Kayla! You can put the gun away!" I called to her. Then, remembering how I hadn't been entirely myself today, I added, "I think." Her tiny silhouette appeared in the doorway, the Taurus in a relaxed grip at her side. With the levels of fear I'd been getting from her, I knew it would be there.

She appraised me while her emotions jittered towards worry. "You look like unholy hell, Amy...you even slept all night?"

"She's dead." My sunken eyes found Kayla's. "This is Leilani. MY Leilani!" The tremble in my voice bordered on hysterical. "She was our *only* lead. And now things have gotten even weirder and...and she's dead!"

Kayla closed her eyes, a steady calmness washing over her concern, not eliminating it but noticeably diluting it. Evoking a small squeak from the couch, she sat next to me. "It appears that way. How sure are you it's her? On a scale of one to ten?"

Numbers were not my friends on the best of days. Kayla's calmness breezed through my fragile mental wall, and I embraced it as my own, resting my head on her shoulder. "One hundred percent," I answered. A short burst of excitement shot through me like an arrow, despite Kayla's attempt to rein it in.

It was flavored with the thrill of the hunt.

"You need to get some sleep. Is your mother gonna be comin' around?" Her manner was stern and immovable.

"I don't think she'll be a problem—I'll just remind her how much she doesn't really care, and she'll go away." I lifted my heavy head off Kayla, meeting her gaze with detachment. "It's what I did tonight." A slow shockwave rolled through my friend as the full gravity of what I'd said dawned on her. "Yeah, I made her not give a shit about anything...wasn't even hard."

"You controlled what she was feeling?" she clarified.

"Like I was fishing in a barrel of gummy worms. Almost killed her too...and myself so...not sure it's entirely a win." Raspy, half-maniacal laughter quivered out of me. "But I could do it again."

My best friend studied me for a long moment through wary eyes, trying to keep the fact that I just frightened her in check and failing miserably. "Come on, let's get you upstairs, I'll have Ma call us in today and dig up everything I can on Leilani while you sleep." She helped me stand, stopping in the kitchen to get a bottle of orange juice from the fridge on our way to the stairs. "Drink this, you look like a mummy." With greedy abandon I took it from her, sharing a fair amount with my shirt and the peeling kitchen linoleum while I was at it.

She was beyond right—without sleep, my thoughts were overlapping and nonsensical. Why had Leilani controlled my emotions? What was Mother doing in the school bathroom in a number thirty-five jersey? Where had I left my red kazoo that was in my back pocket right now?

Once in Kayla's room, I locked the door, as much to keep me in as anybody out, and stripped off everything but my shirt, which still smelled like Daniel...and orange juice. Contemplating the delicious nature of such a mixed drink, I crawled into bed, falling asleep mid-chuckle.

Laugh, and the world laughs with you...

CHAPTER TWENTY-FOUR

"*L*ollipop, lollipop, oh lolli lolli lolli, lollipop." The cheerful fifties tune woke me some eight hours later, announcing a text from Daniel. My phone was off the nightstand and in my hand before I'd fully realized where I was.

11:58 AM: STAPLE GUNNED MY SLEEVE TO A BOARD TODAY DAYDREAMING OF PULLING YOUR HAIR. I KNOW I WANT TO, BUT DO I NEED TO?

The innocent normalcy of his message warmed me, even as the reality of my situation settled in like so much freezer burn. I'd toyed with the idea of telling Daniel some of what was happening, but there was a refreshing angle to him not knowing. He wouldn't look at me the way Kayla had this morning, the way I was now, in the make-up mirror next to the bed.

Who am I?

What am I?

What the hell is going on with me?

My brain did some calisthenics, working through recent developments, while the rest of my body caught on that it was awake. Each bit of progress I'd made with my mental wall only seemed to increase the range of people I could feel.

This, in turn, increased the likelihood that I would be overwhelmed and lose control of my other senses...specifically my body and sense of touch. I might have a ghost in my shell, but maybe my brain was only built for five senses and this sixth one was frying the circuits? And now there was a new defense mechanism at play: I could manipulate people into feeling what I wanted...unless it only worked on Mother for some reason.

I disengaged from my reflection, downing what was left of the warm orange juice in one long series of gulps. Judging by how ravenously hungry I was, even now, and how exhausted I'd been this morning, there was a toll to be paid for these abilities. As appealing as it may have been, I wouldn't be swaying everyone I met—not if I wanted to live. Still, my abilities weren't strictly passive any more, and that was a game changer.

Too bad it didn't bring me any closer to figuring out which game.

Game?

Leilani is dead...this isn't a game.

I put my head in my hands and rubbed my temples, trying to steady my breathing and my bottom lip. My hands grew warm and wet. Tiny pools of sadness and frustration soaked reluctantly into the beaten down fabric of the carpet beneath me. I hadn't known Leilani, but she seemed sweet and innocent, and she certainly hadn't deserved such a gruesome death.

Nobody did.

Leilani had been there for me at a critical time, throwing a menthol life line into the sea of emotions I was drowning in. Part of me had taken for granted that I would talk to her again, and that would never happen now. It was fucked up. The whole situation was fucked up, with a capitol F.U. Every stumble forward brought more questions, more bullshit... more fear.

Leilani is dead...am I next?

Flashes of my hand hovering above those blades chilled me to the marrow. Had Leilani burned herself and then wandered out into the road to collapse? I hadn't finished the article to find out. But Kayla would know. Hell, by now she probably had Leilani's social security number, Pepsi vs. Coke preference, and eighth-grade crush.

Wiping at my tears, I got dressed and went into the bathroom to assess the damage. The raccoon-ish nature of my appearance reminded me that "no run" mascara was a myth. "What's with you and raccoons?" My half-laugh turned into a whole-cry as I washed my face. When I came up for air I was something like human again. Heart thick and heavy in my stomach, I studied my eyes intently...were they getting whiter? I didn't think so but was I really someone I could trust? Tears may wash down the drain, but the underlying stones of grief and horror wouldn't slip away so easily.

Or, maybe they would...

Taking a relaxing breath, I fished within myself, consciously searching for hope and optimism. They both slammed to the forefront with such force I might have gotten a concussion. The fact that I'd been leaning against the sink saved me from a nasty fall.

What luck! I sprang up to greet myself in the mirror. The redness around my eyes was already going away, barely noticeable really. And my God, whatever was cooking downstairs smelled amazing! Vigorously flicking the light off I bounced down the stairs whistling "Lollipop."

The scent of eggs, garlic, and something sweet tickled my nose. Ma had just taken a batch of quiches from the oven and was coaxing them onto a plate. "...take a look at her udders and see what you think, but I'm pretty sure she's getting close to dropping." She was talking to Kayla, who was busily chopping up mushrooms.

"Is that Selene?" I asked, heading over to the cupboard and pulling out three plates.

"The very same," Ma answered.

"I did notice she was a little more...anxious than usual yesterday." I smiled while setting the table.

"Yup, pretty soon we'll have a cute lil calf to spend all day staring at. Hope I'm home for it. I love seeing them learn how to walk. And speaking of, it's good to see you up and so chipper." Ma smiled warmly, bringing the quiches over and taking a seat. "Please tell me it was my cooking that woke you."

"Out of a dead sleep!" I chirped, pouring a giant glass of raw milk.

Kayla smiled, placing the salad on the table. "I swear she was on death's door this mornin', Ma."

"Mmmhmm." Ma was playfully skeptical. "Well, I called Angela and left a message that I was calling you in and haven't heard anything from her." Sorrow hid behind her matter of fact mask. "You know...I don't mind calling you girls in now and then, but you just tell that gentleman friend of yours—what's his name?"

"Daniel." I licked the milk from my upper lip and played hot potato with one of the quiches. Who could wait for Kayla to be done with the spatula?

"Well, you tell Daniel not to keep you out so late on a school night again or he's going to answer to me." She took a bite of her quiche and chewed. "Do I even want to know what you were doing coming out of a laundromat at midnight?"

Kayla stopped eating and glared at me. "Last night?"

Ma shifted her eyes between us, laughing uneasily. "You know...I'm not sure...with these sixteen-plus hour shifts I lose track of the days."

Heat rose in my cheeks, and I looked from Ma to Kayla. I was busted, no sense lying to my best friend about it. "Yeah, we were there. It involves the accidental misplacement of a pool." In between devouring four quiches and three glasses of milk, I relayed the story of running from Mother, including quips about my empathy. Ma didn't register that those parts were anything other than dramatic flare, and cracked up laughing for most of the tale.

"Serves you right," Kayla said when I'd finished. "I'm sidin' with the gnome." Things were light on the surface, but the floorboards under her feet might as well have been on fire.

"He sounds like a perfectly charming young man," Ma said. "Isn't everyone who can take a blow to the ego like that and come out on top. Shriveled bits and all." We all laughed at that. "Daniel...what's his last name? Is he Irish? I bet he's Irish. They've got the best sense of humor." She winked at Kayla.

"Varrick...and I don't know."

"There's a lot she doesn't know about him actually." If Kayla's lips got any tighter she'd spit diamonds.

"Well, you're not going to find out suckin' face like you were...you'll need to talk to him some," Ma teased as she rose from the table. "Exciting as it is living through you, I've got to go make the donuts...or heal the donuts, if you'd rather."

"Thanks, Ma." I gave her a peck on the cheek and a long hug. Next to Kayla's brightness and brewing anger, Ma's emotions were barely existent. "It was delicious...um...whatever it was."

"Glad to be able to feed my girls." Her smile alone could have sustained me. "And there was spinach and artichokes in there—you two didn't even notice." She cackled as she put on her coat, grabbed her purse, and left.

I got up to clean the table off and load the dishwasher, Kayla's eyes fixed on me in awkward silence all the while.

She bit down her anger in small, unpalatable chunks until it was a more manageable shade of annoyance. Pulling her recording device from her jeans pocket, she clicked it on.

"Tell me everything, from the moment I dropped you off, 'til this mornin'."

"I'm sorry to make you upset, runnin' off like I did. We just figured Mother'd be volcanic either way. And boy did she ever blow!" I rolled up the sleeve on my shirt and stared at my arm. "I'm surprised there's no bruises."

I wasn't aiming for sympathy from the gesture, which was good because there was none forthcoming. "She'd have been less pissed if you'd have stuck with our story," Kayla said.

My solid optimism was ever so slowly being dragged through the muck...so I picked it back up again. This time I was ready for the change, and didn't have to brace myself. "Ah! But then I wouldn't have been nailed to the ground like I was, and I wouldn't have figured out the secret..." With eyes full of mischief, I told her what I've recounted here to you, adding in the part about the beast within Daniel that I'd left out of the telling to Ma. Kayla wouldn't like it, but if we were going to navigate through this, she needed full disclosure from me. Besides...I had a feeling it would all work out for the best in the end.

Kayla asked follow-up questions to make sure she understood as I went, keeping the countenance of a reporter throughout. Well, aside from a comment on how Mother deserved far worse and had gotten her long overdue comeuppance. She wanted that noted for the record.

When I got to the part where I nearly sliced my fingers off, cold fear snaked through my best friend. "Shit..." She brought her hand to her mouth and stared off at the rooster cookie jar, as though trying to piece something together, her guilt so luminous I unconsciously took two steps back.

"We're doing all we can, Kayla..." I reassured her.

"All WE can." Her heavy eyes met mine. "I think it's time we brought more people in on this..."

"Hey, it only happens when I'm too stressed...I've got it

under control." My fingers wiggled in front of her face. "No mincemeat hands."

This brought a smile to her and lessened the guilt. "I'd feel better if you got a proper exorcism…I was probably too white to do it right."

"I don't know…Sam doesn't sense anything wrong with me, I'm not convinced we need to go that route." From there, I finished out the events of the morning: finding my kazoo, my run in with Sampson, and what I'd read on Kayla's computer before she'd wisely sent me to bed.

"There's more to Leilani's story than you read last night." We relocated to the couch where Kayla flipped through new pictures of our mystery girl on her laptop. She'd obviously been busy stalking the net while I slept. "Are you still one hundred percent sure that it's her?"

Each new picture garnered my full attention, not because I needed more confirmation, but to appease my friend's obsessive tendencies. Leilani's face and white eyes were damn near etched into my eyeballs; I knew her features almost as well as my own. The images told a story of someone who was loved by those around her. She laughed and rough-housed with her rugby team in her blue and white uniform; number fourteen. There were several frames of her smiling broadly as her teammates came up behind her with a big bucket of water and dumped it over her head. In another series of photos she was at a picnic, finger painting with a toddler using ketchup, mustard, and at first the table cloth, before moving on to using people as her canvas.

There she was, dressed as Little Red Riding Hood with a plastic blood covered ax, looking like she was coming to murder whoever was behind the camera. Tucked away under the hood, a rainbow streak of hair was visible if you knew where to look for it. "Yeah, that's her. You can even see her rainbow hair in this one." My fingers lingered on the screen and I laughed. "There's no need to fear the wolves, Amy…

because I've got an ax!" Despite the dire subject matter I was still in a relatively good mood. "And...this is the part where you tell me that her dying so soon after our bathroom soiree was just a coincidence...right...right?"

Kayla's eyes narrowed before slowly widening, rays of shock spreading through her like dawn. "You didn't do the math did you?"

I winced and raised an eyebrow. "Of course not—I hate math."

She stared at me a moment and then pulled up Leilani's obituary, tapping the screen with her pointer finger. "She was given into God's loving arms on Saturday." Running her tongue over her cracked lips, her eyes fixed on mine. "I've confirmed the date from four other sources...it isn't a typo."

I finally did the math.

What was left of my happy illusion drained away, and my skin erupted into gooseflesh, my heart beating into my throat.

Leilani had been murdered three days before I'd met her.

CHAPTER TWENTY-FIVE

*A*ll our lives we'd searched for proof of spirits, and here it was right in front of us; what's more, we had video evidence to back up our claims. Despite this, my brain scrambled to cope with the conflicting information as I sank back on the couch.

I have to breathe, right?

Breathing is good.

In...out...in...out.

She was dead, after all. No getting around it.

How?

Finding out who Leilani was now raised far more questions than it answered. "But if sh...she was murdered in Utah what the heck was sh...she doing in a school bath...th...room in bum...mmmfuck Maine?" *Am I shaking?*

I am.

"I have my theories." Kayla handed me a glass of water and rubbed my cold arm with her warm, steady hand. "But you need to hear the rest of her story first." She brought the soft, worn white blanket off the back of the couch and around my shoulders in one movement. "Do you need a minute? I thought you knew this morning." Her tone was apologetic, but I was having a hard time actually feeling it from her. My shock was messing with my empathy, washing out Kayla's usually bright emotions.

A welcome reprieve, even as the living room swam and buckled.

A shiver rolled through me, putting jumper cables to my breathing, and the room into focus. After a few long gulps of water I was more in control of myself, still trembling on occasion but not so bad as to spill my drink. "No way I could have handled it this morning...maybe my brain knew that?" I offered a weak smirk, taking another minute to simply stare at the information in front of me and slot it into place with what I knew. "This is cool though...freaky as shit...and I feel sick for her...but man..."

Once I was no longer in danger of fainting, Kayla came alive with a macabre grin. "It gets even freakier. It wasn't her family, like that first article suggested, though they were dragged through hell for nine days before the real killer was found." She opened up another story. The headline read, *"St. George honor killer apprehended. Trial to start Monday."*

"A twenty-six-year-old man named Thomas Obachek became obsessed with Leilani: he abducted, raped, and tortured her for one week before dumping her body in the middle of a suburban road. He initially professed his love, but when she wouldn't return it exactly how he wanted... that's when the torture started. The acid burns were applied slowly, drip by drip, for days before she died of a blood infection. Her pain and suffering was the stuff of nightmares. They know all this because the sick bastard took video of everything and spliced together the worst of her screams into a twisted homage to her."

"Jesus..." My voice was barely above a whisper.

"She wasn't his first victim either, police found five other video sequences matching women taken from all over the country. They were all relatively young, but other than that they shared no similarities. He disfigured and mutilated them such that three of the bodies won't ever be recovered... they were dissolved into the concrete of the ten by ten underground cell he kept them in. He didn't bother cleaning the place for the next tenant either...fucking horrific." Kayla touched Leilani's picture and fell silent.

I swallowed hard, putting my head in my hands, while rocks tumbled in my stomach.

"Are you with me?" my friend asked after a minute, and I managed a feeble nod. "Good...because here's where it gets...interesting."

Interesting? It had all the makings of a Chris Carter novel already. Kayla clicked on another article.

"Honor killer feeling remorse, kills himself in cell."

Thomas Obachek's mugshot took up half the page. He had sallow hamster-like eyes, and a swollen lower jaw and lip sporting a thick purple/black bruise from when he'd "resisted" arrest. He was heavy set, with a bowl cut mullet, stringy blonde hair, and a polo shirt with the top button hugging his neck so tight, he had to have an asphyxiation fetish. If that was how he always wore it, maybe lack of oxygen to the brain could begin to explain some of what he had done.

Too much creep factor.

I turned my attention back to Kayla's much prettier face.

As if sharing my feelings on the subject, she scrolled down until there was nothing but text and an ad for a Christian dating service. "Yeah, so this piece of work was heard weeping to himself, repeating the names of the women he'd killed throughout his first night in solitary confinement. In the morning they found him dead in a pool of his own blood, having gouged out chunks of his flesh with a rusty nail before jamming it into his carotid artery." Her hand ran up the side of her neck, tapping where the artery was. "The words 'I'm sorry' were on every surface of his cell...written in his blood. No one reported hearing anything other than a steady stream of weeping and then silence. No screams, no struggle, no anything."

Kayla paused, letting everything she'd said sink into my already cluttered mind. Knowing that he'd gotten what was coming to him had fired me up and gotten things moving again. "That nail didn't get there on its own...he had help from the guards no doubt." Sometimes the American injustice system was a fine thing.

"Oh he had help alright, but I don't think it was from the guards. I think Leilani possessed him and made him do it... and..." She took a heavy, ominous breath. "I think she might jump into you from time to time..." I pulled my legs close to my body. Was it getting chillier in here? Kayla continued, "Something Daniel said to you got me wondering—what if you're attracting spirits to you, a gravitational pull, like he said? What if this Obachek guy was in Waterville, looking for his next victim, and he brought Leilani's spirit with him, and she was drawn to you?"

My eyebrows furrowed as I shook my head. "That doesn't make sense though, why wouldn't she tell me he'd killed her? Why give me cigarettes and sphinx riddles?"

"That I don't know...maybe she was still in shock herself? She experienced one of the most traumatic deaths I can imagine...and I've got a pretty disturbed brain. Think about how we behave in dreams—do we always make sense? The spirit world and dreamworld are one and the same in many cultures." She had a point; why did any of this have to make any kind of sense on our end? Because it would be convenient?

Kayla smirked, bringing up the picture of Leilani as Little Red again. "But she obviously got herself together enough to kill that scumbag." Adoration mixed in with her excitement, nervousness, and she'd never want you to know it, but fear.

"He could have killed himself on his own...with what he

did, he was facing an agonizing death in general population, anyway."

"More agonizing than silently stabbing yourself to death with a rusty nail? Remember, no one heard him scream from his cell."

"Leilani was the darling of St. George. The cops could have easily either done the killing, or given him that nail and then covered it up. With all that video evidence, nobody's gonna cry for mullet man or take more than a glance at the case." With each defensive word my heart beat faster in my throat. I didn't much care for the possession angle and what it meant for me...

"I'd be on board with you if we didn't have Leilani on video in Maine, three days after she was killed in Utah. If she's powerful enough to manifest to you like she did, there's no doubt in my mind that she had a hand in his death. Kicking a pack of cigarettes and opening that monstrous bathroom door takes more energy than guiding a rusty nail along the floor." She rolled her pen along the table using only the tip of her index finger until it fell off and rolled under the couch.

I hated to admit it, but her narrative meshed with my swaying ability. "You know, in a way, it was like I was possessing my mother...at least in that moment." Hesitating to go on, I bit my bottom lip. "And...upstairs right before I came down...my eyes might have gone white for a second... when I looked in the mirror." Kayla's level of surprise skimmed the ozone layer, and her eyes became saucers a millisecond later. "I said MIGHT!" I shouted, but it was too late: no amount of back-peddling on my part would stop the firestorm of curiosity my words had stoked. "I can't say for sure, could have been a trick of the light or something!"

Bouncing off the couch, she fished in one of the side table drawers, coming up with a small flashlight a few seconds later. Then she was in my face, grinning like a mad woman.

"You don't really *believe* that do you?" The flashlight clicked on. "Look up." I did as instructed, and she proceeded to blind me in the name of science.

"But other than the skin crawlies, I haven't felt anything else this whole time we've been talking about Leilani's death. You'd think I'd feel some kind of strong emotion coming from her if she was in me."

"She might not be...anymore...or maybe she comes and goes? Have you tried calling her up, like an emotion?" Still probing my eyeballs, she pulled my brow up and shifted her angle of approach, correcting my head to look straight when I tried to follow her movements.

"I did have a one-sided conversation with...my hand..." I shot it an accusatory look. "It wasn't very talkative."

"Well..." She turned the light off, but her emotional brightness remained at stadium levels. "...give it a try." It didn't take long for my pupils to return to normal and for my best friend to spot the strain in them. Guilt replaced curiosity as the dominant emotion and she slid off the couch.

"Alright, but do me a favor and shoot me if I try to hurt you...or me...okay?" My tone was light, though I wasn't really joking.

"You want me to *shoot* you to stop you from hurting your-self?" Kayla gave me the side eye as she picked up her back-pack and took out Ma's handgun. Without fail it would have been locked back in its case when Ma was home, but with everything going on, making sure she didn't get caught borrowing Ma's gun without permission just wasn't the priority it had once been.

"Don't just stand there pointing out flaws in my logic," I scolded, assuming the lotus position and pointing to the far end of the living room. "Stand over there...by the window." That would put the maximum distance between us, while still giving her line of sight.

In my mind's eye I pictured Leilani as she'd looked in the bathroom mirror the day we met. *Leilani...come to me.*

Leilani...

I fished inside myself for the particular blend of relief she'd brought me that day. Relief at not only being seen, but understood.

Leilani...let me help you. With each new inquiry, I grew a little more entranced by the flow and feel of the emotional soup within me. It wasn't long before I was lost in the fun of combining different feelings together, and briefly tasting the result before letting it swirl back into the primordial pool. Pride mixed with relief, envy with amusement, disquiet with enlightenment; I was like a kid with a set of finger paints...or a mustard container.

What am I doing in here?

Oh yes, Leilani...

She's not in this inner acid trip.

My one-woman séance is a bust.

My eyes fluttered open. Instead of a gun pointed at my head, as I'd half expected, Kayla's phone blinked its red eye at me.

"I swear to God I thought you were gonna start speakin' in tongues any minute." She was wild with amusement, fear, and relief. "I didn't know it was possible to contort your face into some of the expressions you made!" Her laughter was contagious. In between bouts of hysterics, I explained the emotional combinations I'd been trying out as she played the video back at various speeds, pausing at the most unflattering moments for us to roll off the couch, clutching our sides and gasping for breath.

"How do you do it?" she asked, when we'd finally gotten a hold of ourselves. I was lying sprawled out on the floor, half dead from lack of oxygen. "How do you know which emotions you're messing with when you aren't actually letting them in to feel them?"

I thought about it for a while, filling and finishing a tall glass of milk before answering from the kitchen, "What does the color blue look like to a blind man? My emotion sensors just activate...like retinas do. And once that happens there's an immediate association in my mind and heart with the emotion, at least now that I know what I'm 'looking' at. It used to be a lot more blurry in the beginning. So, I do always kind of feel everything but it's like seeing a picture of the green hills of Ireland, rather than being there and feeling the grass beneath your feet. If I open up and let any emotion in, it gets infinitely more vivid. The difference between looking at a photo of a color palette and coating yourself in a bucket of paint. If any of that makes sense?" I wiped away a sizable milk mustache with the sleeve of my shirt.

"Yeah actually..." Kayla grew pensive, biting her bottom lip as though she were working up the courage to say something. "Do it to me."

"Oh baby, you know just what to say to get me into the mood." My eyebrows raised, winning me a devilish smirk from her.

"And you're dead sexy with that milk mustache of yours," she replied. I ran my sleeve over my upper lip until she gave me a thumbs up. "Just be gentle...it's my first time." Her manner was coy but inside...terror pulsed, bleeding onto her courage and burning chunks of it away like acid.

"No it isn't. I've been wrappin' you 'round my finger since way back when." I laughed, hoping to set her at ease.

"Only by my design." She winked at me, her terror cooling down a notch to fright, one of her favorite emotions. That made me feel better too.

"Alright, but you should sit down and brace yourself, it can be disorienting." She bounced back on the couch without a moment's hesitation. "I'm gonna calm you down some." The confidence in my voice served to settle her nerves a fraction more. And then her anxious, fearful excitement became my anxious, fearful excitement as I opened myself up to her.

It was like trying to count the spots on the sun using only your eyes. I had to keep looking away or risk burning something out within me. I groped around and hit a wall, a one way event horizon; she could shine out, but I couldn't reach in.

What in the—? This is amazing…but why can't I…

Why can't I?

Am I stuck here? Burned in place, like an etched shadow in the wake of an atomic bomb?

My emotional, lead-lined air lock slammed shut, the wheel spinning…spiraling tightly in place. My eyes shot open, and it was cold, cold enough that I might see my breath, but no vapor cloud hung before me. The couch was damp beneath my legs, drenched in sweat, as though I'd just gotten out of the shower and sat down without bothering to grab a towel.

Kayla's eyes were closed and, after I'd blinked at her for thirty seconds or so, she said in all innocence, "I'm ready, whenever you are."

CHAPTER TWENTY-SIX

"Good to know that when you become a super villain I'll be able to stop you." This was all my smart ass best friend had to say to me after I explained what happened when I tried to control her emotions. After the obvious punch to my gut that had come with realizing I couldn't dial her down like I'd hoped, she was immediately trying to pick me back up.

And you know something? It worked.

Chuckling, I gave her a shake of my head. "Stop me? It'll be your plans we're carryin' out."

"This is all new—give yourself a break and some time to get used to it before you go directly into the boss battle." She winked at me. "I'm the boss, in case you didn't catch that." Joking aside, she couldn't hide the flood of relief that had come when I'd told her I couldn't get through.

She adjusted her spot on the couch, evincing an ear piercing squeak, and leaned forward. "I didn't feel anything on my end...but you've gotta remember that I'm all kinds of bull stubborn...so it could be as simple as that." Her eyes followed the cows through the window as they mulled about near the fence some twenty yards off. "Go practice on the cattle...urm...'cept Selene...wouldn't want to give her a still-birth or somethin'." She paused, chewing her lip. "Best to stay away from pregnant women altogether while we're figurin' all this out."

"I could feel two sets of emotions around Selene yesterday, so that was cool. Then the rest of the herd came over expecting some lovin' from me and mom and baby mixed in with the rest. I'm gonna do that—practice with the cows and the horses—it's a good idea." Waking up the computer, I checked the time. "Speaking of, I should probably get going soon, I've got to stop back at my house to get my boots that I forgot to pack."

Kayla nearly choked on her next words. "You need to call in! It's been one hell of a day, your brain's still processing everything...shit *my* brain's still goin' haywire! And you, you need to relax some, especially before you battle with your mother again."

"The ranch is actually the best place for me, the horses make me feel at ease and free, and I can get some practice in, and keep my mind on somethin' else while exhausting my body. That's what I need right now."

Kayla's eyes held me for a long while, as though if she were to take them from me, I might disappear entirely. "Alright, but take my truck, that way if you need to leave at any time you can. I don't wanna lose any time opening this up to the paranormal community." Her arms wrapped around me and I winced, teetering on the edge of emotional heatstroke. I'd been too close to her for too long.

"You master the how of things, and I'll get to the why." She pulled back and smiled sweetly. "Teamwork."

My mind jumbled and, though I knew I replied, the next thing I fully remember was turning the key in her ignition for the—how many times had I turned it? *Curious...*

Was it really such a good idea that I drive? The fine stylings of Mushroom Beard and a cigarette later, and I made my retreat from the light of the Willows to the darkness of my house.

The note I'd left for Mother was still jammed in my bedroom door, wholly undisturbed from that morning. How long did my control over her last, anyway? When I'd made myself happy, I'd needed to do several touch ups as time went on, but maybe since apathy was my mother's preferred state...next to arrogance, of course...that changed the equation? Then again, I liked being happy and optimistic so my theory might have had some flaws in it.

I would have felt better seeing another note from my mother, or a text or even something spelled out in alphabet cereal letters, but the counter was empty. Tonight, getting home right after work would have to be a priority, not because I was looking forward to the confrontation, though in truth, part of me was, but in the name of science. In the name of understanding this new ability, and what, if any, boundaries there were with it. That meant no date night with Daniel...sacrifices had to be made. Opening my phone, I smiled at his last message before calling him on the way out my door.

"Daniel's barbeque and cemetery. You kill 'em, we grill 'em. Home of the midnight red-line special. Looks like I'm out back payin' my respects to dear grandma-ma so you'll need to leave a message."

Still laughing after the beep, I said, "Rapunzel is free from her tower and about to run wild at work. I'm afraid you'll have to pull your own hair tonight, I've got a wicked witch to melt."

~

Apparently not content with my reality, Daniel was leaning against Trevor's truck when I pulled into the parking lot of the Gelding and tried to put a temperamental Green Goblin into park. With a wry smile he walked over to my open window, watching as I struggled for the better part of a minute before speaking in a contemplative tone. "When'd you get your license?"

"It's a work in progress." Was it really a lie with such an obvious bullshit grin topping it off? *Oh, the prayer! How could I have forgotten?* Making the sign of the cross, I recited the first one that came to mind in a passably Irish accent: "May you be in Heaven two hours b'for the devil knows you're dead." The Goblin responded to my attempt by making a shrill clanking sound and rolling forward until I slammed on the brake again. *Shit. Did I get the inflection wrong?*

With a shake of his head, Daniel smirked. "Put it in neutral." As I finished doing so, he reached through the window and pulled the keys from the ignition. His eyes locked on mine, breath so close my temperature rose a few degrees. "Don't take your foot off the brake pedal." He backed out of the window, pocketed the keys, and produced a crescent wrench from his side pocket before disappearing beneath the truck.

How would Kayla feel about Daniel exorcising her truck? Honestly, her feelings about him were all over the place. When I'd told her about the beast I'd seen in his eyes she'd shocked me by saying, "Probably just his sex drive...for some reason you're seeing it in his eyes rather than feelin' it empathically. Maybe you just feel him different...like me."

"So I finally hand you somethin' actually questionable about Daniel, and that's all you've got?" My voice was light and teasing but there was no small amount of surprise in it.

"If anything, this makes me trust him slightly more... slightly mind you. It's typical guy behavior at least. There's still something about him I just don't like...but I'm willin' to admit that I might just be a bit rationally overprotective of you."

"You mean irrationally..."

"I *know* what I said." She was over-the-top haughty in her response. "Still don't like him keepin' you out so late."

"What if I'm compelling him to do that, too? What if I've enthralled him to me without realizin' it?"

"Don't see him for a few days and see how fast he starts stalkin' you," she had said...and now here he was in the belly of her truck after I'd told him he would need to pull his own hair tonight.

"Pull the shifter over 'til it's flush with the 'N.'" Daniel's muffled voice reverberated from underneath the truck, breaking me from my memories. The shifter lilted to one side, having been completely loosened, and without thought I did as requested. "Now, hold her firm and steady." The whole truck swayed a little with the final tightening motions. My mechanic crawled out from the underside of the truck and came back over to my window, holding out the keys. "Start her up and put her in park."

Guided by my hand, the shifter slid easily into park for the first time in six months. "And that..." I paused for emphasis, turning to him with a gigantic smile on my face. "Is how you exorcise a truck." Reaching through the window, I brought him in for a mammoth victory kiss.

"Helps to have such a beautiful assistant." Daniel returned my affection with equal vigor while clicking the driver's side door open. He pulled away from me just long enough to let the door swing open between us, playfully pushing me further inside the truck with each intense caress that followed. Bouts of mischievous laughter erupted from us both with each advance until at last I lay prone beneath him. In the waning seconds I was allowed access to my brain, serious thought was given to calling in sick, and spending the rest of the evening letting Daniel be in control of everything I was feeling.

Thank goodness he hadn't gotten my message...

All the days, not inconsiderable troubles, ceased under his touch.

What empathy?

What dead girl?

What's sticking into my back?

Who cares? There's only the here and now.

And…that upside down horse nostril?

Jigsaw gave us each a thorough sniffing before exploring the rest of the truck's cabin, at least the parts she could reach. I stopped kissing Daniel and my eyes spanned first to her, and then to the rider on her back. Kamrie grinned down at me, knowing full well she was interrupting and not caring one lick. "This your truck?" she asked.

Daniel kept right on nuzzling into my neck as I responded; no attempt was made to move, or hide what we'd been doing. "No, I'm…" Daniel bit my neck and I swallowed hard. "…Borrowing it from a friend."

"Oh. Good! I was gonna have to start questionin' what it is I pay you if this was the best ya could afford." My boss laughed, more than a little twinkle bouncing in her eye.

"She's well loved." I shrugged.

"That explains what's keepin' her together." Daniel gave the cabin a quick once over before returning his eyes to me. "This thing's a death trap. The U-joints are just about corroded through, same with the brake lines."

"And that's bad, right?" Putting the key…or screwdriver in the ignition, gas in the tank, and changing the blinker fluid every five thousand miles summed up my body of car knowledge.

"Only if you want to be able to stop…" A smile slithered across Daniel's face and he jumped me with kisses again. "…Which I don't."

Kamrie didn't much care for what Daniel wanted. Her normally boisterous emotions shifted to displeasure, and the underlying hint of suspicion that had been in the background came riding up to the surface like a bullet train. She frowned down at us, her small frame seemingly larger than life. "You know I got to yammerin' with Allen Clark, he farms taters all 'round these hills, and he was tellin' me 'bout a field o' his a few miles down the way what got all messed with this weekend past. Someone killed a whole heap o' his spuds runnin' their truck through like it was goin' ta supper." It took me a few seconds but I eventually caught on that she was talking about the field Daniel and I had gone muddin' in. She nodded in the direction of Trevor's truck. "Then I got ta rememberin' seein' that white truck covered head ta toe like a piglet's dream that very day and I'm imaginin' that's not by chance."

Daniel propped himself up on his elbows and looked first to Kamrie, then to his friend's truck, and back to Kamrie again, raising an eyebrow just a hair. "You think we went muddin' in *that* thing?" Crisp as an autumn day he laughed, as if what she'd said defied some law of physics. "The U-joints on that piece of shit truck can barely handle this parking lot."

"So who came and dumped a mountain o' mud on the shit pile?" Kamrie, though still suspicious, had cracked a small smile, a growing willingness to trust budding on the outer edges of her emotions.

"Road out to Toddy pond. We're doing some new construction out there and the whole place is a piglet's dream. I may have taken Amy out...for the views..." He raised and lowered his eyebrows at me before focusing back on Kamrie. "I save my muddin' for the second date. Don't want to put all your A-game on the table at the outset." Kamrie burst into laughter, her suspicion slowly dissolving under boisterous admiration.

Daniel slid off me, pulling me up and out of the truck along with him. "But Allen's kind of a dick, you really surprised someone went and ruined his field?"

"True enough," Kamrie said, still chuckling. "He's a right powerful pain in the ass."

Trevor rode up, doing his best John Wayne imperson-ation, which wasn't half bad. "Hey now, that's no way to talk about me when I'm not around." He was an ugly mixture of jealousy and embarrassment that I could have done without.

Jealarrassment?

"You're supposed ta be in the arena doin' laps. What on the greenest earth you doin' out here?" Kamrie's suspicion evaporated, replaced with a strong annoyance that I held both empathy and sympathy for. Daniel had gotten us off the hook, doing with words what I was learning to do with my ability. Squeezing his hand, I gave him a sly smile, letting him know I was impressed with his performance. He returned the smile.

Trevor narrowed his eyes at Nyla, dropping his accent. "Ask her. She apparently likes you all better." This was a case that would get no argument from me; it was objectively true. Nyla didn't care for Trevor any more than, well, any of us, for as near as I could tell.

There was a nauseating, greasy quality to his emotions, especially that underlying dripping arrogance that never seemed to go away—until now. I didn't have to put up with it one minute longer. My mental wall came down and both his and Kamrie's emotions began to blend with my own. Before they could get too entrenched, I reached into Trevor's muck looking for something more light-hearted in nature. It was all so thick, threatening to fossilize me somewhere within if I misstepped. The tip of something lighter, a sort of spirited mischievousness, surfaced and I reeled it up, dousing his jealarrassment, before falling back to my comparatively stable mental ground.

Trevor leaned into Nyla for a moment, as though catching his balance, and she took two steps to the left. I could be relatively certain he wasn't pregnant, right? He sprang up, his eyes fairly bulging from their sockets. Taking command of the reins, he turned his horse around and she whinnied in surprise. "Alright Nyla girl, let's leave some dust trails in that arena!" Trotting off, he called over his shoulder with a shit grin, "Hey Dano! Don't go takin' my truck out muddin' again you asshole!" Having come into the tail end of our conversation with Kamrie, he had to know full well the match he'd thrown behind him.

Kamrie whipped back to us, her anger and suspicion growing by the millisecond and me with my defenses still very much down. Reflexively, I called up the last emotion I'd resonated with, that sense of spirited mischief I'd found in Trevor. It came roaring to the surface within Kamrie, but rather than snuffing out her anger and suspicion it only fanned them both!

Shit! What would that chaotic combination do?

I plunged deeper into the tsunami, grasping around for the right antidote...suspicion's counterpart...um...ummm... trust! Where was it? There, that disheveled thing! Skinny and atrophied, it slipped through my fingers once, twice, three times before breaking the surface, dissolving her suspicion and calming her unpredictable anger. Jigsaw backed up as Kamrie grabbed her mane to steady herself, but had I not been looking for it I wouldn't have noticed that she'd nearly lost her balance. This all happened in a matter of seconds, two, maybe three on the outside.

My teeth ground together and I growled, "Poor choice of words, *Trevor!*"

Daniel's eyes lingered on Kamrie before jumping to his friend. "I'm gonna advance your truck's timing so far you'll see Doc Brown on the other side! Jackass!" he yelled over to Trevor who threw his head back and laughed, disappearing through the arena doors.

Kamrie shook her head, her wide, accepting eyes searching mine. In that moment I could have told her that

Allen Clark was the secret love child of Bat Boy and Sasquatch and she'd have taken it as gospel. My mental wall clicked back into place and I flooded out my anger with a nice sense of calm. Grabbing Daniel's arm, I cocked my head, smiled, and said in a haughty, unamused tone that held the force of my ancestors before me, "If you'd have taken me muddin' on our first date there wouldn't have been a second." Some of that wayward mischief might have still been hanging about. It was pretty sticky stuff…

Now it was Daniel's turn to give my hand a squeeze and an approving kiss on the lips.

"Truth of it is, if I'd have had the time I might have done the job myself," Kamrie confessed with a chuckle. "We had an easement agreement when we first bought this place, meant he could come traipsin' through here whenever he took ta fancyin' it. But God smiled down on me, He did, and chance came ta me ta change those official records such that I wouldn't have that headache no more. Weren't precisely legal, but that's between us and the fencepost. Even with it all he calls me up from time to time like we're ol' friends o' some persuasion." It all almost croaked out of her; this wasn't something she'd shared with many people, if any. Daniel and I shook our heads and laughed along with her. "Anyway," she continued, "Amy girl, I got somethin' I want ya ta get ta workin' on in stable five. Come over that way after you wrap things up here." She nodded to each of us in turn and signaled Jigsaw to canter off toward the stables.

I breathed out, long and slow. It had all worked out—by the skin of my gnashing teeth—but here I was, gradually coming back to myself after only a short trip away. "Well, I *was* thinkin' of callin' in sick and havin' some fun with you… but I've been spotted, so…" My hands trembled as I took out a cigarette and lit it up. "Besides, these things are expensive, gotta pay for 'em somehow."

Daniel took it from me after a single puff. "So quit." With

a flick of his finger, the cigarette broke in two and sailed to separate corners of the parking lot.

The brief thought of life without them, especially given how much my abilities were changing, put a maniacal spin on my ensuing laugh that was just this side of disturbing. "Uh...no. Nope. Not going to happen." After manipulating not one, but two sets of emotions, having a smoke was just above breathing on my hierarchy of needs scale. Food came in a distant second, and I was famished.

"I bet you taste even better without them." Pulling me tightly to him by my waist, his mouth brushed over mine and he nibbled my bottom lip. I'd have bitten him back, but wasn't so sure I could stop myself from actually taking a chunk out of his flesh, ravenous as I was.

The pack of menthols was still in my hand, which now rested near the small of his back. As we kissed I removed another cigarette, turning away from him just long enough to place it between my lips. "But then I'd all kindsa be in a straitjacket, so..." With an impish gleam in my eye, I lit it up and took a defiant, victorious hit.

Daniel watched my every movement, almost as though it were the first time he was seeing me. A smile haunted his lips as he licked them. "You'd look all kindsa nice in restraints." Chuckling lightly, he nuzzled my neck.

"You know...it's an acquired taste. If it bothers you...you could start yourself." I lifted his head from my neck with my free hand, enveloping him in a kiss that sent smoke unerringly down into his lungs. Without disengaging from me, smoke came pouring from his nostrils, measured and controlled, as though breathing fire were a regular occurrence for him.

His hand ran along my right arm with the same deliberate rhythm of our kiss until he'd relieved me of my cigarette for a second time. "How 'bout a quickie before you go?" His eyes held me while he took one long drag from my smoke. "I'll hold this for you." He was grinning like Loki, and true to his word, he held the cigarette steady while I took another hit. My eyes stayed with his as I bent to one knee, unzipped his jeans, and brought him into my mouth. He continued puffing on my cigarette between moans, and some two minutes later, I swallowed amidst his shudders.

Standing up, I took a sizable hit from the smoke, now a quarter of what it had been, blew out thoughtfully and said, "You keep the rest." I smiled at him as I reached into the truck for my lunch bag, no way were the contents making it until break.

Daniel looked at me as though the semen I'd just taken from him had been weighing on his soul, and he was now lighter for having the burden lifted. "I gotta replace the belt on Trev's truck and then me and him are goin' out shootin', but I'll come back later tonight and give you a tow."

I gave him a passionate kiss while slipping three smokes and a book of matches in his shirt pocket. "You just keep gettin' better and better." My next words were whispered in his ear: "And for the record…you taste even better smoked." Why did I want to addict him to cigarettes? I couldn't rightly tell you, but it sure was a fun little game in the moment.

Sometimes, I'm pretty sure I'm evil.

Chomping merrily on my ham sandwich, the official sandwich of all super villains, I made my way up to stable five.

CHAPTER TWENTY-SEVEN

*K*amrie wasn't in stable five when I got there, so I waited outside the main door…which just so happened to give me a perfect view of Daniel down in the lot, working on Trevor's truck. I allowed myself to get lost in my boyfriend's movements such that I didn't register my boss until she was staring down at him along with me.

"So, you and the Varrick boy, eh?"

My face bore the drunken grin of the hopelessly smitten, and I nodded in reply.

"I recollect him scurryin' about here some eight years on, helped build that second story bit there." She pointed to her house. "Solid work ethic you don't often see in the young… present company exceptin' o' course." Taking a step back from me, her eyes widened, bolts of shock lit up her emotional landscape, though the trust I'd evoked earlier still held precedence. "Christ and the man Jesus girl! You look like you need a breathalyzer afore I can let ya start work!"

My cheeks flushed as I faced her and smiled. "No Ma'am. I'm here."

With a wily grin, she peeked down at Daniel again and shook her head. "He's a heartbreaker that one…you can see it in his eyes. Then again so was my ex-husband, but that didn't stop us from havin' a time while we did." Sour affection percolated inside her, hidden well behind an otherwise wistful smile. "On the bright side, if it tweren't fer my cheatin' ex chasin' small fluffy things down big, honkin' holes, I wouldn't have all the splendor you see before ya now...so ya see, sometimes it all works out fer the better." Kamrie was sadistically proud, coming in close to whisper to me, "And now you know why I named my business after a castrated male horse."

Some of her sadistic pride filtered into me, escaping in the form of a villainous laugh. "I didn't notice. But I have a new favorite thing about this place."

The boss lady cackled along with me. "You aren't alone. Not many people know what a gelding is. Even after stallin' here a time. Hilarious, I tell ya!" Her voice lowered again and I caught a wink. "It'll be our secret." Folding her arms, she watched Daniel digging around in the truck bed before speaking again. "Still, I don't want to see you get hurt. I've got a granddaughter 'bout your age I never see. You remind me of her, point of fact. Hell, I almost didn't hire you because of it."

"Why? Is she a slacker?" I asked, rubbing the back of my neck.

Conflict rose within her, fear and vulnerability that were fast eroding the trust I'd sown. I couldn't do this...I shouldn't do this...waylaying her suspicions to get Daniel and I off the hook was one thing...but that was over now...I didn't need it to remain any longer. Then again, Kamrie was always pushing down her emotions beneath layers of boisterousness and a ruthless work ethic...it might do her some good to get things out...

I met with resistance this time, pulling her trust up through the rapidly drying cement around it, but I won out in the end.

"I didn't want the painful reminder." The hurt in her eyes brought tears to mine. "She lives out in northern California with my daughter. I ain't seen her in goin' on four years now."

"Why not?"

"Truth be told I'm a right stubborn bitch who don't know when to leave well enough alone. I didn't agree with her life-style choices, and she was always a daddy's girl. She blamed me for pushing Richard away...can't take an oath this minute it's a lie, either. I'm controllin' and a stick o' dynamite to handle. Same thing that keeps this place goin' so well pushed her far enough away. If I'd dedicate half this much time toward my relationship with her...thing is...and just between you, me, and the wall if ya please...I'm just as glad not havin' her in my life. I could use without the drama."

"I just thought drama was part of a normal moth-er/daughter relationship."

"Nah, ya get ta my age and it's enough. Only so many years and I'd rather they be in happiness o' some sort."

"Happiness is a straitjacket," I mused.

Narrowing her eyes, she pointed her finger at me. "That... that was the other thing I was thinkin' for ya with them googly doe-eyes o' yours." We both laughed, the last of our tension lifting with each short breath. She shook her head as though clearing her thoughts. "Come on, let's get ta dressin' Frodo's wound already, he's waitin' on us."

Frodo was an Appaloosa stallion, with the spots of a Dalmatian dog, who'd been injured two days ago out in the pasture. It wasn't unusual for horses to find trouble, even on the best tended fields. The added responsibility of learning equine medical care, after only being employed for a few weeks, made me giddy. That she trusted me enough to—oh...wait...of course she trusted me, I hadn't given her much of a choice had I? Still, I knew I could handle it and handle it I did. When she was satisfied with the wrap job

I'd done on my third try, she handed me the medical box and told me to go do the same thing to two other horses with similar injuries. She had to go make a jockey out of Trevor.

I'd take dealing with festering wounds over that any day.

My veterinary adventures taught me two things: the usefulness of duct tape has no bounds, and horses aren't the least bit interested in my emotion swaying. Though subdued, I could sense the basic emotions of each horse, but when I tried to pull any particular feeling to the surface it simply dissolved back into the animal. It was like trying to hook a cloud. It stood to reason—if such a thing was allowed to still exist in my world—that if the horses couldn't overwhelm me, no matter how many were around, they must not be entirely on the same wavelength.

So much for training my vicious attack ferrets...I'd have to do *that* the old fashioned way.

Nevertheless, I got the confirmation I was seeking from both Trevor and Kamrie. Mother wasn't the only one I could affect, though she would forever be among the most gratifying.

When I signed out for the night there were three sets of headlights in the lot: two trucks and a sedan. I'd only made it through one chorus of "Please don't be Mother" in my head before her overly jovial voice dominated the air.

"Well, well, what happened here? Besides Karma?" She fixated first on Kayla's truck, and then on Daniel who was unrolling a thick red strap from the back of a black truck I hadn't seen before. A small lift protruded from the back of it, propping up the Goblin on its hind wheels, helpless as a newborn calf. An embarrassing amount of rust lay scattered throughout the gravel underneath.

"There need to be anything else?" Daniel flashed a grin at Mother and her arousal blind sided me just as I entered her range. There were some *serious* hazards to my empathy that wouldn't cross the minds of the casual observer. Christ on a stick!

"Serves the little bitch right." Mother laughed before squinting at Daniel as though she were seeing him now for the first time as something other than a background tow truck driver. "You been seeing my daughter, Amy?"

He secured the left front wheel to the lift, partially drowning out his response through the ratcheting echoes that accompanied it. "Depends on who's askin'."

"Her mother," she said flatly, her arousal vanished, replaced by familiar bitter indignance.

My courageous boyfriend gave a final tug on the strap, catching my eye with a smirk as I walked out of the shadows. "Oh. Then definitely not."

"This keeping her out until after midnight business is over with." Her words were a non-negotiable treaty.

For five of the longest seconds of my life, Daniel stared over at her as though she'd genuinely lost her mind. When he spoke it was with slow, deliberate, authoritative tones. Each word seemed to carry the weight of a punch to the gut, as though what he was laying down should have been as obvious as the night was dark. "Six-teen years to build up trust and a rapport with your daughter, and *you* can't control her." His arm slipped around my waist just as he relieved me of my newly lit cigarette. "*What* makes you think I have a chance in hell of making Amy here do anything she doesn't want to after only *one week*?" He took a quick hit before waving the cigarette wildly in the air, a touch of jubilance returning to him. "You see what happened to *me* when I tried to get her to stop smoking."

With a playful smirk he brought the cigarette back to my lips and I politely obliged his request, kissing him on the cheek before turning to my mother and blowing smoke in her direction. Daniel touched his cheek, acting comically drunk from the show of affection. He stumbled backwards, doing a calculated roll over the tow bar before swooping a second strap from the back of the truck as though that had been his plan all along...which it likely had.

I was afforded a few moments of laughter, and then Mother's delayed spike in anger brought me crashing back to the situation at hand. She was only now processing what he'd said to her. The same speech that set her blood to boiling empowered me, and I responded with a little more snark than was probably healthy for me. "Yeah Mother, I do have a mind of my own you know."

I did...didn't I?

Yes.

If anything, I had more than one.

"Oh, the existence of your mind isn't what's in question here. It's the quality of the contents." She shot a look at me that could have bled mice. "*Get* in the car."

I went to take a drag from my absent cigarette and shook the cobwebs from my brain. "You really think me getting into a car with you is a good idea? After last night?"

"I can't keep doing this Amy." My mother rubbed at her temples. "Just *get* in the car. I've got enough on my plate without you pulling this nonsense."

Ironically, her apathy fought me on its way to the fore-front of her mind. "Then just stop worrying about me at all." Some of her anger boiled into me and I choked it down through clenched teeth. While she was holding onto the steering wheel for balance, I dug around for her trust.

Eww...was that it? It couldn't be. How was I supposed to get in there?

Imagine attempting to pull open a rusty old chest that's been at the bottom of the ocean for centuries, covered with muck, barnacles, and unidentifiable sludge, all while fully submerged yourself and holding your breath. Try as I might I couldn't pry it open, but I did loosen chunks of something like acceptance in the process, and that would have to do.

"I've got all this, okay?" I said, as quick and matter of fact as I could muster. "I'm gonna go in tomorrow, talk with all my teachers and clear some things up. I'll be back on track by the end of the day...you'll see."

For a fisherman's moment, she struggled with the changes I'd brought about, blindly thrashing in search of her comfortable anger and fury. I anchored them each to separate corners of her disturbed psyche and called forth bubbles of soothing calmness. Her eyes closed and she ran her fingertips lovingly over the leather steering wheel. Feeling how locked up she was inside, how crusted over her trust was, broke my heart a little. It humanized her on a level I hadn't even realized was missing. I'd never be able to look at her the same again. She wasn't just a distant, unfeeling ghoul...she was someone who'd been deeply hurt.

Letting the calmness I'd instilled in her wash through me, I placed my hand on her shoulder through the open car window. "It's really not worth getting so upset about...and I'm sorry to make you drive all the way out here...I'll pay for the gas even, but I'm not ready to come home yet. Why don't you go, lay down with some tea and get a good night's rest. Let me take care of my own life." Acceptance had holes in it and was sinking fast, but apathy remained buoyant.

My mother breathed in, with sharp, disappointment-laden apathy. "Fine. Whatever." She pulled away without so much as glancing in my direction. Some twenty yards ahead, where the driveway met the road, the Audi swerved to the side and she threw open her door, immediately retching into the grass.

Sheesh Mother, had giving up control of my life to me been that difficult?

I hadn't made it more than a few reflexive steps in her direction when she just as abruptly slammed the car door shut and took off in a spray of gravel and dust, leaving me staring after her.

"What happened with your mother?" Daniel's warm arms slid around me from behind and he brought my wayward cigarette to my lips a breath later.

With a shaky hand I took it, indulging in the peace it brought, and the silence of his uncomplicated touch. What had happened? How did one answer that question? Exhaling the smoke in a smooth line, I chuckled. "You wouldn't believe me if I told you." Hell...I barely believed me and I'd been there.

Gently, but with purpose, he spun me around to face him, taking my chin between his thumb and forefinger and holding my eyes with something like stern compassion. "Hey. What happened?" Those eyes...I wanted to answer him truthfully, but that would take us down a complicated road at best, one I wasn't ready to walk with him yet.

"I don't wanna get into it right now..." I turned from him, watching the tail lights of the Audi crest a hill and disappear on the other side. Would she be alright to drive home? The first time I'd manipulated her emotions she'd nearly run off the road afterward...

Resting my head on Daniel's chest, I let the solid reality of him bring me firmly back to the moment. After a while I laughed, peering up at him. "You were brilliant with her."

"She doesn't get told off enough. It was my pleasure." He pulled me in for a kiss.

"And you're mine..." I wrapped myself in his embrace and for several minutes we lost our minds together, making our way piecemeal to the side of the black truck. The logo on the door, a stylized shaking fist holding a wad of cash, indicated it belonged to "That Devious Repo Guy." Daniel would later tell me it was his friend Cody's truck, who he sometimes helped with some of his more dangerous acquisitions. But right then, all I cared about was that the hinges on the door worked and it had a spacious interior.

He'd deftly undone my jeans and was beginning to free

them from around my waist when my stomach snarled, bringing me back to my senses. Was that a seat belt buckle embedded in my spine? "Wait…" I breathed out heavily. "Not here…I…not in the cabin of some strange truck."

Daniel pushed himself up, his breathing just as labored, and glanced out the window toward the Goblin. "How 'bout that truck then…it familiar enough?"

Laughing, I playfully shoved him off and rubbed the small of my back. "No…I want my first time to be someplace memorable that doesn't require a trip to the chiropractor the next day."

Daniel mused, "If you don't have to go to the chiropractor, I'm not doin' my job right."

"So, you're not gonna be gentle?" My stomach growled again and I winced at how much of a mood killer it was while simultaneously being grateful for its sobering effect.

"I'm sure we can find some room for gentle somewhere." He took my hand and kissed the back of it before pulling me swiftly on top of him. Another yowl of hunger filled the cabin and the world blurred.

"I don't suppose you have any beef jerky in the glove box?" I grimaced, clutching my midsection.

His little soldier was at the ready, bulging against my sex through the confines of our jeans. My body tingled at the closeness of him. "Not in the glove box…no." He ran one hand up the back of my neck and through my hair, grabbing a handful and bringing me in for a demanding series of kisses. His beast stalked the edges of each one. Damn him… now I was growing faint from lack of air as well as lack of food.

Oh so worth it…

Until you do or say something that isn't you…

Shit. I have a point. This is a good way to wake up covered in blood that isn't mine.

"Mmm…yes but as hungry as I am…" My tone shifted

from sultry to serious as I ran my hand over his bulge, putting some needed space between us. "...I might just take a couple actual bites out of him." I gnashed my teeth together for effect. And you know, in that moment, as I peeled myself from his lap, there was a grisly truth to my words.

Daniel certainly—thankfully—took it that way. It wasn't a chance any guy was willing to take. His eyes went wide and he started the engine without another word, taking off like my mother had a shotgun pointed at us in the rear view mirror. "There's an On The Run down the road a piece. We'll get you somethin' there."

I scored a Choco Taco and nachos and Daniel got a slow, gentle blow job that brought the color back into his blue balls. I'd dodged a bullet in more than one way that night. I'd need to be more mindful going forward.

Only problem was I seemed to be misplacing my mind more and more each day...

CHAPTER TWENTY-EIGHT

*M*rs. Randall's chocolate brown ringlets fell over her slumped shoulders while she skimmed through the day's lesson plans, presumably waiting for the bell to ring. Her emotions were as sleepy as she looked, so I used the opportunity to approach her and make my case for leniency. "Mrs. Randall?" I asked, pulling her trust up to the surface without an ounce of difficulty. She straightened up to my level with a small smile of acknowledgment.

I continued, "I've been…how do I say this…going through some stuff the last few weeks and haven't really been all here." Her sympathy came without coaxing and she nodded. "Well, I was kinda hoping you could take that into measure when coming up with my final grade. I mean, you know I'm a solid C in anything I put my mind to…it's just my mind hasn't been on biology for a while." Well, not THIS type of biology anyway, but that little factoid wouldn't help any, so I left it to rattle around my brain.

"I remember what it was like to be your age Amy—I can give you several make up essays to write that can get you back up to speed."

Make up work? Oh no, that wouldn't do at all. "Thing is… I don't have time to make up every class like that while still dealing with what I have going on behind the scenes. I was hoping you could just give me the C that you know I would otherwise be getting…"

Incredulity came screeching forward, nearly overtaking the trust and slicing sympathy in two. Shit! Why the hell did she have to be so stubborn? Her eyes narrowed, gaze piercing into me…did she know I was messing with her? Trust wasn't enough this time; I'd have to find something else. But what?

Compassion?

Fondness?

Adoration?

Curiosity?

Damn it! They were all slipping through her mind like a fetal pig liver through my fingertips.

"I'm sorry, Amy." She shook her head, leaning against the table and taking in a slow, deep breath. "What—what are you asking me for?" Confusion coated all her emotions now and they each crumbled as I touched them.

Had I broken something?

Burned her out?

Taking a small step backwards, I pulled out of her emotions, heat rising in my head. "Um…sometimes I might need your understanding in being able to run to the lady's room is all." Her emotions shifted to fill in the cracks, with sympathetic annoyance bobbing up as the predominant, if busted, emotion.

Her tone was curt when she turned toward me again. "Yes, of course. If you'll excuse me I think I need to do the same." She left the class room without saying a word to the other students, who weren't really paying attention anyway. I took my seat behind Mr. Skullhead and devoured a candy bar. Manipulating people was clearly more of an art than a science, and here I was drawing vague and nightmarish stick figure people. Would I ever be Monet?

Five minutes later Mrs. Randall was back, her emotions lay beneath a relaxing haze that matched the bloodshot look in her eyes and pleasant earthy smell that accompanied her. While the rest of the class learned about the amazing, mind-blowing nature of stem cells, I wrote what I intended to say to my other teachers, alongside a list of possible emotions that could get me the desired result.

Did I really want to make all my teachers be in love with me? That seemed to be the quickest route to get what I wanted, but had all the makings of a cheesy supernatural sitcom.

It was only temporary…right?

Only one way to find out.

I slipped out of biology early to be sure to get to geometry class before anyone else. In her confused and high state, Mrs. Randall didn't notice. The other kids, as I've mentioned, didn't want to mess with my level of crazy, so all I got was a few blank stares and some slight fear/revulsion as I slunk past. Given my new abilities there was something to be said for the wisdom of that approach.

Mr. Clazmer, and his enormous gut, were erasing the evidence of their last torture session when I walked in. All my carefully laid out mental notes fell into the pit of my stomach. I needed to calm down, and so, one such thought later, I did. Manipulating my own emotions was already becoming second nature.

The dry eraser soaked up the excess sweat in my palms as I joined Mr. Clazmer in his never-ending ritual, to which he replied, "Erasing my boards is not going to help you learn what you need to know Amy, not as woefully far behind as you are."

The ungrateful sot.

We'd see how smug he was when I made him adore me.

Adoration was on the safer side of infatuation...not quite so homicidally prone, so I would start with that and...and...and where were his emotions? He was a wasteland, with not so much as a crumb of arrogance to work with. I couldn't feel his emotions, and I couldn't manipulate what I couldn't feel! The eraser dropped from my hand with a soft thump, and I marveled at him in all of his beautiful, perilous, silence.

"That's no reason to throw things on the floor." He scowled at me, finishing off the top of a pyramid and waddling back to his desk. How in the gates of Christmas Past hadn't I noticed before now? He typed something into his laptop, pudgy fingers eclipsing each key as he went. "There isn't enough extra credit in all of geometry to get you back up to speed before the end of the semester. You were barely pulling a C minus before your absences and that's going to bite you."

"How did you—"

"I've been a teacher for thirty-five years, Amy, no one ever comes to my class early and helps out unless it's about their grades." He clicked the program off as other students shuffled in. That was how I hadn't noticed his emotional silence until now. Each student who filled the class diluted their emotions into the next, making it hard for me to tell where any particular feeling was coming from. He had always been within the bubble of the other students. "Unless you can manage to give me nothing but *A* work from now until the end of the semester, you will be seeing me in summer school." With unfocused eyes, I picked up the fallen eraser and wiped away the end of an arrow, taking my seat as another student walked up to him.

I'd come in prepared to rip his heart out and serve it to him raw, and now mine lay prone on a platter before me. There was a sick kind of justice in there somewhere. On the plus side, I'd learned something huge while my pride was being trounced: Daniel wasn't alone. He wasn't the only one I couldn't feel. Now, as to whether or not that made Mr. Clazmer an alien, that much I still didn't know. But anyone steeped in that much math wasn't making a good case for being human.

I rode out the class, hopelessly lost in the language of theorems while decorating the circles on my worksheet to look like Pokeballs, and the rectangles like Charazards. They weren't even especially good drawings; Mr. Clazmer wouldn't give them an A.

～

"It explains everything!" My best friend took a bite of her cafeteria fiestada, bits of grease dribbling down her chin. If we had to be stuck at school for lunch we could do worse than Fiestada Friday. The weather was even nice enough for us to sit outside, under the shade of an elm tree with "FK + JV Forever" hacked prominently into it. "He's a sadist and a sociopath! That's why you can't feel or affect him!"

"I'll just have to keep tryin', that's all. You can damn sure bet I won't be spending my summer in this prison." I started in on my second fiestada, having devoured the first by the time we got to the end of the lunch line. The food and conversation were already making me feel better about my situation. "But you know this means Daniel isn't the only one I can't feel anymore."

"You gonna insta-love on Mr. Clazmer now?" Kayla teased.

"If I thought it'd get me out of summer school…" I gave her a mischievous grin.

"Ewww! God, Amy!" She scrunched her face. "Don't put that image in my head!" Rubbing her temples with vigor she repeated, "Delete! Delete!"

"Math, science, history, unraveling the mystery…" I sang, and she cupped her hands over her ears, falling backwards into the stubby grass. Taking a big bite of my fiestada, I continued with my mouth full, "Maybe some people just have a wall up that I can't get through for whatever reason. I'll just take a chisel to Mr. Clazmer's every day until I get through."

"You'll have to be in class every day for that to work," Kayla taunted from her itchy grass stronghold.

"Why you gotta point out the flaws in my plan?" I peered down at her. "Now it's a challenge. Mmm...'cept I can't even see the wall to know where to chisel. That could be a problem."

"You could practice on Daniel," she threw in.

"Are you granting me permission to hang out with him?" My snide look was a thing of beauty.

Uncomfortable laughter rolled out of her. "Since when do you need my permission?"

"It'd be nice...just like he's been to you. He didn't *have* to offer to fix the Goblin and he sure as shit didn't need to bring us both to school this mornin'."

Laying there, she took out her phone and flipped through it. "I don't know, I just don't trust him...maybe I got empathy for sociopaths as my power or something? I don't like Mr. Clazmer either."

"No one likes Mr. Clazmer." I rolled my eyes at her, asking my phone, "Am I dating a sociopath?" and souring my lips at the first result—*If you have to ask, you are.*

Glaring at my phone, as though a mere look from me would cause it to repent, I laughed in resignation. "It would figure he'd be a sociopath...I'm really into him."

"Mr. Clazmer or Daniel?" Kayla sat up with all the devils of Ireland in her eyes.

After giving her the smile she'd earned, I shoved her back down and clicked on one of the websites, reading it aloud in one long tirade. "'Seven signs you're dating a sociopath. Number one: they blame others for their failures.' Well the other night he did blame that gnome for the pool incident. But so did I so... 'Two: They lie.' So do I and so do you. Next. 'Three: They lack empathy.'" I laughed. "This is not me, and just last night he wanted to know what was up with me and Mother, so that's a big no. 'Four: Lives life on the edge, without fear.' Hmm…kinda like breakin' into haunted buildings at night?" My gaze fell on Kayla just long enough for my point to take root before I continued, "'Five: They're irresponsible.' He's on time and at work every day, no matter how irresponsibly late I keep him out. Unlike a certain someone who is going to have to whore herself out to pass geometry…" When I looked at Kayla this time, we both cracked up laughing, and my hand accidentally slid into the sour cream. I wiggled my fingers, which sent us into a second bout, only subsiding when I'd wiped the last of the cream onto my fiestada shell.

Through the aftershocks of spent laughter, I went on, "'Six: They have no real friends.' Him and Trevor seem close enough, and he has another friend, Cody, who lets him borrow his repo truck on a moment's notice. Only real friends loan their trucks to each other." My smile was its own kind of magical candy factory.

Kayla sat up again, carefully pulling a twig from her hair. "Yeah, and you bring it back to me all busted up. You didn't say the prayer right, did you?"

In my best Irish accent, I recited, "May your socks be filled with squid, and your ears with kindling?" She shoved me back onto the grass next to her, but I kept reading. "And finally, 'Seven: He's charming and sexually charged.' Guilty as sin on this one. Lock him to my bedpost and throw away the key." I closed the browser and tossed my phone into my purse. "According to the internet we're *all* sociopaths. Lovely. I'm not sure if I feel better or worse after reading that."

Kayla looked down at me and snickered. "I think it might be a little more complex than the seven click-bait signs of

Buzzworldz.com." At least, I think that's what she said—I could barely hear her over the crunch of my third fiestada. Studying me for a moment, as if through glass, she went on, "You know, someone on the forum asked if I was eating more when I used my abilities...I blew it off but maybe I shouldn't have?" My mouth was too full to talk, but I nodded in response.

She'd posted bits of my story as though she were the one going through it. Mainly this was done as a paranoid precaution, to protect my identity, but there was part of her that reveled in the spotlight and wished all this was happening directly to her.

I didn't wish that. If one of us had to be thinking straight I was glad it was the arrow in our duo and not the curly straw.

My best friend leaned against the tree and sighed. "I haven't gotten as many responses as I was hoping for, just a bunch of people with empath stories that are nothing like yours. General feelings of unease around others, or the inability to handle being around people with obviously intense emotions that none of us like, that kind of thing. I started up a few friendships with some of Leilani's friends on Baseline. I'm still feelin' them out, but I'll get 'em to talk, don't you worry."

"I'm more worried for them," I said, dryly. "They were her friends, what do you expect them to know about all this?" The final bite of that fiestada was savored for the nectar of the gods it was.

"They might not know what they know until I know they know it."

I blinked at her.

"Well, one of us understands, so for now that'll do." She stood, dusting herself off and peering into the distance. "I wanna go back out to that barn. I should be getting my thermal camera in the mail tomorrow. I'm gonna have to return it and get the money back, but we can use it real quick before I do."

I got up, the tiny forsaken brethren of my fiestada falling from my lap into the grass like so much ambrosial ant food. Though I didn't want to go back to the Whitaker barn, I could tell by the look on Kayla's face she'd already set her mind to it. "You gonna finish your peaches?" My foot nudged her plate.

"Is that what those things are? Have at 'em." She rubbed her shoulders.

Short work was made of the collection of jellied sugar that passed for peaches, and I played with the remaining sauce, making swirling patterns. "We should bring Daniel. He'll be able to overpower me if need be."

"Pshh...I can take your punk-ass out," Kayla said with some indignation.

"Hey, I've been buildin' some serious muscle shovelin' shit." I showed off my biceps. "Don't be so sure about that."

"That mean you're gonna tell him everything? I want to be there for it!"

"I didn't say that."

"Amy! He should at least know what he's up against in case you go all Gozer on us."

"I don't think I could pull off the hair." I lit up a cigarette. "Besides...why should he know more than us?"

CHAPTER TWENTY-NINE

*D*aniel's work truck idled in the school parking lot, waiting diligently to take us back to the Willows. A pair of girls I'd seen around but didn't know were talking to him through his driver's side window. The lack of oxygen in their combined brains threatened to asphyxiate us all.

With a growl under my breath, I yanked open the passenger's side door like I meant for it to come off its hinges. I was up and over to his lap in less time than it takes to pull a set of fake eyelashes off, kissing him with slow and sensual grace.

At least, that's how it went in my mind, and he certainly returned the gesture with equal fervor. Lying across his lap and propping my elbows against the driver's armrest, I addressed the girls outside the window: "Hey, I'm Amy."

Disappointment washed through them, though not by my direction, and one Barbie dragged on the arm of the other, saying, "We've gotta go, or we'll be late!" Something told me they would have spent all night by that truck had I not come by, but I just waved the tips of my fingers at them and watched them scuttle away like the crustaceans they were.

"Are you jealous?" Daniel smirked.

"Is there a right answer to that question?" Twisting onto

my back, I looked up at him with feigned innocence. "If I say no, it looks like I don't like you, if I say yes, like I'm insecure...um...so...maybe?"

"Now you're indecisive," Kayla added as she jumped in next to me. I removed myself from Daniel's lap, squeezing into the spot between them.

"Who were they? Just curious. I don't know them." I was totally jealous.

"Makes two of us." Daniel laughed.

"Strange girls always coming up and talking to you?" I asked.

"No, sometimes I go up to them." He kissed me while reaching over and popping the glove box open. Inside sat a box of beef jerky. "Present for you."

My smile lit up the cabin.

"I didn't realize you were religious, Daniel. What denomination are you?" Kayla was looking at his necklace that had popped free of his shirt while he leaned over—a plain metal link chain with a small black cross on it.

He smirked at me. "I've only recently converted. Amysh."

"Oh, you are both goin' to Hell." She rolled her eyes.

Daniel laughed and kicked the truck into gear. "There's a whole heap load of people who've got dibs on my soul before it gets there."

"Like who?" I rested my head against his shoulder. He was cool both in touch and in presence, especially as the inferno that was my best friend blazed on my other side.

"My dad, for one. No way that bastard is lettin' me outta work just for dyin'."

"Aren't you skippin' work right now to come pick us up?" I asked. And he'd surely been late to his job site this morning, having dropped us off far out of his way.

"See how devoted I am to my faith?" He gave me the side eye and I just about melted through the floorboards and out onto Elm Street.

"Who else has dibs?" I wondered.

"I don't know…" His eyes lingered on me as we came to a stop at a red light. "…You're workin' on it."

I'd be damned if there wasn't sincerity in those pupils.

"Am I?" I kissed him, tugging on his bottom lip with my teeth. "Lucky for you I never give up…"

After we'd been on the road a while, Kayla looked up from where she'd been staring out the passenger's window. She'd been silent, focusing on keeping her emotions from flaring and roasting me alive. "You missed our turn. Is this the part where you slash us up into little pieces and throw us into China Lake?" There was an air of comedy to her words that overlaid her constant genuine paranoia.

Daniel rolled with it, smiling over at her with a sigh of mock frustration. "Now you've gone and ruined the surprise. It was gonna be my one week anniversary gift to my lamb-chop here, but now I'll have to think of something else."

"Thanks a lot Kayla! I like China Lake." I bumped her playfully before eyeing Daniel. "Lambchop?"

He held onto his smile and made a sudden hard left, slamming the truck to a halt not two feet from an ornate black iron gate. A set of inviting spikes at the top of each rung looked as though they were waiting for their matching severed heads. The gate was big enough for two cars to drive through side by side, and was attached to a stone patchwork fence that engulfed the property. The effect was new money trying to look old, but time had yet to add its weathered touch.

Daniel got out while Kayla swallowed down a string of cuss words. She quickly repeated her relaxation mantra—which also sounded like cussing, only in another language, before I could be burned too badly. Two cameras were focused on us, with one following Daniel as he hit the intercom button to the left of the gate. "Daniel Varrick, here to see the Chevelle."

"See? Now he's getting me a shovel for our anniversary instead. We can bury the bodies together." My smirk was alive with misguided triumph.

"How romantic…" Kayla unbuckled herself and we took in the McMansion before us with wonder. "Would you look at this place? I bet they have a gold-handled plunger in their bathroom," she said.

"Nah, if it ever clogs up they just throw the whole bowl out and start again." I joined her gawking. We were jarred from our architectural reverie by a bout of unintelligible, crackling speech from the intercom. The gate opened with minimal groaning and Daniel motioned us both out of the truck.

"Why are we looking at a shovel? You aren't actually going to kill us are you?" I asked, sliding down from the driver's side and adjusting my shirt that had ridden up.

Daniel stared at me for a long moment, as if really mulling over my question, or perhaps just trying to decipher what I'd said. "No. Not shovel. Chevelle."

"Oh, good. I don't want a shovel for our one-weekiversary. That's right up there with taking me muddin' for a first date…" This caused the knowing smile to return to his face as we walked inside the grounds. Kayla stayed by the truck, indulging in the paranoid fantasies of one too many Stephen King novels, though weren't we kind of in one already? "What's Chevelle?" I asked, before I could overthink things.

Some twenty yards from us a garage door opened. It was quiet and well oiled in a way I didn't think was possible. In all my years I'd never heard one that didn't creak and grind. A stout man in his fifties with a crew cut and the mangled remnants of a handlebar mustache ducked under the door as it rose. Just the little bit of bending and walking it required had him sweating buckets…of fried chicken, if I had to guess. He wore a perfectly tailored suit that tried to hide each of his physical flaws and succeeded, with the exception

233

of the mustache, which could hardly be considered the suit's fault.

"Hey Mark!" Daniel called in a friendly tone, reaching out and shaking the man's hand. With his free hand, he pointed to me. "She doesn't know what a Chevelle is."

"Well, what've you been doing with her?" Mark asked in a manner that truly questioned Daniel's sanity.

My boyfriend smirked. "Not talking about cars, I can tell you that." At this, Mark's emotions took a turn towards lust. The beef jerky I'd eaten earlier lurched in my stomach. Matters weren't helped any by the scent of his cologne, which could have knocked out a yeti. I was beginning to think Kayla had made the right choice staying by the truck when the garage finished opening, revealing a sleek, shiny purple muscle car with white racing stripes and the letters SS on the front grill. "This is the Chevelle." Daniel grinned back at me before disappearing into the garage.

Mark took the opportunity to launch into a fifteen-minute diatribe about the history of the 1970 Chevy Chevelle. It was the pinnacle of manly, muscle car, muscle-ness. Just looking under the hood would cause your voice to lower an octave; driving it your testicles to drop—whether you had them or not. His model was a prime specimen, one which he faithfully took on the road every weekend. In the background of my torment, Daniel was giving the car a proctology exam. The smell of oil and mothballs mingled with Mark's sweat and misspent youth.

"I like the paint colors," I said, when he'd finally given me an opening.

"Actually, it's oxidizing here and here." Daniel looked over at Mark, and the blow to his ego slammed into my mental wall. His embarrassment and feelings of inadequacy dripped into his lust and excitement, creating something close to confused insecurity.

"I-I don't keep it cooped up in the garage like so many. Car like this is meant to be driven," he stammered.

Daniel's fingers tapped along the top of the open hood. "Let's hear her purr." The air filled with the sound of a revving engine and the scent of spent fuel moments later. Mark's pride grew stronger every time he stepped on the gas, but with each rotation Daniel's frown did the same. His eyes flicked from part to part and he reached in, monkeying with something I couldn't see and wouldn't have understood anyway. After a minute he closed the hood and went over to Mark's side. With some effort the man got to his feet, leaving the car to idle.

The car was a sight to behold, and it wasn't a stretch to understand the attraction—something about it just screamed power and sex appeal. Not unlike Daniel...

Was he my Chevelle?

And so what if he was? I glanced back at Kayla, who was sitting on the hood of Daniel's work truck, hopelessly lost in her phone. When I returned my attention to what my muscle car was up to, I found him in the driver's seat with the door closed, revving the engine himself. "I'm gonna take her out and really open her up," he told Mark, who alternated between being embarrassed and incensed.

"I'll need to go with you." Mark started for the passenger's side.

"I'm leavin' my girls and my truck here. I'll be back." Daniel's tone was calm and matter of fact. With some reluctance, and an uncomfortably long gaze at me during which his lust began to resurface, Mark agreed and Daniel peeled out. We could hear the roar of the Chevelle long after we'd lost sight of him.

"His girls?" Kayla peered at me over her phone when I came walking up to her. "I am *not* 'his girls.'" My girl had an impressive ability to eavesdrop, even at a distance.

"That's alright, I'm not one for sharing."

"He could've told us he was comin' to look at a car."

"Wanna see if the toilet seat is really gold plated?" My attention turned to the McMansion.

"Snowballs will fry before I go in that house."

"Nah, Mark's a pervert, but no more than any other guy. Besides, if he tried anything he'd have a heart attack half way through the attempt."

"We don't know that he's alone here," she said, and the point chilled my blood. The sun washed behind gray clouds and the house took on an ominous charcoal hue.

"You really think Daniel would take us someplace dangerous?" Well, that deflection lasted all of a minute.

"I don't know what to think of him. Sometimes he's cool, but then he pulls arrogant shit like this."

"He's human, Kayla."

"Is he?" she replied in all seriousness.

"I found two other people in eighth hour who I couldn't feel. He and Mr. Clazmer are outliers, but they're not alone."

"Neither were the body snatchers..." Kayla all but whispered.

"I spent all period separating out whose emotions I was feeling. It was a strain, but I can do it." There was some pride in my statement.

"Probably best to keep it all to one giant clusterfuck then. No need to tell who exactly has a boner for who."

"Hmm...you know, everyone I can't feel so far has been a guy."

"Body snatchers have an easier time taking over the simpler mind...maybe that's why they just can't win with you."

I smiled at her compliment for the obvious flattery it was. "So does knowing he's not alone make you feel better about Daniel?"

"No, now I'm disturbed at the possibility that the whole

school is getting overrun with rogue spirits. Maybe you can't feel anyone who's already possessed..."

My mind shot to the beast behind Daniel's eyes. "And what if they are spirits coming in and taking people over? Is it really doing any harm?"

Kayla raised an eyebrow, as though the answer should be self-evident, before reeling it in. "Remains to be seen, I suppose. It explains why Leilani's so solid though, doesn't it? Fills in that piece of the puzzle nicely." A thunderous rumble filled the air, growing louder with each passing second. The Chevelle was returning.

"So now Leilani's a zombie and Daniel's a pod person?" I rubbed my forehead, trying to pin these new theories together with what we already knew, while staving off an impending headache. Did this mean I couldn't trust anyone? Get close to anyone? Did I have to lock myself in a shed now, eking out a meager living selling rancid licorice-based moonshine by night?

Kayla scratched her forehead. "No, they'd both be pods, if this theory holds. No zombies...though it does all claw into some gray territory. What if—"

"I can't get paralyzed by 'what ifs,' Kayla!" I snapped, not so much at her as at the whole damnable situation. "I need to be able to live my life, or I'd rather be dead!"

"God damn it, don't say that!" Kayla jumped up as Daniel pulled in, shouting after him while he passed us, "Do you like your fucking car?! Can we go?!" Tears formed at the edges of her eyes as they met mine. I wanted to hug and comfort her, but she was an emotional sunspot just then.

"I'm s...sorry," I managed.

"No, I know...I know what you mean." She wiped the tears away with her sleeve. "You can't stop livin' your life... someone's gotta feed the chickens. I'm sorry...my head gets away from me sometimes." As much as she was obsessed with it, death was a sensitive topic with Kayla when it came

237

to those closest to her. She was mortally afraid of losing either me, or Ma, like she'd lost her dad. My words had been reckless, and my smile, warm and genuine as it was, did little to fill the silence.

Daniel assessed us both as he walked up to the truck but took the wiser course of not saying anything. He opened the driver's side door and reached under the seat, pulling out a padlocked duffle bag. Our eyes were on him as he hefted it back over to where Mark stood near the gate and placed it gently on the ground.

"There's a bomb in that bag, isn't there? He's going to blow us all up." Kayla looked to me with a smirk, her eyes still glossy.

"Nah. I'm gonna go with puddin'. Either red velvet or banana cream," I said.

Daniel sat on his haunches, thumbed in the combination and removed the lock. Without ceremony he unzipped the bag and stood up, nudging it with his foot while holding Mark's attention. "Twenty-five thousand dollars, cash."

"That'll buy a lot of puddin'." My eyes went wide, a matching shade to Kayla's.

"You got another bag with twenty thousand in that truck?" Mark snorted, and he might have had a heart attack that second by the sound of the wheeze that came out of him. "If not, no deal."

"Car needs work. She can either sit here and *continue* to dry rot, or I can give her new life and you can be twenty-five thousand untraceable dollars richer." Daniel's impish smile, the one I'd grown so accustomed to, had vanished from his face, replaced by the shrewd, flat countenance of a business-man. One who was ready to walk away from the deal if need be and not lose a wink of sleep over it.

Mark, on the other hand, was a bundle of nerves and conflicting emotions, his stubborn pride and bravado cowed and shaken by Daniel's no-nonsense exterior. It was kicking up something in him…something like self-revulsion, shame, or submission. I didn't have all the emotions down yet; there were so many nuances and variations. He sneered at the bag and back at Daniel, his pride rising up along well-worn tracks and encasing his more vulnerable feelings again.

So…I derailed the train.

I took that pride and shooed it off into a corner with a broom, bringing up his more agreeable side instead.

Agreeable—well that would have been a useful emotion earlier in the day, Amy…

Anxiety and panic were pressed into service, and just as Daniel was zipping the bag closed, Mark wiped the sweat from his palms on his sizable belly, sputtering, "Okay! Yes. I'll go get the title." With that, he ran into the house faster than that body was used to moving. At that pace, there might be a 911 call in our future.

Daniel peered after him, and Kayla made a pointing gesture between me and Mark, to which I smiled and nodded.

When she'd finished gaping at me, Kayla turned that look toward the money. "Twenty-five thousand dollars!"

"Can I touch it?" I asked, lighting up a cigarette.

"You don't ever have to ask me that question, the answer will always be yes," Daniel said, deadpan.

My cheeks warmed, and I reached in the bag, flipping through the bound stacks of cash with a giddy squeak.

"Where'd you get that much money?" My best friend would be suspicious of milk from her own goat. In fact, she had been two summers back, but that's another story.

"Took a jackhammer to a couple ATMs." Daniel smiled, squinting in the direction Mark went. "That went smoother than I thought it would." His attention returned to Kayla and me. "You two are more powerful than you know."

That was my cue. I had proof that I'd influenced some-one, and it was confession time. Ugh…why'd I have to think of it like that? Confessions always made my stomach queasy, even when I hadn't done anything wrong. "I may have influenced his mind some…" I looked up at Daniel and tapped a congress of Franklins against my temple. "…With my brain." There was no chance for that sentence to come out sounding anything other than crazy.

"Your brain wasn't what was influencing him." He laughed, putting his whole body into it.

Kayla lit up like she knew the answer to the daily double. "That's why we're here isn't it? Pretty young girls to help cloud his judgment." Her bright eyes shifted into something of a sneer…if eyes can do that.

"Didn't hurt." Daniel smirked at her. "You'll have to drive my truck back to your place. Amy and I'll take my Chevelle and pick up the parts for your relic." He grabbed me around the waist and spun me against the front of the car…his car. "And break it in some." That predatory stare again; the other people whose emotions I couldn't feel…hadn't looked at me this way.

That stare was uniquely his.

My mouth opened to reiterate what I'd said, to make him understand that I'd really done something to Mark, when Mr. Impending Heart Attack came shuffling out with the paperwork in hand.

I returned the Franklins to their cozy lair, zipping them in with their brethren.

As far as the government was concerned, the Chevelle had been sold for one thousand dollars. Kayla and I ran the money up and down our skin as though we were bathing in it, laughing hysterically and inadvertently pushing Mark into lust territory again. Good sport that he'd been, I let him stay there.

Daniel gave Kayla his work truck key. "If you're gonna set it on fire, use the high-octane gasoline, she's particular."

Kayla smiled at him. "Congratulations on the car." Daniel

nodded to her before disappearing into Mark's garage and loading the trunk of his Chevelle up with various odds and ends.

I followed Kayla up to the truck. "Well, I tried to tell him..."

"Is that what that was?" She gave me the eye. "We'll tag team him while he's under the Goblin and can't get away."

At the handing over of the keys from Mark to Daniel, Kayla started up the truck and backed out. "I'll meet you at the Willows!"

On my way to the garage, Mark passed me, sweating profusely. He was a jangle of nervousness, self-doubt, and anger bubbling beneath the crust of agreeableness I'd sealed over the top of his emotions. It was a disgusting blend on a day he should just be happy for being twenty-five thousand dollars richer. Ugh...I really didn't want to wade into that mess, but it was almost a defensive reaction to fish for his happiness and gratitude and throw them into the mix. "Have a nice day!" I smiled, running the rest of the way toward Daniel, who was already in his shovel...urm...Chevelle.

A look in the rear view as we peeled away saw Mark waving goodbye to us as the gate closed. He was still fully upright. Mission accomplished.

I'd done good with my super powers. Did that make me a heroine? Sure, why not? I could do a lot more good, I bet, negotiating peace deals between warring countries, ending corporate greed, and bringing about a Utopian world.

But first, we had to stop at Rusty's Auto Parts.

CHAPTER THIRTY

"She's finally mine, Amy. Just gotta get that greaseball smell out of her, and I know a sure-fire way to do that." Daniel eyed me.

"That is a mighty back seat." I threw a glance at it. "Still has seat belts though…"

"I can take those out easy enough."

"Wouldn't that be unsafe?" I smirked.

"We wouldn't be driving while we're back there." He ran his hand along my inner thigh rubbing his middle finger across my sex.

"Hey! You're drivin' now." I placed his hand on the shifter and flicked down the ashtray, something you only found in vintage cars. "Cigarette smoke'll get the smell out too."

Daniel frowned, flicking it back up as we stopped at a cross section. "No smokin' in the Chevelle. Only new sex smell or the entrails of my enemies'll get the scent of skeeve out. I know which I'd prefer." He took off in a squeal of tires and smoke.

Blazing down the country road, he let loose the call of the good ol' boy, a prolonged whoop. "She's been waitin' her whole life for someone to open her up like this." He stared over at me letting the obvious innuendo hang in the air, without additional comment.

Rusty's lot was empty when we pulled in. Daniel danced through the store on cloud eleven, to the stylings of Frank Sinatra, while collecting all the bits and baubles he needed for his new baby and Kayla's geriatric truck. I swung on a star over to the air fresheners to see what might get the smell of skeeve out in a hurry, and found the perfect thing just as the cash register started to beep.

The cashier was gushing "aw" in the direction of Daniel's Chevelle. "Anything else?" he asked.

I threw a cherry air freshener on the counter and slowly met Daniel's gaze with a smirk as the guy rang it up. "There, now you'll get to pop a cherry in her first thing."

Daniel looked me over, like he was considering the merits of a public indecency charge. "There are two cherries here." He tapped each one with his fore and middle fingers.

"There are..." Heat rose in more than just my cheeks. Daniel caressed my hand against the counter, digging his nails in just enough to sting without causing any damage.

"$336.12 is your total." The cashier took a hard gulp. Judging by his nervous arousal, our conversation wasn't lost on him.

"This is for Varrick Custom Builders." Daniel didn't take his eyes from me, bringing the back of my stung hand to his lips.

The cashier hit some more buttons. "That's $268.90 with your discount, Sir."

"Sir," I mouthed to Daniel playfully.

"You know, it occurs to me that I just gave every last bit of my money to Mr. Shiny back there. You'll have to pick up the parts, Lambchop."

"I don't have that much on me. I'd need to go get my check from work and cash it." Or I could make the cashier apathetic enough to let us walk out with everything. But he'd probably end up fired and we were undoubtedly on video… plus wasn't I just saying I was a super heroine? Super heroines didn't steal.

What about Mark you say? Oh, that wasn't stealing, that was redistribution of wealth. He wouldn't miss the money, but it made all the difference to Daniel. I paid cash for the cherries and the cashier set aside everything else for us.

"Your dad has a discount but not an open account with Rusty's?" I asked when we were outside.

"Hell no."

"Why not?"

"'Cause he knows I'd use it for cherry air fresheners." Daniel backed out. "He's a pine tree man all the way."

We were nothing but grins the whole trip out to the Gelding. I didn't think it was possible for him to get any sexier, but seeing the focus in his eyes as he shifted gears in that muscle car, doing 107 on the 137, damn near broke my already fractured brain, and other body parts.

I bounced out of the Chevelle and up to the office to collect my check, eager to soak up some of Kamrie's joviality and add it to my own. What I found was a bucket of nerves, embarrassment, and stress. She looked up at me with a heavy, confirming sigh. "Have a seat Amy. We need ta talk."

Have you ever known "needing ta talk" to be a good thing? It's always followed by words like break up, flammable, or civil lawsuit—and sometimes a combination of all three. As I sat, she rose in an almost unconscious gesture, putting the desk between us.

There was a tremble in her voice that echoed throughout her emotions. "Amy…um…I got ta runnin' my mouth off somethin' fierce yesterday and some things what shouldn't've come out slipped on past. Can't understand what came ovah me." *Oh, but I could.* "I'm a cootin' old fool and ya should forget the share of what I said. Ya feel me?"

It came on instinct. I was inside her frazzled mind and

244

starting to tweak her emotions to calm her down before I even realized it. With a disturbed effort, I withdrew. I needed to get the lay of the land before I went back in helter-skelter. "Yeah boss, no problem, what was it we talked about? Frodo's leg?" Perhaps the mood could be lightened in a more mundane way and with a sympathetic smile.

The smile was returned but immediately darkened. "That's another thing, Clarice ain't doin' so good. Wrap job you did wasn't tight enough and she's been limpin' bad all mornin'." She took in another weighted breath. "Vet thinks she'll have ta be put ta permanent pasture." When Kamrie saw the horror on my face she was quick to add, "Oh it's not on you for the blamin', Darlin'. I should've stayed at yer side 'til I was sure it was sound."

"Yeah but, you...trusted me to take care of it."

You trusted me because I made you trust me.

"Hey, don't you worry 'bout it none, it's awful but it's what happens in life." She dropped an envelope on the desk in front of me. "Take yer check and have some fun with that Varrick boy." She looked out the window. "Now that's a right and propah car he's got." Her smile seemed one hundred percent genuine, but her normal boisterousness had sunken away, replaced by an underground river of anxious uncertainty.

I could bring it back. I should bring it back. After all, it was my fault she was feeling so low. With a flick of my mind I could make her happy again...but would it last? Or would I just make things worse? I couldn't decide, and so the decision was made for me. Kamrie left the office and soon thereafter my sensory range.

Next week's schedule was pinned to the cracked cork board...I only had two days on. It was probably for the best, given everything I was going through, but still, was it a coincidence or was it Kamrie putting more desk space between us? With a knot in the pit of my stomach, I entered the meager schedule into my phone.

My boss was down by Daniel admiring his new ride. When she saw me approaching she cut the conversation short, waved uneasily to us both and went out into the north quadrant with a distant look in her eyes.

She'd be alright...wouldn't she?

"What's wrong?" Daniel asked as I got back into the Chevelle. "She stiff you or somethin'?"

"One of the horses is gettin' put down from something I fucked up with." I sank back in disbelief.

"You gonna lose your job?"

"I don't think so but...my hours were cut back." I watched Kamrie walk across the pasture as we pulled onto the main road. "She seem okay to you?"

"Kamrie? She was all swoonin' over my shovel. Seems how it oughta be."

Yeah, maybe she would be alright. I'd only jarred her out of her comfort zone, and putting down Clarice wasn't a prospect anyone would be looking forward to. I'd give her some time and things would smooth over.

Daniel batted at the cherries dangling from his rear view mirror. "But I think if we're gonna get that greaseball smell out of her we're gonna need more cherries." He eyed me.

We cashed my check and picked up the parts, all in record time. I was tempted to buy out all the cherry air fresheners they had as a joke, but the balance in my bank account didn't share my sense of humor.

Neither did my parents...

CHAPTER THIRTY-ONE

We stopped at my house under the innocuous side quest of both grabbing an extra pack of smokes and raiding the cupboards for grub. My dad's tan Saab was parked askew in the driveway. He usually parked in the garage, with precision, and was never home this early.

Mother.

Did something happen?

I'd only messed with Kamrie a few times and she was already showing signs of being off-kilter. Mother's sessions had been much more intense.

"I don't know what I'm walkin' into here, but I gotta go inside. You go on to Kayla's and I'll meet you," I said.

"Nah, I'm comin' in with you." Daniel's manner was firm.

I at once loved him for it, and was afraid his presence would make things worse. We went in cautiously. I couldn't feel anyone on the other side of the door, or in my dad's den, but I could no longer be certain that meant there was no one there. The tablecloth still lay draped over the coffee table, but the rest of the carnage had been tidied up at some point. Once I reached the bottom of the steps, worry began to lap at me from the direction of my parents' bedroom. Behind me, Daniel took in the ridiculous enormity of my house.

"Kitchen's through there a ways," I said. "Keep going until you're sure you'll die of thirst and then it'll be on the right. Wrangle up somethin' for us to eat at Kayla's while I go..." What? Off to my doom? To make sure Mother was alive and I didn't break her brain? How did I end that sentence? Daniel did it for me with an unflinching, gentle kiss.

As he disappeared into the dining room, I rounded the banister and ascended the stairs. Each step brought a chaotic swirl of emotions drifting and curling around the steady worry. When I reached the top, my parents' bedroom door opened and the muffled sounds of the television accompanied my dad as he came out. He closed the door behind him and ushered me partway down the hall, speaking in a hushed tone, "Amy, I thought I heard you come in."

"How is she?" I whispered, though I knew the answer better than he did. She was a jumbled mess.

"She's um, not doing so great." He pressed his lips together, his voice taut and brittle.

"What happened?"

"I was hoping you could tell me. How did you know to ask how she's doing?"

"She's been out of sorts lately and you two are never home at this time, so I assumed."

"Out of sorts." He laughed uneasily, eyes searching the giant painting of a forest on the wall, as though answers might crawl from the underbrush. "Yeah, that's one way to put it. She didn't go to work today, didn't even call to tell anyone or cancel her meetings. When she didn't show up to her eleven o'clock and didn't answer her phone, Lauren got worried and stopped by the house. No one answered here either, so she called me."

There wasn't a time in my memory when Mother hadn't gone in to work aside from taking her vacations twice per year. Lauren, her assistant, probably expected to find evidence of foul play.

And really, hadn't there been?

He continued, "I activated the GPS on the Audi. It was still in the garage. So I drove to the house expecting..." Nervous laughter and a short breath huffed through his nose. "Expecting to find her dead to be honest." There was love and fear intertwined with his relief...and a twinge of guilt. "But I found her in her bed, watching talk shows, and from what I've been able to get out of her, she hasn't much moved from there since last night. She alternates between telling me there's no point in getting up, and having bouts of vertigo when she does. And yet she dismisses the idea of a doctor like it's me asking if she wants another helping of pie. Just waves her hand at me and gets sucked back into *Elaine*."

Mother hated talk shows...especially *Elaine*.

He glanced back at the bedroom door, the crow's feet bunching together at the edges of his eyes. "She's a shell of herself in there. I'm trying to convince her to go to the hospital and get some tests run but she's ox-stubborn. She finally burned out. I've never seen her like this. What happened between you and her the other night? You woke me up with your shouting, but all she'd say to me was that you were home and not to bother worrying about it."

Well, he was definitely worrying now...better late than never? Underlying it pulsed a genuine, heart-warming love. I'd always felt like more of an obligation than a daughter. Maybe the truth was somewhere in between.

"Let me go in there and—"

"Only if you keep it civil. She doesn't need any more stress. If you apologized for the other night it would help."

Apologize? Dad...she lost it on me, she slapped me, she broke the glass coffee table on my spine! But "Okay," was all I said. Okay, because this was bigger than any of that and I was desperate to fix it. Desperate to know that none of what I'd done was permanent.

Mother's master bedroom could have fit three of mine in it. Whites, blues, golds, and blacks made up the color scheme with angel décor and flowers, some of which were real, scattered tastefully about. A pair of large glass doors, now closed, opened onto her personal balcony, which overlooked the neighbor's new pool, of all things. A white sofa and high-backed reading chair offered options for enjoying the view and sunshine. It all could have come straight from the pages of a catalog. I'd only been in this room a handful of times; the vacant stares of the angel statues were enough to keep me away.

Even with her recent malaise, Mother's room was still cleaner than mine on its best day. A few tissues lay in and around her trash can, and a cup of water, half full, sat on the nightstand. The fifty-inch TV hung on the wall, blaring out the mind-numbing drudgery of some spring fashion line up that was based entirely on fruit. Who wanted to look like a grape?

"Have you eaten?" I asked, and the sound of my voice stirred her emotions, but not enough to warrant her looking away from her show. Dad came in behind me, putting his hand on my shoulder. "Hey, look I'm sorry about the other night." There was some truth to my words—I hadn't liked losing control on her like I had...even if she'd deserved it. Again came the stirring, only this time she looked me over with eyes as empty as the statues around her. The usual fire behind them was gone. As my father had said, she was a shell.

"Meh." She went back to watching her show, pulling her fluffy white comforter up around her a little more.

Sitting on the edge of the bed, I let out a heavy sigh and closed my eyes. Into the inky blackness of her muddled emotions I dove. Not with the grace of an Olympic high diver either; I flailed about screaming like a yeti and hitting the surface with a belly-flop. Her apathy wasn't bleeding back into me like I'd expected. It just sort of hung there, along with her other emotions, shredded and limp, like they couldn't be bothered to seep out. Something fundamental to keeping her going was broken, and the odds weren't long it was because of something I'd done with all my tinkering. Of course, I could be doing even more damage now, simply by being here, but I had to try…I couldn't leave her like this.

We had a complicated relationship, but I did love my mother. There was a flash and something sparkled in the dank and dirty fish tank I was in. Love. There were bits of it floating about here and there. I tugged at them, pulling them to me until I'd amassed a sizable ball and then surfaced, melting the love over her apathy like butter. It had to work— love conquers all—right?

Rock, paper, scissors, love.

"Amy." Mother's hand ran gently along my face where she had slapped me, and I opened my eyes to meet hers. They were brimming with compassion and comprehension. "I'm sorry, I hurt you," she whispered, pulling me in for a warm, generous hug I hadn't known I needed until it was wrapped around me. Tears welled in my eyes; maybe if I could keep her in this loving state I could tell her what I'd been going through. Maybe I'd been coming at this all wrong by keeping her away. Mother was strong and resourceful. She would help me and defend me if only she truly understood.

Her apathy crumbled under the weight of love. Mission accomplished. The Beatles song had been right. Love was all I needed. And who could ever get hurt by making people more loving? Well, aside from the military industrial complex but, fuck those guys. In fact, that should be my first stop to spread some empathy.

But as her apathy sank and melted away it dragged the love down with it, dissolving back into her chaotic soup and leaving us both confused. Mother tensed as a fifteen-foot gator of fear snapped up from the last of her previously tranquil shoreline. My inner gate slammed shut but not before it sank some of its teeth into me.

Mother pulled back from the hug, holding my shoulders and looking on me with wide eyes. "You didn't tell anyone, did you? Oh God."

I couldn't answer. Her fear petrified me in place, and I mirrored her look of horror, my mouth unable to close. There was no way I was going to be able to fix this. I'd fundamentally broken her and she would be like this forever!

She kept going, her voice shaking. "You did, didn't you? You told Kayla and she'll tell Faye and…" Mother's breathing grew short and hysterical as her mind wandered through its own darkest corridors.

Her fear thrashed about as though looking for something to latch onto and give it an outlet. My wall buckled under the pressure but, bolstered by that same frequency of fear myself, it held.

What didn't hold…her anger and fury I'd anchored the night before. The ropes snapped, and the missing spark flew back into Mother's eyes, boiling every other emotion in its wake.

My plea came out automatically, trying desperately to deflect the rising tsunami of anger that I could feel, but which hadn't yet registered with my father. "No, I-I didn't tell anyone!" But all my lie did was add another fifty feet to the water that was about to hit.

It was the perfect fuel.

"You lying little bitch! You did! You did tell and now they're going to come take you away and you know what?! I say let them!" she spat at me.

"Angela! Get a hold of yourself! That's no way to speak to our daughter!" Dad was in shock, though it was hardly registering to me next to the toxic plume emanating from Mother. A plume that now billowed in his direction.

"Oh! Is she *our* daughter now, Matthew? When was the last time you noticed a damn thing she's been up to? Hmm?" Her anger thundered down, spilling over and around me... but my crippling fear acted as an unexpected buffer and my mental wall stayed in place. How was I ever going to get back in to calm her down? Even if I could open my gate, Daniel's introduction to our family would turn into a double homicide and I wasn't likely to be the one left standing in the end. "She's been flunking out, skipping school, having sex, lying about taking her medication, and God knows what else!"

"Smoking!" Smoking would help me focus and get her under control. Wait...had I just said that aloud?

Shit.

Seriously?

"Yes, smoking, you impudent little shit!" She was barely understandable through her clenched teeth, but I read her well enough to jump backwards off the bed, narrowly avoiding her oncoming fist. The metal post on her footboard took the brunt of her wrath. A string of curse words, with the finesse of a snarling badger, issued from her. No way was I sticking around to watch her head start spinning in place!

Seizing my chance, I sprinted toward the bedroom door. With her unwounded hand, she snatched up a nearby stone angel figurine and whipped it at me. It missed by a few inches, hitting the wall to the left of my head as the doorknob jittered against my fingertips. I let out a shriek, bits of plaster raining down on the carpet, and then I was on the other side of the door, pulling it shut behind me like it was my tail between my legs.

"God damn it, Angela!" my father's voice rang out. I'd left him in there with her!

Something big slammed against the door, and the knob turned erratically this way, and that, in my hand. I braced my legs against the door frame and held it shut for all I was worth.

Mother is stronger than me!
She'll win!

Her voice seeped through the cracks, fluctuating in pitch and tone at all the wrong moments. "Is this what you wanted? Me to be as crazy as you? Did you drug me with something? Is that where the rest of your Paraxil went?!"

"Calm down! Whatever Amy's done, we don't hit our daughter!" Horror cleaved through my dad, a hatchet slicing again and again with each heartbeat...or was that coming from me? The pressure on the other side of the doorknob let go, replaced by the sounds of a struggle.

I don't care!
I have to go!
She'll kill me!
She'll kill my dad!

I was halfway down the stairs when this last thought stopped me cold. My hand, still sore from holding the doorknob so tight, gripped the rail, bringing my forward momentum to an abrupt halt. I couldn't just leave him up there with her in such a rage. My fear...her fear...had to be wrangled. Summoning enough presence of mind to sit, rather than continue to flee, I fumbled for a cigarette. The muffled screams of my increasingly savage mother echoed down the stairwell to join me.

Fire sprang to life at the end of a Bic, lighting the trembling cigarette I didn't remember successfully putting in my mouth. Daniel sat beside me, holding the flame. I laid my head against his arm, taking in a few puffs of the smoke. In short order I was able to toss away the remnants of fear and step into a calm and focused mind.

"I don't want to go back up there. She tried to kill me just now." I was matter of fact about it, as if such outbursts happened six times before breakfast each day. On a positive note, I had cured her of her apathy.

"So don't. Let's go while I still have some daylight to work on Gremlin." Daniel seemed completely uninterested in the chaos above us.

"Goblin," I corrected with a smirk, getting to my feet. "But I can't just leave my dad to deal with her crazy."

"Sure you can. It's easy, I'll show you." He got up and took my hands, leading me down the steps one at a time. "One foot, then the other. That's right. It's like you've done this before." That smile of his...erasing the entirety of my second floor just like that.

Of course, there was wisdom in what he was saying. What was I really going to be able to do anyway? If I went in there it would only enrage her further. But...did I have to actually physically go into the room? I could feel her anger clawing out this far without seeing her; maybe I could manipulate her from here, too?

My eyes were drawn to Daniel's, so full of mischief and light. What if Mother's rage bled back into me...as it almost surely would? I'd end up hurting him, or at least trying to, and that would be a fine basket of chud. I glanced over at the coffee table and then at Daniel's biceps. He could restrain me...wasn't that the whole reason we were bringing him out to the barn? But he needed to be warned before I tried this.

"Okay, I'm going to try to calm her down. Now, I need you to understand that I might try to—" The rage that had been battering against my mental wall rushed backwards, releasing all of the pressure against me with a pop! The relentless wave became a flat, squishy field of sinking despair, and there came a boom and a whump from upstairs that shook the house.

Mother sobbed, her wails rising and falling in pitch like those of a banshee in training.

Though my gate clanked and moaned, it held. My knees were a different matter: they buckled, and if it hadn't been for Daniel I would have fallen. The room came in and out of focus, just as when Mother had slapped me the other night.

With my angel's guidance, I sat on the bottom step, tears surfacing at the corners of my eyes.

Through her guttural sobs and my disorientation, I was only able to piece together fragments of what she was saying: "You don't understand!" and "You're never around."

Even inside my fortified wall, my heart broke for her.

Or were there holes in it I hadn't noticed?

Something primal in me wanted to go to her, to throw myself over her, and protect her from whatever was causing her such pain.

To protect her from myself.

I waded into her swamp of sadness to...to...do what exactly? Everything I'd done to her so far had just made things worse. And where was my dad in all of this? I couldn't feel him anymore.

Was he dead?

She killed him because of me.

Where was she?

Where am I?

I shouldn't have done this.

I'm sinking, up to my neck.

I deserve it. Let it all end.

This isn't a gift...it's a curse.

I ruin everything I touch.

CHAPTER THIRTY-TWO

"*A*my." *An angelic voice, so soft and kind.*
Warmth surrounds me in the cold muck.

"Oh, Honey. Honey I'm here." *The light, it's blinding. Heat of the summer sun. Kayla. Her arms are around me. The sludge dries, cracks, and flakes off in withered fragments.*

I'm warm.

I'm loved.

I'm a gift.

Pure love washes over and into me. There's no stopping it, even if I wanted to.

I love her.

A flash and a pulse coil up my spine.

Flash.

Pulse.

Never leave me.

We are one and the same.

My heart quickens, it shifts...turns...clunks back into place?

Sounds of gasping. Scent of oil and...fruit loops...and goats?

Stuttering gulps of air filled my lungs in rasping, desperate rattles. There wasn't enough air! I couldn't hold it in fast enough!

Kayla hugged me to her, stroking the back of my head in her hand as tears burned down my cheeks. Strips of sunlight shown on the leather of the Chevelle's backseat, and my mouth tasted like a stale, salty ashtray. With each shaky breath I purged the remaining sadness from my limbs and embraced Kayla's love for the crushing lifeline it was.

Let me scorch; at least I'd die with her. My arms wrapped around her, mirroring how she held me. "I love you." Was that my voice, so cracked and with all the range of a field mouse?

Kayla swallowed hard and rocked me, kissing my forehead. "I thought I'd lost you."

I pulled back from her, running my hand along her cheek and wiping away the tears as I went. "No...you found me." I kissed her on her lips. "Thank you." My brain swooned, vision blurring, and I fell back, knocking my head against the glass. My heart seized again, as though it were trying to turn over. Kayla's love pulled away, replaced by fear and worry, both of which caused my inner wall to slam reflexively into place.

The residual spinning motion in my heart pulled the fear down and away, bringing up a host of mixed emotions before settling on playful-love. Kayla's ambient love seemed to have left a residue within me. My eyes shot open where I lay, propped against the back seat. A chicken appraised us from just outside the Chevelle's open passenger's side door. I returned her accusing stare. "Well I'm sorry if my freak out is disturbing your day, Red. I'll try to be more considerate the next time I'm stuck in sludge up to my brainpan."

Kayla glanced down at the hen and back over at me, scooting to the far end of the seat. It offered a little relief from her blazing pressure. "From Angela?"

I nodded, rubbing the back of my head. "How'd you know hugging me wouldn't make things worse?"

Kayla blinked a few times, as though the whole situation

were only now catching up with her. "I didn't think about it. Just did it. Daniel sped in here, horn blarin', said you had a bad fight with your parents and he couldn't get through to you—"

"Ah man!" I leaned over the front seat, checking out my raccoon-like expression in the rear view mirror and trying to clean myself up as best I could with my thumbs. If this sort of thing was going to continue I would have to stop wearing eye make-up altogether. "This is not the way I wanted him to find out. Though better a crying jag than trying to punch him, or something." I froze and turned a side eye to her. "I *didn't* punch him, did I?"

"Wasn't really paying attention to what he looked like." She used her sleeve to clear away some of the black around my eye. "What happened with your mother? Bleed-back?"

With widening eyes I sniffed and nodded. "The *mother* of all bleed-back." My memory was still coated in mud. What was buried there? I took out a smoke, and was searching for my lighter when the cigarette was snatched from between my upheld fingers. My hand was wrapped, rather unceremoniously, around a sizable cup of water. It was the biggest thermos in Kayla's kitchen, and I had to drop my purse and devote both hands to the monstrosity to keep it from spilling.

"No smokin' in my Chevelle." Daniel's words held a smooth authority and yet came off as a friendly reminder rather than an absolute order. He was leaning through the open driver's side window on his forearms, tucking my stolen cigarette neatly behind his ear. Before I could respond he continued, "I'm gonna go work a miracle on Gizmo." Removing himself from the car as quickly as he'd appeared, he started toward the Green Goblin, yelling over his shoulder, "If you ladies are gonna make out in my back seat, record it for me." And off he went as though I hadn't just been a hysterical mess five minutes before.

"Th-thank you!" My voice was too sore from crying to carry far. I took several life affirming gulps of water.

"Thank you!" Kayla shouted out on my behalf. Daniel simply raised a hand in acknowledgment and set about jacking up the Goblin. Kayla's normal mistrust and suspicion around him was gone. She felt grateful and even a little guilty.

Guilty…it resonated inside me. I'd pushed Mother over the brink. She'd loved me, and tried to kill me, almost in the same breath. And…my dad.

My dad.

Handing Kayla the thermos, I called my dad's phone. Each ring was a knife in my chest, pulling the air from my lungs.

Answer.

Please answer.

"Hello, you've reached Matthew Durene, please leave a message and I'll return your call as soon as I'm able." His voicemail. My skin went cold at the sound of the beep.

"Dad…um…it's Amy. Call me back so I know you're not dead, okay?" *Thoughts of Leilani.* "Or, even if you are dead, you can still call me back."

Kayla's breath caught. "Did you do something to him?"

"No…well…not directly…I don't think." I paused before admitting, "I don't know." Maybe calling Mother's phone would be worth a shot?

"Hello, this is Angela Durene, Chief Sales Representative with Freedom Timber, the leader in sustainable forestry practices. I'm sorry to have missed your call but please leave a message and I'll generally be back to you within a few hours. Thank you, and have a pleasant day." Straight to voicemail—it hadn't even rung. In her apathy, she probably hadn't charged her phone.

A flash of me standing over her, ready to bash her skull in with my phone.

I hung up.

"I'm worried that she killed him. I have to go back and check. Come with me."

"Oh shit." Kayla's eyes climbed over me for signs I was joking. "Let me go get my gun." She pulled herself out of the car and ran up to the house.

The pressure in my head lifted and I slid back, taking a moment to just breathe and absorb the silence. Red was still watching me from afar. "Nobody here but us chickens," I mused, loosing another cigarette from my pack. "This is *not* what I imagined my first time in this backseat would be like." I got out, lighting my cigarette and closing the door.

My phone rang, a generic unfamiliar jingle. It was my dad's number. "Dad?!" I inhaled too sharply on the answer, and a series of coughs followed.

"Everything's settled now." He seemed calm and just hearing his voice put years back into me. I leaned against the Chevelle, letting out a sigh. "How are you doing?" he asked.

How much should I tell him? "I'm...frazzled, really. But I...I pushed her into this."

"Your current rebellious streak isn't helping, but there's more to her meltdown than that. I've never seen her lose control anywhere near those levels. Not even on Grandma, and that woman has made a science out of button pushing."

"You got any pot?" I asked in all seriousness. Hey, it worked for Mrs. Randall.

My dad laughed. "She's up, combing her hair, and getting dressed as we speak. We're going to the hospital to get some tests run. If she needs medication, they'll figure it out."

I wanted to go with, but the thought of being in an enclosed space with either of them turned my stomach. It was also potentially dangerous, given the strength and severity of Mother's mood swings. "I can meet you there."

"No. I need you to stay home. I'll call you when we know something," he said. "Is this a number I can reach you at?"

"Yeah, it's my phone." My hand brushed against the mass of fur that was Delilah. She licked me, not seeming to mind my cigarette, and I scratched behind her ears absent-mindedly.

"Oh. Okay. That explains why I couldn't get a hold of you earlier. When'd you get a new phone?"

"Three years ago." An awkward silence stretched between us. "How're you doing? Did she hurt you?" Kayla came back outside, the screen door slamming shut behind her, and I held up my phone along with a giant thumbs up.

"No. No, I'm fine," he said, and I could taste the lie through the phone. "She's coming down the stairs now and we've got to go. I'll call you later." Without waiting for my reply, he hung up.

"Okay," I said to the empty air. Taking a few more drags of my smoke, I processed everything. Mother going to the hospital was probably for the best. They could at least stabilize her, and with any luck she would return to normal without me continuously tinkering around in her emotions.

"He's not dead." I looked over to Kayla, who was a respectable distance away, waiting for me to say something.

"That's good, but how can you tell with him?" Her delivery was perfectly deadpan, making me smile.

"Really, how can we tell with anyone anymore?" I pushed off the Chevelle, opening the door and reaching for the grocery bag on the floor. My stomach clenched and grumbled. "Let's talk inside while we make some food or I'm liable to eat that damn chicken, feathers and all." We left Daniel undisturbed in the belly of the Goblin and went inside.

Once at the kitchen counter we discovered he had plundered my freezer of six steaks, all labeled from Lobo's of New York. "Oh no! Beef Tournedo!" I tossed two cuts of beef bearing that name at Kayla who screamed in appropriately fake fashion but caught them both.

"Inferior beef! Argh! My weakness!" She stumbled

around, falling to one knee before reading the label. "Oh! Oh wait! Damn. I take that back, this is blonde aquitaine!" Her eyes bulged and through clenched teeth she said, "You know how much this stuff is per pound?"

"No. Is it any good?" Not that I cared; chicken feed was looking palatable to me just then.

"Don't know, but I aim to find out." Kayla had a massive outdoor grill and set about getting it going while I washed my face in the upstairs bathroom. I could hear her and Daniel talking below but couldn't make out the words or feel her emotions.

I had no memory of him bringing me here.

Again, I checked my eyes. They still had their pupils. "Leilani? Leilani, talk to me." I pulled a string of wet hair off my face and peered deeply into my mirror image. "Or do I need to say your name one more time?" This was probably not wise, but I had to know. "Where are you hiding…Leilani?"

Nothing happened.

I flipped off the light and repeated in quick succession: "Leilani, Leilani, Leilani!" The sight of the shower curtain bunched up behind me gave me a fright when I turned the light back on, but other than that small comedy, nothing happened.

Then again, why should she answer to me?

Downstairs, I raided the Rodriguez milk supply to tide me over until dinner. "I can't keep doing this," I told Kayla as she came in.

"Mi leche, es tu leche." She smiled, washing the dirt from a potato.

"Lechery aside, I'm swearing off messing with anyone's emotions, ever again. I'll be lucky if I didn't permanently fry something in my mother's brain…or my own." I filled her in on the situation with Kamrie and my mother. "I was lost in her sadness—if it hadn't been for you being the lighthouse you are, I don't know how I would have gotten out. There was no time, no physical senses, no me, just endless sorrow." I shuddered. "You saved my life."

She tossed a potato my way, and I barely caught the slippery little spud. The smiley face she'd carved into it stared up at me, making me laugh. "You'd have found your way out on your own eventually," she said. "I don't think you give yourself enough credit. All you've been through the last few weeks and you're still here, able to laugh at a potato."

"It's a good call backin' off for now," she continued. "We've got enough spuds in the fire as it is." She took Mr. Potato Face from me and summarily wrapped him in tin foil.

"Thanks." I smiled warmly. "There's so many unknowns, even within my own memory. Potato or no potato, that's enough to drive me mad right there. I better go see if I said or did anything to Daniel I need to apologize for. He say anything to you?"

"Asked how you were. I told him you were tightenin' your corset and you'd be back out in a bit. Then he asked for some rags and for me to keep Goblin in my thoughts and went back to work. Oh! He didn't have a black eye…I checked this time."

"He brought me here, exactly where I needed to be to get out of that funk." I picked up the plate filled with wrapped potatoes and headed for the door. "You think that's a coincidence?"

Kayla followed me out with two plates full of steak. "He had enough sense to bring you to me when it mattered most —that says somethin'. Maybe we can trust him with all this after all."

Tipping the plate up, I let the spuds fall into the fire. "And maybe he knows more than he's lettin' on." Daniel's weight shifted underneath the Goblin and I narrowed my determined eyes at him. "I aim to find out."

CHAPTER THIRTY-THREE

*A*ll four tires were off the Goblin, and Daniel was fiddling with a cable, when I slid underneath and into his automotive cave. His arms and hands were smudged black. I lay next to him for a moment, trying to make sense of what he was doing, before slowly turning my head to look at him. He dropped the wire he was working with and grabbed my face in his greasy hands, pulling me in for a heated series of kisses.

In those kisses he said everything he needed to: that he understood, that he was here for me, and if I wouldn't fuck him in the Goblin, maybe I'd fuck him under it?

What had I come down there for?

"Go pump the brakes." Daniel's warmth left me.

"But I don't wanna stop…" I pulled him back down.

He kissed me a few times before pulling back again, this time holding my head by the chin firmly against the cold gravel driveway, so I couldn't rise to meet him. "Brakes." He touched my nose with his pointer finger and went back to fiddling with his wire.

I kissed his cheek, leaving a dab of grease from my nose on him, and slid out from under the jacked up truck. Around the front, I caught my grease-covered face in the side mirror. With a few adjustments it made for some decent war paint. Over the next ten minutes I got my fill of pumping brakes by hand for my next three lifetimes, but by the end Kayla's brakes were no longer the certain doom they had been.

Daniel then set about taking apart her U-joints. The process was loud, involved a blow torch, and was not conducive to me giving him the third degree. He enlisted me to spray the thing down with penetrating oil, letting the innuendo drip to the ground with each pull of the trigger.

Did that count as foreplay?

Kayla called us for dinner just as we set the second drive shaft back in place. Yes, I now knew what a drive shaft was. Aren't you proud of me? We went inside and washed up. All the while he gave no indication I'd said or done anything terrible in the time I couldn't remember.

"They didn't thaw properly. I did what I could with them, but you can tell," Kayla said, taking small, measured bites at the kitchen table. "Such a shame." She looked up at Daniel, who had won Mr. Potato Face in the lottery and was looking down at it curiously. "Next time you raid Angela's private stash we'll give it time to thaw." Leaning forward she added, "And pleeeaaase let there be a next time."

Daniel gave her a knowing smirk. After further consideration, he split the smiley face in two with his knife and slathered the mutilated spud with butter.

"Now you've turned Mr. Potato Face into a Batman villain," I said, peering over at him.

Picking up the ketchup, he turned his whole plate into a bloody crime scene. "A short-lived Batman villain." He scooped up a forkful, ate it, and immediately offered me the next round. I happily accepted. "Now you're an accomplice," he said, with a wry smile.

"And a cannibal?" I asked, still chewing.

"Mmmhmm. No matter what though, we're in this

together. If we keep our mouths shut…" He tipped my chin up, closing my mouth. "…No one will ever know." I melted at the prospect. We were in this together.

But, he still had a blindfold on.

"Thanks for getting me out of my house earlier." I smiled at him. "I'm sorry you had to see that." He had a mouthful of steak but responded by feeding me another forkful of murder potato.

"How'd you know that bringing her to me would snap her out of it?" Kayla asked, watching him intently for subtle facial cues while he chewed. I hated that framing, it made me sound like a mental case…which was only a half-truth. "Do you have a sixth sense?" she continued.

"Is *common* the sixth one?" He stabbed another piece of steak with his fork, letting his gaze linger on Kayla before turning to me. "Why wouldn't I bring you here?"

I hadn't considered that question. We were headed here anyway, to work on the Goblin and eat. And really Kayla was my sister-wife, so it only stood to reason that she'd be able to help me. I probably flipped through a few shades of pink then—why had I immediately jumped to the conclusion that there was something freaky going on?

Oh yeah, all the freaky shit going on.

I'm allowed to be paranoid sometimes, too.

"Common is a sixth sense." I laughed. "More rare than empathy or ESPN."

"ESP," Kayla corrected. "Extra sensory perception…not extreme sports personality neurosis."

Daniel laughed and kept eating. He gave no indication he knew anything about what we were alluding to. I swallowed hard and bit the bullet. "I thought maybe you knew more than you were letting on…like maybe you had a sixth sense…like I do." His eyes swept over me as I spoke. "It's how I knew to get out of that first room we were kissing in at the church. I told you at the time, remember? I used it again to get away from my mother the night we...went swimming."

Daniel looked in thought for a moment. "Ayeah, I remember."

"But the flip side is I can get overwhelmed by strong emotions...like what happened with my mother today... that's why I lost it on the steps. I felt what she was feeling, her heartache bled into me." I braced myself for him to laugh, to brush me off and leave, but he didn't.

He wrinkled his nose. "Your mother is psycho."

"Only because I made her that way." My guilt bubbled to the surface.

"No, no. She's always been psycho," Kayla interjected. "Don't take all of this onto yourself. That nut was cracked long before you went anywhere near it."

"Kayla's right, and even if your mother knew EVERY saintly thing we've done this week, that doesn't justify attempted murder," Daniel said. Kayla blossomed with respect at his words. Were they bonding over a mutual hatred of my mother?

Hey, I'd take it.

"Yeah, but I *really* messed with her emotions. I swirled them around and called them up like I was playing notes in a symphony...poorly...with my kazoo." I rifled through my purse, emerging with the red plastic instrument. "This is what liberation looks like, by the way," I said, blowing on the kazoo.

They both looked at me sideways before Kayla spoke up, "Of course, I know what you mean Amy, but I think it's time we showed Daniel the results of our experiments, so he can know too." She pushed her chair out and went into the living room.

Daniel leaned over to me. "You make beautiful music. Let's go and you can practice your humming on me."

I stuck the kazoo in his mouth. "I'm still eating." I was on my third steak and second baked potato, and had eaten enough lettuce to feed a warren of rabbits. He hadn't left, which was good, but he wasn't exactly taking any of this seriously either. Not that I could blame him. "And what Kayla's going to show you is gonna explain a lot. I'm not crazy."

Daniel spit the kazoo onto the table. "Yes, you are." His lips closed over mine, tongue joining the mouthful of warm baked potato I'd just taken in. Buttery goodness oozed down my chin, spreading up onto his face. Most of what was in my mouth ended up in his, and he swallowed it while pulling back from me. "It's one of the things I like most about you."

Laughing at the mess we'd made, I licked the excess potatoes from his face. Partly to be sexy, and partly because I was still hungry.

He was returning the gesture when I was blindsided by a wave of frustration. Kayla's anguished shout came from the living room seconds later. "Fawwwk!"

"What's the matter?" I called back to her.

"The file's corrupted!" she cried.

"All of them?" I asked.

"Even my backups don't want to open." She was clicking the mouse with a force that carried into the kitchen, as though hitting it harder would make some kind of difference.

In a voice meant for my ears only, Daniel said, "I'm collecting my tools and then we're out." He licked a last bit of butter, real or imagined, from the corner of my mouth, and headed down the stairs.

Watching him go, I reassured Kayla, "We can always redo them." While continuing to eat, I cleaned up bits of fallen potato from the floor with a wet rag.

"Sure, if we need to, but these are the pioneering tests—I don't want to lose them." She growled, coming into the kitchen. "Might be that last system update I did. I'll install an

269

earlier version and see if that helps...I'm not giving up so easily."

I looked out the window at Daniel jacking down the Goblin. "Daniel doesn't believe any of it. He thinks I'm crazy...but he finds crazy to be sexy, so it balances out? I don't think he knows anything about what's going on either."

"Well, we saw today he's got one hell of a poker face," she said, and I couldn't argue the point.

"He wants to go." My tone was thoughtful and almost apologetic. He wasn't the only one who wanted to. Setting one of the uneaten steaks into Samson's bowl, I added, "I owe Sam for helping me the other night."

And Kayla, for helping me every night.

"Yeah, that was blonde aquitaine worthy, for sure. He's such a good boy. Yours is startin' to learn his manners too." She grinned. "Just needs a flea collar and an oatmeal bath." Tilting her head, her grin became a genuine smile. "Hey, it's gonna take me a while to rip my computer apart, anyway, so go have some fun and relax. You earned it with all the shit you've been through today."

Empathy for empaths.

She blew me a kiss, which I caught, touching my hand to my chest and releasing it. I kissed my palm and wound up like I was throwing a baseball at her. She fell backwards into the living room, falling over the couch with a squeak.

"And don't worry about Daniel!" she called out. "We'll get him to come around once I get my files fixed, or we'll redo the tests with him here to see it firsthand." There was a smugness to her emotions. "Then he can see my equipment is more than flashing lights and sounds."

Outside, Daniel was locking up the last of his things in his work truck. "Got a smoke?" he asked. I gave him the one that had been dangling from my mouth and took the last one from my pack. With all the insanity I never made it to my room for another one.

The blue light of his blowtorch gave an eerie incandescence to his face in the dark of the night. He lit his cigarette from the flame before holding it out for me to do the same. Certain I would roast myself, I declined with a shake of my head. Daniel took the cigarette from my mouth and replaced it with the one he'd just torched, before repeating the process on this second cigarette.

"I don't know how you can do that," I marveled at him. "I'd be afraid I'd burn my face off."

"Why do you think I don't have any hair?" Daniel inhaled, running his hand over his shaved head as I chuckled. His work truck rocked slightly as he jumped in the back and secured the lock.

"We need to stop at my place." I flipped the empty pack upside down and shook it. "But you want me to follow you back to your house in your work truck?" I hadn't seen his mothership since the lightning storm last week.

"No, I've got it covered." He looked down at me from the truck bed. "Besides, you don't have a license."

"But, I have charm." I smiled up at him. Could I charm a cop if need be? No...I wasn't doing that anymore...remember? "And you let Kayla drive without one. She's only got her temps."

He jumped down, frowning. "I didn't know that." With his hand firmly on my waist, he pulled me close to him. "You fucking hoodlums." Under a kamikaze kiss, we made out, our cigarettes whittling down to nubs. He flicked his into the tall grass, blowing his last bit of smoke slowly in my face while asking, "You ever used your wicked wiles on me?"

The question startled me. Had he taken me seriously after all? "No...well...yes...but no. Only my natural ones, not supernatural." Could I be sure of that? "Not knowingly, anyway."

He studied me with unreadable eyes for a long moment before opening the passenger's side of the Chevelle and

271

gesturing me inside. We backed out and took off down the road against the orangish purple backdrop of the setting sun. Hazy white clouds flanked it on either side, spreading into infinity.

Daniel fiddled with his phone, calling someone as we drove. One thing the classic car lacked was hands-free calling. "Got a job for you...in Albion." After a pause, he rattled off Kayla's address. "Shit man, off a cliff." He laughed. "My place." Another pause and then he held the phone against the dashboard of his car, speeding around the corner and down my street like a madman. We screeched to a halt in my driveway.

Bringing the phone back to his ear, he asked, "Did you get all that?"

With a smile and a shake of my head, I left Daniel idling in the driveway and ran inside to get the smokes. My house looked ablaze in the light of the setting sun, and it might as well have been for all the trouble I'd caused. The door was locked, a good sign that I might actually complete my quest this time around.

My cigarettes were right where I'd left them, amidst the junk in my side table drawer. I jumped on the opportunity to freshen my make-up and hair in the bathroom before heading for the stairs. The door to my parents' bedroom was open, with the doorknob itself wrenched to one side and hanging down at an unhealthy angle. Wood splintered out a few inches above and below the latch.

Just inside the room, a chunk of plaster peppered the carpet white in uneven sprays. The heavy stone angel Mother had hurled at my head seemed undamaged. I picked it up and put it back on its pedestal near her bedside, as though doing so would set everything in order.

Mother's metal bedpost was bent where she'd tried to clock me.

Jesus.

Lit only by the grace of the hallway light, several paintings hung crooked on the walls, curtains were partially torn down, and…was that blood on the floor? Yes, a sizable smattering of random drops trailed from near the antique vanity, whose drawers were askew as if the whole thing had rocked forward and back again. Propped against it was a busted mirror that had once been attached.

I picked up a loose shard, streaked and tacky with blood. It shone in the dull light.

Whose blood was on my hands?

Absentmindedly, I fit the piece back into place, staring at my fractured reflections. In each of them, my surroundings dimmed. Long shadows wove between the shallow light, snuffing it out. Seven figures came into view behind me, each shrouded in darkness save for a thin, brilliant aura.

I froze.

No. Not figures, figure…one shadow projected back seven times.

The name came out hushed and strangled, as though stolen from my last breath. "Leilani?"

CHAPTER THIRTY-FOUR

*I*f I look away, if I so much as blink, she'll disappear.

She answered my summons.

A bit late and in the wrong mirror, but she answered.

My stomach twisted, bile rising in my throat.

I should be happy.

Why aren't I happy?

And, why hadn't I felt her coming?

Why can't I feel her now?

Each step toward me evened the light around the figure, bringing them out of the shadows.

…

…

…

Until it was Daniel standing over me.

Our eyes met in the shattered mirror.

What? What had I just seen? A hallucination? Wishful thinking? Had Kayla been on to something with their names being so similar? Daniel was actually Leilani? In the darkness I stared back at him, a maddened creature, looking my boyfriend over as though it were my first time seeing him.

"Daniel...if you were a ghost, you'd tell me, right?" My voice was fragile and distant, barely mine at all.

He laughed to himself, taking a knee by my side. His hand cradled the nape of my neck as he came in for a slow, sensuous kiss that I reciprocated on autopilot. "If I was a ghost, how could I do that?" Such a calm, reassuring presence.

I peeled myself from the mirror, facing him. "I...I don't know, an alien then?"

His features softened with a sympathy that belied his serious tone. "Amy, why's it so hard to believe somethin' good is happening in your life? I'm here. I'm real." He took my hand and brought it under his shirt, pressing it to his chest. "I only have one heartbeat."

My fingertips pulsed with the steady thrum of his singular heartbeat, each repetition bringing me incrementally out of those illusionary shadows, and back into myself.

Thud-thup

He is here.

Thud-thup

Am I?

My hollow eyes searched his, and I asked the question too long on my lips: "Then...why can't I feel you?"

He tilted his head, narrowing his gaze. "You can't feel me?"

"No. You're silent. It's...it's one of the things I love about you."

Did I just say love?

Daniel's grip tightened over my hand, fingers interweaving with mine. His free hand caressed my neck and jawline with gentle consideration. "I don't know. But, if I make things easier for you, maybe we're meant for each other." There was a candid warmth to his words, as though he were figuring them out as they left his mouth. "I wasn't supposed to be out there with Trevor that night. Somethin' told me to go."

I perked up. "What was that something?"

"Fate. God. The devil. Don't think it much matters." He coaxed my chin up, locking his eyes with mine. "You're beautiful, wise, funny, and sinfully reckless. I count my luck every time you let me touch you. So, I don't give a damn why, Amy Durene, all that matters is what we do with it."

"Aw hell, Daniel." The inches between us melted away, my lips closing over his without remorse. Let him drag me into the long shadows; I had my lighter and a full pack of smokes. "You're a vampire aren't you?" I said between kisses. "Gettin' me to fall for those lines…?"

Pressure bore down on my jugular vein. My spine seized, and a scrap of involuntary breath rushed into my lungs. His slick tongue lapped at my tender flesh before sucking in with a vengeance. He brought us to our feet while I squealed and shrieked with laughter, sparks of pleasured-pain setting me to fits of delirium.

I am here.

I am.

He growled, gnawing on me one more time for good measure. "Let's go."

The blood in my brain had moved on to greener pastures, making me unsure of my footing. Surveying the floor, I half expected to find fresh droplets of blood, but only the old guard remained. Soon it would set into the carpet, a permanent reminder of what I'd done.

"I can't leave the blood. I have to get it out before it sets." I balanced myself against Daniel.

He scanned our surroundings. "It enhances the décor. Maybe your folks will want to keep it." With his hand on the small of my back, he led me toward the light of the hall.

I stopped short of the door, looking back at the tattered room. "I can't leave things like this. It's my fault."

My phone, which I'd left in the Chevelle, was pressed into my hand. "You got a message from your dad. Answer him and I'll take care of it." He made his way to my parents' bathroom and opened the cabinets in quick succession. It didn't take him long to find what he was looking for: a bottle of hydrogen peroxide.

Whether he truly believed me or not, he was taking all this remarkably well. And now here he was cleaning up my crime scene without a second thought. If he wasn't an angel, he was from somewhere in that general region.

To the hiss and fizz of the hydrogen peroxide hitting blood, I unlocked my phone.

7:45 PM: STAYING THE NIGHT AT KENNEDY MEMORIAL FOR OBSERVATION AND TESTS.

With quick fingers, I replied,
7:53 PM: HOW IS SHE?

He didn't make me wait long for his answer.
7:54 PM: STABLE AND SLEEPING. DON'T WORRY.

I shot back, almost without thought.
7:54 PM: THANKS. PLEASE KEEP ME POSTED.

The ball of lead in my stomach turned over with each new fizz and pop coming from the war-torn room in front of me.

Don't worry...

...right.

I'd stop worrying when Mother was yelling at me again, in her normal pitch.

And then there was the matter of my mind playing connect the dots, on a blank page...or a bloody mirror if you like. What was I supposed to make of that? Either my angelic boyfriend was hiding something, or my mind had slipped into the couch cushions.

Neither option appealed to me.

But today had been a whirlwind of crazy, and this emotion ability was centered at least partly in my brain, making stress induced hallucinations a real possibility. Doctor Nimans's diagnosis of "exhaustion" came to mind.

Hadn't Kayla prescribed some fun and relaxation tonight? As it stood, I was a soaking wet, lead-lined blanket. Daniel deserved a better Friday night than playing forensics lab. Hell, we both did. I couldn't change the clusterfuck of a situation I was in, but I could change how I felt about it. Messing with anyone's emotions may have been off limits, but I wasn't anyone...I was me.

Wasn't I?

Watching Daniel pour the peroxide, I dissolved the metal ball of despair in my gut, letting an effervescent happiness bubble through me. "We've got the house to ourselves tonight!" I sang the words, grinning like a maniac and bouncing on my tip toes.

Instant upper.

Daniel chucked the empty bottle into the overturned trash can. "Luckier and luckier. Where's the liquor cabinet?"

CHAPTER THIRTY-FIVE

The letter organizer on our kitchen wall held a legendary amount of keys. Most had lost their locks to the ravages of time long ago, but one of them opened my dad's den. Whether this was intentional or an oversight on my parents' part, I'd never brought it to their attention.

Daniel let out a long whistle as we entered the low light of the den. An oak and marble bar with rounded stylized edging took up a quarter of the space. The glass case behind it housed every liquor available in rural Maine, including some local rotgut. The middle of the room was dominated by my father's prize pool table. His awards, trophies, and coveted golden cue hung on the wall nearby. In the front, next to the curtained bay window, was a surround sound theater, leather sectional couch, and a sizable collection of movies.

On the underside of the bar, affixed to a magnet, was the liquor cabinet key. "What's your pleasure?" I asked, opening the cabinet with a little too much enthusiasm. Several bottles had to be readjusted so they wouldn't topple out.

"Fifty Stone." Daniel unfolded the black leather cover of

the pool table. He switched on the LED surface lights, bathing the purple wool surface in an incandescent glow.

"That white remote over there syncs the lights to music," I said, pouring his whiskey into a glass. A few chunks of ice, some Coke, and a maraschino cherry on top and we were good to go. Well, I stopped to wipe some spilled cherry juice from the bar. The biohazard red chemical cocktail tended to stain, and if something was going to betray our presence here, we could do better than red dye #40.

Dead Operation's newest album started up as I delivered Daniel his drink. He was feeling out a pool cue, sliding it between his fingertips. "You any good?" he asked, in a voice as streamlined as the stick he held.

Reaching under the table, I came out with a triangular wooden case. Opening it revealed a set of sixteen billiard balls polished to perfection. "You'll have to play me to find out."

Daniel threw me a half smile, eyes sparkling with intrigue. "Let's make it interesting—for every shot I make you take something off, and vice-versa."

I laughed, placing the rack on the table. "8-ball."

When Daniel was down to his boxers I gave him control of the game and mixed us up some Blind Draws: Irish cream, tequila, and the aforementioned rotgut. I had to leave my socks and shirt at the bar by the time I was done.

Our shot glasses clinked together. "Thanks, Lambchop," he said, smirking.

"Don't thank me yet." I downed my shot, and after a moment's hesitation he did too. Our eyes teared up, but everything stayed down so I must have mixed it right. "Lambchop?" I wheezed.

"You don't have a pet name for me?" He coughed, banging on his chest.

Bending to line up my shot, my cheeks flushed. "Call my phone." I knocked number thirteen in but scratched. "Damn.

So close." Picking up my phone, I increased the volume so he could hear when it rang.

I plucked the cherry from his glass, momentarily wincing at the foul taste of Fifty Stone while sucking on the sweet fruit in a suggestive manner. My phone played out "Lollipop lollipop oh lolly lolly lolly..." Leaning on the pool table, I held up the source of the song, feigning innocence.

Daniel returned a look that said he'd expected more maturity out of me and yet found every note more flattering than the last. A playful respect grew in his eyes as he closed the distance between us, focusing on the cherry in my mouth. "That's gonna get you into trouble."

The cherry disappeared between my teeth and I pulled the stem from it, offering it to him as I chewed. He lifted me onto the pool table, parting my thighs with his body. I laughed, my brain humming from the Blind Draw, and he arched me over the table like I was his shadow.

"Notice we both consider each other food." Sinister amusement dripped from each of his words, and he ran his tongue up my chest to the base of my ear, making me squirm.

He lingered there, brushing his cheek against mine, his hot breath down my neck. I swallowed. "It's your turn...I scratched."

With one arm Daniel brought my whole body onto the middle of the pool table, stalking up after me. Billiard balls shuffled in our wake, clacking into each other, though none went in. The slab was unforgiving, and the wool, once soft to my touch, burned against my bare back as I slid across it.

Thump.

The six-ball dropped into the side pocket, followed by the heat of Daniel's lips over mine. He unhooked the clasps of my little red satin number like he was snapping his fingers. I tossed it over the edge of the table without removing my mouth from his.

Click. Clack. Click.

Thump.

Thump.

Thump.

The table to my right was cleared, though Daniel kept his focus on me. He kissed down my neck, devouring my breasts and popping the button free on my jeans. I bent my body upward and with a few good tugs the blue denim joined his on the floor.

We each had one piece of clothing left. Daniel brought the coveted 8-ball to my navel, rolling it around in a small circle while his eyes drank me in. Two hundred proof alcohol begging for a flame. I plucked the shiny black ball from him and sailed it toward the corner pocket.

Thump.

It went in.

"I win," I said, pulling his boxers, wet with his anticipation, to his knees. My mouth opened, eager to take him in, but he held me by the shoulders, guiding me back onto the table.

"You win." His kisses trailed down my chest, roaming over my stomach, and pausing at the threshold of my panties. He took his time there, pacing his tongue back and forth, tension coiling at my core with each pass. I closed my eyes, reveling in the electric sensation, and at the slight chill setting in on the far side before he doubled back.

Fire at the gate!

Guided by his nimble fingers, my panties slipped off.

He lowered my knee, shifting between my legs, continuing toward his end goal. After a moment's admiration he plunged his tongue into my bits, digging his fingers into my thighs and restricting my movement. I gasped, arching my back. The feel of him in me…it was right.

Lust coated every other emotion, fusing with the prevailing happiness. Indulging in the primal waterfall, I got lost in its meandering cascades, letting it flood away my other senses. I didn't notice his tongue leave me or his arms become pillars at my sides. But when his cock throbbed against my sex the waterfall scorched to steam, struck by the bolt of lightning now surging through my body at his touch, slamming me back into my abandoned senses.

Oh my God…

…is this happening?

Now?

"Tell me you want me." Daniel's gaze was piercing, as though he already owned a piece of my soul, and the rest was a formality. Threadbare chains held his beast in place as his erection swelled against me.

Lunging up, I bit his bottom lip, pulling him onto me. His mouth was thick with my scent and I licked from one corner to the other in one action. "My lollipop tastes like brimstone," I replied in a low breath, heart pounding in exhilaration at everything that statement represented.

My hips ground into him, tender flesh in need of his potency. But he seemed to be waiting for me to answer directly, or tormenting me as I'd done to him all week. I couldn't tell, and I didn't care. "Yes, I want you…all of you," I whimpered.

Shink…

Clang…

Ca-chink…

Off came the chains.

His calloused hand trailed over my thigh, midsection, and breasts, nails digging into my flesh with possessive hunger before coming to rest on my neck. He curled his fingers into the hair at my nape, thumbing my throat and jawline. The applied pressure ordered every muscle in my body to tense as he entered me, raw and as unyielding as the slate I lay upon.

I sucked air in through gritted teeth.

He can't go any farther…

He can't…

But he does.

And it hurts…oh God it hurts!

My voice was stifled by his grip. Thin wisps of breath were all that escaped under my ever-widening eyes. He watched me, seemingly just as pleasured by my reaction as by my warmth around him. His intensity…as though he were etching this moment in stone within his mind.

I tried to move, to rise to meet him, but his grasp tightened around my hair, holding me fast to the table. The strength of his body pinned me in place while he slipped deeper inside me.

A relentless descent.

He'll break me in two.

He'll…

I can't…

"Daniel!" His name trembled off my lips.

He came in for a kiss, carnal and vicious, thrusting forward past the point of all tolerance before drawing back. A rush of brutal ecstasy rippled through me in his wake. His grip eased up on my throat and the air flowing into my lungs brought its own simple euphoria.

I am here.

I am alive.

He moved my hips, settling into a sensuous cadence. Our eyes didn't waver from each other. My heart surged, turning over…and over…turbulent emotions writhed together in breathtaking anarchy. Within my chest came a spark, red hot and all-consuming. It spiraled with the unstoppable momentum of a supernova before condensing into a black hole of need and desire.

Daniel yanked me to him by my hair, sitting us both upright so I straddled him. His mouth muffled my startled cry. "I bet you can feel me now," he growled.

"Yessssss." A primal moan trailed from my lips to his. I

could feel him, rigid inside me, rough hands guiding my body, making us one. Shockwaves of ecstasy and love cascaded through me at the thought. "Yes," my voice quivered, "more…" The pair of emotions obeyed, sizzling to the surface, incinerating all others in their wake and spreading like wildfire.

My chest tightened and even as his arms enfolded me, even as he worked inside of me, he was too far away.

I need to feel his emotions…

…to dive into him and never see the light of day again.

This aching obsession fell upon his vivid hazel eyes set into flawless skin that glistened with the sweat of our effort. I licked several beads from his temple, savoring the salty, bittersweet taste. His scent, layered with whiskey, earth, and oil, made a potent aphrodisiac. Laughter rolled out of him, mixing with his perfect moans. The sound reverberated through me as he brought our lips back together, vigorous and decisive.

My fingers clawed at his chest, wanting to merge with him, wanting to swim in his soul. The craving swirling at my center hunted for even the tiniest sliver of an emotion to latch onto, but was met with an empty void. I cried out, hands shaking with need, digging into his flesh—if I could remove it…

Daniel's hands closed over mine, pinning them to my chest without effort before I could do any damage.

I can't hurt him…

I can't…

He shuddered, giving me some of what I longed for. Part of his life now swam inside me. My body spasmed, pure euphoric love and ecstasy exploded into each of my cells, Daniel's every feature coding in behind them. "I love you…" My voice ached with the words. They weren't enough, they would never *be* enough.

Daniel responded with a tender kiss, savoring the aftershocks that ran through us. Each of my breaths seemed borrowed from him. My angel...who was now hallowed ground.

He began to pull out. "Don't." My thighs locked over his. "Don't leave." I stole a shaky breath. "Teach me...teach me everything you like...everything that makes you happy."

His eyes, hollow and devoid of emotion, fixed on mine for a long moment before he continued to pull out, bringing a mixture of clear, white, and red fluids with him. He coated four of his fingers with the concoction before placing them in my mouth.

One by one, I licked them clean.

A distant part of me knew I would have balked at the gesture five minutes ago, but that might as well have been another lifetime.

Daniel kissed me, laughing under his heated breath. "That's a good start."

CHAPTER THIRTY-SIX

"Is this a hand print?" Kayla snatched up an open pizza box from under the kitchen table. A Chicago-style crime scene lay in evidence: five saucy lines dripping from the middle of the pizza and across the upper lid of the box. Cold cheese and Canadian bacon dangled over one corrugated edge.

"That's where that went!" I liberated a fragment of the mangled pizza and took a bite. It was still good after several hours on the floor. The miracles of modern food science. Kayla shoved the box into me with a shake of her head and a smile just this side of an eye roll.

"When I said go have fun, this is kinda exactly what I meant." Soapy water squished from the rag in her hand and down the tomato speckled leg of the table. "I am NOT cleaning that up, though." She pointed to a smear of white goo on the chair.

"It's ice cream." I chipped away at it with my fingernail. "I'm not gonna waste Daniel's happiness like that."

"It's not exactly a rare commodity." Her hand mimicked a repetitive vulgar gesture in the air. "He's probably already made more on his way home. All over his car thinkin' of you."

I laughed. "Probably."

Hopefully.

Definitely.

"Could have stayed and helped clean, though," she said.

"Well, he did pick up some before you got here." I looked back at her in all seriousness. "His shirt and shoes from the den floor, his boxers on the couch, and his pants from over there."

Kayla snapped the rag at me, missing by a wide margin and flinging bubbles onto the wall. "Your parents could come through that door any minute and you're crackin' jokes. Did the stain come out?"

"Won't know for a few hours." The felt in the middle of the pool table was a distinctly darker shade of purple than it had been the day before. Having used the last of the hydrogen peroxide last night, I'd called my best friend in a panic to bring some more.

I ran some water over the drink glasses and washed them in the sink. "How long did you bleed after your first time?"

"I don't know, a few minutes maybe. It was light too, nothing like the episode of CSI you've got goin' on in there."

"What about the next time?"

"Just the one time, I think, why?" Her concern ran in sheets against my wall, sliding off like suds on glass.

I turned around and toweled my cup dry. "I bled this mornin' too."

She thought for a moment. "Maybe you tore somethin'? Lookin' at this place, I wouldn't be surprised."

"There's no pain."

Except when he left me this morning.

"Sex hormones are potent, especially your first time— they can numb you up. Remember how stupid I got for

288

what's his face?" She shuddered. "And we didn't need a clean-up crew."

"Yeah." I snickered, stopping short of dredging up any specifics, like having to bleach her jeans to get her "married" name of Kayla Kearney out of them. "Also, I may have cranked the emotion dial to eleven before busting it off and burning it to cinders. That could have messed with my hormones some."

Kayla raised both eyebrows at me before knitting them together. "You think?"

"I regret nothing!" I raised the glasses above my head and scurried into the den.

My smarter half was leaning against the den doorway with her arms folded across her chest when I popped up from behind the bar. Her concern flared and I kept the bar between us.

"What happened? Why'd you change your mind about going fishing?"

"My mind had nothing to do with it." I laughed. "It just kinda happened." My thumb rubbed at a smudge on the oak wood trim. "I called it up, you know, harder, faster, deeper, more."

Was that my fingerprint or Daniel's? In my mind's eye his reflection moved in time with mine against the side of the bar, my sweaty fingers unable to grasp anything but him. The same thing I craved at my core. To hold him. To whip and drive his ecstasy to monsoon levels and drown us both in the rushing tide.

My torrential rains evaporated under a supernova of shock that threw me off balance and into the glass case. Kayla! The door to the den clicked shut. She was moving toward the stairs in a panic. Another set of emotions joined hers seconds later, jumping from relaxed, hopeful, and lusty, to shocked and uneasy alongside my best friend.

"What are you girls doing here?" My dad's muffled voice came through the door.

Shit!

I pulled myself from against the glass case with the deliberation of a sloth, willing the bottles not to rattle. They didn't make a sound and neither did I as I crept over and folded the top back over the pool table. The hydrogen peroxide was fizzing under cover of darkness when the doorknob jiggled.

I dove under the pool table, cringing at my stupidity even as I did it. It would take them all of three seconds to see me. I pulled my knees up to my chest. *I'm an ant. I'm a dust bunny. I'm a*—Kayla's sing-song voice piped up, interrupting my small thinking exercise. She was filled with forced excitement faker than anything I could have put there. "We have a surprise for you!" The ground shook, as though she'd jumped from the steps, and she was louder now: "But you've both gotta close your eyes and come with me. Oh, come on! It'll be fun!"

Her enthusiastic performance had me wanting to go see too, and I crawled to the door. All of them moved toward the kitchen. My best friend was a genius. The millisecond I thought they were out of view I slipped into the foyer and up a few steps. I bounded down them like a herd of elephants, and skidded across the kitchen floor right into a man who was not my father, though he shared his same salt and pepper hair. He looked down at me through coke bottle frames, a night's worth of scruff, and a sheet of hundred-dollar cologne. He was familiar, but I couldn't place from where.

"Sorry!" I stammered.

The man laughed, a bit of mischief dancing in his eyes. "Never admit culpability."

My dad scratched at the white bandage plastered above his left eyebrow. "So, what's the surprise?"

Crap. What *was* the surprise? I met Kayla's equally frantic eyes. "We...cleaned the kitchen! Ta da!" I made a big display of showing off how shiny everything was. "Figured it would make Mother feel better." Hey, if I could lie to a priest you better believe I could lie to my dad.

"Yes. It's very nice." He glanced around without actually looking. Given the smushed pizza box in the overflowing trash can that was probably for the best.

"Where is she?" I asked.

"Still at the hospital," my dad said. "I could use your help, since you're here. She wants me to gather a few things from her room. Marty, her office is just down the hall there."

Marty? Martin, Mother's lawyer. He nodded. "I remember." Mother's keys jangled in his hand as he disappeared down the hall. He'd discover my red kazoo was missing and report it to Mother and—*oh shit...not **my** paranoia.*

Deep breaths, Amy. Deep breaths.

"Come on, Amy," my dad called, and I followed him up to the post-apocalyptic landscape of their bedroom. He winced when we first walked in, sadness mingling with fear through glossy eyes.

"I got the blood out of the carpet." My voice was small and unassuming. Remembering my neck and the enormous hickey that was surely there I covered it posthumously with my hair.

"Oh? Good...good. Can you gather her brush and make-up?"

I bent down and picked up some lip gloss.

"The doctor thinks it's pre-menopausal hormone fluctuation." He opened her top drawer.

"What does *she* think?" A jar of powder lay open on its side, covering the blemishes beneath the bed.

"She fired him." He laughed but there was a ball of stress wrapped around the humor. "Somehow got a neurologist from Augusta to come up and see her this afternoon."

I laughed with him. "Sounds like she's getting back to

normal already." And there was real relief in me. The silence stretched while he assessed the room, seeing more than just the task at hand. He had a distant look and feel to him, like only part of him was in the present.

"How many stitches did you get?" The lid to the powder was cracked but it screwed back on without issue.

"I'm alright. When your mom gets back she's going to need less stress, so we're both going to have to pick up the slack around here. I'm trying to convince her to cut back some at work and I'll do the same, be around more for you after school. Some things are going to have to change around here. Are you with me?"

Oh, things were changing, but I wasn't so sure it was in a way either of them were going to like. Still, I nodded. "She loves these earrings." The crystal teardrops hung limp in my hand. "She says they dazzle people."

He took them from me. "Keep all this in house would you? I'm betting Kaylee knows, but that's as far as it goes, okay?"

"Okay." I found my shattered reflection in the mirror. "Dad, do you believe in ghosts, or psychic powers?"

"You think your mother's possessed? She'd probably take kindlier to that diagnosis than the one her doctor gave her." A streak of amusement colored his sadness, but nothing else. He'd been more surprised to find Kayla and I home than by my question.

"Do the Durene's have any abilities that run in the family? ESP, Empathy, talkin' to dead people? Or a history of mental illness?"

He chuckled, zipping up her bag. "No. All the crazy is squarely on your mother's side and you never heard me say that. I can handle getting everything together from here. I'll tell her you cleaned the house for her." Pausing, he looked thoughtfully around the room. "First you, now Angela. I'm wondering if it might not be this house. Something in the construction or a leak I don't know about that's turned into a mold problem. Marty says it's not unheard of to cause the sorts of things you and your mother have been experiencing. Can you stay at Kaylee's for a few days while we figure it out?"

Could my dreams come true? Yes please. "Yeah, that should be cool."

"Alright. Go fill your suitcase and take as much food as you want." He reached into his wallet and gave me what I'd make in two weeks at my job. "In case you need anything else."

"Th-thanks Dad." For an unsure minute I thought of hugging him, but he busied himself in Mother's suitcase and I backed into the hallway.

"Kayla!" I yelled over the railing. "I'm movin' in with you!"

Her face appeared below, and she grinned like a mad angel. She took the stairs two by two and whispered as we entered my room, "You do somethin' to your dad?"

"No, it's temporary, just until he sees the stain on his pool table and murders me." I pulled out my luggage and unzipped it. "He thinks mold in the house might be making me and my mother nuts. He wants me to stay with you until after he spends a fortune figuring out that's not it."

"I never considered spores as a cause of this. I'm sure that barn was full of them." She pursed her lips together.

"What if my dad decides to play pool before the peroxide can do its thing?"

"I'd say you should have thought of that before roaming all over his prized table with Daniel's beast, but...I don't know how to end that sentence." Kayla's smugness was growing brighter by the minute.

I lit up a cigarette, mindful of where my dad and Martin were and the waves of sympathy, guilt, and regret coming from them. "I could always make 'em both uneasy 'til they leave. Spook 'em out."

"Haunt your own house?" She cocked an eyebrow.

"Fawk. No. I said I wouldn't..." Blowing out my smoke, I stared into Cormack's blazing eyes. "Knowin' my luck they'd end up too scared to function, pissin' themselves on an endless loop." We both laughed and I shoved some random clothes into my bag, confident they would make a cohesive outfit in my time of need.

The sooner I was off my dad's radar, and he mine, the better.

CHAPTER THIRTY-SEVEN

"*S*elene's calving." Ma was up to the driver's side window before Goblin could be put ever-so-smoothly into park. "I'm keeping her close, so you girls will need to go inspect the summer fence for me." She squeezed Kayla's cheek. "Unless you'd rather we switched places?"

Our ATV whined through the mud as Kayla and I made our way to the northwest section of fencing. A creek ran along the outer edge, flanked by an otherworldly grove of weeping willow trees. They were coated in fog and swayed in the chilly breeze like a veil between worlds. It didn't take long to find the first broken stretch and get to work.

"Got my new thermal camera this mornin'." Kayla beamed at me and unraveled the spool of wire. "It has a wider range of temperature differentials than the one on my phone. If there's anything hangin' around us it should be able to tell."

"You're gonna take a picture of me and find some vapor flipping us off." I picked up the fencing pliers, the Swiss army knife of medieval torture devices.

"This one can do video." Grinning, she measured a length of wire against the mangled fence. "What the hell came through here, a moose?"

"Toss a stone. You ever recover those files? Or does it not matter since we're gonna redo them with your fancy camera?" Those first tests, even just a few short weeks ago, were such a strain on me. Now, I bet I could do them in a fraction of the time, and without passing out.

"'Course it matters. I told you, this is history we're makin' here. But God condemn it all, I spent the last of my youth in uninstall purgatory last night. I'd dig around and take something out only to restart and have it change nothing." She twisted the wire tightener. "I pop over to Coffeecake's tech forum to scream for a minute, and what do I discover? All my most recent threads dealing with Leilani, and 'my' empathy, were ghosted."

I pounded a staple into the post. "They deleted them?"

"I messaged the admins, and they're usually active at night, but I never got a reply. So, I bring up 'Bump in the Night' and get a 404 error. The whole site was down. Rinse and repeat for all the forums I posted to about any of this stuff in the past few weeks. Either the site wouldn't load or my recent threads were MIA."

"Oh shit..."

She met my wide eyes with an excited, sidelong glance. "You took the poetry from my mouth."

"What'd you do? Why didn't you call me?"

"I set up my equipment in the living room, drizzled honey on an apple and offered it to Leilani, along with an apology for putting her story up without permission. I asked her to talk to me through EVP or the box so we could help each other."

The EVP had different colored lights, and the box flipped through radio stations at a rapid clip. Ghosts could supposedly manipulate the lights and chaotic static to communicate. We'd had mixed results with the box, but in the dead of night in a vacant house that echoes and groans, we'd had our hair raised by a word or two that seemed to be answering our questions. When she played the video back later, we didn't always hear what we thought we had again, or sometimes we'd hear something completely different.

Kayla kept going. "I didn't get a response, but the session was interrupted by a tow truck pulling into the drive at half past midnight. Same one Daniel brought Goblin home with the other night. Except out steps this black-haired, tattooed breath of the wild." She let out a measured breath of her own.

"Cody?" I smirked at her. Otherwise known as "That Devious Repo Guy."

"Oh my God, Cody..." She feigned fainting. "Yeah, so my night got derailed. The box was on my belt and that got us talkin' about ghosts and then I just never shut up. Ended up talkin' to him 'til two-thirty! We swapped creepy stories and turns out he's got a possessed truck of his own." With a sigh and a vacant smile she leaned against the fence.

"You didn't entertain this gentleman unarmed, did you?" One utterly facetious eyebrow raised at her.

Her eyes tracked me under half lids. "I had my Taurus on me the whole time." The rebuttal hung thick in the air. "Anyway, I'll get into him more later...or him me...I sincerely hope." We both giggled and she continued, "After he leaves, I go back inside and apologize to Leilani again...but, I mean, come on, did she *see* who was at my doorstep? After a few more questions, with a lot of static for answers, I kinda fell asleep on my laptop. This morning, I woke to find my computer rebooted." She paused, turning to me slowly. "ALL the files were there. Like they just went out for pizza. And every one of the forums were restored."

I gave her shoulder a good tap with the pliers. "Why didn't you tell me this when you came over?"

"Girl, I barely yanked your neck from the noose as it was," she said, and I couldn't exactly argue. If we'd have been idle for one more minute, my house would have become a smoking pile of rubble when my dad caught me in his den.

Lowering the pliers with sheepish grace, I made a kissy face at her. "Love you…"

"…more than a sock full of barbed wire," she chimed.

"If she can delete the files, why not type a message to us?"

"The deletion was the message. 'Stop looking for me out there.' Final question I asked her—does she want us to go to the barn—and then all the files came back. Seems pretty clear to me."

It was about as clear as the fog creeping through the willow fronds, but I wanted answers, answers Ms. November 1975 could hold in her faded gaze. A lump formed in my throat. If things hadn't gone as planned before, would whatever was there be able to correct the problem? And what would that mean for me?

Kayla could see the worry in my silence. "You're stronger now, you know, than when we started. You ain't shied away from me once today."

"I've noticed the more relaxed and rested I am, the more I can handle. And Daniel sure wore me out." I laughed, throwing the pliers into the toolkit.

Sporting a determined smile, she hopped on the ATV. "Maybe Cody can do the same for me."

The afternoon stretched with talk of double dates, details of her conversation with Cody and my night with Daniel, and even Frisbee with Sam and Dee. Somewhere in there, we managed to mend a few miles of fence. By the end, she'd grown unbearably bright with anticipation of our trip to the Whitaker barn, and I had to drive back while she focused on being a Zen master.

"Woohoohoohoo!" She ran across the cattle lot and rode the top of the fence, waving her fuzzy pink earflap hat around like she was in the rodeo. "Time for blackjack and hookers!"

"More like menthols and moonshine." I snorted, climbing up several yards away from her and sitting at the top. One missed call from Daniel flashed at me when I turned on my phone. At some point he must have replaced his picture with an 8-ball, and I chuckled at the sight of it. Hitting call, I brought the phone to my ear and looked out toward the house.

One ring completed before I hung up.

Daniel was sitting on the patio table, watching us.

CHAPTER THIRTY-EIGHT

I vaulted the rest of the way over the fence and ran toward him. Daniel caught me as I leapt into his waiting arms, wrapping my legs around his waist and melting fevered kisses over his welcoming mouth. He laughed between short breaths, devouring me in turn.

With every touch and every taste, I was home.

"Hey! Hey! I'm right here! Get a room you two!" Kayla hollered, walking past us. "And no, you can't use mine!"

"There are plenty of other rooms," I whispered, biting his earlobe.

"No there aren't! You take that shit to the shed!" My best friend snickered and caught my eye, untethering her fierce expectation as she passed and letting it slam into me at full strength. "I'm loadin' up Goblin."

Did she just weaponize her emotions?

"Show me to the shed." Daniel nuzzled against my cheek and his words coiled through me, wrapping a constricting wire around all other thought...

...except Kayla's expectation, which had branded into me.

"Kayla wants to..." I swallowed down hard. *Just get the words out.* "...we need to go to the Whitaker barn." Eternity gazed back at me through hazel hues, and the seconds stretched into lifetimes.

Daniel loosened his grip and swung me to solid ground. While I steadied myself, Kayla came out with her hands full of equipment and set it all meticulously in the bed of her truck. She was humming with infectious excitement. "So, you in, Daniel?" she asked.

My boyfriend lit a cigarette and blew a gradual stream of smoke while surveying her. "Here's the problem." He looked down at me, liquid mischief sparkling in his eyes. "Dead Operation's playin' in an hour in Bangor and if me and Amy don't leave now, we won't make it."

"You have tickets?!" Kayla gasped. "That show's been sold out for months!"

His eyes didn't move from mine. "Lambchop's been through a lot, it's just what she needs."

I glommed onto him with a zealous hug that checked his balance. "Sweeter than candy," I sang softly, taking in the grounding scent of leather from his coat. His smile broadened against my temple while he stroked the back of my head.

Kayla shifted her tripod, familiar worry creeping over her. "What's the Fifth Quarter hold? A few thousand people? Amy, you sure you're up for dealing with that many at once?"

"Damn. Don't bring logic into this," I mumbled, smooshing myself further into Daniel.

"Like any muscle, it needs to be worked regularly to be strengthened," he said, grabbing my ass, and grinding my thigh subtly against the brick in his jeans. Heat swept through me, and though I'd meant to say something, all that escaped was a quivering whimper.

"At most she's dealt with forty people at once. She should probably ease into it," my best girl countered.

Daniel pulled back from me, wearing a smile that promised he was up to the top of Mt. No Good and the view was amazing. "Or dive in." He offered me his cigarette, which I took between numb fingers.

"I can't be the North Pond Hermit my whole life." I inhaled the smoke while talking, lending a compressed, wheezy quality to my tone. "I'll have my cigarettes and Daniel makes everything easier, seriously—you're at street lamp levels since he got here."

Kayla coughed and waved her hand in the air as she approached us, disappointment just beginning to cloud her excitement. "One night of sex and you're already droppin' me for a pair of eyes?"

"A night and a morning and a Dead show." I bumped into her playfully and put the smoke out on my shoe. "I know I suck, but the barn'll still be there tomorrow…"

"We don't know that." The edges of her smirk were weighted. "Remember Poltergeist?" Spoiler if you haven't seen it: the house implodes at the end. "You don't suck, I get it. I'm green, you *know* that, but I get it. At least bring me back a keychain or somethin' would ya? Get Flynn to sign your left boob and we can press ourselves together."

"Nope." Daniel stuck his icy hands under my jacket and cupped each breast while I shrieked. "Only one giving autographs'll be me."

Ma joined our circle of chaos, while laughing at us and toweling off her forearms. Kayla smiled. "I'll have date night with you, Ma. Whattya say? We can paint each other's nails corpse-purple and watch pulp horror from the seventies."

"You don't want to touch me, I've been up to my elbows in bovine amniotic fluid." She waggled her glistening fingers at Kayla, who shrieked the same as me and jumped away. "I had to go in and get him, but we've got a new bull."

"A bull?" Kayla perked up. "That mean I get a car?" Beloved as Goblin was, he guzzled just about every fluid ever made like it was last call at the Blind Pig.

Ma gave her a semi-irritated side look. "We can discuss

302

it." But there was an underlying generosity and excitement in her that had me grinning and nodding vehemently to Kayla.

"I bet Daniel knows the places to get a good deal, don't you?" I snuggled in and kissed him.

Ma turned her attention on us. "Hello, Daniel. Are you Irish by chance?"

"No." He smirked. "By blood."

Ma laughed. "Oh, you can call me Ma, and you're staying for dinner."

"Raincheck on that, Ma." He opened the passenger's side door of the Chevelle and escorted me inside. "Amy and I have a show to catch."

"I'm holding you to that!" Ma pointed to me as I got in the car. "And to keeping my treasure safe!"

"Yes, Ma'am." Daniel shut the door and I rolled down the window.

"Bye, Ma! Congrats on the new bull!" I waved to her as she walked toward the house.

With equal parts pride and embarrassment, Ma replied, "You too!" Kayla opened the door for her and held up one finger for me while she disappeared inside.

Trying to salvage something of myself after a day in the field, I ran a brush through my hair, stopping after a few strokes. "Hmm." I strained the mirror to examine my neck as Daniel got in. "No hickey. Guess you didn't autograph me as hard as I thought." I shot him a fox's glance.

"Oh? I can fix that." He slid on top of me and chomped on my neck while starting the Chevelle. I squealed, and after a few seconds he sat upright, shifting the car into drive.

"Wait!" I put my hand over his as Kayla came running up. She wasn't prepared for the honey-laden smile I threw at her. "So...maybe we can hold off on telling Ma I'll be staying with you until tomorrow? You know...just in case I end up somewhere else tonight?" Daniel shifted his hand so it covered mine, playing with the edges of my fingertips like piano keys.

A subtle symphony of desire hummed along with each caress.

Leaning in the window she peered at me, no doubt seeing the threads of everything that could go wrong with my plan. "I won't say anything, *if* you both promise to come out to the barn tomorrow…"

"Yeah, we alrea—" I said.

"—at seven in the morning," she interrupted, letting the wickedness drip from each syllable.

"Seven?!" I choked out. "Kayla! Be reasonable. How about…one?"

She clicked her tongue against the roof of her mouth. "Eight, and I'll meet you out there so you don't have as far to drive from…Bangor, or Monroe, or whatever field this beast ends up parked in." She patted the car door. "How's that for reasonable?"

"Anything before noon on a Sunday is unholy," I countered.

She gave me a deadpan irreverent smile. "Nine. I've got a shipment at two."

"Are you proposing nine a.m. or disagreeing in German?" Daniel asked.

I opened my mouth to bid for eleven, but Kayla cut me off again. "Halb zehn. Keine Minute später." Her lips were pursed but turned up at the ends.

"Angemessen," he replied, and seeing the look of confusion on my face added, "Ten-thirty. Not one minute later." He sat back in his seat. "Reasonable."

Kayla eyed him, trying to hide the upturn of her eyebrows under a stalwart demeanor. "If she gets overwhelmed, you get her out of there and away from people." She pulled the Taurus from her jacket and waved it at him in a jesterly manner. "Or I might get angry. And Amy doesn't like me when I—"

The kitchen window flew open and Ma's voice cracked through the air. "Kayla Isabel! Is that my gun in your hand?!"

Beside me, Daniel chuckled to himself. In one smooth stroke, and without thought, I swapped the gun for my cigarettes.

"N-no Ma! Just a pack of cigarettes!" Kayla shouted, holding them up in wide-eyed surrender.

"Didn't I teach the both of you better than to smoke?" Ma bellowed, and the window clanged shut.

Kayla brought her other hand slowly to her neck and made a choking gesture while staring at me. "From noose to necktie…" she said.

We'd both catch heat for smoking and probably have to watch some videos on lung disease, but it was better than Ma finding out her gun was going on adventures without her.

My best friend leaned down and gave me a smiling, grateful kiss on the lips. The pressure in my head instantly vaporized, and my mental wall came down in a landslide. Her gratefulness and shock spilled over me like liquid granite. I braced for incineration, only to come up for air engulfed in a primordial radiance. The same pure love that guided me out of Mother's darkness cradled each of Kayla's emotions as they flowed around me, so many lily pads on an endless river of warmth.

Is this the searing light that separated us all this time?

A single universe apart.

What changed?

Roots of the euphoric love I'd crystalized with Daniel glowed within me. A near perfect match to the light I was immersed in. I could match Kayla's frequency now? She was bright, but no longer blinding. Inwardly laughing, I swirled her sugary love around my fingertip like cotton candy at a carnival.

Come play, Kayla.

Baleful need scaled my insides one thorny tendril at a

time, anchoring itself as it climbed. Its vines constricted around my heart, cruel yet somehow comforting. I sucked in an ecstatic breath to the feel of Kayla's lips still pressed against mine.

Or is it the other way around?

Taste of almonds and chocolate...

Scent of...sunflowers...

Our favorite.

A vicious, penetrating howl split my foundation, shredding me in two. Amidst squealing tires I was ripped from Kayla. The Chevelle tore onto the road, whipping the horses into a froth under its hood. Daniel held the steering wheel with white knuckles and I flipped around to see my dusty silhouette growing smaller in the distance.

My silhouette?

CHAPTER THIRTY-NINE

"*W*-wait! I've got her gun and…" *I need to touch her more.* "…And that was my last pack of smokes!" Was *my* throat the one vibrating? *Do I really sound like this?*

Daniel wrenched the gun from me, threw it in his glove box, and slammed it shut. "No more kissing her like that!"

I faced forward, trying to glue together the fading pieces of a kaleidoscopic dreamscape. Had I kissed her, or had she kissed me?

"Kayla?" My words glazed over, unsure and distant. It still felt like the gun was in my hand. "She's my sister." *Is she?* "That was just—"

The Chevelle skidded to an ear-splitting halt in the middle of the street. My hands slammed against the dashboard, keeping my forehead from doing the same by a small miracle. Daniel swept his molten-hot tongue into my mouth. His exacting fingers kneaded the hair at the nape of my neck, twisting it just tight enough to bring the situation into focus. He maneuvered me back to my seat and released me before I could process any of it.

I stared, blank and unassuming, into vivid eyes I might have once blackened for such a stunt.

"No more." His breath was a cool storm against my smoldering lips.

He regarded me in a silence broken only by the idling engine, as though weighing my response. Each scattered path my mind stumbled down was overgrown with the need of him, to see him smile, to hear him laugh, to be in that moment and only that moment. And above all...to love him.

My angel's gaze fell away from me and to the road. He'd been understanding, and selfless, through bouts of crazy thick enough to send lesser beings wandering off Frye's Leap during a dry spell. All he asked was that I not kiss my best friend on the lips. It was important to him and I'd brushed it aside because I...

...because...

Be here...

...and now.

The Chevelle jolted forward, though my attention remained on Daniel. I'd hurt him, and I hadn't meant to. It wasn't in the vocabulary of my DNA anymore. I ran my fingertips along the far side of his cheek and down his rough neck, using the leverage to straddle him in one motion as he drove. With lips hovering near his, I whispered, "No, no more." Soft kisses of atonement grew in passion and devotion as he returned them.

This was how I would make him happy.

He veered onto an access road and threw the car into park. For all my worry about the seatbelts, they hardly made a dent in my spine.

∼

By the time we pulled into the lot of the Fifth Quarter we had missed the opening band and most of the second. Not that I minded; I was exactly where I wanted to be. Daniel swung into a spot near the entrance and reached under his seat, coming up with a red handicapped placard. He hooked it on the mirror and got out. "This way," he said, and we headed in the opposite direction of the front doors. I'd never been to the venue before, maybe there was a side entrance?

We walked for two blocks and turned into a narrow alley. Daniel did a running jump, parkouring off a gated window and onto the roof of a Scrub n' Suds. He bent to offer me his hand, but I was already mid-jump. The gutter on that roof may still be crooked to this day, but I made it. From there we navigated a maze of close-knit buildings, the music, and emotions, growing ever closer with each jump.

"I need a minute," I said, resting against the industrial air conditioner and peering out over the tranquil beauty of the Kenduskeag River. The lights on the State Street Bridge made fireflies on the water's surface.

Daniel lit and handed me a smoke. "You can feel them through the roof?"

"Yeah." I laughed. "A lot of them are numb and the rest are anxious."

He tilted his head while nodding. "Sounds right." Such gentle acceptance made me smile.

"How'd you know about this?" I gestured at the labyrinth we'd come through.

"Roof rats get to explorin'."

With a knowing smirk, I asked, "So, you don't have tickets to the show?"

"That's our ticket." He pointed to the edge of a stone balcony some thirty feet and a very steep slope away. "Or we could stay up here all night." My chin got a playful tweak. "Whatever you need. I already have what I want." Kissing me, he sucked the smoke from my lungs while freeing the cigarette from my hand.

He'd driven all this way, made these plans, and was ready

to chuck them off the roof if that's what I needed. I leaned my head against his shoulder. "You really are an angel."

After a long exhale, he snickered. "Fallen, maybe."

"Still counts." A violin solo serenaded our Hallmark moment. Dead Operation was opening with "Hyperion."

"I want to go...I need to go. But if I pass out—"

"You won't," he interrupted, taking my hand. "I make things easier, so keep your eyes on me." He coated me with a saucy glance. "It's where they belong, anyway." My feet lurched into motion as he pulled me down the slope at a run.

Focus on him.

I did, letting the reality of that 100-foot drop slip from my mind like suds off a tailpipe. We hurdled over the rail and onto the grand balcony, vacant except for a small table and folding chairs. A coffee can, half-filled with sand and cigarette butts, invited me to snuff out my smoke while Daniel opened the steel door with casual resolve.

With the intricate spell of "Hyperion" weaving through the air, no one noticed us come in. The tightly packed emotions of the floor beneath hammered against my kneecaps, but I stayed upright. Daniel squeezed my hand, running a stamp over it and smearing the ink with his thumb. It wouldn't hold up to scrutiny, but in the dark and from a distance, the initials VCB, Varrick Custom Builders, looked a lot like the VIP everyone else sported.

From the upper echelons we could see the band no matter where we were. The crowd was thick, but not to the level of the sardines below. With some trial and error, we found a spot above a large pillar and next to the outer wall that gave me ample room to breathe. I lost myself in the music, I lost myself to Daniel's touch, but I didn't lose myself to the emotional whims of the crowd. By the end I was sweaty, exhausted, and hungry enough to eat a vending machine sandwich.

I scored a D.O. plague doctor shirt, and got Kayla a pair

of skull-shaped pocket maracas. Joined with my liberty kazoo, we could form a band. As we left, I broke in the maracas to a chorus of honking horns and slung curses in the parking lot. My growling stomach provided the bass.

People were either jubilant or pissed off; there was very little middle ground. As tired as I was, everything threatened to merge into a giant ball of happy anger. I hooked an arm into Daniel's and beamed. "Thank you for tonight. You were right, sometimes you gotta dive in."

His body tensed and we came to such an abrupt stop that I stumbled forward a little. Following his insanity-infused gaze, my hand shot over my mouth. Deep gouges, as if from the claw end of a hammer, criss-crossed the body of the Chevelle.

Each word Daniel spoke next had its own zip code. "What in the frothy pink fu—!" His face connected with the windshield and I went sprawling into the side of the car, cracking my head against the window and sliding to the ground.

A malicious knot of anger loomed over us, blood dripping from his knuckles as he spat through clenched teeth. "That's for Emily, you piece of shit!"

CHAPTER FORTY

"She's up in County because of you!" the angry bull screamed. His rage charged the door to my china shop mind and splintered it down the middle.

Shit! I can't let him run loose!

Focus!

"Daniel…" I put my back against the car and turned my head toward him. He blurred in and out as he rolled off the hood and stood beside me. The pavement became a canvas of splattered ichor at his feet.

Hands up and palms out, the way you might try to calm a wild horse, Daniel stepped toward his attacker. In a low nasal tone he said, "Hold up a lick there, Tim. Before you go cold cockin' a son of a bitch, you need to hear my side of things." He spat a wad of blood off to the side.

Tim strained against two good Samaritans who'd each taken an arm. The bull's mad sunken eyes fixed on Daniel. "I ain't hearin' shit! You used her! Emptied her bank account, filled her head with roadkill! Made her hate us!"

Daniel's brows drew together. "Whoa. I don't know what she told you…" He strayed closer, each word growing hushed. "...But we broke up because she's a pathetic, frigid, unlovable cow with the personality of a house plant." At this last sentiment, he stomp-kicked Tim in the chest.

Tim and his chaperones flew backward, and Daniel fell on the bull in a flurry of black boots. "That dumpster fire was lit before I got there! Nearly burned my dick off in it!"

Scrambling to their feet in a slew of curses, the Samaritans grabbed for Daniel. One got an elbow to the jaw and the other a fist to the gut for their trouble, and my matador kept on kicking.

Outside my china shop door, one bull became three.

The door exploded inward in a stampede of red.

Get off my angel!

I seized both rodeo clowns' anger by the throat and cranked their fear past the boiling point. Every other emotion drowned or evaporated in a scalding cauldron of terror. Clown One clutched at his chest, tripping against the brick building. Clown Two ran like his pimp was calling him for mac n' cheese, parting the assembling crowd of gawkers.

Daniel pinned his knee against Tim's chest, snatching the flailing cockroach up by the collar. "I don't know how she is for you, but when I was fucking her, I thought I was gonna get arrested for desecrating a corpse!" He conducted an orchestra of satisfying cracks with each punch to Tim's face.

Fighting against an uncooperative ground, I slid up the passenger's side of the Chevelle. What sound would pocket maracas make against a real human skull? I was about to find out.

But the problem with blind rage is, it never learned braille and wouldn't be caught dead reading a warning label even if it had. I'd set into motion a blistering tidal wave of fear that overflowed my targets and flooded into me. My once raging bull melted into jittery tallow.

The hood clanged under my shaky hand as Daniel tossed

Tim onto it. Terror hardened around me, fixing me there. Tim's swollen eyes and lopsided jaw were savaged into the scratches he'd presumably created, and he gurgled out a whimpering yowl.

Daniel, his nose and mouth awash in blood, took on a matter of fact, almost disappointed tone. "Your sister tried to drink Drano and failed, so you thought you'd come take it out on my innocent Chevelle?" Grasping Tim by his greasy locks, he slammed the boy's face into the hood once more and let him slide to the curb.

My fallen angel cocked his head and examined the glistening streak Tim left behind. "I like red better, anyway," he said, as though he were picking out swatches at Rusty's. "I'm getting a new paint job and you're gonna fuckin' pay for it, you mouth-breather." Sneering, he looked down at Tim's groaning form and flipped him onto his back with one foot. "Once they pull your balls outtah your throat. Now, get the fuck outtah here."

Can Tim get anywhere but to a morgue?!

A girl sporting three short braids ran over and knelt beside Tim, calling his name. Blood poured over the concrete as he struggled to respond.

Jesus!

The white rabbit never mauled anyone!

You don't know that for sure…

Besides, don't invite yourself for tea and then complain when you get second degree burns on your lips.

My rabbit touched the bridge of his nose and winced. Drawing in a sharp breath, he blew a clot of blood all over Tim. "Fuck!" Daniel screamed, through gritted teeth, "Broke my fuckin' nose!" Seemingly as an afterthought, he kicked Tim the rest of the way over the curb. The girl with the braids shrieked and jumped back.

Daniel snagged the D.O. shirt from my statue-like grip. I

flinched, but otherwise stayed cemented in place. He dried off his bloody fists and brought the shirt to his nose.

His broken nose!

He needs a hospital and I can't move!

You can't pull yourself together!

You scalded away "together."

Fear is all there is…

…oh God! For the rest of my—

"Amy. Come on." Daniel's voice poured through me, melting the brackish tar in which I stood. A matrix of patterns, hard-baked into my foundation, glowed beneath the sludge. Everything hadn't burned away…

…love remained.

Fear and love aren't as different as you might think. Both are bright, strong, and overwhelming. Both cause us to fight, flee, or freeze. And both are engines of survival. Or so it was for me. From one of these glowing bastions of light stretched a tiny sprout, its roots absorbing the pitch around it as another leaf unfurled.

I huddled next to the seedling, coaxing love to flourish within a dark and tremulous valley. Pieces of fear sloughed off the sides, rolling to a stop at my feet. The slag brightened in pockets of green before bursting into an oasis of wildflowers. Clover bloomed between my toes, tickling me as I took a playful step back. A dagger poked between my shoulder blades and I froze, only to be met with the scent of roses.

Of course, they were there.

The frosty touch of the Chevelle's door handle returned me to my body. I'd actually taken that step back.

You overdid it this time. Fried something.

I'm gonna pass out.

No…he said I wouldn't.

Daniel needs me.

More flowers blossomed. Roses, orchids, daisies, and…sunflowers.

Rabbit needs you.

I leaned into the handle, steadying myself before opening the door and bumbling into the front seat on gelatin legs. Rabbit was bent forward, his face buried in my souvenir shirt.

Betraying a tremor, I asked, "You want me to drive to the hospital?" As if it were in any way a good idea.

He laughed in a short huff. "No." Sitting up and releasing a measured breath through his mouth, he pulled my shirt away. Black, blue, and purple half circles cradled his eyes and extended over the bridge of an obscenely slanted nose.

My stomach tightened.

Daniel looked in the mirror and brought his fingertips to either side of the demolished bridge. After a few seconds of feeling around, he jerked it to one side with a sickening crunch.

Tears welled in his eyes and we both hissed through our teeth. On reflex, I cupped my hands over his nose, as if to protect him from more pain. At the feel of his broken cartilage, my heart jolted, unraveling layers of chains at the core of me.

A second gruesome snap filled our sanctuary.

What did I—?

From my fingertips pulsed a faint luminescence. Smoky tendrils wove into his skin, and through the bridge. Half-moon bruises faded from purple, to pink, to white, beneath wide, unblinking eyes that mirrored mine.

Cold…I'm so cold.

Hitching my breath, I pulled back with some effort. It was like disengaging two electrically charged magnets. I stared at my shaking hands, wisps of pale light retreating into fingertips abuzz with vitality. My gaze returned to Daniel. Aside from the blood around his nose and mouth there was no sign he'd been hurt.

How had I—

The rest of my body joined my legs and I collapsed into his warm rigid arms. In a breathless voice that echoed in the darkening corners of my mind, he said, "Holy shit! You aren't fuckin' around!"

No, but I was passing out...

...even though Daniel told me I wouldn't.

CHAPTER FORTY-ONE

*G*rumble.

Gruuuuuuumble.

Grrrrrrrrrrrrrrrrrrrrrruuuuuuuuuuuuummmmmble.-

I woke to a stomach twisting itself into knots over the finer points of self-cannibalism. My mouth was a desert, my face an oasis of drool soaking into a pillow that smelled of earth and musk. A buzzing sound crackled somewhere close. One sliver at a time, I opened my eyes through lids that seemed coated in rust.

Darkness, save for a dim green glow at the foot of the bed.

Pale blue-white glow from my fingertips.

Was that real?

Each movement of muscle was its own decathlon, but eventually I made it across the finish line and propped myself up on my elbows. The source of both light and sound was a mini-fridge with a jagged, neon "M" sign humming inside. Two shelves housed a dozen Monster energy drinks in tall slim cans. I crawled to the fridge and pawed it open, pouring the drink down my gullet before I could register the taste.

Might have poured it into the garbage for all the good it did. I opened and slammed another. The flavor reached me by the end. It was the finest orange puree on the planet.

Monster? I stared at my fingertips in the cool misty air rolling off the fridge. *Is that what I am?*

I moved onto another can, and after that another. Ma said people had heart attacks after drinking too many of these. Maybe I could kill whatever was in me.

A shiver crawled through my spine and I shot upright, fully awake for the next century or so. The room brightened enough through my dilated eyes to see the outline of a doorway and light switch. I shuffled over and flicked it on, bringing a corner lamp to life. My hand brushed lightly against a sheet of paper taped above the engaged deadbolt. It read: "Don't leave this room."

Daniel's handwriting.

His capital Ds look like shooting stars.

Or maybe a capital A that didn't quite make it home after a night of drinking.

On the other side of the door, a bullseye drawn in Sharpie masked a fist sized crack in the wall. Black ink had seeped into the crumbled gypsum in places, but overall it was a meticulously symmetrical piece of art.

Mounted over a series of shelves, each cluttered with X-Station paraphernalia, loomed a large TV. Drawers hung half open, spilling unmatched socks and inside out t-shirts onto the well-worn hardwood floor. Thick black curtains covered each window. I lifted one and gazed out onto an early morning landscape. I was on the second story overlooking a giant garage surrounded by white vehicles, each carrying the face of one judgmental eagle.

My stomach growled again, turning at the thought of another energy drink. Gun cases, snowboards, and a pair of boxers hid under the bed, but not so much as a single bag of stale chips. His closet brimmed with clothes, hunting gear, snow gear, and a playboy bunny Halloween costume still in its packaging. My purse, and subsequently my phone, were nowhere to be seen; however, I had a more pressing problem.

I'd downed four energy drinks in twenty minutes.

And Daniel's note had said not to leave the room.

I lay back on the bed, holding a stomach that simultaneously felt hollow, and like a Xenomorph would burst forth at any second. Groaning, I eyed the empty Monster cans. There was no way my aim was that good, especially with how jittery I was. As if to mock me, the heavenly scent of Italian perfection began a subtle dance under my nose. Had Chummy Cheese heard my grumblings and come through with a zeppy peppy pizza?

If not, could I please hallucinate it?

Whining, I stared at the note. Why was I prepared to take this to *Secretary* levels? My stomach turned to quicksand at the thought of not doing what he'd asked. It rivaled the other two needs in urgency. He'd written it for a reason. He hadn't said don't leave the house, he'd said don't leave this room.

But he hadn't planned on me drinking enough Monsters to fill a bathtub.

He wouldn't want you in pain.

Yeah. I'm right. He wouldn't.

I strained an ear to the door and, not hearing or feeling anyone, opened it. The bathroom was just across the way, its shining white tile gleaming in the sunlight. I'd be there and back again before you could say Chummy Cheese chops, chews, chokes, and chases chattering children challenging chocolate chickens to cheer, three times fast.

Okay you, I wasn't done by then, but I *am* impressed.

Fifty Chummy Cheese cheers later, I crept out into the hallway on feathered feet. Below me, two sets of emotions blended together in a soup of passive frustration. And at the end of the hall, on a pinewood coffee table, sat the source of my salivation; a meatball sub cut in two and drowning in cheese.

The spicy siren never stood a chance. Sweet and savory sauce oozed through my fingers and into my mouth, and I played hot potato with the meatball on my tongue while scampering back to Daniel's room. I closed the door, sat on the bed, and took another taste bud obliterating bite of pure deliciousness.

Everything was right with the world.

The floorboards shook in measured stride, and a swell of anger and frustration kicked open the door like a shotgun blast seconds later. "God damn it, Danny! You are not—" A well-dressed girl in her twenties stopped in her tracks, slowly lowering her foot to the ground. "You...are not Danny..."

I kept chewing, tightening my grip on the sandwich as I stared at her through wide eyes. Her brows, nose, and ears resembled Daniel's.

Without looking away from me, she called out the door, "Maaaa-um! Danny's brought a girl home...and I think she's feral."

Shaking my head, I replied, "I'm Amy," and took another sizable bite.

She crinkled her brow and cocked her head. "Well, Amy, this is MY lunch." The plate was snatched from me, spilling a trail of meat and sauce onto the floor.

I squirreled the last of the half I'd been holding into my overstuffed mouth.

Moments later the plate was returned to me by an older woman with her hair pulled into a bandanna. A few more meatballs were sacrificed to the floor on the way. "Christina, that's no way to treat a guest in our house! Look at the poor dear, she looks like she hasn't eaten in days."

"Days?" I choked down a bite that needed more chewing. "What day is it?"

"First girl he brings home and she's a meth addict." Christina rolled her eyes. "Figures."

"I'm not a meth addict, I'm just...well..." I examined my saucy fingers. "I don't know what I am."

"You don't know what you are? What kind of an answer is that? What? Did Daniel *make* you? Out of his Weird Science kit?" my sandwich rival hissed.

"Christy! Go make another sandwich." Maaaa-um pointed out the door.

"Yeah, Christy, make me one while you're at it." Daniel came in, sneering at her as they passed in the doorway. Placing the plate on the bed I sprang up, enveloping him in a hug that he returned with gusto.

Happiness fluttered from Maaaa-um, birds on the wing, while Christy tumbled into insecurity and bitterness. She scrunched her nose at him. "Your science experiment stole my food! At least have the decency to chain them up." Throwing her hand in the air dismissively, she stormed down the hall.

I picked up the sad remnants of my sandwich, stopping short of chomping down. Two instincts struggled within the same hand. Eat the sandwich or bring it to Daniel's mouth. I did the latter, grateful when he shook his head "no" and I could take another bite.

Maaaa-um watched me. "I'm glad you like it—Amy, did you say your name was?" I nodded and smiled through my full mouth. "I'm Tina, Daniel's mum." She patted her son's belly. "I'll reheat some more. We've got three tubs left over from Kiwani Days to get through. So we're eatin' Italian 'til the Fourth." After giving us both a satisfied once over, she strolled out of the room.

Daniel smiled at me. "Not the way you're going. We'll be crackin' that second tub by sundown." He closed the door, threw the deadbolt, and ripped down the sign he'd left.

"I'm sorry," I said, mid-chew. "Nature called...but I came

right back." I picked up the plate and waved it around. "With a slight detour."

He crumpled the paper and tossed it on his desk before sitting beside me. "You say anything to them about last night? Your empathy, any of it?"

"It wasn't a hallucination?" I brushed his nose with my fingers. "Did I really?"

Lowering my hand to his lips, he closed his eyes, kissing each fingertip with a gentle reverence. "You tell them?"

"Just that I don't know what I am...they think I'm crazy, like you used to." I put the sandwich on the plate and flexed my fingers. A crack scattered through my voice. "I don't know if I'm possessed, or an alien, or an X-girl, but I'm some kinda freak."

Saying it aloud made the surreal real, and my eyes welled with unsung tears.

He brought my hand from his lips to the side of my face, cupping it within his and stroking my jawline with both our fingers. "You're beautiful." His lips closed over mine with the same adoration he'd shown my fingertips.

I caressed his hand as he held mine, heat and pressure swirling through me like a tropical storm. Tears warmed my cheeks and I took in a deep, unsteady breath, returning the kiss in fevered waves before resting my forehead against his.

He massaged the back of my head, speaking in a soft tone, "We're gonna figure this out. 'Til then, keep it between us."

I nodded, whispering, "And Kayla."

"And Kayla," he agreed.

"And Leilani." I pulled back, thinking a moment. "Aaand the raccoons."

He cocked an eyebrow at me. "You've got a lot to tell me." I opened my mouth to add in the owl, when he stuck a meatball between my teeth. "Not here." Reaching under the bed, he pulled out the gun case. "Fill me in on our way to see Kayla."

"What time is it?" I asked.

"Little after nine." Daniel gathered boxes of ammo and his crossbow from the closet, while I cleaned meatballs and sauce from the floor. Tina was making more...no need to use my tongue.

"Where'd you go so early?"

"Early? I'm up at five most days." He chuckled. Given the hours we'd been keeping, that mini-fridge was just as much a necessity to him as it had been to me. "There were fires to put out from last night."

"How'd it go?" I put a few cans of Monster in his camo backpack for good measure.

"I ain't in jail." Shouldering the crossbow and ammo bag, he added, "And this ain't the place."

No jury in the world would convict him. I'd see to that. "We goin' zombie hunting?"

He unlocked the deadbolt. "Could be."

We were heading down the backstairs when Tina called after us, her voice echoing off the narrow hallway walls. "Amy, come here for a minute won't you please? Let Daniel take all that out to his car."

Daniel smirked and motioned toward her with his head, continuing down the winding steps. I set the backpack down with a thunk and crept into the kitchen. A giant tub of meatballs lay open on the counter while four sandwiches spun in the microwave.

Tina smiled at me and said, "We're out of mozzarella, so I used swiss, I hope that's all right."

"Yes." I smiled back. "Thank you."

"Plain milk? Strawberry? Or chocolate-caramel?" she asked. Why did it feel like my answer would reveal more about me than an ink-blot test?

"Oooh! Strawberry!" I grinned.

This won a round of approval.

Christy sat, spine-straight, on the couch with her feet up

in the exact spot I'd liberated her food from. She glared at me with a mixture of jealousy, shock, and insecurity sloshing around.

I might get sea sick if I didn't focus somewhere else...or make it stop. "I'm sorry Christy. I was just so hungry and—"

"Obviously!" she snarled.

Just a slight attitude adjustment...a small one, really, to make her more pleasant and happy. Wouldn't we all win? That's where I'd gone wrong with Mother. I should have made her happy. What harm could there be in that?

I don't know, a category five hurricane?

How are those good Samaritans doing?

"Christy, go down and see if that invoice came from Dave. Let me know when it does." Tina shot her the "mom look."

See? Mum's on the case. Just focus on something else.

The open tub of meatballs sat on the counter, beckoning me to bury my head in it and inhale. It seemed like a great way to solidify my status as a meth head.

"Can I help with anything?" I asked Tina. Anticipation bounced around her like a wayward super ball, though it didn't show as more than a pleasant smile on the outside. She poured a glass of milk, put a spoon on top of a container of strawberry Lightning flavoring, and slid both over to me. I opened the container, weighing the pros and cons of dumping the whole thing in all at once.

How many scoops did they recommend? Two? Or was that raisins? Here I was in my moment of need and marketing was failing me.

I put in three and stirred, turning to a picture of the Varrick family outfitted in superhero costumes as I put the lid back on the Lightning and shifted it across the counter.

Nothing could have prepared me for how adorable a five-year-old Spiderman Daniel would be. He looked like the perfect ending of a Star Trek Transporter accident between his parents, manifesting all the best features of each. His dad was Captain America, sporting a hubcap emblazoned with his judgmental eagle, while Mum rocked the Wonder Woman look, complete with measuring tape lasso at her hip. Daniel was flanked by two competing Supergirls and the toddler version of Flash.

"Cuuuuute!" I pointed to the picture. "Three sisters. Is that why he started shaving his head, so they couldn't do his hair?" I laughed.

"It never saved him from the make-up, though." She laughed with me, but underneath swept a current of sharp and hollow pain that bit a chunk from my wall.

Okay, move on.

"You've got a lovely family," I said, starting in on my drink, which could have used another spoonful of strawberry, and taking in the rest of the portraits on the walls.

"Ha!" Christy spat. She hadn't moved from her place on the couch.

As the portraits progressed, there were only two older sisters and Daniel. The Flash was missing. Next to the portraits, a faux chalkboard read: "Please excuse the mess, the children are making memories" only "making memories" was scribbled out and replaced with "being assholes."

Christy spoke up again. "Danny has a girl overnight and you're not layin' into him. You're feeding her and chatting! He's just eighteen. I was almost twenty when Noah stayed over and I'm still catchin' shit for it!"

"Yeah, wasn't her catchin' crabs punishment enough?" Daniel came in and slammed the lid on the tub of meatballs, drowning out Christy's response. "I'll put this back in the garage fridge." He gave his mum a peck on the cheek and she handed him a glass of Lightning-less milk.

"Your dad could use an extra pair of hands out in Fairfield. Tanner called out sick."

He chugged the entire glass in one go, putting it down

heavily on the counter with a little spin to it. "If I find a spare pair, I'll drop 'em off."

"It'd go a long way if they were yours!" She smiled at him against the ding of the microwave.

Daniel picked up the tub. "We'll take ours to go."

Tina placed two sandwiches in a steel lunchbox and handed it to me as I finished the last of my milk.

I took Christy's plate and set it in front of her. "I don't like swiss," she said, frowning at the sandwich. When she went back to typing on her phone, I opened the lunchbox and made to dump the sandwich in with ours. "Hey!" she snapped, "I didn't say I wouldn't eat it! Geesh, what are you pregnant?!"

I returned the sandwich and stared down at myself. Why *was* I so hungry all the time? The feeling in my heart...did I have a chest-burster inside? My breath dried in my throat and the room grew chilly. No, no...I had scans at the hospital, they'd have noticed an alien egg...wouldn't they?

Those scans were all around my head.

And my cytokines were high...

"I could eat up some grandkids!" Mum chimed in and Christy's jealousy oozed around my frigid feet. I backed up, square into Daniel.

"What if the grandkids eat up you?" I said under a shallow breath.

"Then we'll know for sure they're mine." He nudged me down the hallway with the weight of the meatball tub. "Come on Lambchop, before she starts pickin' out names."

"I can't be pregnant with your Xenomorph, I don't even know your middle name..." I didn't resist his herding as I processed this troubling new possibility. "It was nice meeting you both!" I shouted back to them.

"You too dear! Come back anytime!" Mum said.

"His middle name is Douche-Canoe!" Christy added. "With a hyphen!"

"Oh, it is not! It's Ethan!" Mum chided. "After my great grandfather who lived to be one hundred and seven, with *twenty-two* grandkids."

I squinted as we stepped out into the sunshine; it was one of those days that promised hints of summer against a cruel, chill wind. "How many aliens you figure it'd take to overrun the world?" Opening the lunchbox, I bit into my hot sandwich. It was way better with swiss.

"One." A giant sheet of plastic crinkled in the trunk of the Chevelle as he popped the tub inside, next to his hunting gear. "In case you need to refuel." He threw a knowing smile my way and closed the trunk. The poor scratched up car looked even more wretched in the light of day.

"I just might swim in it," I warned, holding out the other half of my sandwich for him.

Taking it, he looked up at the house. "Christy can't handle me bein' the favorite." He donned a Loki grin. "On a scale of one to ten, how jealous is she?"

"Grinch green for not sharing her sandwich with a meth head." I laughed. I'd been afraid to lose the sense of normalcy our relationship had gifted me with this past week, but here he was bringing it with him into my surreality.

Our surreality.

CHAPTER FORTY-TWO

"*P*urse isn't here!" My heart marinated with the meatballs in my stomach. My life was in there, and not an insignificant amount of cash. "Can I use your phone?"

"Broke last night," he said. "It's for the best. Phones have ears." When I cocked an eyebrow at him, he added in a pleasant announcer's voice, "NSA, FBI, CIA and other nefarious abbreviations are listening."

Kayla had taken video of so much of our journey, and even put some of it on the internet. Our phones were right there, every step of the way. If someone was listening, they already knew everything.

Not everything…not last night.

A man jogged by with a Golden Retriever at his heels.

Is that earbud for music, or taking instruction?

Daniel started the car and backed up, the wheel sliding under his bruised knuckles. I reached for them, but he blocked me gently with his elbow. "Looks worse than it is," he said.

Right. No good risking passing out again, if I didn't need to. Except, I did *need* to. *Look at the cracks on his ring finger, glistening deep red every time he flexes—that's fresh blood, and under that fingernail there...it's almost black! He's suffering. He's suffering, and you can make it stop!*

No! You stop it, he doesn't WANT me healing him now, it's not a good idea. I fiddled with my fingertips before sitting on both hands, in case they decided to grow minds of their own again.

It was some kind of torture to do it.

Peeling onto the highway, he asked, "How do raccoons figure into all this?"

I told him the whole story as we drove, and I kept my hands busy with more meatball subs. On occasion he'd interrupt, extracting one innocuous detail or another with surgical precision, but on the whole he listened.

"And now my hands are smoking without a cigarette..." I said, twisting some sauce off them with a napkin. "What'd it feel like when I healed you?"

Heal him.

He wriggled the bridge of his nose with his fingers and considered the question. "White hot. Then numb. Then like I could do an eight-mile line of coke."

I laughed. "It was the opposite for me. Cold and draining, but also comforting somehow." I tried to will the wisps from my fingertips, but only managed to create a distorted jackalope shadow puppet. It leapt across the dashboard in the morning sun, stopping to nibble at Daniel's unnecessarily purple knuckles. I stared a long moment, not only resisting the urge to heal him again, but replaying Mother slamming mine against the floor. Over and over she'd done it, yet I hadn't bruised...not even a scratch.

Checking in the side mirror, I rubbed my neck. The hickey I'd been sure would be there hadn't been, either.

I dug my penknife free from my pocket and unsheathed the blade. Blood pooled into a tiny canyon as I sliced into my forearm.

Daniel glanced over and then back at the road.

While I spoke, my eyes never left the wound. "I dropped a twelve-pound bowling ball on my foot three frames into my free birthday game at Splitz. Hurt somethin' ugly with a bruise to match. Ma put ice on it, and I limped through the rest of the game. Didn't give it much thought on account of the two Vodka Cokes I'd snagged, but I walked out just fine not two hours later. Next morning there was no brui—"

The canyon walls meshed together, tossing the blood clot up and out, still wet. Reddened flesh flared with the heat of someone snuffing a hotbox from a cigarette out on me.

"Oh shit!" I jumped back, as if I could get away from my own arm. "Shit! I'm doing it! I'm healing!" With the last traces of the wound and pain fading, I brought my forearm square with my face. No wisps.

I cut my arm in a different spot, bringing it beneath my shirt into the darkness. Still no light show, just throbbing pain followed by pinching, burning heat. With gritted teeth, I pulled back out in time to watch the second wound finish sewing together, and the Chevelle squeeze through the partially open entrance gate to the Whitaker barn.

"What the fuck?! You see this too, right?" Hard as I tried, there wasn't enough air in the cabin to fill my strangled lungs. "Tell me you see this too!" Shadows pulsed at the fringes of my sight and I slashed my arm a third time.

A cry echoed in the distance.

Keep cutting…bleed IT out…

Daniel's voice bled through my hailstorm, carrying a soft, detached authority. "Hey, hey, that one went a little deep." His hand cupped the wound, blood pooling against it with each of my erratic heartbeats. "You've got arteries in there." With his free hand, he brought his shirt over his head, down his arm, and wrapped it around my gash.

My understanding of human anatomy consisted entirely

of what I'd gleaned from sleeping behind Mr. Skullhead in Biology class.

Dem bones, dem bones, dem dry bones.

Dem bones, dem bo—

Was I even human?

We'd stopped moving. Condensation clung to the inner windows, muddying the daylight. Why was I in a refrigerator? Blood trickled over my shaking elbow, pattering to the leather seat below in uneven drops.

Pit. Pat. Pat. Pat...

The dull throb in my forearm exploded with heat and I cried out between clenched teeth.

That echo in the distance...had it been me?

I didn't think I'd cut so deep...

When the stream subsided, Daniel unwrapped his shirt and my muscle and sinew finished their grisly intertwining dance. Swallowing back bile, I searched his eyes for answers they couldn't possibly hold. My heart screamed in my chest, erupting as an increasingly frantic whimper through each harried breath. "Am I...am I the ghost?"

Daniel shifted me on top of him, his tone firm and relaxed. "Calm down." The emotion radiated from my spine without thought, dissolving mountains of anxiety and fear in gentle waves. The screaming quelled to a dull disagreement. "And breathe," he continued, "Ghosts don't breathe."

I sucked in a full breath warmed by his closeness. The shadows retreated in slow draws from my vision as his lips graced my neck. With each kiss, more of my senses returned, only to slip down the rabbit hole of his perfect touch and be lost all over again.

"You're alive Amy," he said, coiling his tongue against the soft flesh below my earlobe. Every nerve in my body stood at attention. "And don't you forget it."

"I won't forget..." My hand anchored into his, steadying the tumbling earth.

His scouring fingers arrested my neck, blood trailing down from them in cold rivulets. "And, you belong to me."

"Always..." The word rolled from my tongue to his as though it were an extension of me. He grew hard against his jeans. So that's which way was up. Drifting on a fathomless kiss, I fumbled with his button and zipper, slipping my hand down his pants. A handful of seconds later he came, coating his stomach and chest in short bursts and treating my ears to an angelic chorus of moans.

Outside our windows, a watercolor world of splotchy greens and blues rolled by. We stared down at his wellspring of life and then at each other, smiling. He grabbed his bloody shirt and cleaned himself off in one long, deliberate sweep.

With a click of the door handle, fresh, cool air swirled around us. Daniel lifted me up and onto the pebbled remnants of the road. Every manner of weed grew in the cracked and worn crevices. Bumblebees flitted between violets and lilies while the wind whistled through the forest canopy, broken by an occasional bird song.

In the decades of neglect, the woods had claimed sections of the crumbling barn. Indeed, the trees were all that seemed to be holding the building together in spots.

A strange symbiosis.

"You wanna go in there now?" I skirted behind Daniel, who was rummaging around in the trunk, and put my arms around him, peeking down the front of his jeans with a fool's grin. "I mean, we could do other things..."

He picked up a sawed-off shotgun and gave me a long backward once over. "I could fuck you all day and declare Monday a national holiday, but we need to go in there and figure out what's going on before I decimate you."

"Right, it's best to conserve my energy, given the circumstances. Not nearly as fun though." I stared at the barn, unease struggling for purchase but sliding off the prevailing calm like it was made of ice.

"You don't want to go in." It was as much a statement as a question.

"No. I can't help feeling like somethin's wrong with me and if I go inside it might get fixed. Whatever's fighting for control will finish the job."

Within my chest, strings tightened, thrummed, and slackened all in the same heartbeat. A tug, coming from—

"You're already possessed." Daniel lit up a cigarette, took a drag, and held it toward me. "And I don't share."

I accepted the smoke with a half smile and a shake of my head. I was already possessed. There was an odd comfort in that. "Yeah, the hotel's full, no vacancies."

"How many times you healed today without so much as a yawn? Handled that crowd last night without breakin' a sweat. Whatever's fightin' for control is you. So, finish the job. Knock its teeth in."

Did it have teeth?

I was a little tired and hungry, but nothing like the night before. Taking a hit, I asked, "How is it you're so calm about all this freakishness? I had to 'influence' myself." Influencing...that had a nice sanitized ring to it.

Daniel gazed out over the field, resting his forearm against the top of the trunk and narrowing his eyes. "For a long time, people couldn't figure out how those little bastards could fly." He pointed to a bumblebee hovering over a patch of wildflowers. "Violated the laws of aerodynamics. Yet there it is bouncing from flower to flower, ass to the wind for the law. The impossible bumblebee. Just because we can't understand something, doesn't mean we never will, or that it's unnatural, or something to be feared."

"Bumblebees can sting." I zoned out on my cigarette hotbox.

"Treat them right, and you can pet 'em." He handed me a shotgun before closing the trunk. "Lead the way, Lil Bumblebee."

Taking one last deep hit, I tossed the smoke to the ground and snuffed it out with my shoe. "Over here."

A dense undergrowth of thorn bushes had sprung up since our last visit. They concealed an army of mosquitoes that took flight as we tromped through. What if I healed over a mosquito's needle while it was still filling up? Would it be stuck in me? Would I even react?

Honeysuckle vines crept up the side of the barn and through the hollow windowsill. A bumblebee hung upside down, shoving its face in one of the thin flowers. The warped door knob turned in my hand, still unlocked from our hasty retreat. Stopping short of opening it, I eyed the bumblebee and then Daniel. "How do they fly?"

He grinned. "On mini tornadoes of their own making. Controlled chaos."

Laughing, I shouldered the door open and wedged a piece of wood under it. My sneakers squeaked on the glass littering the floor. We squeezed through the double doors and into the barn proper. The place brimmed with sunshine, though our entryway lay in the thick shadow of the loft. Had the roof caved in?

No, the large rear doors were open.

"Those…weren't open before…" I whispered, taking a step back. "We should go. The owner might be here." I couldn't feel anyone, but that didn't mean anything.

"Good. We've got questions." Daniel prodded me forward with the barrel of his gun, a chilling but reassuring reminder we'd be able to defend ourselves. Never mind that we were the trespassers, or that I normally couldn't hit the broadside of a barn. While standing inside one, with a shotgun at my hip, I couldn't miss.

We stuck to the shadows along the wall of the loft, the earth growing increasingly damp and muddy with each footfall. I was just about to peek around the corner when I hit a mushy divot and slid, slamming my body against the wall to

335

keep upright. Ancient tack clanged and thumped together. A hooked chain tore free, narrowly missing Daniel on its way to the ground.

Rats, their bodies slick with oil, skittered underfoot, leaving muddy worm trails in their wake. The muck I'd slipped in congealed, cold and unwelcome, into my shoe. I winced and stifled a gasp while Daniel steadied me. After a ten count, we chanced a look around the corner.

Not all the rats had been spooked. A fat, grease spattered one squatted and hissed between low, sloppy bouts of chewing. It gnawed, the way a dog might on a chicken bone, on a delicate young finger, nails painted a purple that matched the surrounding skin.

It wasn't oil coating those rats and congealing into my shoe. A petite frame lay impaled through the spikes of a rusty tiller. Her hand hung just above the blood-soaked earth, bloated fingers dangling and missing in places. She'd tilted to the right, her upper half swollen, eyes bulging and vacant. Ichor flowed from her mouth, staining her ginger hair black.

I screamed, guttural, visceral, and deafening.

The rat kept on chewing.

CHAPTER FORTY-THREE

"No! No! No! No! No!" I half-screamed, half-whined, slipping in the muck and running to her side. "No!" I punted the rat off her fingers. It shrieked and tumbled into the muscle car. "Kayla! Daniel, help me! Help me get her down! I can heal her! I can—I can heal this!"

Daniel lifted her off the tiller, her heart and part of her lung sloughed back into her body cavity with a sickening slurp. He lay her on the ground and a small rat emerged from her stomach. It scurried away coated in blood.

My hands slammed against her chest, slipping into her rib cage. "Heal! Come on Kayla! Heal! Heal! Damn it!" But nothing happened. No light. No wisps. Not a godforsaken thing.

"Please! Pleaaase!" Wincing, I reached in and mashed the pieces of her heart together. "HEAL!" The scream tore at my throat, choking me to my marrow, and carrying through the barn.

Flies crawled over her blue lips. I turned to the side and dry heaved into the dirt. There was nothing but bile where meatballs and strawberry milk should have been.

Daniel held my hair back. "Let's go outside and—"

337

"No. I can't leave her!"

"Amy, it isn't good to—"

"I don't care!" I sobbed. "I'm not leaving her to be eaten." I whipped a broken board at one of the rats eyeing us from the corner. "Fuck you!" The tears came in sheets too thick to tell if I'd hit.

Straightening up, I pinched the flesh above her heart and lungs together through shaking fingers. "Heal. Come on! Heal! Little wisps please! Pleaaaase. Bring her back! Please!"

Daniel lowered my hair and ran his hand along my neck and shoulder. His knuckles erupted in a soft light, reflected in the blackish red pools of ichor I knelt in.

"Yes! Yes! Now on her! On her!" I just about vaulted Daniel over my shoulder to shove his still glowing hands onto Kayla's heart. "Heal!" In my mind's eye, the wisps surged from his knuckles to her heart like ethereal jumper cables.

In reality, his knuckles shifted from purple, to pink, to white, and the glow died away.

I padded my pockets for the penknife that lay on the floor of the Chevelle. "I-I-I need a knife-or-or-some-something sharp."

Daniel pulled a tactical knife from his boot and handed it to me, handle first. I locked ragged eyes with his. "I need an artery."

The shadow of a smile curled his lips and he laughed under his breath as if I'd just told the punchline of a cosmic in-joke. He flipped my arm so the underside shone, and eyed it before looking back at me. "You sure you've got the energy?"

"No. But if I don't try it'll kill me." I had no business asking it of him. He'd be well within his—

"Son of a bitch!" I cried as he sliced into my arm with ruthless efficiency. Blood bubbled from me in a gushing fountain. It was the same spot, same angle I'd cut earlier, only deeper. I really had been close.

My wound vanished into Kayla's chest, pouring life into her like something out of a vampire novel. Through gritted teeth, I howled, visualizing her heart beating as sharp, dry heat gnawed at my arm.

Catch fire.

Come on!

Catch fire.

Catch…

Catch fire…

Catch!!!

…

…

…

Long after the embers in my arm grew cold, I laid over her. To open my eyes would be to permit a reality I'd never be ready for. I'd healed. Kayla hadn't.

"What good is it? To find out you can heal only to be too late?" My voice squeaked and lurched out of me, itself a deadened thing. "It's cruel."

Daniel picked my arm up, ran his hand over the smooth skin, and set it back against her.

"What were you doing here by yourself?! Why didn't you wait for me? Wh-what were you—" My wild eyes shot open and I slowly pulled up from her. "Are you still here?"

Surveying the barn, Daniel said, "Her equipment's all over. Some of it's set up, some of it's in pieces."

Clipped to her belt was the meter with lights on it. "M—make the Smurf detector do something Kayla…if you're here." It was caked with blood and when I tried to wipe it off, I only made it worse.

Daniel wiped it on a clean part of his jeans and turned it on. One green light flickered before holding. The rainbow of other colored lights remained dark.

"Is that…is that good or bad?" I asked.

"Neutral," Daniel said, calm as ever.

"Maybe that's what's missing...why I can't heal her. Maybe...maybe her spirit isn't here. Sh-she doesn't want to come back." Kayla believed in Heaven and had earned the right to be there. "No. No, she wouldn't...w-we agreed to give each other a sign, a sign if one of us died." I turned back to her, my face tight with tears. "Make the...m-make the lights go. Make 'em go."

The lights didn't go.

"She fell from up there. Trying to set up that camera. Looks like the edge of the loft gave out."

Her new camera...

It lay under the tiller, attached to a mangled tripod. The camera itself seemed intact. "See—see if she caught anything."

Daniel scooped the camera up, turned it on, and wiped grime from the display. "No memory."

Molten lead poured through the crevices of my mind and I slumped over Kayla, rocking back and forth. Shadows snaked around the edges of my watery eyes. What would she do? She would...

She would...fall to her death.

My mouth opened in a desolate cry. It languished in my throat as the thin rope that had tugged at my heart shifted to a set of steel cables. They twisted around my core before I could catch a sliver of a breath. Deep gouges carved out a hollow space that would *never* be filled without her.

I would *never* be whole again.

I stared at the remnants of the tiller, and then at the buzz saw lodged in the table I'd once stood on. I could stand on it again. I could be with her.

Fall at just the right angle on those blades and...

"Hey, I've got you. Stay with me," Daniel's voice boomed through a twilight haze.

When had I gotten to my feet?

I was halfway to the table and leaning into him.

Stay with him...

The cables hooked into my heart corroded, breaking into flakes of rust.

...you belong to me, he'd said...

"Always." The word slurred out of me, along with my desire to jump. And suddenly Daniel was all that was keeping me upright.

CHAPTER FORTY-FOUR

*M*a said, "Let me see my baby."
We held each other long after I blacked out from grief.

Dad said, under his breath, "…I've been calling her Kaylee."
But it was Kayla in that coffin.

Mother said, "You should be with family."
I went home with Ma.

Abuela said, "Faye overdosed this morning, on my grand-daughter's grave. County Psyche has her."
And Emily.

Mother said, "You should be with family."
My family was six feet under and in pieces.

. . .

Mr. Feeney said, "Kayla was the brightest."
    He had no idea how right he was.

Kamrie said, "Take what time you need, Sugah Cube."
    I'd take three days ago, please.

Amy said, "Anything before noon on a Sunday is unholy."
    The bell tolls longest then.

Mother said, "You should be with family."
    I went home with Daniel.

Daniel said, "You're alive Amy, and don't you forget it."
    I won't forget it…

…

    …

    I forgot.

CHAPTER FORTY-FIVE

*I*t wasn't that I died exactly, only that breathing alone doesn't make you alive.

But part of me died in that barn, cut in half, as if I'd made that jump. What was left bled into the ocean of grief that soon surrounded me, like so much viscera sinking into a barren earth.

The police said the loft gave way under years of rot. It was an accident. The barn was no place to be exploring. It was preventable. What were we doing out there?

Was that what happened?

Every time I closed my eyes, I saw her.

The boards cracking under her feet.

Half a heart dangling off twisted metal.

Rats chewing on bloated fingertips.

"Chicken tacos?"

I drifted out of my malaise on a cold sweat, legs sticking to the shredded backseat of a minivan in Daniel's garage. Plastic sheeting ran from floor to ceiling, dampening the whir of a power drill.

Mother had wanted me to come home.

Home was unscrewing a panel on his Chevelle.

Mum set a Taco Time bag down on the wooden spool table in front of me and tossed a handful of hot sauce packets onto it. "There's a mix of hard and soft shell."

"Thank you." You wouldn't have known I meant it by the robotic way it came out. I unwrapped a taco and took a bite. I'd been staying there for I didn't know how many days and she'd been gracious, making food for us, letting me shower, and even buying me a travel pack of essentials.

Today, instead of leaving, she sat next to me, staring out the industrial doors at a striking blue sky. Birds swooped and dived outside, enjoying their "Bug Time." Without looking away from the show she said softly, "A piece of you is missing. People say it fills in, but that's not true. Some days you don't fall all the way in, but the hole's always there."

Yes, that was it exactly.

"Lost my youngest daughter to this road. Truck hit her. One of ours, too." A flood of old grief seeped up from between the prevailing acceptance in well-worn patches. "She was playing tag with Daniel. He saw the whole thing."

I watched him work, focused and diligent. Is that how he stayed so calm under pressure? Practice?

"Chelsea would be sixteen this year. Same as you," Mum said.

"I'm sorry." The words had been said to me so many times I'd nearly choked on them and here they were again, inadequate as ever, but all there really was.

"Sometimes life doesn't make any damn sense at all." A small fire of bitterness burned away her grief.

On the street, a dump truck rumbled past, shaking the ground. "How'd you stay on the same road?" I asked.

"All my memories of her are here. I'm not going to let one horrible one take them from me. I had three other children who needed more than just memories of their mum, or I might have gone with her." Patting my leg, she slowly stood on knees that cracked from the effort.

With the flick of a switch on the nearby wall, Daniel's drill fell silent and half the overhead lights went out. "Food's on!" she shouted, leaving without so much as another glance our way.

Daniel dumped the contents of the Taco Time bag over the table and picked out three soft shell tacos. He haphazardly emptied most of the hot sauce packets over his conquest before sitting next to me and digging in.

"You lost a sister too..." My voice was just above a whisper.

He closed his eyes and tilted his head up, as though reveling in whatever meager nourishment the taco offered. "Yeah."

"And you saw her die?" The words were still robotic, trying to process the information rather than feeling it.

"They say it fades, but I can still feel the folds of her shirt on the tips of my fingers." He wiggled his fingers and took another bite of his taco, finishing it. "Truck bed damn near took my face off."

I touched his cheek. A flash of him, raw and bloody, came unbidden to my mind's eye and I shook it away. "How old were you?"

"Six."

Flares of sympathy were swallowed by my sea of numbness before they could do more than flicker. "No sense at all." I pulled my knees up to my chest and gazed out over the labyrinth of shadows the garage had become. A bird slammed frantically into the metal sheeting in the far corner, too panicked to find its way out.

"How'd you go on?" My hollow voice seemed to dampen the ambient sound. "I'm so numb."

Rough hands slid over mine and pulled me to my feet, leading us across the crinkling plastic. Taking me by the shoulders, he gently kissed my forehead before pulling a painter's mask and goggles over my face. A sander was placed in my hand and switched on. Its vibrations jarred me to the bone until he guided me down to one of the panels.

Back and forth we went, applying pressure and releasing it in a subtle dance until the purple paint and the key marks gave way to smooth silver. Once I had the hang of it, he got up, massaged my neck, and went back to disassembling the rest of the car.

Wax on, wax off, Lil Bumblebee.

CHAPTER FORTY-SIX

*C*ody and Trevor came by a few days later to help and offer their sympathies. Trevor's arrogance chewed at the edges of my malaise, rather than being consumed by it, as every other emotion had been.

Progress.

"She thought you were cute." I gave Cody a bittersweet smile. With his black wavy hair tied into a short ponytail, pencil thin mustache and goatee, and stylized compass tattooed on his forearm, he looked fresh from the Caribbean.

"Wish I'd have gotten to know her better." He swirled a pile of dust around underfoot. "You try to...how do I say this...contact her?"

Flashes of sunlight pulsed—like the lights on the Smurf detector—reflecting off the panel I'd been polishing for the past hour. If I didn't stop soon, I'd be down to raw metal and it would have to be repainted...again.

I shook my head. "No luck."

"Well, let me know if I can help, if you try again, or whatever." He turned just about as red as the Chevelle's fresh coat of paint.

"I will, thanks." Maybe we could use her spirit board, if

Abuela hadn't found and set fire to it yet. The entire Rodriguez clan had circled the wagons to keep the Willows running. I'd been shooed away after Ma's suicide attempt, as if the whole thing were my doing.

A white girl, courting trouble and playing with things she didn't understand.

In a way, they were right. I had no idea what I was doing. My manual was a pack of menthol cigarettes, a book of cheeky matches, and some cryptic bullshit about lions from a ghost girl.

I'd been too numb to argue. Hell, I still was, and the fear of losing Daniel was one of the few emotions to ripple through me on occasion, so I hadn't left his side much since.

Trevor sneered, first at me, then at Daniel. "I put that horse up for sale. Don't know why I let you talk me into buying the stupid nag in the first place."

"Because you're his bitch." Cody laughed.

Daniel looked into the middle distance a moment, and then nodded his approval.

Trevor kept talking, as though he hadn't heard the comment. "That's okay though, I'm gonna end up making my money back and a tidy profit to boot."

"Where you gonna find someone who's a bigger fool than you?" Daniel asked.

"Internet." Trevor came over by me, plastering a fake smile on his face. "So, Abby, maybe you could help move the horse along? Talk it up?"

"I shovel enough shit, *Tyler*," I said, continuing to polish. *Wax on, wax off.*

Cody brayed with laughter. "I see why you like this one, Dan."

For the sake of Nyla and the Gelding, I turned and gave "Tyler" my undivided attention. "Look, Nyla's a good horse, she just needs the right owner. Be upfront about how spirited she is and how it's a strength, and you'll find the right buyer soon enough."

Trevor blinked several times through ever-widening eyes. "The right buyer is the one with money. And the name's Trevor, not Tyler." His arrogance butted into me, making a crack that was quickly swallowed by my void.

"Trevor wishes his name was Tyler, then he could make all the flowery soap his pretty little heart desires," Daniel said, lifting the panel from in front of me.

"There's an investment for you." Cody laughed, hooking chains to the engine.

Chains to the engine…

Chains in my heart…

I rubbed my chest at the shadow of a feeling.

"Only way I'm investin' in soap is if Daniel agrees to start takin' showers," Trevor said, and they all laughed.

"Speaking of showers. Cops gave me a scalding the other night, hauled me down to the station and everything. Somebody finally beat Tim Bennett's ass, and they got it in their heads it was me." Cody pulled one of the chains tight and threw a sly eye at Daniel. "I was in Waterville, staking out a job, but I'm sorry I missed it."

"I heard Tim cold cocked you Dano, broke your nose." Trevor smirked.

"That pansy couldn't break a sweat." Daniel didn't look up from tinkering with the engine. If I hadn't touched his broken nose myself, I'd have had no idea he was lying. One hell of a poker face, indeed.

"Remember when Dan busted his nose at Mt. Doom? He looked like a damn raccoon for weeks." Cody snickered.

"It was such an improvement." Trevor laughed.

"Tim's full of shit, and he's gonna wish he hadn't gone on record as having keyed my car. When I'm done writing this monster bill, he'll be paying for the Chevelle, the face lift I was planning on doing anyway, and for me and Amy to take a nice long vacation to one of those islands with like, three people on it." Daniel caught my eye and I moseyed over, slipping my arms around his waist. The back of his neck tasted salty against my lips. Under all that numbness, I loved him. Not as much as I would come to, but close. And love, as you may know, is as blind as justice.

"He von't pay, but his parents vill." Trevor modeled a thick German accent. "I vanna be a pig on zat vall vhen zay open ze envelope, unt from ze gentleman who deflowered zeir frauline unt zent Lord Font La Roy to ze hoosegow no less."

"You gonna drop the vandalism charges if they pay?" Cody asked.

"We'll be even. No need to have him moochin' off the taxpayers." Daniel wiped a bit of grease off the side of the engine.

"I'm just glad you ain't gotta bum rides off me no more." A flare of jealousy slithered through Trevor's arrogance.

"You'll miss me." Daniel smiled, and I was sure he was right.

Cody and Daniel lowered the engine back into the car and fiddled to hook it all back up. I leaned in, occasionally asking a question that either Daniel or Cody would answer. Trevor fiddled with his phone.

"She's beautiful, but I can't believe you spent $50,000 on her. Not with the work she needed," Cody remarked.

"Pffft. I gave him half that." Daniel grinned and rolled under the car.

"That explains Uncle Mark's heart attack!" Trevor popped up from the backseat. "For that cheap bastard to give anything away for less than he thinks it's worth would be the day he damn near drops dead."

"Is he okay?" I asked, something like sympathy and worry bubbling up through the sludge of numbness. I'd forced him to go against his nature without the slightest understanding of the side effects at the time. Then again, hadn't he been one hamburger away from a coronary when we'd met?

"Guess so." Trevor narrowed his eyes at me, as if to wonder why I cared. "Cleaning lady had to jolt him a few times with that fibulator thingy. Zap! He's home now, gonna be selling his place, so my Pops is there preppin' it." Pride sprang from Trevor like the rising sun, giving a patch of my malaise a nasty burn.

"So, what happened to buying a truck and going into business with me?" Cody asked Daniel casually enough, though each word was strung together by an underlying wound.

"Chevelle's purtier than you, and trucks are easier to get than my sister," Daniel mused, sliding back out and standing up.

Cody's dejection healed over with the warmth of hope.

"Slap a magnet logo over one of these trucks." Trevor gazed out over a lot filled with Varrick Custom Builders' vehicles, each shining in a neat row. "Repo work is done at night anyway, and your dad won't miss one. Sell it to him as a second business idea."

"The whole point's to do my own thing, dingus," Daniel said.

"Yeah, would you wanna be under that old man's nutsack the rest of your life?" Cody said to Trevor. After a brief pause he added, "Don't answer that."

As if on cue, a white truck whipped into the parking lot, sending its struts into a squeaking frenzy as it screeched to a halt in front of the doors. On the radio, Electric Ian shouted in his nasally voice, "Minnesota was rocked by a three-point-nine earthquake just daaaaays after my ex-wife moved to the land of ten thousand lakes. There are no coincidences, folks!"

Without turning the truck, or radio off, a 6'5" landslide of anger got out and slammed the door. "Danny!"

CHAPTER FORTY-SEVEN

"*O*h shit! Ol' Man Nutsack!" Trevor's eyes widened. "Ain't we got fireworks to pick up, Co?"

"Right you are. Amy, you comin'?" Cody was halfway to the side door.

Mr. Varrick's anger ground into my numbness with each step he took, breaking it into piles of rubble and dust.

"No." I shook my head, putting the Chevelle between me and the walking earthquake. Daniel was elbow deep in engine grease, and I wasn't leaving him.

"Pick me up a couple M80s and a King-Sized Ball Buster." He glanced at his dad. "I know I've already got one, but he gets lonely in the night."

The boys reached their escape hatch as Mr. Varrick breached the garage. "How come I got Gabe telling me you haven't been in Stockton all week?!"

Daniel didn't look up from tightening a screw. "Gosh Dad, we just found a dead body a few days ago. I'm great, thanks for asking."

With how collected Daniel had been, I hadn't considered how her death had affected him.

"So, see a therapist. I want you back at the site tomorrow before the rooster gets his first hard on."

"I'm taking a long overdue vacation."

Under his tucked in polo shirt, Mr. Varrick's gut shook with seething laughter. "Not an option. We already have guys out. You're gonna be working by candlelight as it is."

"Then hire more guys." Daniel tossed me a little smile. "I've got other priorities."

Mr. Varrick crossed his arms, giving the impression he was squeezing the blood to his balding head. "This what you've been doin'? Working on this piece of shit car you set your money on fire for? Fuckin' some runaway?"

Runaway?

"Yeah." Daniel closed the hood of the Chevelle, checking to make sure the black racing stripes matched up.

I giggled at his brazen response.

"Angela Durene called me. We do a lot of business with Freedom Timber, you know that?" His eyes sizzled first on Daniel, then on me. I stopped giggling.

"She asked that I send you home if I saw you with my boy. Didn't figure you were in my garage this whole time." He took his phone out. "You gonna go, or do I need to call her?"

His anger jack-hammered through my numb bedrock, invasive, unsettling, and every bit as deafening as the real thing. I didn't want it touching me, to risk opening up to turn him down.

I'd have to do it manually.

Daniel straightened up and walked toward his dad. "Amy needs me. She isn't—"

"No, I'll go," I interrupted. "And Daniel, you should go in to work tomorrow, I'll be fine." I caught his eye. "No need to make your dad any *angrier* than he already is." I hopped in the Chevelle, as though being inside would shield me from being buried alive by rage.

It shielded nothing, but my words had the desired effect.

The hammering slowed, replaced with vindictive satisfaction. It hung like smog around me, choking but mercifully silent.

"Good to see one of you has some sense." Mr. Varrick's vindictiveness melted into a slimy soup, heavily seasoned with guilt and sympathy. "I'm sorry for your loss, Amy. It's a terrible thing, but I agree with your mother, you need your family at times like this."

Dive in...make him understand your family is here...

"Daniel. Please," I pleaded, and he opened the driver's side door to get in.

Mr. Varrick stepped closer, pockets of anger rising from the soup. "This isn't over. You take her home and get back here."

The Chevelle purred to life, crisper and cleaner than the last time she was together. Daniel's dad left my range before I could act on the growing impulse to make him as docile as a kitten.

"He needs anger management." I let out a deep and simmering breath, my shell of numbness now snail-sized.

"No shit." Daniel clicked his tongue off the roof of his mouth. "You okay?"

"Yeah. No. I don't know."

We idled at the end of his driveway, semi-trucks shaking the car with each passing. "You got a preference about where you want to go?"

"Ireland." I leaned my head against the window, checking the side mirror.

"Is that a right, or a left?" Daniel smirked.

"No, I better go back to my house before Mother sends the cavalry." How had she found me? "We have to stay around here. There's unfinished business at the barn, and still so much we don't know. Plus, I can't leave Ma, she's gonna need me when she gets out."

A lot of good you did her before...

"You'll be alright by yourself?" He studied me as he drove.

"As much fun as it would be, we can't live life joined at the hips. And it isn't gonna get any easier. I'll probably always be terrified when you aren't with me." I snuggled into him.

"Ordinarily I'd say that's healthy, but this situation shot past ordinary quite a piece back." He put an arm around me. Though he'd toweled off, he was still slick with grease in spots. I took in the acrid scent, losing myself in the bluish black puffs that colored the half-moon sky.

"She was in charge of the why, of the research. I was in charge of the how, of accepting and integrating whatever the fuck I am."

And doing a poor job of it.

I don't know, you're still able to laugh at a potato.

Well, numbly giggle at one, anyway.

"I'll take over the why." Daniel kissed the top of my head.

"She showed you how to use her ghosty equipment, didn't she?" Hope sprang across my desolate landscape, planting seeds of optimism and excitement as it went. "I know the Smurf detector didn't work before, but sometimes a spirit has to be dead a few days before they're allowed to return...I think."

"So they say."

"Good. Cause this time we've got something we didn't have before." My smile was broad and manic, apt to swallow the moon if left unchecked. "An ally on the other side."

CHAPTER FORTY-EIGHT

*S*moke trailed through the screen in my bedroom window, tiny phantoms escaping into the misty morning rain. Taking in a steadying breath, I flicked an ash into my "World's Greatest Dad" mug. I knew he was there of course, a bundle of nerves just outside my door; what I didn't know was why. It was nine o'clock on a weekday.

The knock came, firm and resonant, and above my manic heartbeat I answered, "Come in."

My dad opened the door, lingering on the handle as his eyes fell on my makeshift ashtray. He took several steps inside, unable to look away from it and laughing with melancholic resignation. "You think so little of me?"

Behind him, Daniel slipped around the half-open door, shoes and shirt in hand, and disappeared into the hallway.

I tipped the cup as though I were reading it for the first time, and granted my dad a small smile. "I just grabbed something…"

"Don't let your mother catch you doing that in here." Dad leaned against my dresser, the scar on his forehead barely visible beneath his natural creases.

"Where is she?" I snubbed my cigarette out in the mug.

"Work. She's got a lot to catch up on." His eyes darted around the room, never resting anywhere for too long, as if he were afraid of what he might see. That was probably wise —I was pretty sure Daniel had collected all his clothes, but mine were strewn about in hurricane fashion. I wore a hastily thrown together mismatch of smiley face pajama shorts and an inside out, moth-eaten "over the rainbow" tank top. Neither had seen sunlight in two years, but I hadn't seen a washing machine since my adventures with Daniel in Waterville. By the time I sensed my dad was in the house and heading toward my room, being choosy about my wardrobe wasn't an option.

"No mold in the house." He scratched the stubble on his cheek. "Found a family of opossums living in the shed, but that's all the excitement."

I nodded, shifting against the wall.

"Well, that and the stains on my pool table." His eyes dropped to me.

"That didn't come out?" I winced.

"No. Were you and Kayla in there?" He carried some residual anger, but it was cut heavy with remorse.

"Yeah. You're not mad?" I straightened up.

"I was. But when your daughter finds her best friend in… that state, it puts things in perspective." He swallowed and stared out the window. "Could have been you."

Could it have been? Or would I have healed?

"Was it cherry juice?" he asked.

"Yeah," I said, raising an eyebrow at the absurd accuracy of the statement. My sheets were stained red with "cherry juice" from last night and that morning. An unexpected side effect of my healing was that every time was my first time.

Doubtless, he was thinking of maraschinos. Red #40 had become an unlikely ally. Us biohazards had to stick together.

. . .

After some silence, he took in a jagged breath and held it. "I quit my job." The sentence hung in the air, sinking slowly. "I'm going to start something up here, on my own, eventually." My jaw slackened and he let out his breath, biting his lip. "Something your boyfriend told your mother, about having blown sixteen years of rapport. I can't get back that time, but maybe we can set a new clock." The words seemed to pile on top of one another. "You can show me how to ride a horse."

"I-I hardly know myself. I mean, Kamrie's shown me a little but…"

"Then we'll take lessons together. How does that sound?"

Was it too late?

I stared at him, jaw still slack. "Nice. It sounds…nice."

They say you can't go home again, but could I build a gingerbread version?

"Good! Set it up with the um…the Galloping Gelding, right?" Embarrassment splashed through him.

"Gilded." I chuckled.

"Think we can get in today yet?"

"As long as I'm back by three. I've got some things to take care of…unless I'm grounded." In which case I'd have to make sure Daniel brought a ladder. Nothing would keep me from that barn.

He pursed his lips, eyebrows furrowing as though he didn't know what my official status was. "We can be back by three."

Kayla's quest for her father had ended in tragedy, but if a second chance for me and mine rose out of the ashes, well there'd be poetry in there somewhere, wouldn't there?

In life she'd been my guardian angel; I wouldn't put it past her to pull these kinds of strings in the afterlife if she had the chance. I looked to the sky and smiled, warmth flaring through me to melt off the last little chunk of numbness encasing my heart.

Taking out the Fugitive, I called work. On the third ring,

a familiar boisterous voice bounced through my receiver: "Amy Durene. How are ya Darlin'?"

"I'm better. Doin'…better. Wonderin' if me and my dad could come out for some riding lessons today, or sometime soon?" I smiled at him leaning against my doorway, looking as content as he felt.

"Oh good, you're with your dad. That mother of yours called looking for ya. I figured you was with the Varrick boy if you was with anyone, did I guess right?"

"Right-a-rooney." So that's how Mother had tracked me down.

"She was mighty worried about you. We all are. You come on out here and ride as long as your backside'll allow it. On the stable."

My heart grew three sizes, flushing with more warmth.

"Could I take Nyla out? I hear she's for sale again." The desire to make my dad generous skipped circles around me. I'd pay twice the price for that horse to get her out of Trevor's hands.

Just a little generous…

"I'll get her ready, Sugah Cube."

"Thanks Kamrie, see you in about an hour." I clicked *end*. "That sound good, Dad?"

"Perfect," he said, strolling into the hall.

"I'm gonna shower and change and I'll be ready to go." I trotted to the bathroom and turned on the water, stopping short of grabbing a washcloth from the linen closet.

My dad stood in the hallway, fear blending with nervous contentment amidst swirls of sadness, remorse, excitement, and anger. "I haven't been there for you, and I'm sorry." His glossy eyes focused on the banister.

I hadn't messed with his emotions, had I?

"Aw Dad…" I walked toward him, arms outstretched. "We can start a new day." His "Breeze of Costa del Sol" cologne mixed with my "rugged mountain axle grease" as we hugged.

Primordial warmth radiated from him and my heart turned over again, only this time without clunking. I purred like the Chevelle: crisp, well oiled, and fueled by a glow nearly as bright as Kayla's had been.

There was no need for a wall.

I twirled in the love, dancing and laughing as the feeling flowed through me, just like I'd splashed in the ocean one sunny day on a beach in Bar Harbor. I was there again, in my mind's eye, searching for shells and sifting through sand with my pink plastic sieve. A wave stole it away and my dad waded out to get it back for me.

There were eddies in the water and I didn't want her going out after it. One of them might suck her under. "Stay on the beach Amy." I called to...myself?

These are more than emotions...they're memories.

The current takes me/him/us under.

We can't breathe!

My dad shoved me hard against both shoulders, his shrill screams mixing with my own. I flailed back, crashing onto my tailbone; he struck the railing and flipped over it. The house shook from the impact as he hit the first floor, glass shattered, and his cry abruptly ceased.

The whole scene played on repeat a few times before I understood it was my current reality and not a memory.

"Dad!" I ran toward the overhang. Mid-stride my spine seized and my legs went out from under me, slamming my head into the rail. Searing barbed wire coiled around the base of my skull. Overhead, the light flickered, and my eyeballs strained out of their too-small sockets, bursting like two undercooked hard-boiled eggs. First one, then the other.

Everything went black.

My ears hissed and popped, hot fluid trickling down either side, leaving me with only the vibrations of my screams.

Then, even those were ripped from me.

CHAPTER FORTY-NINE

I fell out of myself, and into unfathomable cold.

I gasp, but there is no sound.

I cry, but I have no voice.

I scream, but I have no mouth.

I'm everywhere and nowhere.

Spread out, and impossibly small.

And falling, perpetually falling.

"You're in sh…hhock. Ffff…ocus on my brrr…eathhhh…ing."

There was no breath. No Daniel, except in what passed for my memory.

"…feellll the fuck off…ff ccc…c…old."

Yes…

The memory spread thin, stretching far and away, so I no longer understood why I stopped fighting the cold. Or why I was.

But I stopped.

Even though the cold will consume me.

Feel it.

A picture formed inside and around me, painted with brushstrokes of emotion.

I was dangling over the edge of an event horizon, a slow

and eternal vortex of pure desire spiraling beneath me. There was no place, surrounding this black hole, where I didn't exist. Its thorny edges were sewn into me, saving me from being pulled into the abyss. Alongside the thorns, my blue-white wisps shifted through thousands of flavors of compassion.

Spiderwebs of fear crept outward in ever-widening veins.

What is this?

Where am I?

The answer formed along with the question. An instant intuition.

Inside…

…myself.

Stripped of my senses…

All but one.

All but the sixth.

How do I get back to the others?

The question rippled from me, illuminating a giant glowing tendril of curiosity that stretched upward in the darkness, Jack's beanstalk. It wrapped itself once around the thorny edge of the swirling abyss…around me…and spiraled down into the void. The same void that lay coiled in my chest, painted here in the only medium it could be seen. Emotion.

Did that tendril just shoot up in response to my question, or had it been there the whole time?

The whole time.

The whole…time?

And before that…

I'm not me.

I hadn't been strictly talking about other people's emotions overwhelming me, had I?

Curious…always so curious…

This is curiosity, yes, but it doesn't shift, not even slightly, into anticipation, fear, excitement, or anxiety.

I had no control over it, there were no other seeds of emotion to pull from. Just solid curiosity.

Maybe if I match it...

Shifting to mimic its bright tone, I sank inside it at the point where it touched me. No resistance. A flash of current catapulted me upward, pitching me onto a canvas of blazing white light. Patches of brown, yellow, and black filtered into view. Actual colors?

A blue-white aurora shimmered and snaked over the color swatches, bringing them into sharper focus with each wave.

Healing...

Now there were shapes, too. Row after row of long, blurred outlines...like prison bars.

Are these my eyes?

The angles are all wrong and...

...I can't blink or move them.

But the shapes and colors were moving.

Yellow circles smiled up at me, stretched over thighs that leaned hard against the wooden banister. A yellow butterfly rested on fingers that groped for a shiny brown rail, but overshot, and grasped air. We fluttered and tumbled down the stairs, face first, like a carelessly tossed plastic doll, without any attempt to protect ourselves.

Our? Yes, the curiosity is here, all around me, in my limbs, jerking me forward with the grace of a toddler.

There wasn't any pain as we fell...

...I wasn't connected to the nerves. MY nerves.

What the?!

Give me back my body!!!

I was knocked out of my vision and pinned under the crushing weight of myself. My arms shot over my head as I slid to a stop on the bottom step. The upper half of me throbbed with the raw heat of a wicked carpet burn, while the lower snarled at the bite of a twisted ankle. Grunts and wails rattled through my vocal cords, but fell on deaf ears.

Careful what you wish for, Amy…

There was barely time to get uncomfortable when I was torn from the pain and flung into a bell tower of endless ringing. I made to cover ears, which didn't exist within this singular sense of hearing, with hands I had no control over. Not that it would have made a difference; the sound was residual, there was no shutting it out.

Crashing waves, moans, and growls accompanied the ringing in ragged bursts. Somewhere in the wet sand, a wounded beast dragged itself from the water…

…but were they waves at all?

Fuck! I need more than my ears!

The thick taste of smoke, almonds, acrid flowers and chemicals poured over me in metallic sheets.

Not what I had in mind, but I'll take it…another sense is another sense.

Flavors of flowers and chemicals?

It wasn't waves I was hearing…it was carpet…shuffling along carpet.

And that taste…

*Are you **dragging** my tongue across the carpet?!*

Oh, gross!

Rising on the heels of indignation, I shoved my way back into the pilot's seat of my own damn plane. My body lay face down on the carpet, tongue lolling out like I'd just woken from a night of licorice moonshine. Rolling onto my side, I spit a clump of fuzz from my mouth and grit my teeth through the pain gnawing its way up my leg. Before I could finish a groan, the connection to my sense of touch, to my motor functions, sparked and wavered, tossing me out.

I landed in the fragrant air of Costa del Sol, on a bed of lavender, sunflowers, and…coppery blood.

Wait!

I pleaded without a voice, to an entity without compassion.

Stop! Listen. We can talk this through! Figure it out!

Without the capacity for compassion.

The waves began again. My body dragging against the carpet. But I'm not moving it!

It was pure...

Tell me what you want!

...curiosity.

Not human.

And I am already giving it what it wants.

A faint puddle of confusion and anxiety soaked the edges of my empathy.

The waves stopped and the breeze of Costa del Sol became a tropical storm. I could taste the cologne now, sharp and biting.

Dad...he's close...

Please, don't hurt him! I can help you!

Labored breathing—scratching, clawing, and dry— became a sand belt in my ears.

"Please."

It's my voice...but not me speaking.

"Him don't you can, I help please hurt."

Every syllable is grating, as if vomited up.

What?

"What?"

Oh shit!

"Oh shit!"

Somehow, the frail connection to my vocal chords still worked through bent and crossed wires.

Dad!

"Dad!"

Dad! Wake up!

"Dad! Up wake!"

If I could feel his emotions, I could change them. What

emotion would be strong enough to wake someone? Excitement? Anticipation? Fear? What if I gave him a heart attack? But I *had* to do something otherwise…otherwise—

Warmth and light flooded through me, cleansing my thoughts, washing them down a peaceful, lazy river…

—otherwise nothing…

I had nothing to fear.

He was here with me…right now, my dad.

Wrapping me in love, a soft blanket on a sandy beach in Bar Harbor.

I don't have to be alone anymore…no, never again.

But, I want to be left alone…don't I?

Alone at the mahogany dining table.

My blue eyes in its reflection are his blue eyes.

*The only thing I gave her…were those eyes…*he thinks/I think.

My/his hand touches my/his cheek, it's both young and old, smooth and stubbled…

How is this possible?

I sifted back into the vein of otherworldly curiosity at the question, and shook out into my remaining senses. Through blurry, stinging eyes with lids that refused to shut, the outline of my hand came into focus. My hand clasped around Dad's arm.

I can't let go…

*I don't **want** to let go…*

All I need to do to feel this close to anyone, is to touch them…

It's beautiful…

The warmth feeds into my fingertips, into my palm, spiraling through me…

…and into…

…into—

"No!" I shouted, tugging to free myself against an electromagnetic pull that held the force of two suns locked in orbit.

The letters "N" and "O" dripped from my wrists in trickles of my blood and sweat.

Searing barbed wire strangled each of my senses again, wriggling and spreading into me like hellish worms. My body seized under another internal electric shock, but my hand remained where it was, and this time, so did my consciousness.

My muscles strained, impossibly rigid against their very skin and bone, constricting my own airway and choking my screams into silence. The earthy scent of sunflowers and bittersweet taste of almonds suffocated what precious space remained.

I couldn't black out…

…there'd been enough free rides.

This is my body you curious bitch! Get out!

Anger flared and fell away.

No oxygen for the flames.

No oxygen for me.

Only curiosity…

The tendrilous worms wriggled deeper.

Maybe…I shouldn't resist…

Maybe…we can see where this might lead…

Maybe…it will bE INtEReSTING.

YeS…iT wILL Be…i CaN StaY MATchED tO Our "CURIOSITY"…aN ASseT. wE UNderSTaND THIs CoNSTruCT, HoW tO mOvE EFfiCIEnTLy, We CAn PeRFOrm BEYonD eXPECtAtiONS THiS WaY.

THINgS arE FinALLY goING AccORDiNg To pLA—

No!

Shit!

Curious fingers bore into each of my five senses, haphazardly operating them like a ham-fisted puppeteer. Blistering worms spilled from the unfilled spaces, squirming in uneven clumps as they fell into the nothingness. I hung on by bare threads, the tendril wrapped whisper tight around me, separated only by a thin sheen of jittery tallow.

What the fuck?!

What is this THING?! Oh, God! I don't want to be worm food! Get IT off!

IT fused with me before, just now…h-how had I gotten free?

As if in response, Jack's alien beanstalk slipped against the sparse barrier of melting jittery tallow.

Fear! Fear, that's how!

Fear is the enemy of curiosity!

Fear, I could work with.

A fifteen-foot gator of fear clamped its jaws around the base of the curious tendril, twisting and turning in a death roll that tore the source of my subjugation from my head in frayed pieces. Like the roots of a pernicious weed, it clung to me, volcanic thorns burrowing further with each rotation.

I didn't stop. Mangled and raw, I ripped us both from my senses, plunging us into pitch black silence.

Into a sea of reptilian fear.

I invoked a feeding frenzy then. Gator after gator: swarming, leaping, tearing the tendril to shreds and pitching it into the spiraling abyss from whence it came.

An abyss that was no longer a freezing void. It swirled with warmth, love, anxiety, confusion, and…terror.

Down…down…and away…pulling them to the underside…like an eddy in the ocean.

"Stay on the beach, Amy."

Dad?

No!

Stop!

My blue-white wisps, veined through with shocks of fear, shot across the event horizon, interlocking and blocking it off. But the river of emotions kept flowing, gathering over the cap I'd made like shells in a sieve. Flashes of math equations and a memory of ordering socks spilled over the edges and became me.

Math? Internet socks?

Those are the kinds of things my dad would be—

I tracked the memories to where they rushed into me; names, places, and emotions bubbling up, like ghosts. I had to stop it! *How* did I stop it?

My wisps shot to the entryway, pulling me into a distant, thrumming, iron glove. It bore down on me, an ill-fitting crushing dead weight.

That thrumming...a heart beat...MY heartbeat. I pulsed in time with it, matching it, unlocking my pass code and hitching into my veins. I raced through my body, as lightning grounds to earth, and collided with the base of my skull, slamming into now familiar slots.

My senses.

My hand jerked free from my dad and I didn't stop scurrying backwards until well after I hit the wall under the stairs.

The heat in my palm died away and the swirling, that god-awful void within me, ground to a smooth and steady halt. My senses flickered, buzzed, and went numb in rolling waves, and pressure surged, tight against my skin. I would split open any moment, split open and pour onto the lavender-flavored carpet.

If I didn't drown in my own body first.

CHAPTER FIFTY

I don't know how long I sat there, afraid to move and split open, unable to process who I was or what happened. Each thought divided into two, into four, into six, and plunged back into a foggy haze before a single thread could be followed.

Thinking through a kaleidoscope. One plus one, equaled one.

At some point I began to understand that I existed. Fragments of sound faded in and out. A grumbling stomach, the distant rain of a runaway shower pattering somewhere above, and a quaking voice offering prolonged whispers of "I'm not me."

It was all I could do to breathe. To stare. To blink. Hell, I couldn't even do that.

Almond scented smiling faces winked out as I brought a/my hand to a/my face. Fingertips slid through something thick, stopping halfway up the/my cheekbone at a squishy mass.

An eye.

My eye.

Out of its sock.

I need to order more.

Eyes aren't supposed to run out of socks.

This is bad…

I should correct it.

With trembling fingers I tucked one eye, and then the other, back into their beds. To dream the dreams that only eyes can know. There wasn't much pain, not that I would have probably noticed if there had been. The aurora shone, rippling brightly over sixteen fingers that smelled red. Everything was in blurred multiples, but they were at least at the general angles they ought to be.

Progress.

As I blinked the tears away, a figure on the floor, some distance in front of me, muddled into view. For an out-of-phase second, it was *me* lying there.

Me?

I ran my hand across my temple, skimming off a sheet of sweat. The cool metal of my mood ring offered some tiny relief to my overheating body.

I am orange. I am orange. I am orange.

I am hungry.

I am Henry the Eighth I am, Henry the Eighth I am, I am…

My butterfly ring flitted through a field of colors, not settling on any one for long…but the outline, the outline remained silver…a nice, steady silver.

I am, Amy.

And my ring is silver.

Sunlight fell long upon the hand across the room. The one that might have once been mine.

It has a ring, too.

Gold. It's gold.

Heavy on his finger.

He loves…but is not in love…

Not with her…

Dark pools on the carpet around him.

Spilled Kool-Aid?

Delinquent paint?

Cherry juice?

Sunlight crept away from his hand to huddle against the front door.

Blood.

He's hurt.

I can unhurt him.

With that singular thought, I crawled in his direction. The twenty foot journey became a quintathlon of me stuttering through my senses with every movement. My screws weren't just loose, they were stripped.

The only constant was my empathy.

How's that for a gangly bucket of chum?

He'd settled into a calm anxiety, one without peaks or valleys. Each breath was erratic, wheezing, and edged with a scream. Without hesitation or comprehension of what happened the last time I'd touched him, I cradled his head. Wisps jumped from me to him, weaving a faint blue-white glow beneath his matted black-white hair.

The pressure within me eased, even as my chest grew tight.

Inner chains rattled, loosening as my heart purred in reverse.

Reverse?

Swirling…

Like a…

What happened, Amy?

…black hole.

Only…backwards…

A white hole…

Pulling free this time took all the effort of opening a freezer door. *Why did I think it would be harder?* I stared at my palm and scooted cautiously back until I huddled with the sunshine by the front door.

It was warm.

Down in the living room, a sea of glass glittered in the carpet, cloaked in a cloth that hung on the bones of our coffee table. I couldn't have told you, then, how it broke. How I'd nearly killed Mother in that spot. Only that the cloth was coated in guilt. Guilt that clung like mold to every surface of the house.

Sometimes, I heard gentle screams coming from myself, as if my vocal chords understood something I didn't.

Something I couldn't.

Sunlight, warm and cozy, abandoned me to stretch across the never-ending kitchen floor.

Dad didn't wake.

Because I'd healed his body…but not…

…his—

My stomach wailed, a low continuous grumble that merged with the rumbling of an engine.

In a Pavlovian display, I rose, staggering out the door on limbs that tingled, burned, and spilled me onto unforgiving concrete. A stuttered cry, at a volume only dogs could hear, squeaked past my trembling lips, and my eyesight collapsed. Cherry red paint glazed my tongue and brushed the air, guiding me to the side of the Chevelle. My senses were either jacked on, missing, or crossing each other, while performing in a synesthesia circus.

Into the driver's seat I climbed, only to fall over and listen vacantly to the swirling underside of multiple dashboards. A cacophony of dried beef and spices sang from the cracks of the glove boxes, coaxing me to sit up and twist them open. My fingertips shuffled along uneven cardboard and vacuum sealed plastic, coming to rest on the barrel of a forty-five. I grabbed it, put all six of them under my chin, and pulled the triggers.

"Not in the Chevelle." Daniel's voice lit up the night beside me, dimming the hollow click of the gun. He reached through the window and took the instrument of death from me, though it would be some time before I registered this. "And not at all. You're not fucking killing yourself, got it?"

The car door opened, and he set something on the floor behind me. Getting down to my level, he studied me as I gripped a phantom Taurus and stared out the front windows. "Besides which, you had it aimed at the front of your chin. You'd have blown that pretty face of yours off and not much else. We'll find a less messy way to clean you up."

Some of the pressure eased, allowing a handful of thoughts to connect. Daniel was here. He would take care of things. He would know what to do.

I could relax.

But not enough to kill myself.

Or slip out of myself...

I had to concentrate on that, stay in my senses.

What happened?

That tendril...

...came out of nowhere.

Tore me from control.

I fought. Threw it into the...abyss...sealed it off.

But...it could...

...come back.

375

Come back and break through.

It WILL come back!

Will it?

Did it ever leave?

Now, I'm curious...

Flashes of hugging my dad skipped through my mind in oversized flip-flops, and tripped.

If I touch someone...

I can't let anyone touch me.

It'll come back if I do!

Oh God! Daniel! I can't let him—
I opened the car door and bolted as far and as fast as my benedict legs would take me.

That turned out to be seven steps as the crow flies. Or as the crow slams into the Goblin-green wall. Luckily, I didn't feel it.

I toppled into the overgrown grass, still wet with the day's rain.

What's Kayla's truck doing at my hous—
Leaves rustled in the canopy overhead.

This isn't your house.

Crickets fell silent mid-chirp under the shadows of faded knot-prone boards that stood in defiance of the years, in defiance of the odds.

The Whitaker barn.

What am I doing here?

CHAPTER FIFTY-ONE

"*A*my!" Daniel called. His footfalls on the ground tasted like cherries.

"No! Don't come any closer!" My words mutated into incomprehensible screams as they escaped.

I ripped open the Goblin's door and clambered inside, locking it as Daniel's shape darkened the window, and the left half of my body went numb. Pieces of his muffled speech evaporated in my ears.

I have to get away. For his own good.

Before...

Before what?

What happened, Amy?

...

My mind wouldn't connect those black dots...not just yet.

377

Feeling under the seat for the screwdriver, I jammed it into the ignition and turned.

Please let this work!

Please! I'll pour you a bowl of Lucky Fucking Charms!

The truck sputtered, gasped, and started up.

Irish prayer accepted.

Now to keep my eyes in focus without my legs losing feeling.

Just outside the grime encrusted windshield, another ten walls of Goblin-green sprang up. The truck jerked as the engine choked and died. Daniel dropped the hood and leveled his gaze on me.

"Lambchop…"

"…you're in…"

"…no condition to…"

"…drive."

His silhouette blurred at the passenger's side window, and glass shattered inward.

Was it the coffee table? How was the coffee table here?

No…the passenger's side window.

His arm reached inside.

"No! Stay back!" The command choked in my throat as a faint frantic scream.

I pulled my door handle and lurched onto legs fueled solely by an Irish prayer and the terror of what I was capable of.

What's that?

What are you capable of?

I ran into the barn with its siren buzzsaw.

I can end this.

Daniel's words tasted of earth and axle grease. *"You're not fucking killing yourself..."*

I veered away from the saw, sending a tangle of ghosty equipment sprawling behind me.

His shadow fell long over mine as I careened down the hall littered with rusty tack. Something heavy hooked into my arm, tearing it open, but I had too much momentum to stop. I barreled through the double doors into the office and lost every sense but the squelching sound of my bare feet meeting shards of scattered windowpane.

Shit!

Twisting my internal wiring, I cranked feeling into my upper body in enough time to grasp the half-open office door. I teetered against it for the barest of seconds before it slammed shut, driving me hard against the rotted wood. Banshees of pain wailed through my fingers and arm.

Heat gusted past my ear and down my neck, while my eyes flickered through shades of gray. Daniel arched over me, his palm flat against the top corner of the closed door. My legs buckled and I shifted my weight against the wood, sliding to the dirt-strewn floor beneath him.

"Don't touch me..."

No words, no screams anymore, only fitful heaving breaths shifting the prevailing dust in mini tornadoes.

Daniel lowered to his haunches in front of me, chains rattling in his hands.

I stared blankly forward, vision throbbing in time with my heartbeat, my muscles shaking and unresponsive. I was the rabbit now, flush with terror and having run myself into exhaustion.

Exhaustion? Give Doctor Nimans a raise.

No! Be like her! Be a doctor!

Don't let him touch you, oh God!

Heal! Heal the faulty wiring!

Don't let him—

Needles of heat threaded through my arm and fingers in tiny flares, but my internal wiring remained cold and loose. Edges frayed into ghosts of themselves with each attempt to splice back into my senses. As a small favor, this ghosting extended to the pain, turning what was an operatic song into a frail intermittent whimper.

Nothing was pulling me from my senses this time. This time the enemy was me. I'd done this when I'd torn that *thing* from me. I didn't care at the time, I didn't think, couldn't think, I just pulled, and...and *stripped my circuits bare.*

Oh God.

How was I supposed to know?

Drawn and quartered, stretched too thin, there wasn't enough "*me*" to complete the connection even if the threads weren't bare. I'd unspooled one yard of rope too many, casting a net over that...

...black hole...

Would I be stuck here then, in this place between life, this purgatory, gawking at a world I couldn't affect? But the world would be safe with me as a sentinel, making sure that spiral never moved again.

Daniel would be safe.

If that *thing* were going to come out again, it would have by now.

Wouldn't it?

Something tickled the tips of my fingers, familiar and comforting, it held for a wink before falling away.

A cigarette?

I could use its help with the bullshit now.

How was it that I'd gained a sixth sense at the expense of the other five? The former ran through my heart, rather than my mind, at least as near as I could tell, and it hadn't been torn to shreds.

So it wasn't true that I couldn't affect anything. I could haunt people from my purgatory.

"Haunt your own house?"

A bright twinge of pure love shimmered through me.

Kayla?

It faded, folding back in on itself, back into me. Had she walked through me, or touched me from the other side? I lowered my defenses and cast a wide net for her. Stalking past the soft fear of the small critters in their hidden hovels, I burst into the feral courage of the forest beyond the barn. There was no way to measure, but it was farther than I'd sensed before, by a lot. Free from the noise of my other senses, I might just stretch across the whole Universe.

I'd find Kayla and life would be different, but she wouldn't be lost.

She'd be the very thing she'd always sought. A spirit.

Another small twinge pulsed at the thought of her. I chased it, through playfulness and paranoia, back through wild courage and tiny soft fear…

…back to me.

Kayla?

"Haunt your own house?"

The same playlist.

A memory, bright and beautiful.

As unchanging as the voice messages I'd listened to until the Fugitive's battery died.

I'd plugged it back in.

But...I couldn't plug her back in...

Kayla...

Despair coated my frayed wiring, shorting out the remaining threadbare connections in fits and sparks.

She's not here...

Daniel's outline in the darkness faded from gray to black to oblivion.

...and neither am I, anymore.

Not one pane of glass left in my purgatory window.

Brick lay upon brick, surrounding me, damp and earthen, exhaling the breath of the grave with each hollow scrape of the mortar and trowel.

No!

I don't want to be sealed in! Stuck in my body! Imprisoned in darkness!

No!

Please!!

Daniel!!!

CHAPTER FIFTY-TWO

*L*ove and longing went supernova in me, bursting out in a brilliant flash that burned away the encroaching brick tomb.

It settled, so much firework dust over the pitch, and cold.

Outside of myself a faint response shone. A matching afterglow of love and longing erupted in a chain reaction, like stars in a nearby galaxy.

What is this?

A stairway to Heaven?

Footprints in the sand.

My footprints…

Impressions of my emotions, separate from me…but ingrained.

Coiled in my DNA.

From the first time I'd been with Daniel.

Reinforced every time thereafter, with reckless abandon.

Tiny impressions of that intensity, that euphoria.

Hooked into my body.

…if you can feel it, you can manipulate it.

Can I still?

A delirious mix of love, euphoria, obsession, and lust uncoiled from my DNA in great strands at my call, roots holding tight to the cells that contained them. Billions of tiny anchor points.

I only needed five.

Thorny vines, ripe with roses, sprouted and grew, curving wildly just outside the bricked up walls of my prison. But not through it…not to me.

The veil.

They're tied to the physical and can't breach it. They're right there, at the tips of my fingers…or whatever passes for them here. Just a little breeze or…a stick…or…

…a bit of suction!

The black hole within me, that awful, beautiful abyss, spun at my desire. One smooth click of the dial pulled on the mixture of love and obsession, threading it through my estranged senses. Then the vines pierced the veil, bridging the gap and weaving into me as tight and unbreakable as the red string of fate.

Ash and tar coat my tongue.

Acrid smoke burns my nose.

A tiny mountain of embers eats away the darkness.

Lips of fire consume mine. Broad talons, tight upon my neck.

Gentle thunder swirls into my lungs.

My Plutonium Dragon engulfs me.

I surfaced into Daniel's nicotine kiss, inhaling the smoky lifeline as I reclaimed all my senses, or as close as I would come for a good long while.

"Dan…iel…" My voice, brittle as dust on a puff of smoke, caught on the corners of his perfect mouth. If I'd been over-grown with the need of him before, what greeted me now was uncharted, lush, and without limits. A cluster of wisteria blooms growing off the edge of a mad world.

The edge of *our* world.

The only one that mattered.

Static filtered through my limbs, which shook and convulsed, waking from their zombie status. Haphazard

fingers slipped up his arm, sparks of euphoria trailing behind them like fireworks.

Home.

Yes.

I've found my way home.

My tongue curled around his, pulling him deeper, swallowing him as though he were ambrosia. Tension mounted in my chest at my desire to feel him, to merge with him…just as it had that first night we'd been together.

It had tried to spin then.

It had tried to—

No!

No, I won't allow it!

Allow what?

What happened, Amy?

…

I'll never hurt him!

Never let him be hurt!

Five senses would be enough. We'd make do. We'd explore every last one and top them with a cherry! Under my pounding heart, the supernatural tension ceased and fell silent.

My lips trembled as I held his gaze. A plutonium dragon peered out of those endless eyes. "I-I…I can't hurt you. I won't allow me t-to," I stammered without breath. "*I love you.*"

Those fucking words, those stupid fucking words! They still weren't enough! Grabbing his neck, I pulled my chest to his, nuzzling his velvet cheek and biting his ear. My words tight-roped an orgasm. "Break your chains Daniel. Ethan. Varrick." Rolling my tongue across my lollipop's jawline, I addressed his beast again, panting sharply. "Show me what pizza you like…any toppings you want. No limits."

Primal heat blazed between my thighs and I moaned as I bucked into him, beckoning him to top me. His fingers dug

into the hair at the nape of my neck and pressed me against the door. Breathing heavy, he pinned my legs to the side with his, leaning in just out of reach of my lips.

"Amy. Rachael. Durene." Daniel's steady chuckle tangled with my scream when the agony in my feet became a full length feature. I wailed through gritted teeth. Why had I wanted back into my body again?

"You ran through fucking glass, barefoot." His lips brushed across mine as I cried. "You probably don't want to move."

My brain flipped between the pleasure of his touch and the torture in my feet. Smoldering flares punctuated the pain. Was I healing over wounds with shards still in them?

"I need you to focus, and tell me what happened to your dad?" Daniel said, his tone smooth and calm.

My dad? What happened?

Details were already fading into the ether, a nightmare covered in mud and bubbles, riding toward the dawn and *spiraling down the drain.*

I don't want to connect the dots.

The dots are black holes…

The dots are—

"Amy." He took my chin between his thumb and forefinger, catching my eyes and enunciating each word. "What happened with your dad?"

Those eyes…not the death of me at all, but the life. How could I *ever* do anything but what they asked? No choice but to connect the dots. No choice but to answer truthfully, or what passed for the truth in my fractured memories.

Memories that aren't all mine.

Why aren't they all mine?

For the same reason I'm not passed out.

The same reason I'm not even tired, in spite of the healing, in spite of not eating, in spite of the trauma.

. . .

The reason my skin felt a size too small for a while.

What happened, Amy?

"I-I drained his soul," I whispered, as if doing so would shelter me from the weight of it. "Right down the garbage disposal in my chest."

CHAPTER FIFTY-THREE

I'd drained him...no...not me...IT...something...else...
It wasn't me...

Wasn't...
Couldn't have been...
Could it?

My arms latched around Daniel's neck and I winced as he lifted me, my whole body trembling. Each time my feet swayed, fresh pain spiked through them. He brought me out of the office, past the tack, past the discolored darkened patch of earth above which Kayla had taken her last breath. I snuggled into him, and closed my eyes against the onslaught of reality.

I hated this place.

He bent and scooped up the scattered equipment with his free hand before setting both me and it on the bed of Kayla's truck. If I hadn't already been shivering, the steel under my thighs would have set me to it. *But it isn't as cold as where I was.*

And where was that?
Where was what?

Daniel reached into the Chevelle, and came away with a

handful of Rustic Ray's jerky and a can of Coke. Half of each sip dribbled down my chin, while he shuffled around in the passenger's side of the truck.

"You broke Goblin's window?" I whispered, as much to him as to myself. It was already a hazy shadow-laden memory.

Glass pattered to the ground as he pulled the blanket from under the seat and spread it next to me. I scooted onto it, offering him some of the jerky I munched on while smoothing the blanket out.

What a fine night for a picnic under a galaxy of stars.

"Shit, Amy, course I broke it, after how I found you in my car? Figured you'd jam that screwdriver in your fucking neck. This somethin' I gotta worry about with you?" He stabbed the tripod into the ground and switched on the camera.

I shook my head absently. "No. Not in the Chevelle and not at all…"

His cool assessing eyes, both piercing and distant, studied me, as if processing my words in layers and languages far above my pay grade. Finally, he nodded, some warmth returning with whatever understanding he'd gleaned. "You'll get control of yourself, or I promise…" He came in for a slow kiss that steadied my lips, his tone effortless. "…I'll kill you myself." Reverent knuckles dusted my cheekbone, and I nuzzled into them.

There was a strange comfort to the idea. A backup plan. He understood the gravity of what I'd been through. No bull-shit. No platitudes.

He took off his shirt and plopped it over my head. It was warm and smelled of his sweat. I climbed inside with a grateful sigh.

"Where the fuck were you gonna go in this, anyway?" He smirked, glancing at the truck cabin.

"Into a ditch, most likely." Had I really tried to drive?

389

What had I been thinking? I tugged back and forth on a tough piece of jerky like the feral creature I no doubt resembled.

He picked up my foot, mild annoyance spreading from his face to his voice. "See what happens when you run from me?" Glass shards poked out of the soft pad. My skin had healed over each one, sewing them in as perfect extensions of myself.

"Oh God." I looked away.

Daniel?

Daniel is God…

What?

Had I just thought that?

"Don't run from me again." He brought his boot up to the tailgate, rocking the truck forward, and sliding his tactical knife from its holster.

Somewhere deep within my muscle memory, the reflex to pull away from him, to kick him and tell him I'd run a fucking marathon if I felt like it, twitched. The obsession that had anchored my soul to my body now snaked around it, crushing my small uprising into a fine powder of confusion and submission.

"I-I was afraid I would hurt you, too," I stuttered.

Gently setting my foot against the blanket, he leveled his gaze on me. "That logger's chain that took a bite out of you damn near set up shop in my neck. And wouldn't that have been fine, me bleedin' out and you catatonic one room over?"

"I-I'm sorry." I checked his neck for scratches in the dim light. Thankfully, there weren't any.

"Point is, every path's dangerous, Lambchop. Especially now. I need to know you're gonna be back to back with me, not runnin' full bore in the opposite direction. If we ain't got each other in this mad shithouse, I may as well slit both our throats right here." The knife twirled between his fingers like they were a second home, fully furnished.

"We're in this together. You let me decide if I want you to run or not."

He let out a measured breath. "I know this is fucked up overwhelming territory, so I don't want you making any major decisions without comin' to me. That includes killin' yourself. You aren't just you, haven't been for a while. Keep that as your North Star."

I'm not me.

I'm we.

He is the reason I'm here, and not alone in the darkness.

He is the reason...

"*You* are my North Star." My eyes, brimming with innocent wonder, followed his every movement.

Something like concern touched his brow, and he handed me a flashlight. "Hold this steady, right here, and concentrate on answering my questions. Don't know how much time we got and if we need to move, well, you need to be able to move." The knife blade gleamed in the artificial light.

Was he going to...?

"What happened with your dad, after I left your house this morning?" He bent, holding my foot down and narrowing his eyes at the task before him.

He was.

He was going to...

I was an animal, caught in the blade's glare. "U-um...we talked...he, uh, he apologized for—" With surgical precision Daniel pierced my skin around the biggest shard.

I gasped and jerked my foot free. "Faaaaawk!"

"You got to stay still," he said curtly. "I need to go get that chain?"

"I-I can't do this!" My eyes squeezed shut.

But I will do it.

If he insists, I will.

Bits of jerky churned in my stomach, as much at the pain as at that certainty.

A certainty that was morphing, even now, into an automatic function, like breathing...or my drunken hyperactive heart beat.

I couldn't say no to him.

The knife firmly in his grasp, he pressed his knuckles against the tailgate and leaned toward me. "Okay. We'll just skip into the hospital and explain that you have healed over glass in your feet. There'll be a media shitstorm before the anesthetic hits your system, and we won't be able to go anywhere without people knowing who we are. No more bowling, no more concerts, no more quickies in the laundromat."

I scrunched up my face. *No more laundry mat quickies.* I'd be on a slab, getting more than just my feet dissected. Exhaling slowly, I chipped away my anxiety and thawed it into a puddle of calm.

"Do it."

He held my foot against the blanket, firmer this time, exciting parts of me that had no business being happy right then. "What happened right before you drained him?" he asked.

"He was sad so I-I hugged him and his emotions lit up l-like s-s-sunshine." I grit my teeth as the pain carved trenches into my calm. "I melted into it and...we were at the beach and then I was h-him-him, looking at me, but also I was me...and then he...fell over the rainbowwwww ow ow ow ow!" The flashlight dropped with a clang half of Albion must have heard. It rolled through the gap between the bed and tailgate and thunked on the grass. "Over the rail, I mean. He...he fell over the...over the r-rail." Sweat beaded on my temples, and a whimper hung at the beginning and end of each breath. I could quiet my soul and occupy my mind, but my body understood what was happening to it.

Daniel picked up the light and shone it on the bloody aftermath. The two inch shard that once occupied my foot now lay on the edge of a once off-white blanket. On the thermal camera, a red light fluttered until the burning in my sole died away.

And did the flashlight dim?

"What did you do when he fell?" My surgeon handed me the torch and started in on another embedded fragment.

"I-I blacked out, hit my head on the rail and things are f-fuzzy after that." A good black out sounded nice right about then. Hell, I'd have settled for some Fifty Stone. "My senses got all tangled up and I tripped over 'em…down the stairs." I narrowed my eyes, flipping through the corrupted files in my head.

Who labeled these?

They're all out of order.

"Felt like I had to fight to stay in control." My hand erupted in a tremor, and the flashlight beam danced across the inky black of the barn entrance.

"What were you fighting?" Daniel placed his hand over mine, steadying it and bringing me into focus.

What *was* I fighting? The answer pulsed under layers of my fracturing calm. "Curiosity."

Oh shit!

Was IT back?!

IT'S BACK!!!

Keeping in time with a rampant heart beat, fear slammed into the underside of my calm, spreading tiny fissures, but the pulse of curiosity remained unmoved and unphased…at once alien and familiar.

Familiar?

It wasn't back at all…it had never left…it couldn't leave… because…because it was *part* of me. MY curiosity.

Me…fighting my own curiosity?

Could that be right?

That *felt* right.

Ever try to nail down mist in a hurricane?

So much of what happened, from the time I hugged my dad to when I woke in Daniel's embrace, was rolling gibberish, splattered randomly across my subconscious mind, peeling off in places and evaporating in others. It would be a good long while before I'd stitch together what really happened when I was disconnected from my body—and then under circumstances that would see me looking back on having glass cut from my feet with fondness in comparison.

For now, I was working with ghosts of fragments.

Suffice it to say, I wasn't lying to Daniel, or myself when, through a locked jaw and spasmodic breathing, I said, "My curiosity took over, almost with a life of its own." But I wasn't exactly telling the truth, either.

"Robotic. Something I *needed* to do. *Needed* to experience. Then fear sn-snapped and...my back was...against the wall." Green flecks of paint underscored my fingernails. "Thought I would burst outta my skin." *Like I want to now, oh God!* "...Like there was too much me inside."

I'm not me...

...because I was him?

Was that it? Was it so simple? Had I been fighting my dad for control? Him trying to get back to his body all that time? It made a nauseous kind of sense.

"Curiosity that's mine, but not mine..." I said in an uneven sing-song voice before shooting bolt upright, the sweat pouring off me in sheets in the chilly night air. "My dad!" I swiveled to hop off the truck bed with single minded, adrenaline-fueled idiocy. "I have to get to him! He's not finished—"

Daniel swiveled me back, with little effort. "*You're* not finished either. You've still got another foot to go." Next to me on the blanket, a chunk of flesh the size of a mouse dyed the last few white fibers red. Bile rose in my throat: the jerky I'd eaten, already a ghost in my stomach, already replacing the lost rodent.

"He's fine." Daniel picked up my other foot.

Jesus, how many feet do I have?

Using his thumbs, he massaged the sole of my second foot, hitting a patch of crushed glass that lay just beneath a smooth, healed over surface. Pain scattered like buckshot up my spine, holding me hostage and making me sing soprano.

Just because I couldn't *see* the glass, didn't mean it wasn't there.

"Been monitoring the police channels and there was an ambulance out to your house half an hour ago. On its way to Waterville Memorial, now." He set my foot flush with the crimson blanket.

I closed my eyes, tilting my head back and indulging in some much needed oxygen. "An ambulance. Not a hearse." *Sure thing...they'll give him an IV full of Souliprax and he'll be good to go. Souliprax: ask your doctor about it today.*

My emotions are dangerous...with lives of their own...if I'd have stayed on Paraxil...

Was that all I had to do to end this? Take that stupid, soul numbing medication?

"What isn't he finished with?" Daniel asked. The stars blurred and the truck spun in tepid half circles. I could close wounds yes, but I'd lost a fair amount of blood. Blood that didn't seem so quick to come back.

"The daily crossword puzzle!" I screamed through gnashed teeth as Daniel dug out a small chunk of glass. "No, that's not right, well it is, but it's not what I...what I meant."

It *was* right...two across was some kind of airplane...

"What did you mean?" He examined the hellish ruby between his thumb and forefinger.

"I don't know." Shivers rolled through my body. "I'm sorry, I'm...I'm missing things...I can feel them melting away like snowflakes on the tip of July."

"There's grown men who'd be bawlin' to their mamas if they were in your feet, and you're settled back recitin' poetry." He creased his brow, shook his head and smiled. "You're beyond the call." "

"I'm cheating, keeping myself calm. But what about you? Aren't you afraid I'll take your soul?" Why wasn't I more afraid of that myself? Was it the power of love, or wishful thinking so I could touch him?

"Putting aside, you already have it?" He rubbed the top of my foot, up my ankle and back again, sending happy tingles through an area that had gone numb after being held down so tight. "I trust you."

"I'm not always me—" I whispered, an ache settling in my overtaxed lungs while heat blazed in the sole of my foot.

Was it over?

In the silence that followed, I caught the path of a shooting star that turned out to be a satellite. "Demons feed on souls. That's what I am...or what's possessing me."

Curiosity that's mine, but not mine...

Daniel's impish grin played hide and seek with the deep shadows cast by the flashlight as he stood up, his glazed eyes capturing mine. "Been to church too many times for that to be true."

My whole world was spiraling into insanity, and there I was smiling, chuckling even, as I dove. How else was I going to survive the trip? "Could be a Protestant demon."

Running his thumb over my cheek with reverence, Daniel said, "You're not anything so mundane." He took my hand, guiding me off the truck bed. "Try out your new wings. See if I missed anything."

I stepped tentatively down, wiggling my toes in the mud. My soles were tender, the way skin that's been sheltered by a scab for weeks feels when it finally falls off. But both were mercifully free of glass.

"Ready for take off," I said, giving a salute. "Thank you, Doctor Daniel." I bounced on them a few times before giving him a quick peck on the lips that lingered, electrifying into something alive with need.

What would new lips feel like on his?

"I can't...stop..." I managed.

"Why would you?" His hands, slick with blood, swept up my throat, fingers combing through my hair and clamping tight, bringing me to attention on my fresh tip toes.

"I'm freezing and filthy...deranged and dangerous...never know what might happen next." The words offered by what was left of my brain were sound, but not high frequency enough to penetrate the haze of lust in which I hung.

"Mmmm," he moaned, low and resonant, licking my lips as though my words were flavors of candy. "Yeah."

"Could be venomous...or grow tentacles...where tentacles shouldn't...be..." I cupped and rubbed his bulge, bringing feeling into my numb fingertips.

He flipped me around, pressing me into the rusty tailgate. Cold, wet steel touched my waist, slicing through one side of my smiling shorts and then the other. They fell to the ground, exposing my bottom half to the night. Laying the knife flat against my stomach, Daniel laughed, his breath a jungle against my ear. "You won't hurt me..." He unzipped his jeans and ran his manhood, thick with precum, across the screaming flesh between my thighs. "...I can't promise the same to you."

I leaned back and returned his playful laugh. "I can heal."

With slow deliberation, he licked my neck, biting the soft skin just under my jawline between his canines until I cried out. "That's my girl," he mused. Bending me over the bloody blanket, he hiked up my shirt, pulled it over my head, and tossed it aside. His knife blade ran down my back with just enough pressure to feel its edge without penetrating.

My muscles tensed and I inhaled a sharp breath I didn't dare release. Was he...was he going to cut into me again?

His cock slipped inside me, hard and resolute, pausing

when he broke through my hymen for what must have been the fiftieth time. He always paused then, a half-drunk grin plastered on his face, before demolishing me. This time, his thrusts were tempered as his blade skated my skin.

Cloaked in a heady breath, he whispered, "No limits."

More paint underscored my nails; I was whole with him inside me. Things were silent, and together, and I was whole. In a hushed, half-drunk tone, I sighed, "Yes...God... Daniel...yes!"

One and the same.

They are one and the same.

The knife sliced into my left shoulder blade, methodically parting a red sea until he reached the very small of my back. I sucked in a shock of air that gave way to waves of high pitched, stuttering cries, even as I tightened around him.

We repeated the pattern on my right side.

Oh, God! What am I doing? What is he...

Placing a thumb over each wound, he gently ran the length of them, fanning out the blood. "Don't heal," he demanded. My wails shifted to orgasmic moans, pleasure and pain stirring together and pouring into each heated broken cell of my body.

In and out he pistoned, hypnotic, soothing, ecstasy.

I want to do what he asks...need to...

Flares rushed over my back, betraying me.

My cry from its pain was twofold.

I want to do what he asks...

...need to...

As one wound closed, he opened another near to it.

Don't heal.

I bit into my arm. This stroke was deeper than the last.

Please...don't heal!

The next was deeper still, more jagged, less controlled.

Daniel moaned, spreading the blood over me like I was his canvas.

Is he going to skin me alive? Am I going to let him?
"Break your chains."
This is what I'd asked for...
"Break your chains."
...if not what I'd envisioned.

For an eternity trapped inside five minutes, Daniel painted me with wings, only to have my body dismiss them.

Still inside me, barely relenting his pace, he arched me up to him, spilling tepid blood down my back and over his stomach. Was the world out of focus because my head overflowed with fuck-me hormones, or did I need a transfusion?

"Daniel, please!" I whimpered.

Please what? Please stop, please don't stop...please don't heal. What the fuck do I want?

It doesn't matter what I want...

"No limits..." *Isn't that what I wanted?*

He caressed my throat with force, the knife blade flat against my jawline and coaxing me to turn my head far to the side—to look up at him. His cold, lifeless stare ensnared me. Saliva dripped over his parted lips, oozing down my shoulder and breast, sweltering at first and then increasingly glacial in its descent. A barbed wire chuckle surrounded his words. "Want to *revise* your previous statement?"

Daniel wasn't here, or perhaps more accurately, all of him *finally* was. A plutonium dragon as apt to slit my throat as to kiss it. Did he expect me to say yes? To recoil at what lay beneath his skin? And how long would I last if I...

But I was too far gone for any such imaginings—wrapped firmly around his fingertips by a red string I'd cut and twisted myself.

I tore my gaze from him and enclosed a trembling hand around the saturated blade, grimacing as it pierced the underside of my fingers and palm. Biting back a scream, I tightened my grip, returning my eyes to the hollows of his. How could I summon a dragon, MY dragon, and then berate him for what he was? Blood rained upon the grass and I let go of the knife, reaching back to stroke and smear his face with what belonged to him.

Words aren't enough…but blood scratches the surface…it begins to be.

It's a "good start."

My dragon's smile curled within my hand, nearly as sharp as the blade that slid over his palm on its way to the ground. Without so much as a wince, his fingers wove through mine. He squeezed our palms together, silencing my cry with a wet kiss soaked in honeyed moans.

I have his life. He has mine.

And I knew death…

…the little death, yes, and the final death of the me that was. The me capable of seeing the world, seeing that dragon, as it was, and not how I wanted it to be.

How I *needed* it to be…

Red flags aren't as bright through rose-colored glasses. Glasses I'd fused to my soul on the dirt floor of that barn, not an hour before.

Daniel's chest rose and fell rapidly against my back, his eyes now shining and wide, his brow slightly furrowed. "I've never done anything like that before," he said, a smile edging the corners of his blood smeared mouth.

"I know…" *"Break your chains."* I'd told him…had I *made* him do it…or *allowed* him the freedom to?

Still holding his hand, I turned around and snuggled against him. For comfort, for warmth, and for balance. The trees bled into the Chevelle, which bled into the grass; a world of oil paintings, but Daniel was here…he was solid.

"I love you…*all* of you." I closed my eyes, kissing the salty skin above his pounding heart as the night's tears broke free of me in great, guttural sobs.

My Love put an arm around my shaking body and stroked my back.

It wasn't only for him I cried: it was for me, for my father, for Kayla, for Ma, for all the things I didn't understand about what was happening to me...to us...and for the few things I did.

Among the sadness, mourning, confusion, frustration, fear, and pain that poured from me, were tears of relief and yes, even joy. Joy at the edges of that smile.

His smile.

After a time, Daniel tilted my chin up, peering into my swollen eyes with adoration. Hot blood gushed down my wrist, chased by deep, gnawing pain. Unclasping my trembling hand from his, I stared at it before again finding his eyes.

Laughing over my tears and the crack in my voice, I stammered, "I...I didn't heal."

Daniel took my hand gently in his own, which I also hadn't healed, and kissed it, grinning.

"Don't heal."

Control...he's teaching you control...

Yes, he'd been trying to help me get control...if I could get a handle on this ability there's no reason I couldn't control the others, or anything else that came my way...our way.

I smiled and softly kissed his lips.

There was nothing we couldn't do together.

Nothing I wouldn't do for him.

CHAPTER FIFTY-FOUR

*D*aniel opened the trunk of the Chevelle and took out a pair of shop towels. He wrapped one around my hand and tied it as I winced, then did the same for himself, tying it off with his teeth.

"Let me heal you." I moved to take his hand, and heat flared inside me...my hymen healing on its own.

"Not a chance." He stepped back, playfully. "Let it scar." Smiling, he pulled my suitcase out with his good hand.

"When did you..." But I knew the answer already, when I'd been a million miles away.

"Did a once over of the place, and snagged what I could off your floor quick. Turned off the shower, checked that your dad still had a pulse, and grabbed some food." He'd been level headed in the chaos, always thinking of me, always a step ahead of what I needed.

Always, what I *needed*.

And hadn't he come to me at my loneliest point? As if summoned? Or by a gravitational pull? *Black hole.* Hadn't he saved me from the oblivion of Paraxil? Taken up smoking and become increasingly possessive and emotional with each passing week? And now he wanted to let his hand scar after…after unchaining his beast.

Like I'd told him to. I couldn't feel him, but that didn't mean I wasn't affecting him.

"Daniel?" Crimson flowers bloomed through my towel.

"Hmm?"

"What if I'm makin' you love me?"

"You mean with your wicked wiles?"

"Yeah."

"Then I'm the luckiest son of a bitch standin'." He yanked a wet wipe from its box in the trunk and ran it across my forehead and down my nose. "And I wouldn't change a damn thing." Gently kissing the tip of my nose, he placed the wipe in my free hand. "So, clear your conscience on that front. We'll fill it with something fucked up later."

I laughed over trembling lips.

Exactly what I needed to hear…

"Get cleaned up, while I start a fire with my body heat." He reached far into the trunk and came away with a can of gasoline. "Then I'll char us up somethin'." Pulling a handful of wipes, he rubbed down his neck and chest while walking backwards into the darkness. "Glove box has more beef jerky in it if you need somethin' now."

"Yeah, I heard it in there," I said absently, turning toward the passenger's side of the Chevelle. Switching on the dome light, I assessed myself in the side mirror. War paint of a different sort ran down my cheeks now, as though I'd cried blood. *Or popped my eyes back into their sockets.* I looked away, blinking back the hazy memory.

Fuck. That hadn't happened…had it?

Much of me was soot black, streaked through with gray on my backside and right arm where the blood had run. The soles of my feet, however, were stark white.

Had I looked like this all night? And it hadn't bothered Daniel at all?

Why would it? If the situation were reversed I wouldn't have thought twice. I'd have just been glad he was okay. Well, intact maybe; how could there be anything approaching okay, given this royal clusterfuck of a situation?

I went through the rest of the box and several shop towels, shivering as I scrubbed the barn grime from myself. Twice, my bandage had to be swapped out, having soaked through. If my hand didn't quick-heal on its own I would need stitches, and Daniel too. From my suitcase, jeans, a sweater, and a pair of ill-fitting novelty socks proclaiming my love for Spam passed the smell test, and I sighed into their warmth.

I was in sore need of make-up, but could pass as human. My default setting from here on out.

Ceramic mushrooms stuck out from under the rear passenger's seat. I slid the gnome out and chuckled, kicking the door shut and walking toward a now roaring fire. "You don't forget a grudge, do you?"

Daniel, back in the shirt he'd let me borrow, threw two planks of wood onto the blaze. Sparks swirled into the air some thirty feet from the barn entrance, shadows dancing off the buzzsaw and table inside. "Nope," he said.

I sat, cross-legged, on a makeshift bench of crumbling cinder blocks and rotted planks not far from the fire, and lit up a smoke, blowing some of it into the gnome's mushroom bagpipes. It trailed out the little guy's mouth along with the musty scent of gnomish halitosis. Giggling, I repeated the process, tapping on the back of the figurine until a series of smoke rings came out.

My smile widened.

One of the rings encircled Daniel, who was crouched over the coals, sporting a pair of tongs last seen hanging on my neighbor's grill. The very same neighbor who'd been dispossessed of the gnome which was now wedged comfortably in my lap. On the outskirts of the fire, a Lobo's of New York label curled into ash.

Picking two foil wrapped packages from the flames, Daniel opened them on the bench next to me and cut into one of the steaks with his tactical knife. Blood and juice sizzled on the foil, dripping from still pink flesh.

"Kayla wanted to try these again," I said, taking it from him. The thing could be mooing for all I cared.

Daniel sat next to me. "I remembered."

It wasn't possible to love him more, but here I was.

"Grub's on, Kayla. Blue Aquafina, just like you like." I held a stabbed piece up by the knife and waved it around.

Crickets chirped.

Wood cracked, hissed, and popped.

Because she isn't here…

You KNOW she isn't.

Ignoring myself, I set the steak beside me and cut into another, stopping short of chomping down to cast an eye at the gnome. I never had ordered that pizza. Chunking off a small piece of my steak, I popped it in the little guy's mouth. Better late than never.

Daniel put an arm around me and I rested my head against his chest as we chewed in silence for a time, staring at the pops and swirls of the fire.

Swirls like water down a drain, like eddies in the ocean, or…cotton candy around a fingertip.

Hisssss.

Pop!

A twinge plucked at my heart and I stopped chewing.

That kiss…our last kiss…the last time I saw Kayla alive, something had popped. The bright barrier had come down and…

Had I drained her?

I had been confused about where I was afterwards…as though I were looking at myself as we drove away.

And in the days after her death...I'd seen her falling...

Maybe not in my mind's eye at all, but a memory. Same as my dad.

I had drained her.

I drained Kayla and what's more...

"I killed her." My breath came out quick and clawing and I jolted forward, the gnome sliding off my lap. Daniel caught it one handed.

"I-I killed my sister." I clutched and wrenched my chest, knotting my sweatshirt and unwittingly pinching the skin beneath hard enough to leave a bruise, however temporary. "That's why she isn't here. Her soul's wherever this comes out. Oh God. Daniel! I threw her into the fucking abyss!"

Collapsing to my knees, I whined like the wounded animal I was. "For days afterward, I saw her falling...when I closed my eyes. Part of her was in me, IS in me still."

Yes, that was as real as the damp earth seeping into my jeans. "She wouldn't have come out here alone, but she'd have come out here for me!"

CHAPTER FIFTY-FIVE

*D*aniel remained where he was, still chewing. "You couldn't have killed her. You never left my room. I've got an eye on it."

"Physically, maybe, but we have no idea what I'm capable of! Weird shit just keeps piling on, more and more and more!" One handed, I yanked out clumps of grass while repeating "and more" until the earth was an upheaved semicircle around me.

Visions of the black hole in my chest growing and consuming the planet gnawed their way to the front of my mind's eye, as real as her falling. Was this next? The inevitable outcome?

"You wouldn't kill Kayla." Daniel snapped me back to reality. My nails were broken and jagged, fingertips numb from clawing mud and rock.

"I-I started to drain her the last time I saw her, but you drove off. Something happened, something…unlocked when she and I…when we kissed. Like a key fitting into a slot or a circuit completing. I don't know why then? We'd hugged, and kissed, and touched countless times since all this began.

But that time the pressure in me changed, my heart stopped clunking and started spinning."

Again I wrenched my sweatshirt and skin, the pain grounding me, letting me finish my thought. "I took some cotton candy from her, and for a minute, after we left, I was her! Just like with my dad on the beach! Exactly like it!"

Daniel pursed his lips together and furrowed his brow. "You stopped draining your dad, but not Kayla? That don't sound right. No way you'd have let that happen. I watched the video from my room and you didn't do much more than drool on my pillow. If there was something like that going down, even at a distance, you'd fight like a she-bear."

He was right, I would have fought like hell before hurting her. Yet, how many blackouts had there been, where I had no memory of anything? Maybe I had fought? A shudder swept across my chilled frame.

"Death's a powerful thing," Daniel continued. "Could be taking that little bit connected you, so you got a flash image of her final moments."

"It wasn't the holey barn roof I saw when I closed my eyes. It was her falling, as if I was above her."

"People who report near death experiences say they float above themselves. Something like that probably factors into forever death too." His words offered an odd comfort that tucked itself in beside me. What a small and horrible gift if this was the case: a piece of my best girl with me, connecting us for the rest of my life, and beyond her short one.

Of course, with how things had been going, mine might not be much longer.

"Forever death." A serrated shadow flickered in the light of the fire, rolling back and forth over the hollowed out muscle car. "I wanted to kill myself on that buzz saw more than once—it was like a compulsion, or a call almost. She could have gotten the same call, only there was no *you* there to stop her." I glared at the barn. "We need to run those tests on this fucking place."

Daniel flipped through the images on the thermal camera. "I've been running Kayla's tests since we got here. Only thing that came back as an anomaly so far is you." He leaned over and showed me the footage of my feet. "There's an increased heat signature when you heal, at the site of the wound, and every time it activates, the camera fades, glitches, or turns off. Same with the flashlight and EMF detector, though with that we only got a slight blip when it was right up against you."

I turned from the video, stomach fluttering. "I believe you." Hell, I didn't want to be there when it was taken, much less relive it. Snagging the thermal camera, I took a panoramic video of the barn, settling back on first me, and then up to Daniel. Kayla had wanted to capture him on her new camera.

After a few failed attempts, I got the camera to play back what I'd shot. Two thermal humanoids, a handful of blobs that might have been raccoons or rats, and a great glowing fire that washed out the entire screen. "I have no idea how to read this thing." I handed the camera to Daniel with a heavy sigh, and a laugh that jumped the asylum fence a few yards back.

What had I been expecting? Kayla to photobomb the thing?

Yes.

We'd promised each other.

But she isn't here.

I looked at the barn, swallowing a bout of tears.

"Why'd you come out here by yourself?" I demanded of the piece of Kayla inside me. "Being reckless is *my* job, *you're* the responsible one!" Tears meandered down my cheeks, soft and unerring, and a picture sketched across my mind in the crackling aura of the fire. *Kayla getting a jump on set-up so*

when I finally got here, probably running late and dripping with
excuses, we could do the tests without making her late for her ship-
ment at the Willows.

"If I'd have gotten up earlier..." I grit my teeth, picked up
a grassy dirt clod, and hurled it at the barn. Left handed as I
now was, it barely made it past the fire, sending bits of mud
hissing into the flames. I went back for another, and another,
and another, until the ammunition and my tears ran dry.

Daniel ripped out a clump at his feet and refilled my
freezing hand. "Just don't stay too long in the land of what
might have been," he said. "I need you here with me." The
grass clod drizzled icy muck down my arm and off my
elbow.

He was right, I could spin my tires in the muddy ruts of
the road not taken for eternity and not get anywhere. Didn't
I owe it to Kayla, Daniel, and myself to keep moving forward
and figure this out? I threw the clump into the fire and faced
Daniel, straightening myself up. "I'm here with you."

"Good, 'cause whatever's goin' on here is bigger than this
barn." He snicked his Zippo open and lit a cigarette. "Not
everything is spooks, Amy." Narrowing his eyes, he surveyed
the woods and the hillside beyond the barn. "Least not the
kind Kayla was chasin'."

"What do you mean?"

"When you're a hammer, everything's a nail. When you're
a ghost hunter, everything says boo." He sat on the grass
beside me, resting his elbows on his knees. "Splitz only gives
free games on your actual birthday, the owner's a fuckin'
skin-flint. So unless I'm missing something, you had to have
dropped that bowling ball on your foot and healed it a week
before you were out here the first time."

Shit. Being bad at math had come back to bite me again.
How long had this really been going on? When was the last
time I'd hurt myself on anything substantial before that ball
hit my foot? Maybe a nick or three while shaving, but those

hadn't been severe. I'd barely noticed them...but was that because they'd fast healed?

"I got a helluva splinter last November jumpin' Kayla's front fence. That was bandaged and nasty for days, but Ma thought it was odd it didn't leave a scar..." Could it have been my healing kicking in slowly? After all, we seldom grew a foot overnight.

Ah, foot...poor choice of words.

"You think it's been me all along? And the barn is a coincidence?" It never crossed our minds...

Why would it? I'd first felt emotions that weren't mine out here. But, I'd first gotten my period at summer camp; that didn't mean summer camp caused it.

"The emotion swaying happened out at the Gelding...the soul drain at my house...or Kayla's actually." My stomach churned, and the world spun beneath me. "We've been so narrowly focused...what else have we missed?"

Daniel grasped my hand and pulled us both onto the bench. He handed his smoke to me and I took a few silent, steadying hits.

"How does a girl die three days before you meet her?" he asked.

"I'm terrible at riddles. Um...an embarrassed zebra?"

Really? That's what we're going with? Where did that even come from?

"That's what's black and white and red all over." Lifting the cigarette from me, he took a drag. "In which case I'd also accept us, about an hour ago." He kissed my temple and brought me in close, flushing me fifty shades of red.

"I'll give you a hint," he whispered. "The girl never died."

An ember popped from the fire and I flipped around to look at him. "But Leilani's death was all over the news. Sh- she had tons of Baseline posts from friends and family mourning her. Why would anyone make up such a horrific story?"

"Who says it's made up? You can heal. So she figured out she can, too." He cocked an eyebrow at me. "Special as you are, you really think you're the only one?"

"To find out you could heal that way...coming back from acid burns?" My hand trailed over my face. "So she went along with it...let people think she died? After all that, maybe she had to. But why not explain everything to me? Why come to me at all, just to leave me with some cryptic bullshit and a cancerous crutch?" I plucked the cigarette from his fingers and took a hit.

The question hung in the air, dank and unappealing, as it had since the beginning. From the pitch black of the tree line, an owl hooted and another responded some distance away.

"You're being watched." Daniel picked up the gnome, turning it slowly side to side. "*We're* being watched. And after what just happened with your dad, I'm betting the watchers will become the wardens soon enough."

"Wardens? They gonna put me in prison?" Wouldn't it be the safest place for me after what I'd done tonight?

"It won't be sold that way. Least, not if they're smart." He pulled a bloody shop towel from the bag beside him and began cutting and tearing strips with his knife.

"I'm not goin' anywhere! Not without you." My throat went bone dry.

He stopped tearing and set his gaze on me, his tone level, but weighted. "If some kinda organization shows itself, you play ball 'til we figure out what field we're on. No use becomin' a thorn in a lion's paw without knowing how many mice might be around to chew you out."

"I'm a lioness...I don't fear wolves..." My stomach sank. Had Leilani been warning me of what was to come? That the wolves were circling? And now there might be mice too? "Ghosts are far less disturbing. Let's go back to them. Kayla was communicating with Leilani, she gave her milk and honey and got her to bring her files back."

"Kayla's ghost in the machine feels like a glitch in the spook to me. Someone, it could have even been Leilani, got the wrong memo and ordered your X-file deleted before they were ready to move." The certainty with which he said it made my stomach trip down a few more stairs.

"That's a pretty thorough fuck up," I said.

"Just increases the likelihood we're dealin' with a government agency." He smirked, tipping gas from the can onto the strips he'd just made.

"How are you so sure about this?"

"Kayla plastered your story all over the internet, you think people don't watch for that?"

"She never mentioned me, she said she was the one with the abilities. They'd have been watching her—" Had they thought she was me? Was that really why she was out here so early? Had they killed her thinking she was me, or when they'd found she wasn't?

No, she came out to get a head start on tests...didn't she?

Was that the only reason?

Daniel snickered. "One look or listen through the grapevine and that illusion shatters real quick. Neither of you were careful around your phones. No need to be when you're dealing with ghosts."

"But if we're not..."

I thought the only way Mulder and Scully would find me was if we sought them out. Or made enough noise. I swallowed hard; between Mother, Kayla, and my dad, I'd been rather loud the last few weeks.

"Of course, I don't know for sure, I'm just a boy scout." He set down the gas can, each strip thoroughly soaked. "Bein' prepared."

"So then, what if they don't come, these wardens?"

"Then we pick a place on the coast to hold up a while, and figure things out."

It sounded wonderful, as do many things that never come to pass.

"There's a place I know in Bar Harbor," he continued, "across from the Thirsty Lobster. We can eat the finest kinda steamer omelettes, lay on the beach, and go sailin'. You know how to sail?"

"A little."

"I'll show you the ropes." He stuffed a strip into the hole in the underside of the gnome's boots. "I think we could be ready for that."

The innuendo warmed itself by the fire until it clunked me in the head and I gave him a wide-eyed "O" expression.

"You don't have to tie me down." My lips curled into a smile.

"No, I don't," he agreed, shoving the last of the strips he'd covered in gasoline inside. One end hung out like a fuse.

"Molotov gnome?" I asked, flicking my cigarette into the fire.

He smiled and brought a leather ammo band filled with M80s up from the bag beside him. "Thought we could blow off some steam by blowing this fucker through the center of the earth."

"I just settled our account with him. We smoked on it and everything." I patted the little guy's head. "Can't we call it even, live in peace?"

"Yeah, about a million of 'em." Daniel fastened the band around the gnome's waist. He got up and surveyed the area, kicking some logs and bricks around as he went, as though doing so would maximize the feng shui of the coming destruction. The ceramic figure was set some five feet in front of the barn entrance, and he dug his lighter from his pocket.

"Wait!" I shouted, swiping the pile of leftover strips off the bench and hurrying to his side. I haphazardly wound them around the gnome's head until his eyes were covered, tying it off as best I could with only one fully functioning hand. I lit a fresh cigarette, placed it in the little guy's mouth, and stood. "There."

If I couldn't stay the execution, I could make the condemned a little more comfortable before he went. Maybe that would count for something on the little folk luck scale.

Daniel gave me a side smile and touched the hotbox to the main fuse that wound through the M80s. He backed up, grabbing my hand and pulling me behind the Goblin, where he ducked and covered his ears. I did the same. A series of thunder claps shook the ground, patters of dirt rained down on us, and something flew over our heads to land burning next to the Chevelle. Hollow whooshes followed in quick succession, and the shadow of the truck grew longer.

I peeked over the bed. The earth where the gnome had been was scorched clean. A swaying sea of orange and yellow consumed the barn entrance and all that lay within, like a roving high tide.

Where was this on the luck scale?

"Shit! Daniel!" Terrible and beautiful all at once, the blaze mesmerized me. Waves of flame and heat roared through the windows, up the trees, and into the night.

My heart lightened. Good. Let it burn. A long overdue service to the town of Albion and humanity. An old rotted hellscape just waiting for lightning to strike or a Molotov gnome to happen by.

No one else would fall to their deaths from these rafters, by accident...*or otherwise.*

The constant pressure within me lessened, as if seeing the place in flames had released a burden on my soul. Bright, unbridled, peaceful serenity warmed me, eclipsing all other emotions for an all too brief time.

Kayla?

Yes, but...pressing from outside, not within...and distant, unfathomably distant.

Hot debris and embers crashed down around me, sucking the air from the moment and my lungs. When had I gotten so close to the barn? Daniel was beside me, his hand encircling my bicep, about to pull me away, and I stepped back with him as the rest of the roof collapsed in rolling flames.

"She's at peace." I laughed and cried in the same dreamlike breath. Daniel pulled me back further and held me as I coughed, and we stared at the inferno. "I felt her. For just a second, but I felt her."

She kept her promise.

Of course she had. She's my best girl.

Daniel patted out some embers taking root in my clothes and hair.

"Are *you* at peace?" he asked.

I put my arms around him and buried my head in his chest, sighing. "It's not entirely mine...but yeah."

"Good. We gotta get goin'. This fire's hungrier than I anticipated. Almost ate you."

"I wasn't trying to kill myself...I..." What was I doing? "I guess the connection was strong and drew me toward her." *Like the buzzsaw...*

Even though she wasn't here...she wasn't...and then she was...

I rubbed my forehead against his chest. "I'm not right in the head, or heart, or probably my goddamn pinky toe."

"Yeah, and you do it all so flawlessly." He kissed the top of my head and led me toward the Chevelle.

"Did you start this fire for me?" I glanced at him.

He grinned and opened my door before going around to his.

Some boys give flowers. Mine commits arson.

I looked back at the blaze and up into the billows of smoke filling the night sky. "I hope you found your dad. Found your answers." I paused when the Chevelle's engine purred to life. "I promise, I won't stop 'til I find mine."

Daniel's door slammed shut and I threw a smile at the

Goblin and the sky. "More than a five alarm fire," I whispered, and got in the car.

We sped away from the Whitaker barn, the flames barely visible by the time we hit the main road.

"I need to help my dad," I said.

Daniel turned right.

My peaceful high remained throughout the ride to Waterville Memorial, throughout our shower and second wardrobe change in one of the vacant rooms, and through signing in and walking down the hallway to the intensive care unit. The nurses all shared in my tranquility.

Yes, everything was as it should be.

Right up until I entered room 103.

CHAPTER FIFTY-SIX

*M*y father lay on a bed with every kind of tube and wire going into, around, or over him. Colorful buttons flashed on monitors, and a small army of dials were flipped this way and that. So many patches covered his sunken chest it scarcely counted as bare. His mouth hung open—there wasn't a choice with the number of tubes down his throat. One was connected to a breathing machine that pumped up and down in a steady rhythm.

His emotions were scattered, thin things that couldn't form letters, let alone sentences. Echoes of fear, anxiety, and confusion drifted about. At least that was my best guess; it was like trying to tell what a drawing was with only two lines to work with.

Like identifying someone in the aftermath of a shark attack.

I'd been that shark.

I'd left him, we'd left him, like that. How long had he laid there, and who found him?

I went to his bedside, tears stinging in streams that pattered onto the hard plastic rail surrounding him.

Deep sorrow, full and vibrant, pulsed in the chair by his

side. Red eyes, puffy and underlined with dark gray circles looked up at me, startled from a heavy daze. "Amy." Martin's voice was dry and soft. He coughed to clear his throat and got to his feet, picking up his glasses from the side table. "I'll leave you two alone."

"He loves you," I whispered as he passed me.

Marty smiled wanly, and nodded. "I didn't realize you knew."

"I do." My focus remained on Dad's gaunt face. "And I'm glad you're here." Never mind *how* I knew. Instinct, more than concrete knowledge, though it did put the lust and shock I'd felt from both of them last week into a new perspective...

I didn't have any facts or figures, I didn't know how long they'd been together, only that my dad loved him, was IN love with him, in a way he never was with Mother. There was a light tug in Marty's direction, his own gravitational pull.

Hug him.

Comfort him.

Tell him it'll be alright.

What if I drain his soul too?

What a fine couple they'd make then. Side by side ICU beds with matching pajamas. Marty turned toward me, his arms opening, and I held my injured hand up between us.

"Don't take this personally, but I don't want to be touched right now. I just...want some time with him," I said.

Marty nodded again and left.

A piece of my heart ached to see him go.

But it wasn't my heart, was it...

"I'm sorry, Dad." I reached out to take his hand and stopped short, hovering over it. Was I taking it for comfort, to heal him, or to drain whatever was left of him? What a hellish version of rock, paper, scissors to play. Comfort, heal, or drain.

I pulled back, opting out for the moment.

"I don't know what happened, or how to fix this, but I'm going to try, and I need you to try with me, okay?" My voice squeaked, catching on itself. "Change your emotions if you can hear me...um...get mad or sad or happy...or something."

Anything.

The fragments of emotions continued jostling, so many ripped and torn streamers in a light current. I dove in without a hint of resistance, wading through the wreckage, coaxing confusion to fully form. It shredded to bits at my mental touch, like soaked tissue paper.

Shallow screams drifted from him; if I hadn't been so close, I might not have heard them at all.

Something!

I willed fear, the next biggest emotional remnant, to heal in my mind's eye. It broke apart in sopping pieces.

My stomach sank along with the flotsam. So far, I'd only ever healed by physical touch.

Daniel had stayed out in the hall when I'd been sure it was Mother's sorrow on the other side of the ICU doors. I turned to wave him in and jumped back, rattling my dad's bed. Lines swung back and forth and the tone of one of the beeps heightened.

Daniel was already behind me.

"I'm gonna get you a cat bell." I laughed through the tears.

He smirked and hugged me with one arm. "I'll just get it caught on the neighbor's fence."

"Gotta try to heal him. Stop me if..." I trailed off—how would we know what was a good reaction or a bad one? Healing was always messy.

"I got you." He kissed my wet cheek and spun me gently back toward my dad before letting go.

Laying my palm across Dad's clammy forehead, I fished for a shred of anxiety and called for the wisps to thread through it. To knit it together, strong and brilliant. The heart monitor beeped, and beeped, and beeped, an untold number of times. It was like trying to gain a foothold on a cloud...and then it took. Tension in my chest relaxed and a faint luminescence wove through the places where the IV needles met his arms.

A high pitched choir of shrieks and flashing lights erupted from the tangle of machines, and several nurses rushed us aside.

My heart stuck, a dry and hollow lump in my throat.

Dad's emotions remained unchanged in the chaos...like he wasn't a part of it.

We backed into the hallway, narrowly missing Mother, who gave us a fleeting glance before running in.

"He's an echo." I shivered, staring at the door as it clicked shut. "Like he's haunting his own body." I rubbed my arms and backed away, until the cluster of calm but alert emotions in his room faded. One of the most devastating nights of my life was just another day at the office for them.

Of course...what else were they supposed to feel but calm? Hadn't I seen to it?

"H-he can't even form a whole emotion. But when I tried to coax one from him, he screamed...and now this, after touching him. He *knows* who did this to him." Clenching my injured hand into a fist, I thrummed it against my chest, as though doing so would somehow steady my erratic heartbeat.

"Your ability set the machines off." Daniel squeezed my shoulders. Yes...like the stuttering flashlight and twitchy camera earlier. "And the screams mean he's in there somewhere. Could be the soul is like the liver, it needs time to regenerate. You just need some rest, and so does he."

"I can't go home. I have to fix this. I'm the only one who can." I rubbed my fingertips against the bandage on the back of my hand fast enough to start a second fire that night.

"How do you have malfunctioning machines in an ICU

421

unit?!" Mother's voice carried through the door and down the hall, followed by several muffled responses. The door thumped open and she stalked out, her hand digging into her forehead and pushing up her hair. She closed her eyes and took in a shaky sizable breath. "The sooner I get him out of here the better." Anger, frustration, fear, and worry competed for top billing, but were all doused in numbness, either from shock or the pharma cocktails she'd been cycling through since I'd pushed her over the edge.

Or maybe it was a combination of the two.

A few tears escaped her, rolling tentatively down each cheek. Her choked words came out in a whisper: "I'm so sick of hospitals."

"Mother…" I started in her direction, halting when waves of low nervousness rippled through her, buoyed by the numbness. She wiped the tears away with her thumb and faced me, taking a small, seemingly unconscious step back.

"They aren't sure what's wrong with him," she said. "Physically he's fine, no sign of stroke or concussion, but he stops…stops breathing every so often, so I *don't* see how that can be. You don't just stop breathing when you're *fine*, but that's what this hospital's best and brightest have to say." Her glassy eyes held mine, fear clawing its way across them in bloodshot veins. Whether it was fear for my dad, or of me, I couldn't tell you.

"You look like bloody hell," she added, with a burst of flat indignation.

Bloody? Had I missed a spot? My distorted reflection in the buzzing Coke machine across the hall appeared clean.

"How'd you know he was in the hospital?" she asked.

"Police scanner," Daniel responded before I could register that I had no idea what I would say. His answer was true enough, but it wouldn't have been the first train I hopped.

Mother gave him a lingering side glance, her lip curling. "It's not really appropriate for you to be here."

My boyfriend moseyed up to the soda machine, put in a dollar and pressed the button. A can of Coca Cola clunked down with enough racket to wake half the unit. Maybe that was why it was there? Picking up the drink, he leaned against the machine and cracked it open, meeting her glacial gaze with a loud slurp.

Mother's frustration and indignation swung around her like a mace. The numbness encasing both emotions acted as a buffer against my worn and crumbling mental gate, making it more like a Nerf mace than a real one. Still, as exhausted as I was, it might get through eventually.

I tossed a wry but worn smile to my rebel. "Would you please give us a few minutes?"

He handed me the Coke, kissed my cheek, and headed down the corridor without another look back.

"Daniel's been helping me." My own frustration bubbled as I turned to Mother. It was always someone else fucking up my life, as if half her DNA were incapable of such base debauchery.

"Helping you destroy your life." She watched him until he got on the elevator. "Helping you repeat your Junior year while he helps himself to your body and what passes for your mind."

"I'll do online summer school or something, I don't know, is any of this really important right now? What happened to Dad?"

Or rather, what did *she* think happened? I'd been there and I still wasn't entirely sure.

"The upstairs rail gave way and he fell." She hugged herself. The railing hadn't been broken when he'd fallen... had it? "I don't know when it happened, but I found him when I came home at seven. There was blood on the carpet beneath him but *they* say he doesn't have any cuts."

An arrow of suspicion shot through her nervousness, cleaving it in two. "What happened to your hand?" she asked, eyes narrowing. "Were you bleeding in the house today?"

"This? No, it just happened a little while ago." Shit! How was I going to explain it?

Tell her.

Show her!

I can't...

"That boy had his bandaged too, same hand. Did you join a cult?" She put her palms out toward me and spoke slowly, eyebrows raised. "You know, don't answer that. I've got enough on my plate tonight. I've got to get your father into Kennedy and out of this inept death trap." She headed for the waiting area, swiping her phone, her nervousness dwindling with every step.

The shortest fight in the history of Mother.

Because she can't get away from you fast enough.

Hey, a gift horse is a gift horse. Don't knock it.

And speaking of horses...

While I waited for Daniel, I used the phone at the nurses station to call Kamrie and fill her in on why we'd missed our riding appointment—minus the soul-sucking details, of course. Dad was in the hospital following a nasty fall and I was only just now getting around to calling after a crazy day.

"It's just one thing after anothah, isn't it Sugah Cube?" she said when I'd finished. "I wish I could give you a big ol' hug."

"Me too," I said, tears welling as I let her go.

Would I ever be able to hug anyone without fear again?

Daniel wrapped his arms around me and whispered in my ear, "Got somethin' for ya." I still feared hurting him, in spite of his reasoning to the contrary, but basked in his warmth all the same.

He led me up the elevators to a third floor room at the end of a hall with an angry fluorescent light that hummed in alternating octaves. A sign reading "UNDER MAINTE-

424

NANCE" was taped firmly to the door. Two sheets of paper filled with codes and legalese hung just below it.

"Your room awaits." Daniel opened the door and ushered me in. After we broke in the bed, I fell into a blissful sleep beside him.

Not that it lasted for too long at a stretch that first night. I woke screaming from half-remembered nightmares half a dozen times, convinced my dad had flat lined. There was no going back to sleep without checking on him each time.

And getting some chocolate pudding from the cafeteria.

For the next few nights, that out-of-bounds room was our home. No tentacles sprang up from any of my crevices, and I didn't develop a hunger for souls. The nightmares gradually receded, but my dad remained the same.

However, the machines he was hooked to continued to malfunction.

I wasn't giving up on him.

~

"They can't just give up on him like this! It's only been three days!" Mother yelled as I shambled past the ICU family room, with its stiff, unwelcoming furniture. "He can't breathe on his own…not regularly. Blood sucking parasites think they know better than his doctors!" There was irony in there somewhere, but I'd promised Daniel I wouldn't commit suicide so I kept the sentiment to myself.

"Tell me there's something you can do, Marty. What have I been paying into all this time, if they're just gonna let him…" Mother buried her head in her hands.

Marty put his hand on her back and rubbed. "I'll get an injunction and contact the press. They won't get away with it."

But, Mother couldn't feel his doubt.

Neither of them noticed me, and I kept on my way. No

worries, I would use my influence to grow the hearts of the paper-pushers by three sizes. I'd have to find a way to track them down. But Daniel could help with that when he got back from work.

I wandered through the hospital, glimpsing frail hands and worried faces through each half-cracked door. How many were fighting this same battle right now, on top of their illness? Could I make it all go away with a touch? No one would even need to know I'd done it.

Or maybe, I should say fuck it and make a giant spectacle of my healing. Daniel was sure that if I did, the lines would never stop and people who made money off of suffering would want me dead. People who thought what I did was the devil's work would, too.

Given the state of my life, there might have been a kernel or two of truth to that devil theory.

Could I squander this cursed gift, or did I have a moral obligation to at least try to use it for the greater good, no matter the price tag?

It was too much to think about.

So I smiled at the overpriced clown balloon hanging in the gift shop window instead. The same one Dad had sent me when I was here not long ago. "Laughter is the best medicine," I said as I bought it, along with a king-sized Snickers and a Monster drink. The clerk groaned inwardly while smiling outwardly, and handed me my change.

"Either that, or you'll scare him awake." I grimaced at the shining, freakish clown.

Did the methods matter if the results were the same?

My footsteps echoed down the ICU hall, past the empty family room and the lone nurse at the desk. Numbness crept out of Dad's room, biting into my mental wall. Mother always was the frost queen; now her emotions matched. Whatever they had her on this time was—

I froze halfway through opening the door. It banged hard against my shoulder.

A man stood, looking out the window, wearing three days scruff and a wrinkled white dress shirt open at the collar. He'd been emitting solid concern and pity that I'd mistaken for Marty, but as he appraised me, wariness took root around the edges.

"Hello, Amy," a familiar voice spoke from the shadows of my father's bedside. She had a Utah accent, so Colorado had been a close guess. "It's time I gave you more than just a pack of cigarettes." The bone-tired eyes of a dead girl met mine, her rainbow streak long faded in her jet black hair.

CHAPTER FIFTY-SEVEN

"Greens aren't just a pack of cigarettes, they're a flavor sensation." Walking to the bed, I didn't take my eyes from her. "They're a lifeline," I said, and her smile tinged with the same numb melancholy her soul wore. Setting my food on the bed, I took my dad's hand in both of mine and asked the only question that really mattered: "Can you help him?"

She shook her head. "I can't. But you may be able to, with more experience and understanding of what you can do."

"Understanding? Experience? I never want to *do* this again!" I blinked in rapid succession, my enunciated words stumbling out in cracked, breathless squeaks. "You must not have been paying too close attention, this is a fucking nightmare!"

"Oh, it's a shit show alright, and we're the stars." The creases under her reflective chestnut eyes belied a weariness beyond her years.

"Who's we?" I shifted my gaze from her to the man, wariness still wafting from him like dry ice.

Whoever he was, he was smart.

I didn't even trust me.

"The name's Alistair Wolcott, and you're already aware of Ms. Polumya. I'd say it's a pleasure to finally meet you Ms. Durene, but it isn't, not like this." He nodded toward my dad, his voice grave. "We're here to help you navigate this cluster-fuck, to the extent that's possible." His vowels had a British or Scottish elongated edge to them, dulled beneath brash New English stone.

"Leilani?" I turned back to her, sucking in a short breath. "You're Mulder?"

She considered the question. "I suppose in a way I am. I search for others, like us, to try to uncover the truth. I'm swept up in it, same as you. But whereas you sense emotions, I sense you, and other aberrations, except my memory sucks. It's spotty, and I don't always remember every encounter."

"Blackouts..." I whispered, bringing my hand to my mouth.

She nodded, biting her full lower lip.

"Your family, your friends, they all think you're dead. Did all that stuff really happen to you?" For a long moment, the steady beep of the machines offered the only response. I shouldn't have asked the question so bluntly, but I had to know.

Pity drizzled through Alistair in the silence, soaking into my heart. He cast somber eyes over her, his tone gentle but matter of fact: "She doesn't like to discuss it."

Leilani rolled a six ton glare his way, holding it for a five count before softening on me. "It's a complicated mess, the whole thing. It's better I be thought dead. Safer for my family that way. I got involved with some *very* bad people and not all of them have found the tactical knife of justice yet." She sneered. "Some are still slithering about."

"So, you never actually died?" What was this rash of disappointment spreading through me, ugly and itchy?

Because if she could come back, so might Kayla.

429

"Not physically. Though there were days, *are days*, I wish I had," she said.

"Am I in danger from them? Is Daniel?"

"Yes." She looked from me to Alistair, resuming her stone glare. "We all are."

Alistair rested against the wall, folding his arms and smacking his tongue against the roof of his mouth, annoyance steadily replacing pity. He caught her glare and held it.

"Then why'd you leave me with no explanation?" I demanded.

She shuffled her feet, cheeks flushing red. Embarrassment bloomed through her numbness, slowly frosting over and withering as she spoke. "I told you, I just end up places, I get pulled to find others. One day I'm in Utah trying to make sense of my life, and the next I'm sitting in front of a thirty-foot-tall Paul Bunyan statue in Maine with no idea how I got there. I didn't know that you and I had even talked until Alistair showed me a transcript and the video."

All this time, we'd been wondering about her, thinking she held all the answers, and she didn't even remember meeting me.

"How long have you known?" I asked Alistair.

"When Ms. Rodriguez went digging for information on Ms. Polumya, it sent up flares," he replied.

"That was three months ago! Why wait so long to contact me? Maybe we wouldn't have to be meeting like this if you had!" Tears welled in my eyes and I gestured at my dad. They'd removed some of the tubes in his mouth, but it still lay open, his lips dry and cracked. "Hand me that lip balm." I pointed to the table next to Leilani and she tossed me the vanilla mint Chapstuff.

"We have a protocol we follow," Alistair said. "We watch and decide what level of threat you pose before risking lives by engaging directly. You were pegged as an empath with mild emotion control abilities, but when your mother, Mrs.

430

Rodriguez, and your father were all hospitalized, and given Ms. Rodriguez's death, we bumped you up on the priority list."

"Bumped up? How many others are there, besides me?" I put the Chapstuff on my dad's lips; at least I could make him a little more comfortable.

"Several each month, and very few of them sane. They're time intensive and then there are the emergencies: someone killing people, bringing buildings down, or hacking into restricted areas. So those have to be addressed quickly," he said.

"That three-point-nine in Minnesota wasn't an earthquake." Leilani leveled her eyes on me, her tone grim. "It was a person."

"Oh, shit!" I plunked onto the bed, twisting the lip balm out past all decency.

"Yes. Well put," Alistair said.

"What are we?" I swallowed a lump in my throat that punched a hole in my stomach. The air seemed thick as cotton candy.

"Extraordinary. Aberrations. Gods and goddesses reborn? Angels? Demons? Virulently insane?" He rattled them off with a nonchalant shrug.

"I prefer humans, with a twist. But I think you're onto something with that last one." Leilani gave Alistair a hard, lingering side eye.

"Mental abilities *do* take their toll." His face lit up with the infectious grin of a mad man. "Which reminds me, how far away can you feel other people's emotions, Ms. Durene?"

I smooshed the cap back on the Chapstuff, coating my fingers in vanilla mint relief. "The nurse at his station. The couple in room 106, but just barely."

Alistair narrowed his eyes and clicked his teeth together. "Forty-five feet, give or take. That's an impressive range to still be feeding yourself. As far out as you can sense, most psychics are catatonic outside of three months. But here you are, with your clown balloon." He threw me a bemused smile.

I fiddled with the gauze bandage on my still unhealed hand. I was far from stable—and possibly contagious—but never considered it could be worse. Hadn't I come razor close to catatonia...if not for Daniel? The balloon wavered back and forth on the wings of some unseen draft and I unlooped it from my wrist. "What's your ability?" Staying focused on Alistair, I tied the balloon to my dad's rail, stopping midway to wipe excess Chapstuff onto his sheets.

Could he hear all this? Might he wake up any moment with all the answers from wherever I'd sent his soul?

When had life ever been that convenient?

"I cut through red tape like every day's a grand opening." Alistair leaned forward, a far off twinkle in his eye, and I couldn't help but chuckle.

"*Never* underestimate the power of bureaucracy, Amy. Alistair got my father out of jail and brought the hammer down on Tom Obachek with a phone call." Leilani's breath dipped at Obachek's name and her anxiety spiked, momentarily tearing through her numbness.

"Well, it was a bit more than one, but it's nice to know I'm appreciated." Alistair smoothed down his vest.

Leilani swept up the tattered copy of *Chicken Soup for the Soul* I'd been reading to my dad, from the small table next to her, and quickly thumbed through it. Flurries of melancholy and anger settled in her as she gazed well beyond each page. There were more emotions present, but distinguishing them was like trying to read a book beneath several feet of ice.

The Bureaucracy King took a deep breath through his hawkish nose and turned to me. "I'll level with you, Ms. Durene: we need your help as much as you need ours. What are you? Frankly, we don't know, but it's the mission of the Centaur Program to find out."

"The Centaur Program?" I asked.

"Don't ask me why it's called that. Some stodgy old bastard thought it made him sound educated, I suspect. I keep pushing to rename it Freak Show but we'd have to change the stationary, and what would we do with ten thousand Centaur-themed Frisbees?" He scratched his scruffy chin in what looked to be serious contemplation.

Was he aware that *he* was a stodgy old bastard? He wasn't gray yet—in fact he sported a full head of thick, dark brown hair reminiscent of greased chicken feathers—but he had to be older than Mother.

It's best not to ask how I know what a greased chicken looks like.

"Are you government or?" Popping open my can of Monster, I took a drink. Hopefully I could keep it down.

"Public purse strings, private everything else." He laughed.

"Speaking of..." Leilani reached into a black leather bag by her side and pulled out my small plush purse, the one I'd lost in the concert parking lot.

"My purse? How did you get this?" Bouncing up and down, I spilled Monster on my dad's hand before setting the can on one of the pinging machines. The nurse would yell at me, but he wouldn't stay mad long. I zipped open my purse. Phone, wallet, and kazoo were all intact, but no maracas. Scooping the money from my wallet, I counted it without thought.

"Some jerk took it home and stripped the phone for resale. One of Centaur's techs recovered everything for you," she said, clasping her bag closed and picking the book back up.

"There's twenty dollars more in here than there was when I went to the show!" I squealed.

Alistair smirked. "Our people are good at persuading unsavory characters to do the right thing. You can understand that, can't you, Ms. Durene?"

I snickered. "Yes."

"If things work out, you may be one of our people some day." Straightening against the wall, he scratched his chin while letting his eyes roam over the room. "Or at the very least, we can equip you for what you might be up against."

"The bad people?" My phone booted up, displaying several unread messages from Kayla. My heart flushed and I soaked in the icon. After a few seconds, I placed the phone back in my purse.

I'd read them later, when we could be alone.

"—angerous, malicious, self-righteous, reactionary, lurpy, half-wits stuck in the right hand lane of a roundabout." Leilani scowled, gritting her teeth. I'd missed part of what she said, but got the gist of it.

"Don't scare the girl." Alistair threw an annoyed look at her before softening on me, his chin raised. "Nothing you need to worry about. Those troglodytes don't have a presence around here, and we've got you monitored."

As if the constant monitoring wasn't disturbing on its own, here it might actually be the lesser evil? Did I want to live like this?

A stone sank in my gut.

Had they monitored Kayla's final hours?

…Or been responsible for them?

Would Leilani remember, either way?

Play ball 'til we figure out what field we're on.

"So, you want me to join you? You aren't going to put me on a slab? Dissect my brain? Lock me away in a glass warehouse on tiny alphabetical slides?" *Don't give them ideas, Amy!*

"We're in King country, Ms. Durene, but we're not the Institute. Any tests we perform will be with your consent, and you can stop any time you wish." Pity drizzled over him again. "You've been through hell, we don't need to make that worse. I'm sorry we couldn't get to you sooner, that we have to meet like this, I truly am. But you've demonstrated tremendous mental fortitude, and understanding how and why will help us keep others from walking in front of a Greyhound."

Leilani huffed and stared at the page she was on so intensely she might have been reading the coding behind the Universe.

Alistair let his eyes rest on her for a stretch, running his tongue over his top row of teeth. "Now, if you're a threat to yourself or others, we will step in as needed." He sighed, switching to me. "I hope you'll understand."

Leilani peered in my direction, her tone deadpan, emotions crisp with nihilistic acceptance. "I can't take a piss without someone watching." She tilted her head, eyes flipping up to Alistair. "But, it's marginally better than walking out into traffic or waking up in an unmarked van with a hood over my head."

"I think I'd want you to stop me, if that was the case." I flattened a piece of tape on my dad's arm. Wasn't it already the case?

"Good, then we're on the same page," Alistair said, "and Ms. Polumya can go *back* to hers."

Her half-lidded eyes glowered at the empty space in front of her a moment before doing just that.

"So the blackouts, the hallucinations, they're common?" Turning the smooshed lip balm between my fingers, I skimmed off chunks to flick into the garbage.

"Mental abilities put a tremendous strain on the mind, and physical ones on the body," he said. "We've developed tools that can keep this at bay, and training methods that may stop you from exhausting or driving anyone else you love insane."

Ouch. Straight for the jugular. All this time it was me possessing myself? Overloading my own circuits? Is that what I'd done to my dad? Tried to possess him? Why did that feel *curiously* half-right?

I twirled one of his IV lines in my fingers, until something let out a screeching beep and I quickly dropped it. "What do I have to do? If I join this program?"

"You'll need to move to Detroit while tests are run." Alistair sat in the windowsill, the bright lights of the parking lot casting a halo around him.

"Detroit? Oh, Mother will never let me go." I snorted.

"Since when would you let that stop you?" Leilani smirked, not looking up from *Chicken Soup for the Soul*. For someone who didn't remember me, she sure had my number...and so much more, I bet.

I preferred her hiding in my mirror. But then, she'd never been there, had she? Just a hallucination of an overwhelmed mind under tremendous strain, if they were to be believed.

"We can fill Mrs. Durene in on what's happening with you. Or if you'd rather she remain in the dark, we can fabricate just about any story you'd like." Alistair thrummed his fingers, long and lean as the rest of him, against the window's edge.

I got up and gazed out the small window in the door, half expecting Mother to be on the other side.

But she wasn't. Her plate was too full for that. "You could tell her I got into an elite program for the gifted...it wouldn't be too far off."

And it would give her a healthy dose of crow to eat.

"Well, we have to stay within the bounds of credulity, Ms. Durene." Alistair frowned, raising a slight eyebrow. "Perhaps a school for at risk youth would go down easier. We'll present it as a once in a lifetime opportunity and a chance to be mentored by the *glitterati*." He'd clearly done his homework, on all fronts. Mother might actually go for it.

Was that a good thing?

"What about Daniel? Can he come?" I wouldn't go without him.

"Mr. Varrick, who hacked a maintenance request for

room 302, and tied it in a knot of back ordered parts and people on vacation so it won't be touched for at least another week? All so you could be close to your father?" Alistair laughed, cynical admiration frolicking through him. "The young man's resourceful. I don't imagine we'd be able to keep him away even if we tried, and as you're unable to sense him, he can help with some of the testing."

My dragon *was* resourceful, crazy smart, and scary observant. So much of what he'd predicted that last night at the barn was playing out in front of me, and he'd had the equivalent of a matchstick and a piece of chewing gum to work from. That Alistair recognized this, with admiration, boded well.

Daniel would come, he was ready to go to Ireland with me and Detroit was much closer. A weight lifted from my chest only to be replaced by another in my stomach. Did I even want to go? Miles away with people who knew how long I took to brush my teeth but who I knew next to nothing about?

The watchers or the wardens...

My dad's short, shallow screaming thundered in my ears, though it could barely be heard over the heart monitor. I went to his side, stroking his face, while heat and pressure built behind my eyes.

"They want to take him off life support..." My breath hitched and I seized Alistair's gaze, stopping just short of diving into his emotions and making him amiable. "Can you superglue the red tape together and keep him on?"

His mouth quirked up, amber eyes sparkling. "Yes."

My hand trembled against Dad's cheek as I unsuccessfully blinked back a stream of tears. Relief washed through me, and Alistair, though I'd done nothing to evoke it in him.

"Anything we can do to ease your stress, so your focus can be where it needs to be. We can also see to it you graduate your sophomore year, the health of those you have 'swayed' is monitored, and that Mrs. Rodriguez doesn't lose her cattle ranch while she's away."

Ma? The Willows? Here he was with a solution to a problem I hadn't thought of yet. My lips quivered and I closed my eyes, taking in a sharp stuttering breath. "You think I did somethin' to Ma? Mrs. Rodriguez? I didn't, I—"

I didn't know that, did I? Everything was such a blur after Kayla...

I might have...

Cool silky arms encircled me and Leilani set her temple against mine. "There's no blame here, Amy. Even if you did, you can't be held accountable for abilities you have no control over. There isn't a manual for any of this, but intent matters."

I melted into her embrace, this living dead girl who had some understanding of what it was like. Some empathy for what I'd been through, even as she'd seen so much worse. And knowing what I was capable of, that I might turn her into my father at any moment, here she was anyway. A deep undercurrent of acceptance flowed beneath her glacier of melancholy as she stroked my hair and I silently sobbed into hers.

Her touch...was everything.

Maybe I couldn't be held accountable, but I could be responsible in how I dealt with the aftermath. I could do everything in my power to get a handle on whatever was going on with me. So I didn't hurt anyone else, so Ma's life wouldn't get worse, and so they wouldn't pull the plug on my dad and make me a murderer before I could find a way to heal him.

In the end, my choice to join the Centaur program was never a choice at all. There was only one way it could have ever gone.

"Okay," I said, my blurry eyes fixed on my dad. "I'm game."

CHAPTER FIFTY-EIGHT

By 9:05 the next morning, my father's life support extension was not only approved, but he'd been cleared for a spot at Kennedy Memorial's long term care wing. Mother was therefore in a much more relaxed state of mind when my acceptance letter to the "Mount Pelion Institute" came.

Two of her most pressing problems, solved in one day.

Father's new accommodations were far from posh, but were clean and serviceable. I set a pair of small ceramic horses on his nightstand, and moved some wires out of the way to give him a kiss on the forehead. "I'm gonna be gone for a little while, figuring things out, but don't you give up, alright?"

"Where was this daughter the past few years?" Mother stood in the doorway, numb uneasiness pervading her, seeming to accuse me of having something more to do with my dad's situation than I'd let on.

"It's hard on Marty, you know. Has been for a long time." I stood back from the bed and turned around.

"The situation isn't exactly oppressive, they can do what they want. All I ever asked, for the last sixteen years, is that they keep up appearances. Something your father agreed to, by the way."

As I passed her I stopped, compelled to say more, and she shifted her weight away from me. Sixteen years? Because of me...or because of her job? I focused on a worn spot on the floor several feet ahead of me. "When Dad wakes up someday, let him go. You've got your career set, I'm grown and won't be around to get in the way of you climbing even higher once I'm gone. It'll be a second breath of life."

Her voice tightened and cracked. "You think I care about any of that? At a time like this? You really do need that school."

"Yeah...I do." I looked down the hall at a nurse delivering medication, the wheel on her cart sticking as she trundled along. "They're gonna take me out there early. Try to get me caught up."

"Already?"

"They gave me the option, and after everything that's happened, I need a new location."

"What about that boy? Or did he leave you after getting what he wanted?" She plucked a piece of fuzz from her shirt, rolling it between her fingers.

"We broke up," I said, holding my breath. "He didn't want me going and it's too big a chance to miss for some boy."

"Good," she said, without so much as an "I told you so."

"I'll call once I'm settled."

"Okay." There was no asking how I would get to Detroit, no offer to drop me off at the bus station or airport. She just folded her arms across her chest, putting her hands in her armpits like she was cold. Internally, she was. Bubbles of apathy froze solid in sheets of nearly transparent numbness. Numbness worked something like dark matter: I could only sense it based on the behavior of the emotions around it, otherwise it was invisible.

I left, glancing back once to see the door to my dad's

room closing with a long hiss, and Mother sitting at his bedside.

I took a back exit into the parking garage and jogged up to the idling Chevelle. You didn't really buy that we'd broken up, did you? Well, the important thing was Mother did—if she thought he was coming she might change her mind and yank me from the program. Although, with how apathetic she'd been, that was far from the certainty it once was.

Climbing into the car, I stopped short at Daniel's crooked smile. His left eyelid shone black and purple, the mottled discoloration continuing down his cheek and popping up again across swollen lips.

"What happened?" I gasped, bringing my hand to his face. Under blue-white wisps, sprung at my touch and without thought, the bruises began to fade.

"The old man took exception to me giving his empire of dirt the middle finger, for some girl." He snickered.

"Did you tell him I'm not just SOME girl? That I'm the love of your life and you'd rather drink Drano than be without me?" Every muscle in my body tensed and I sneered, narrowing my eyes as he opened his.

He gaped at me, a mad twinkle forming in his fresh eye, and a devilish smirk on his dwindling lip. "It was motor oil, but yeah."

"I don't want you drinking any toxic substances, besides me," I said, and he slid his hand over my cheek, devouring me with a kiss and making slurping noises until I broke out in laughter.

He was making sacrifices for me, burning bridges with his family to be by my side.

"Are you sure about this? We can always stay, or elope to Mexico, or Canada, or Ireland."

"No, we can't." Daniel sat back and put the car in drive. "Program's the best place for you right now. They'll be time for Ireland later."

"Next closest thing then, I gotta stop at Kayla's after my place and pick up some things before we go." It was Friday; I had to be at the program by 9:00 am on Monday. Alistair had offered to fly us out, but Daniel wanted to bring his car and wouldn't let anyone else touch it, so we opted to drive.

∼

My house smelled of new carpet when we entered, and the railing had been fixed and raised. "Did you break this?" I asked Daniel as we topped the stairs.

"I didn't know what happened with your dad, so I made it look like an accident." He grinned. "But, I'm also the one who fixed it." Smacking it a few times with his palm, he nodded his head as though satisfied with his work. "And I got paid to do it."

Of course, Varrick Custom Builders would have been the ones Mother called for this job. There was some delicious irony there. Now I had to hope that his father and my mother wouldn't get together for brunch, and exchange notes, until after I'd turned eighteen.

"Wanna test out how strong it is?" Daniel asked, still holding that grin.

I tugged on the rail. It didn't creak or move a centimeter. That wasn't the kind of test Daniel had in mind, though, and I raised an eyebrow at him. "I'd rather test how strong this is..." I grabbed his crotch and pulled him against me, running my leg up his thigh and arching against the banister.

After a few minutes of us testing the railing's structural integrity, I packed a suitcase of dirty clothes and essentials and left without looking back.

It had been my house my entire life and never felt like home.

Home was the Willows.

The front of which was now guarded by a featherless crow.

"What do you want?" Abuela squinted at me as I got out of the car. Was she reading my soul or getting distracted by my shiny earrings? She was emotionally silent...so it wasn't just males, after all.

Samson and Delilah came bounding up, sniffing and snuffling me and Daniel furiously.

"I've got to pick up a few things," I said, petting Samson's head and staring at Abuela. I hadn't noticed the lack of emotions at Kayla's funeral. By the nasty look she was giving me, I ought to be grateful for this turn of events.

"Be quick," she grumbled, "and just you, not him. I'll have a hard enough time cleansing the place when you've gone."

Daniel stayed back, wrestling with the dogs as though he hadn't noticed her at all.

"You and she went looking for trouble, with your hunting for Satan. You found it. It took my granddaughter and it will take you, unless you throw yourself on the mercy of Jesus, Holy One, Son of God, the True Vine, Shiloh, Prince of Peace, Lamb and Light, Faithful Witness..."

She trailed off behind me as I went inside and up the stairs to Ma's room. Someone had been sleeping in her bed, which was meticulously made with military corners. Crosses loomed in various locations, a scattering of poorly painted Jesus figures beneath each one. Abuela was the acting overseer of the Willows until Ma returned.

If she returns.

Pulling *Chicken Soup for the Soul* from my purse, I set it in the nightstand. I'd considered going to see Ma at County, trying to help her recover from her breakdown, but until I could be sure I wouldn't make things worse, this would have to do.

A note inside read:

Ma,

For the cold mornings.
I love you,
Amy

A Jesus figurine fell over as I closed the drawer. "KAYLA 7" stood out in painted block letters, the "Y" taking up half the space. I set it in a compromising position with another savior and moved the cross half an inch to the left. Then I got up and did the same to a few of the others before heading down the hallway.

No one had been sleeping in Kayla's bed, not since I'd been there, and everything was as she'd left it, otherwise. I gathered a bag of clothes, including some of her shirts that could fit me, and sat on the bed in the quiet room, listening to the barks of the dogs playing with Daniel below. Pulling out my phone, I re-read the last messages she'd sent.

7:16 PM: TELL DANIEL HE'S AN ASSHOLE. RIGHT NOW. I'LL WAIT. OKAY. NOW TELL HIM AGAIN. NEARLY TOOK MY FUCKING HEAD OFF PEELING OUT LIKE THAT! IF I HADN'T BEEN REELING BACK FROM THAT HOLY FUCK STATIC SHOCK WE GOT HE WOULD HAVE!

7:17 PM: WHAT IS HE? JEALOUS? HE SHOULD BE. I'M A MUCH BETTER KISSER.

9:02 PM: WATCHING *NIGHT OF THE LEPUS* WITH MA. YOU'RE MISSING OUT. PBBT. NO YOU AREN'T. FLYNN'S PROBABLY ELBOW DEEP IN YOUR CLEAVAGE AS I TYPE. CAN YOU FEEL MY SEETHING JEALOUSY FROM HERE? I BET YOU CAN.

10:23 PM: CODY SAYS HE MIGHT STOP BY TONIGHT! WITH LUCK HE'LL BE HERE IN THE MORNING.

10:48 PM: HOPE YOU'RE DOING ALRIGHT. I'M STARTING TO WORRY. MESSAGE ME WHEN YOU GET THIS NO MATTER THE TIME!

10:49 PM:

I snuggled and rocked with Ralph the Love Raccoon for a moment before texting back.

7:46 PM: I'M HERE, BUT WON'T EVER BE ALRIGHT AGAIN.

7:50 PM: I MISS YOU.

7:52 PM:

Her solar powered candles glowed in each window, flickering in and out, in and out. Just as Kayla had that last night at the barn. *She wasn't there...and then she was.* That feeling

444

stuck with me long after most of the chaos had settled into a dreamscape. An itch I couldn't quite reach. I picked up one of the candles and placed it in my bag, tugging the drawstring tight.

Abuela's rosary hung heavy over Kayla's headboard, snug in the groove it had carved into the soft wood in its short time here. Jesus, His Holy Crab Cake, Lemming of God, Silence of the Lambs, had his chance to help the first time my best girl put this over my neck, and he hadn't stopped any of what was to come.

I swiped the rosary off her headboard, slung my bag, and Ralph, over my shoulder, and hammered down the stairs and out the front door.

"Your rosary is broken." I shoved it at Abuela without looking at her as the screen door slammed shut behind me. "Or it might be your God."

I fell into the great white fur of both dogs and embraced them while they baptized me in drool. "Take care of Ma when she comes back." Delilah whined at her name. I looked at Abuela, now muttering in Spanish so fast I couldn't follow her if I were fluent. "Stay out in the field as much as you can until then," I whispered.

"Tu nieta está ahora con Dios. Hubiese pensado que era un poco mayor para Su polla, pero supongo que todos somos niños ante Sus ojos," Daniel spoke in a solemn tone, making the sign of the cross over himself.

Abuela whipped the giant rosary at his head, getting more distance than her waif thin arms had a right to. He ducked and it went sailing by, skidding into the dirt. Samson and Delilah gave chase, tugging it between them before dropping it in Daniel's hand. He rubbed their ears and set the necklace in the backseat of the Chevelle.

"¡No! ¡No puedes quedarte con eso, Diablo Blanco! ¡Devuélvemelo!" Abuela's gravel-laden voice carried across the county.

"Oye, lo tiraste, solo mantengo a Maine hermosa." Daniel got in the car and I followed, putting steel between me and the volcanic avian woman flapping her arms at us.

"Jesus! Daniel! What did you say to her?" I asked, checking the sky for locusts.

"She cussed you out, so I reminded her we are all children of God." He smiled, starting the car and pulling a half-circle around the driveway.

She scuttled toward us, quick and lithe. "¡Te mataría, cara de panocha! No me jodas!"

"¡Ahí no hay peligro! Tengo tu rosario para satisfacer mis deseos nocturnos." He gestured to the back with his thumb. "¡Está incluso lubricado con baba de perro! ¡Prima!" With a wave out his window, he took off.

I leaned out my window and added, "Besame el culo, Abuela!" Kayla had taught me a few choice phrases in Spanish, and "kiss my ass" stuck. The racist old crow threw handfuls of gravel to match her voice, while Sam and Dee jumped and barked on either side of her.

"Chances are she'll be dead next time I'm here, right?" I asked, flipping around in my seat to stare, wide-eyed out the back window, my heart thundering in my chest. "I didn't know you spoke Spanish, what else did you say?"

"She said we can keep the rosary, and I said gracias." He glanced in the rear view and beamed.

"I didn't hear that word…" I pursed my lips at him before turning away to watch the candle in my sister's window, now fading from view. Sighing, and resting my chin on my seat back, I said, "Kayla wants you to know you're an asshole. Twice over."

"Oh, way more than that." Daniel gave me the eye, and then furrowed his brow. "You talkin' to her?"

"It was in her last texts. Her dying words."

He put his hand over his heart. "Well then, I'll do my best to honor them."

Half-smiling, I shoved his arm playfully and faced forward, taking my cigarettes and lighter from my purse.

"No smoking in the Chevelle." Daniel drummed his fingers over the steering wheel and flicked on the radio. "Road trip doesn't change that."

Setting my smokes back down, I hooked my arm in his and kissed his cheek. "Already living up to your word in fine form." I laughed and groaned in unison.

It was going to be a long drive.

And with all I've told you in these pages, from those first steps into that godforsaken barn to now, we've barely left the dooryard.

I'll catch up with you again in a bit. This next part I've got to take a breath for, have a few thousand cigarettes, and drink a bathtub full of wild cherry moonshine. Until then, stay sane or as close to it as you can stand.

I'll keep a light on for you. 🖤

Far from...
...The End.

AFTERWORD

*Oh, Amy, what are you getting yourself into? Detroit? Really?
Ireland is so much greener, but okay—I'm here with you. Let's do
this.*

~

Hey, Darlin' Reader,

You made it this far, eh? Good, I'm glad you did, and I
hope you enjoyed part one of Amy's swan dive into the
mouth of madness. Maybe it was more like a stumble and a
belly flop, but either way, she's on her way. If you had fun,
laughed, cried, threw the book across the room, gnawed on
it, or couldn't put it down, come find me and let me know.
I'm a new author and love hearing how people interpret my
stories. Once they leave me, they're not strictly mine
anymore; they become ours, and some new ~~abomination~~
creation is born.

There are at least nine books planned in the *Bittersweet
Empathy* series. *The Spiral* is a foundational pillar. Much care,
and several bouts of insanity, went into making sure it can
hold the weight of what's to come. Not everything was

answered here, and some of what was may not be the whole of it, but we'll get there in due time.

It's taken me seven years to write this novel, to learn the craft, do copious critiques, and experiment with different styles until I settled on the one you've just read. I've still got much to discover, and I don't know that I'll ever be a book-a-month kind of writer, but rest assured that I—and Amy—are working on her next adventure. She's already woken me up screaming a few times, in anticipation.

The best way to stay updated on my latest releases is to join my newsletter, if you haven't already. . When you do, you'll get an e-book of *Red String*, a novelette which will give you a glimpse into Amy's future, and perhaps why she wakes screaming.

I'm going to skedaddle and get back to work. You can help me write faster by sharing my stories with others, engaging with me on social media, and of course, leaving a review. Even if *The Spiral* wasn't your cup of tea, stating the reasons why in a review may help someone else discover that it's theirs. I've got odd tastes, so I often find the one to three-star reviews even more helpful than the fives. 😶

Fives are good too though, don't get it twisted. We've got enough of that going on in the Tragedy of Amy Durene.

Thank you for taking a chance on me. This book is dedicated to my husband and daughter, but I also wrote it for you, and I tried like hell to do it justice.

Brightly yours,

Nikki DeKeuster

JOIN MY NEWSLETTER BY VISITING WWW.NIKKIDEKEUSTER.COM

ACKNOWLEDGMENTS
IT TAKES A VILLAGE TO WRITE A NOVEL.

Legions of people cheered me on throughout my writerly journey. If you were one of them, at any point, I thank you, sincerely. Every bit of it helped me cross the finish line.

But some of you went beyond the call, and there really are no words, but I'll take a stab at it anyway.

Even though I'm not supposed to have knives...

Brian DeKeuster, this book is dedicated to you but that isn't enough, it will never be enough. Your soul and influence are alive in every word of this book: from that first brainstorming session when Amy was a spark in my eye, to me forgetting to eat because I can't stop flipping through the beautiful shiny pages of this completed novel.

Thank you, gracias, danke, спасибо, go raibh maith agat, ありがとうございました, Þakka þér fyrir, and Ni 'lassui.

~

Michelle Kroncke, my life twin, who shares my light and dark with equal grace. No, I mean that as a compliment; this has nothing to do with you tripping over the coffee table.

Your support and enthusiasm for this story were key stepping stones in me seeing it through to completion.

Stepping stones toward world domination.

~

Jennifer Hatfield, my alpha reader, with the strength to survive my piecemeal torture and enthusiastically—or masochistically—come back for more. Your fortitude never ceases to amaze me, on every level.

You are this book's aunty and holder of the world's largest collection of Bittersweet fan-fiction on the net. The existence of which is enough to fuel my soul through the rest of the series.

~

Allison Erin Wright, who encouraged me as I took my first wobbly steps as a writer. You helped me see that I not only could do this, but I must, so you could one day hold the finished tale in your hands.

It took a few minutes, but I got there.

~

My team

Editor- Allison Erin Wright
http://wrightediting.com
Proofreader- Jennifer Hatfield
http://www.phoenixrose.net/about
Cover Artist- Grace Zhu
https://www.artstation.com/gracezhu

~

CRITIQUE PARTNERS/BETA READERS

Brian DeKeuster, Jennifer Hatfield, Allison Erin Wright, Michelle Kroncke, Debbie Wingate, David Green, Kirk McDougall, Monica Grier, Stephie Kuhn, Ann DeKeuster, Gidget Ferguson, Katherine Kroncke, Linda Holtz Skelton, and Lyndsey Ellis-Holloway.

ABOUT THE AUTHOR

Nikki DeKeuster invites you to sit around the fire as she weaves you dark tales of mischief, mayhem, and mad love. Stories that stick to your ribs long after the lights have been doused and your head hits the pillow.

She enjoys crunching leaves underfoot while exploring the bluffs of Lake Michigan with her daughter and husband.

Her work can be found in numerous anthologies, a novelette, and this, her debut novel.

ALSO BY NIKKI DEKEUSTER

Red String (Free when you sign up for my newsletter at NikkiDeKeuster.com.)

Vivid and well-paced. I was rooting so hard for this supernatural Bonnie and Clyde. ~ Stephanie Scissom, author of The Reckoning.

This is not a love story. It isn't a knitting story either, so if that's what you're looking for, try the DIY section four rows over. As for me, all I want is a normal date night at the carnival, eating funnel cake, scoring prizes, and snuggling in the Tunnel of Love. But when one of the rides ends in a death toll, it trips my need to help in a world too often void of it. Problem is, I'm supposed to be staying on the down-low, and playing the hero is high profile.

Now, my boyfriend and I are on the run, with more mayhem, carnage, and Carolina swamp muck than you can shake a radioactive raccoon at. If we can't rig this high-wire game of pursuit in our favor, I'll be wishing for the inside of a body bag.

Will our red string be severed before we can cross the state line?

HAPPY OLDEN DAYS

A ROWAN AND CORMACK TALE

HAPPY OLDEN DAYS

*C*andy canes can be sinister. Oh, they act all sweet, but suck on them long enough and they can turn sharp and mean. Pulling mine from my mouth, I admired the fine point I'd honed. I lay on my stomach, sinking into a dire bear-skin rug in front of my great stone hearth. My home was alive with warmth and the scents of pine wood, berries, and fresh gingerbread.

The fire popped, expelling a fat, shaggy soot sprite, who singed the book I held before bouncing to rest beside me, its eyes askew. I stabbed it through with my candy cane and raised it to my lips, blowing a smidgen of north wind over it before sliding the treat between my teeth.

"Thank you," I said to the fire as the sprite dissolved over my tongue, a savory marshmallow delight. "It's the perfect weather for soot sprites."

The front door clunked open, letting in a flurry of snow and frigid air along with the *love* of my eternity. His white face matched the snow covering his cloak, making a game of discovering where the snow ended and he began.

I twitched my Luna moth-esque wings and the snow sifted off him, gathered into a ball, and rolled into the hearth. It hissed, became steam, and floated to a cup on the table beside Cormack's overstuffed chair. The steam swirled down, steeping cinnamon and bone meal in hot water. On display next to the cup sat a magnificent ginger-bread house, a few more windows than planned chewed into it.

"Hello love! What's a five-letter word for a small glowing magical creature that starts with 'F'?" I asked.

Cormack kicked off his wrinkled leather boots and raised an eyebrow at the book in my hand. "You haven't slept, have you? Why are you torturing yourself like this, Rowan?"

"National Crossword Puzzle Day is coming up, and I'm going to be ready for it." I narrowed my eyes at my cross-word book. "Isn't that right?"

The book said nothing. No matter how many times I had threatened to throw it in the fire, it remained stalwart and loyal to its function.

"Firefly," he said, his tone gentle.

I dusted soot from the page, penciling in the word and stopping at the second "F." I would have to borrow a square from nine down, but twenty-eight across had an extra it wasn't using. Setting my candy cane point to the paper, I shuffled the squares to their new locations and filled in the "L" and "Y" with my pencil.

"Beautiful!" I purred. Maybe with one less box, nine down's prompt of "nightshade" would be illuminated.

"It certainly is." Cormack sank into his chair, turning the plate this way and that before breaking off a side of the cookie house and chewing it. His smile wavered a fraction at the corners, and a shiver crawled over my spine.

"Is everything alright, my darling?" I set the candy cane in my book and closed it. "Is it not to your liking?"

"Oh, no, it's good, just... something's off." His brows knitted together.

I got up and peered in the tiny windows of my decadent

masterpiece. "I noticed too. I think the ginger I used may have been a dye job."

"Artificial everything these days." He sneered, took another bite, and sighed. "I'm sorry to be grumpy. Your baking is lovely, as always. I've just had a day, is all."

Caressing his cheek, I kissed his pale lips and drifted to his lap. "Tell me about it."

"One of the backup channels on the Styx overflowed into Domhan Eile," he said flatly.

I gasped, my hands shooting to my mouth. Domhan Eile was a place for the honored Irish dead—such a disaster might take lifetimes to sort out.

"Yes, precisely. No one puts a coin under the tongue of their dead anymore. Not even on the eyes, which was bad enough. Of course the Styx is overflowing. Add to it the lack of a funeral watch, and they aren't at rest when I deliver them, either. Today, one made it out over Lake Michigan. I only just reached him with my scythe."

He sighed again and picked up his tea. "It's taking its toll on me... ironically."

I rubbed his knotted shoulders. "No respect for tradition. It's all silly nonsense to silly people. They've no regard for the world they live in, let alone ours."

Footsteps crunched outside, and a boisterous knock rang through our home. Three humans, bundled in layers and bearing fraudulent smiles, gawked at us as we opened the dark oaken door. Our Fae forms were unknowable to most, so they must have been struck by Cormack's handsome visage.

My heart rose. Wassailers? Perhaps I had judged humanity too soon.

One of the young men stepped forward. "Good evening sir, miss. Are you happy with your internet service?"

Cormack scowled down the path to the closed cemetery gate. "Did you jump my gate?" he asked, nostrils flaring.

"That's the length we'll go to for higher quality internet, sir," the second man said with a fool's grin.

Cormack's scowl deepened, and the girl took a wise step back when a marvelous idea caught me.

"Darling, what if we brought some of the traditions back to Milwaukee, starting tonight?" I slithered an arm around his and gazed up at him. "*Fari Lwyd* comes to mind."

A twinkle lit my love's eye.

"Th-that's right," stammered the girl, "AS & S is dedicated to offering high-quality broadband to everyone in the greater Milwaukee metro area b-by 2055."

Cormack raised a hand like a conductor, and the trio burst into the opening hymn to Grianstad an Gheimhridh. A song not heard by human ears in a millennium. The solicitors clutched their throats and held each other's wild eyes for only a moment before their bodies joined in the merriment.

I stepped outside in my bare feet and sundress and hummed to the earth, my blonde hair whipping long in the wind. From beneath the ground shimmied the skulls of a horse, a deer, and a chipmunk. I threaded them with vines and placed a crown atop each of the wassailers, blowing kisses of fire into the empty eye sockets of the animals to help guide their way.

A raucous smile erupted on my love's face as we sang along with them. Why hadn't we done this sooner?

When we'd finished five songs, I handed each mortal a chunk of gingerbread house. That was very important. If we didn't feed them, they'd have the right to ransack our house, and once inside they'd never find their way out.

Maybe if one of them were a ginger, that wouldn't be a problem, but they were all brunettes.

We walked them to the gate, and Cormack motioned them through. "Thank you for brightening my night. Now go forth and brighten the neighborhood." They crossed the street and brought traffic to a screeching, swerving, beeping halt, wassailing all the while.

"How long does the enchantment last?" I asked, waving to them.

"'Til dawn," he said, wrapping an arm around me and kissing the top of my head.

"Oh! Dawn! That's the answer to nine down!" I cuddled into him as we strolled back to our hearth amidst the howling winter wind. "And it frees up an extra square."

"Efficient, and clever," Cormack mused.

National Crossword Puzzle Day didn't stand a chance.

-End-